Ontogenesis:

On-to-gen-e-sis/ˌän(t)ōˈjenəsəs/
(n.) The development of an individual organism or anatomical or behavioral feature from the earliest stage to maturity.

Acephalous
Book 2

Amanda Marsico

Red Ink Enthusiast™

Published by Red Ink Enthusiast™
Murrells Inlet, South Carolina, U.S.A.

ISBN: 978-0-9984209-4-3

First Edition

DEDICATION

For the changers.

ACKNOWLEDGEMENTS

Unending thanks to my editors, beta readers, and cheer leaders. Writing is a solitary endeavor. Publishing isn't. You make this possible.

"I often see how you sob over what you destroy, how you want to stop and just worship; and you do stop, and then a moment later you are at it again with a knife, like a surgeon."

Anaïs Nin

Prologue

Breena bounced around in the passenger's side of Vos' dilapidated pick-up truck. He bought it off of a farmer for five-hundred dollars after insisting on settling in the Grayling area.

"It's necessary to be close to my queen." The words rolled into the stuffy car with more gravity than Breena thought necessary.

Bree couldn't help but roll her eyes. "Don't get me wrong, Vos. I'm glad I have you around for advice. I don't want to rely on Atlas anymore. That's why I called you instead of his guy, R. Who goes by a letter for a name, anyway? Someone who doesn't want to be found, that's who. But I'm not queen yet—technically there *is* no queen—and so you don't need to feel obligated to—"

"I am obligated to you. Forever."

"Well—"

"Nope." He playfully flung a hand over Breena's mouth.

She bit into his hand and he dropped it. "That's not how you treat a queen."

"'Technically there is no queen.'" He smirked. "You either accept my help and allow me to afford you the respect due, or you accept my help and let me treat you like my petulant little sister."

"How do you know that's how people treat their sisters? Atlas told me families from Hell only have one child."

"They do, but that wasn't always the rule. Your mother—" Bree wrinkled her nose. "You're exactly like I always imagined a sister would be. If my sister was the queen."

She huffed. "Well, I can never be queen if I don't get my astral connection back." Breena's wrist gave a phantom throb. Her thoughts drifted back to the illusory hotel room in Myrtle Beach. She had resorted to killing her spiritual body to escape Atlas and Tabitha.

Her wrists and forearms were free of visible scars, the effects of the shard of glass used limited to her astral body, but she could still periodically feel the pain twinge deep inside her. She flexed her wrist and grimaced. Since coming back into her physical form, Breena's ability to manipulate and travel through dreams, and to create illusions, had not healed. She sighed, knowing it would take something drastic to knit together the fissures left in her spirit. "How long 'til we get to Hell?"

Vos howled a laugh, swerving into the other lane when he threw his head back. Breena flung a hand out to brace herself against the door. Vos continued to chuckle into Breena's glare. "You really thought I was taking you to Hell? *Driving* you, in a pick-up truck, to Hell. As if it's a location on your map?"

Breena stared at him wondering if she should be embarrassed. *There* is *a 'Hell' on my map. Hell, Michigan. It's two-hundred miles south of here.*

"Breena, I can't take you to Hell. Only you can get yourself there. I picked you up so we could discuss your request in person."

"OK, then. If I have to get myself there, where do I go first?"

"You're thinking about this in the wrong way, Breena. You don't *go* anywhere. You have to *die.*"

****

Tabitha melted through the black, mesh-like space of purgatory. Her being—it couldn't be called a soul—strained through the thick space. As she sifted through the layers of nothingness, her particles spread and collided, not in the rush of a hadron collider experiment, but in the sludgy soup of time. Although she didn't fully buy into such a human concept as time, given her eons of existence, she couldn't deny that the process of returning to Gehenna was not immediate, or constant, or already complete, any of which might suggest time was a circular or spherical thing rather than a linear progression as taught and followed on Earth.

Her moment or ages or instant spent slipping through allowed her to consider what had just happened. Her daughter had dethroned her. It was hard for Tabitha to accept that her reign was ending, that she was the last of Gehenna's daughters to rule. Passing her Right over to a *granddaughter* of evil concerned her purist sensibilities. It wasn't that Breena was diluted in terms of lineage, but in terms of upbringing.

Did I make a mistake allowing her to live with humans? Would Breena have turned out as a better queen if she had grown up in Gehenna? Lucifer, or rather his team of subordinates, had raised all of his daughters in their home, but he had insisted on sending Breena out, just like the gentry children, to get a better sense of humanity and to be the first in a new line—a new kind—of rulers.

The first of anything was frightening, even for a woman in Tabitha's privileged position. Knowing that an almost impossibly young, human-raised, human-loving girl, her matricidal daughter, would take the throne made her ears ring with fury. By the time Tabitha reached Gehenna, her form had coalesced, though it shook as she tried to hold in her flames. She stretched, straightened her shirt, and smoothed her slacks.

"How naïve, that daughter of mine."

****

"No, no, no." Jo's volume escalated with each iteration as she paced the room. "We are not making this into some sappy support group where we sit in a circle and share all that's happened to us because of Reid Case." The static caused by her shuffling across the carpet made her thin, straight hair rise, bits of the mousy brown lengths hovering above her shoulders like the energy of her enthusiasm emanated in unseen waves. The glint in her deep-set eyes held the same message. "That wasn't even his real name. Atlas Thorley played us from the start. I'm sure the actual Reid Case is dead."

Leigh nodded her head from her place in the back of the room.

"We are going to be people of *action*. We can do something about him rather than wallowing in self-pity."

Leigh's conviction swelled and her slow nodding turned into clapping. She pushed away from the wall where she leaned and waved her hand indicating all of the others sitting in the rented meeting hall at Christ Church. "What are you guys doing? Are you going to sit there and be angry or are you going to do something about it?" The layers of her short, choppy haircut swished as she turned her head to look each attendee in the eye. *"Well?"*

A murmur circulated, some resisting the active approach the two women advocated and others working up their nerves to join in the rallying spirit.

Leigh crossed her arms over her red and black flannel shirt. "Jo's waiting. . ."

Jo cleared her throat and moved to stand beside Leigh. "Let's slow down for a second. I'm not trying to pressure any of you. If you wanted a support group, go find some real group therapy. There's no shame in that. I want to make it clear, though, that is not why I'm here. I called this meeting to raise your spirits, to see if we could band together to give Atlas the reckoning he deserves."

A shrunken, nervous little man raised his hand.

"Ted, you don't need to raise your hand to speak. What do you want to say?" Leigh crossed the room to put a hand on his shoulder.

"I'm, I'm worried that. . . no, never mind." A hush fell over the room, everyone waiting for the continuation of the sentence they knew would come. As much as Ted played at shy and averse to confrontation, it was mostly an act to soften what he wanted to say.

Leigh tapped her combat boot. "Just spit it out already, Ted. For the love of—"

"I don't think we should take any action because then we'd be no better than those psychopaths doing the rioting, and I, for one, am *sick* of being called a psychopath." His face reddened. "I just want people to like me."

Jo pursed her lips, restrained, but Leigh couldn't stop the derisive snort that escaped.

"Those rioters aren't seeking justice. They're only fighting for themselves." Jo pulled a chair around to sit in front of Ted. She leaned forward, resting her elbows on her bare knees, the holes in her jeans large. "They are doing exactly what Atlas wanted—to tear away the structure and logic to our society, to make his twisted version of happiness through chaos and acephalous culture—"

Ted inhaled and held his breath, blinking rapidly, full of skepticism.

"—and it doesn't matter that he had that Linda woman clean up behind him and un-instruct everything he told us to do. She took her coaching seriously, but I still think that was an act he put her up to. As much as I hate to say it, those zealots are just as much victims of Atlas as we are. Some of them are like us, hotline callers that just wanted help and a listening ear. They're the ones Linda couldn't retrain, either because she didn't get to them, or they were too taken by Atlas' charisma. And maybe she was, too. The others are just sheep trapped in a mob mentality. There are too many of them for us to stop, but there's only one Atlas Thorley."

Leigh's hand absently drifted to her side where, under her baggy flannel and unbeknownst to the group, she concealed the small pistol she had registered to carry since the start of the riots. She grinned.

Chapter 1

"Breena, why don't you go get in bed? I'll take care of the maintenance, and then I'll be right up."

"No, I got it."

Jordan shook his head and hoped it came across as frustration with her stubbornness rather than pity. It was both. "Bree, it's good to see you trying to reconnect with your skills, but I know you're exhausted. I can keep taking care of it for now."

She was quiet.

After killing Tabitha, Breena thought she'd be able to breathe again, that things would go back to normal. As she'd crossed the stage at her high school graduation, she actually believed it had.

For the moments between climbing the little stairs toward her diploma and then descending the second set careful not to step on the hem of her purple gown, Breena didn't think about the sensation of forcing her fire into her mother, about how it reminded her of squeezing a lump of play dough through the little toy head to grow its hair, except in reverse. It was like pushing something way too big, too strong, into a weak container, the give and melting away of resistance sickening.

In the last week of rioting, Tabitha's zealots still on the loose, Breena received a cryptic text from Linda—sent with a burner phone and no help in locating her brother Ari—that people would likely be after Bree for revenge. Since that point, she and Lilly had been staying at Jordan's, and he was using his gradually-improving psychic skills to shroud the house in an illusion of riot destruction, hoping that none of Tabitha's fanatics or lackeys looking for Breena would check a place that already looked ransacked.

The reality of her naïveté, that all she had to do was get rid of Tabitha, sat heavily on her chest. *Vos was wrong, I swear. I don't need a one-way trip to Hell to get back to normal.* She snapped back to the present, Jordan waiting for her response. "No, let me try to build the shield again. I'm so close."

"Look, I can literally see the effort pulling on you. The strings of your energy used to be knit tightly together. Now, they're getting further apart. My illusion is on the verge of transparence, and your energy is threadbare. One of two things is about to happen. You're going to pass out from trying and I'll have to let the guard down to focus on you instead of it, or the illusion around the house is going to fall on its own because we're standing here arguing about it instead of fixing it. Either way, it's going to be very obvious that the house is fine and people are living in it. Someone's bound to be watching." Jordan scanned the sky for signs of eavesdropping birds. He didn't trust anything with feathers since Tabitha had spied on them as a dove.

"I know, I know. I'm just as worried about them finding us as you are. I'm going to fix it." Breena shoved back from the desk she was using as a table and left her bowl of spaghetti.

"Want me to put that in the fridge for you, Bree?"

"Thanks, Lilly, but I'll only be a minute. Tonight's the night I'm going to do it!" *But if I can't believe myself, why should they believe me?* Breena stepped over Lilly's sleeping bag and went out of the room. Jordan followed at a distance.

On the porch, Breena surveyed the weakening illusion of damage with her hands on her hips. The sticky summer air smelled like wet grass, and a lone breeze carried in the faint odor of dog mess from a few yards down. Her nostrils flared as it hit her, and she turned to go back inside. Breena gasped then recovered. "Shit, Jordan. I didn't know you were there."

Jordan stood in the doorway with a worn expression and dark circles under his eyes. His lips curled, but the smile didn't light his face. "Sorry." Jordan looked out into the yard. "I know you feel like something is missing, not being able to use any of your power, but this is my illusion, and I don't mind maintaining it. You taught me well."

"I can do it."

"You shouldn't."

"Jordan, we've been through this. It's my mess and I need to clean it up." Her mouth threatened to quirk up at the oxymoron of cleaning the situation they were in by making the house and yard look sloppier, but annoyance with Jordan kept the humor at bay.

"You *need* to get better. You *need* to get some rest. I wish you'd go sleep for a solid day and leave things to me and Lilly for a while. You're running yourself into the ground. What if you lapse into another coma? What if you never wake up? Do you know what it would do to me if I lost you?" His hands dove roughly into his pockets. Jordan's wet hair curled in the humidity. Breena could smell his shampoo over the sweaty July air—sandalwood, his favorite— and orange on his face and hands from the snack he'd had before dinner. "I've thought about it so many times, and so many times it seemed like you were gone already. Your time in London. . . you never called after I left. And all that time in the hospital. The way you crawled back to Atlas even though he destroyed you every time." He had pulled his hands back out of his pockets, clenching his fists. "Don't push yourself to a place you can't come back from. You taught me well. You need to let me save—"

"I don't *want* you to save me!" A bird startled out of the gutter above them. Jordan reflexively glanced at it. Breena stomped down the steps and into the darkness. She came to rest against an illusory tree trunk hanging at an odd angle over the fence. As she leaned on it, the image allowed her to sink into it, little by little. *The image is failing. This tree is like a cushion.* Jordan's tense form approached in her peripheral vision, and Bree heaved an exhausted sigh.

"What is wrong with you?"

"Nothing." *Nothing except that I have to choose between dying to be myself or living as a shell.*

"Not nothing, Breena. You've been acting weird for two weeks. Acting like you don't want me near you, like I annoy you. What did I do?"

"You *do* annoy me."

Jordan pulled himself straighter, affronted. "I'm trying to help you."

Breena pinned him with her eyes. "I must be losing my voice for how many times I've told you I don't want your help because you don't seem to hear me anymore."

He closed the distance between them. His chest, all lines and long muscle visible through his clinging white t-shirt, pressed against hers. Jordan braced his hands on the tree trunk behind

Breena's head. "I hear you, Breena." She tried to put some distance between them, but the tree was still too sturdy to pass fully through. His closeness made her ache, and breathing harder only made the space feel smaller.

The arguing began weeks earlier when Jordan found out Breena texted Atlas for help with her connection before graduation. This was as close as they had been since.

"I hear you startle from your sleep calling for him in the middle of the night. I hear you coaching yourself to breathe when you think no one notices you're having a panic attack in the bathroom, and I hear you hold your breath when the news comes on, like you're waiting to see his face. I've never been able to tell if that's out of dread or excitement. And I hear you tell me you don't need my help. But I *see* the life draining out of you, yet you ask me to ignore it, push me away. Why?"

She couldn't look at him. Heat rose in her cheeks, giving away her anger and embarrassment. *I hate it when he calls me out.*

"You still love him, don't you?"

That broke her resistance. The last thing she wanted was to talk, but she couldn't allow that idea to live. "No! I hate him. He's just as bad as Tabitha. If it wasn't for him, I wouldn't be a part of this world at all. I wouldn't have had to become a *murderer.* Jordan, I *killed* someone. My own biological mother! It doesn't matter that she was evil. I came from her. I *am* her. And he's no different, either. He killed, too. It doesn't matter which side they fought for. Both of them wanted to upset the balance of peace and chaos. I'm so angry at him. You're in danger because I chose to use him to get at Tabitha. It's *all* my fault. If I wasn't always looking for an escape he would have never found me. He was in my dreams for years, Jordan. Years. I never told you that, did I? Before I even went to London. He and Tabitha found me because I went searching for something better than being awake. And you know what? I kind of want him to find me again. Even though I hate him. Even though I told him he was a pawn and nothing else. Because I miss being in the fray, and I never belonged here anyway. Or with you."

Jordan shoved his toffee hair back with both hands. "You think I don't hear you? Do you even hear yourself?"

Breena opened her mouth to hurl a retort at Jordan when Lilly flicked the front porch light on and popped her head out of the front door. Jordan sprang back from Breena. Lilly called out to them through the shadows. "Everything going OK? Doesn't look like you've gotten much work done. Breena, I went ahead and put away your spaghetti."

Bree called back a dismissive, "'Kay." The air between her and Jordan was dense and heavy while they waited for privacy. Once Lilly was back inside, Jordan found Breena's face, brushing across her cheek with his palm.

Don't lean in to him.

He stepped towards her.

He's just a habit.

Jordan wrapped his free hand around her waist, pulling her against him.

I can't keep this up.

At her ear, Jordan whispered. "Just be happy here. Let me be enough."

His cinnamon gum made her eyes water. That's the reason she attributed to her threatening tears. *Being together just endangers him, and he wants me to need him so much. It's not like I'll be around much longer, anyway.*

"Why are you so eager to escape?"

Breena straightened. *Self-sabotage?* "Jordan, it's over." Not lingering to witness his expression or suggest she'd answer his question, she turned from him and walked back to the house. Memories of the first time she'd used her fire to sway Atlas prickled at her conscience. She shook her head and ascended the front porch. *It's easier being free.*

In their bedroom, Breena gathered her pillows and blankets from the mattress and drug them down the hallway to Arthur's study. *Jordan's dad won't mind. It's not like he's ever here for his family, anyway.* Bree smirked to herself. *He would* definitely *mind.* She dropped the bundle on the floor, satisfied that her action spited both Musil-family men at once, and considered taking one of Arthur's fancy cigars as a cherry on top.

Though she was thankful to have Jordan's spacious house as a safe haven, it never stopped bothering her that Jordan's parents had stayed in Berlin when the rioting started. She figured most parents would have risked themselves to travel back for their child, that even *they* would have wanted to make sure their son was OK, but Arthur and JoAnne Musil were business people, and business people like them held one value above all: The customer is always right. Arthur's client demanded they remain close by to monitor the status of their investments in the face of the global upheaval, so they did.

Pace yourself. Save some vindictiveness for another fight. With the next trip between rooms, Breena thought about her own mom. Lexa hadn't come to be with Breena, either, but at least she had made the attempt to get Bree to stay with her and her boyfriend, Grant. It was Breena's stubbornness, not Lexa's lack of care, that kept them apart during the riots. She exhaled. Fumbling the zipper into place, Bree moved her suitcase of clothes, an organized person's nightmare-mixture of clean *and* dirty apparel, and the TV tray she'd kept beside Jordan's bed stacked with books and various electronics' chargers.

She heard Lilly coming up the stairs, but made it to the study door too late to escape her questioning.

"Why are you sleeping in here?"

"I broke up with Jordan."

Lilly stomped her foot. "What? No. Why?"

"Ask him. I don't want to talk about it. I'm tired." *Tired of owing people explanations.*

"Yeah, I'm sure you are. OK, well. . . if you need—"

"I'm fine. Good night." Breena used the door to push Lilly the rest of the way out of the bedroom. *I'm such an asshole friend.* On the floor in front of Arthur's desk, Bree spread out her comforter and then layered it with other small throw blankets. She'd left the t-shirt cotton sheets on Jordan's bed, but taken the rest of his covers and pillows, which she threw to one end of the blanket pad. Standing in the middle of the spread, Breena pulled her tank top over her head and threw it across the room, followed by her jean shorts and socks. She drew back the corner of the top two blankets and climbed into the pile, trying to lie at an angle where her feet and shoulders were both covered by the patchwork. With pillow under her head, she exhaled a slow breath and then reached out to her right searching blindly for her phone. Feeling in an arc with her arm, she realized the device was still on top of Arthur's desk.

Breena struggled out of the blanket cocoon with an irritated huff and seized the phone, her shimmering sword against insomnia. Her fingers slid across the screen swiping away the darkness as she clambered back under the heap. From her back, she gazed up at the phone she held above her face, arms up, elbows locked. She stared at the blank text message form. Her thumbs danced above the keyboard, typing a few words and then erasing them, typing a few more and giving up again. As Breena let her arms fall to the floor, her phone flopped out of her hand and smacked her in the face. "Ah. Dammit." Breena groaned and rolled to her stomach.

Lilly's concern was always like a disembodied voice in the air around Breena, cautioning. Lil was her alarm and conscience. Now, her voice came in from the hall in the same way. "Everything OK in there?"

"Yeah." Elbows pushing into her pillow, she propped up to give her courage one last chance.

-OK, Jet. Where do we meet?-

"And. . . send." *Nnn, my stomach.* Breena shoved the phone away and wrapped her arms around herself. Since killing Tabitha, Bree suffered stomach aches when she worried, migraines when she attempted dream manipulation, and unmanageable mood swings—mostly rage and guilt.

The ping assigned to numbers not in her contacts list sounded. Jet Sala replied to her text, instructing Breena to meet him the next day during his lunch break at the canoe rental stand where he worked.

****

Atlas looked back at his empty living room. Dusty footprints from the movers clouded the sheen of the polished floors, but they still reflected all the memories he made with Breena in the space more than a year earlier. The window sill she liked to sit in, the small dining table where she pretended—terribly—to like wine, and the corner where they attempted to build an indoor teepee using impossible instructions they found on a "50 At-Home Dates to Try This Friday Night" list online. The finished product had looked nothing like the picture on the website. *I miss that.*

He swung his apartment keys around on his finger, steeling himself to leave his home, and the Breena he first met, behind. With clenched teeth, he set the keys on the counter and rolled his final suitcase out of the door. It clicked shut behind him with an aching permanence. *Things went so wrong here.*

By the time Atlas arrived to the airport for his flight from London to Michigan, he had waffled between wanting her back and continuing their silence so many times that he had eight draft emails, four unsent text messages, and one scripted voicemail written out. *Indecision is pathetic. It's not that I even want her back, not unless she would do things my way. . .* Atlas shuffled out of his shoes and walked through security. *Actually. . . for once, she might.* He put his hands above his head as the agent waved a metal detecting wand over the buttons on his pants. *She doesn't want to ascend. She said as much when she called me after Tabitha died.*

"Thank you, sir. You can move through."

Atlas nodded. *Maybe I could get her to— No. No, I wanted a simple life.*

****

Breena didn't know when she had fallen asleep, but she woke up feeling more rested than she had in weeks. *Maybe the anticipation of regaining my sanity helped me pass out.* Still in her bra and underwear, Bree shuffled down to breakfast, bacon and something bready burning by the smell of it.

"Hey."

Jordan studied his charred toast like he was about to take an exam on it. She could see the dark waves of animosity rolling off his shoulders. Her energy, unusually replenished from sleep, allowed her to see the aura without focusing much. Acid burned in her chest, forcing Bree to grit her teeth against the recognition that she was the cause of the offending tension. "Can I have some of this bacon?"

"Do what you want." He stood, shoving his chair back with his knees, and gathered up his plate and utensils. They clattered into the sink and Breena fought the urge to peek to check for broken plates or glasses. Jordan was out of the room before she had pulled free of her involuntary withdrawal into herself, something loud noises had always caused her to do.

Breena flopped three strips of mostly-crisp bacon onto a blue plate and stood eating the cold meal over the sink. When she finished a minute later, she let her plate, which she didn't know why she had bothered to use, fall from her hand and into the sink like Jordan had, half-heartedly praying something would break and relieve the pressure.

Jordan sat upright in lotus position on the couch. Since the riots, he had increased his meditation sessions to an hour each, twice, sometimes even three times a day. When Lilly questioned him about it, he had said it was because he needed to gain endurance to take Breena's place in protecting and shielding them in case she fell into another long sleep or never fully recovered her connection to her psyche.

Breena noticed him as she crossed through the room and to the stairs. His sleep-ruffled hair fell in front of his eyes, which she assumed were closed, and he wore light grey sweatpants two sizes too big. Her heart fluttered at the steady rise and fall of his chest, the sun-drenched skin she had kissed so many times, and the constant heartbeat that used to lull her to sleep. Vague nausea dawned on her with the realization that she had no reason to be that close to him anymore. When her breath returned, she pivoted to continue to her room and dress for the meeting with Jet, but Jordan spoke, holding her in place.

"You're staring at me."

"No I'm not."

"Yes you are. You're looking at me like you've never seen me before."

"I wasn't looking at all." Breena spun on her heel and bee-lined for the stairs.

"You never were."

****

At the canoe shop on the Manistee River, Breena got in line behind a loud family of four and a couple acting like newlyweds. *By the time I reach the window I'm going to have missed Jet's entire lunch break just waiting to rent this dumb boat.* Jet insisted that she come as a customer, rent a boat, and sign all of the typical waivers for it. He explained that he'd already gotten in trouble once for taking out boats with friends during his lunchbreak, and he couldn't afford to lose his job.

She brightened, stepping up to the window. Jet was waiting for her with the paperwork and wristband. She shoved a twenty under the slot in the glass and went around the side of the building. Jet exited a few seconds later with a paddle in each hand.

"Hey, glad you came. Thought you might chicken out."

She shook her head.

"Here." He handed her a paddle and laid his on the ground. "Is it the right length for your height?"

"Yeah. Thanks."

"Good. Put that over there and help me get this canoe off the rack."

They walked underneath the boat and straightened their arms over their heads, lifting the boat off of the shelf.

"Walk it over there, and we'll set it down. We can come back for the paddles and then throw 'em in the boat."

On the water, Jet did most of the rowing to get them quickly away from shore. "So, new customer, aren't you?"

"You know I've bought from you before."

"That one time didn't count. A one-pill deal is hardly a deal."

Breena shrugged, content to let him put stock in his own assumptions.

"Ground rules, then. You tell me what you're looking for; I see what I can find. If I find it, I'll give you a price. Take it or leave it. I don't waste time negotiating."

Breena nodded along. *Like a bad movie.*

"I found the pills you asked for easily this time. Good intro price. Twenty pills, sixty dollars."

"Deal." She fished the remaining cash from her pocket and handed it over. Jet's rough fingers grazed her palm briefly as he dropped the bag in her hand and retrieved the money. She shivered at the contact. *I hope he didn't notice that.* The smooth pills rolled between her fingers through the clear baggie, and Breena looked at them for a long time before realizing Jet had been looking at her just as long.

"So, uh, you want to paddle around for a little longer?"

"Well, I, um, I was going to—" As she tried to come up with words, she noticed how the sun made a white circle of light where it shone on his almost-black hair, which fell straight in a long layer over the closely buzzed sides of his head. Her hand twitched with the impulse to brush it away from where the strands shadowed his lightly-freckled, sunny skin and rich brown eyes. "—I want to. . ." *see their details.*

"Just say no."

"No, no. I was just worried your lunch break was over. You still have time?"

"It's fine."

Breena nodded and stuffed the pills in her backpack.

"Help me row."

"'Kay." The canoe floated downriver until the rental building was small and the screaming children playing on shore didn't bother her. *This is nice.*

"Want some music?"

"No thanks. It's quiet out here. It's a good change."

"Lots of people in your house?"

"No, just two people who talk too much."

"I gotcha." Jet pressed his oars through the water a few more times, looking out to the tree line. His thick lips pressed shut.

"I'm sorry. I didn't mean you couldn't talk to me." She shuffled on the hard wooden plank. *This should not qualify as a seat.* "So, Jet. Do you take all of your clients on a peaceful river excursion after a drug deal?"

He snorted. "Hell no."

"Why me?"

"Why not? You're pretty, you came alone. . ."

Breena startled, and Jet could see it in the set of her eyebrows and the way she bit her lip.

"Shit, that sounded creepy. I'm not, I swear. You just seem like someone I want to get to know."

You wouldn't want to know it all. "That's. . . sweet? I think. I will admit it's fun talking to someone else for a change. Everyone's been so holed up since the riots that there haven't been many opportunities to get out and treat this like a real summer break."

"You say that, but business here has been better than ever. All the people who normally would have traveled to big cities are finding other ways to vacation."

"True. I'm surprised people are vacationing in Grayling at all. It seems so ordinary."

"Well, you grew up here, right?"

"Yeah."

"And that's why it feels plain. Think of all the people who live in huge cities where there was big time looting and arson. It must not look so bad here in comparison."

Breena surveyed the trees lining both sides of the river. Uprooted ones hung over the river, their longest branches dipping in. *There's no "better here" or "better there." I caused it all. It's all bad.* She shrugged, unable to find the silver lining.

"There are two types of people. The ones who stay and clean up when things go to shit, and the ones who escape." He swiveled around on his so-called seat and stared down-river. "The people who've come here are the latter."

"You've got that right." A smile spread across her face at the thought. She knew it wasn't something to smile at, but Jet's comment gave her a sick satisfaction, like she was in the right company even if *she* wasn't right. Jet turned back to face her, and the sun, which had shifted as they floated along, caught his eyes. They illuminated to a glowing red-amber hue, and Breena felt her heart thump one out-of-sync beat.

Jet rested his paddle over his lap. "Can I ask you something? About the Halcion pills."

Her face contorted in disapproval, but she said yes anyway. Bree stopped paddling, too, after realizing her one-person effort was guiding their boat into a circle.

"I'm assuming they're for you, not to sell?"

"Yeah. . ."

"Why? What do you need them for?"

"They're sleeping pills. . . I have insomnia."

"If you actually need them, can't you just go to a doctor and get them the legit way? Why risk it?"

"I can't get them from a doctor. I have dependency issues."

"You mean addiction."

Breena glowered. "I hate that word."

"All addicts do."

The sunlight shifted as the afternoon warmed Breena's face, and eventually the canoe-return hut popped into view around a bend in the river. Jet rowed toward shore as the current carried them closer to the building. When the boat sidled up to the mucky bank, Jet shoved a paddle in the mush to hold the canoe ashore and jumped out. Breena stood when the boat stopped rocking and grabbed on to Jet's hand. He helped her up the steep incline and went back down for the boat. By the time he got it and himself to the return shack, he was covered in thick black river filth. They walked out to the parking lot to wait the ten minutes for the next shuttle.

"You can't go back to work like that."

Jet kicked at the gravel. "Eh. I'm already an hour and a half late coming back from lunch. They don't expect me back at this point."

"Jet! I hope you don't lose your job because of me. I'd feel terrible. You even told me you couldn't get in trouble again, and I kept you out there so long." As she said the words, Breena acknowledged guiltily that she didn't actually feel their meaning. Jordan's face came to mind. *I only act like I care. Why?*

"Pff. It was my idea to float down. I don't care anymore anyway. It was worth it. Had a really good time, Breena." He faced her and stepped in.

Is he going to kiss me? Stepping back would say I assumed he was going to and that I'm rejecting him. I don't want to look presumptuous. It's conceited to think he'd want to kiss me already, anyway.

No one else was at the pick-up site. He reached for her hand.

Or is it? She held her position as he leaned in and planted a firm kiss on her lips. Breena inhaled sharply at the fire that bloomed behind her eyelids, and Jet responded by shoving his hands into her auburn hair. She let the kiss deepen until Jet pulled away and pointed up the dirt road, still catching his breath. *Like when I first met Atlas. . .*

The shuttle bus rumbled around the curve and stopped in front of them. She ascended, dazed, and Jet followed Breena up the steep steps and into a sticky vinyl seat. They sat, shoulders touching, in uncertain silence, and the bus puttered off.

In her car, Breena poked at her sunburned arm, watching the skin go white under her finger and the red flood back in when she lifted it. *Lilly and Jordan are going to notice this.* She pulled down the visor mirror and looked at her face. The pink sunburn accentuated the mossy green overtone her chestnut eyes sometimes reflected. *And my lips are so puffy. Sun and kissing do not mix well on me.* Thinking about her lips made Bree realize they were stinging from sun and friction. She flipped the visor back up and rifled through her backpack for lip balm. *Guess I don't have any.* She saw the corner of the plastic baggie poking out from under her wallet. On a sigh, she dropped her shoulders and pulled them out. The stress she held melted away at the thought of taking a pill. *It's been so long.* She pulled one from the bag. *And in a few minutes, this suffocating ache will be totally gone.* She dry-swallowed it and leaned her head back against the seat. *Bye-bye Atlas. Bye-bye Jordan. Bye-bye reality. Bye-bye guilt.*

****

As Breena slipped into her pharmaceutical bliss, Vos received a call from the one number he was obligated to answer.

"Sir?"

"I'm getting involved. This is taking too long. We need her."

"No, let me handle it. If you show up, she'll think I betrayed her."

"Like you betrayed Tabitha? Exactly. This is in my hands now. Don't go near her unless I tell you to. Galo and Mestif will handle this from now on."

"Fine." Vos hung up before he said something he would pay for later. As he stared into his muted TV, his heart ached for what he knew awaited Breena.

****

Atlas jumped up from his seat the moment he felt the familiar tug. For the first time since he had cradled Breena's bloody form as her psychic life drained away, she was back. Her connection was soft and nonspecific. There was no agenda, no command. The link flickered in his excitement, so Atlas lay out on his new living room floor to bask in it. He inhaled her relaxation. *It's been really lonely, Love.* Random thoughts and ideas trailed through her subconscious. *And what's this?* One scene in particular looped through like she was trying to make sense of it.

Atlas marveled. *That's my house. This house. I wonder if she knows I'm in Grayling.* In the memory, which he viewed through her eyes, he saw the window in the corner of the spare room, the room where he murdered Reid, where she killed Tabitha. A shadowed figure stared inside. There was no mistaking the energy that emanated from him, even though his face was unfamiliar. Chills crawled across Atlas' arms. *Ah, hell.* No one scared him as much as that man, and it infuriated Atlas. Sacrificing the rare moment with Breena, Atlas stormed into the kitchen.

Atlas rummaged through the cluttered drawer beside the refrigerator where all of the random junk and notes written on scrap paper landed. Between a book of coupons and a ring of keys to unknown locks was a sticky note with R's phone number, the last of his contacts from Tabitha's days. *I thought I was finally rid of all this.*

After shouting into the phone for a half an hour, Atlas left R with what *he* thought, but R couldn't seem to grasp, were simple instructions: Contact whatever rioters he knew, have them contact everyone *they* knew, choose a name for the group, pick a target, and destroy it. He needed to send a message that the rule-makers of society had not regained any ground since the riots died off, and that those rioters' feelings about the balance of powers had not changed. And, with any luck, Atlas could send a message to the man lurking in Breena's periphery that he was no match, not for Atlas, the world, or for Breena's iron will. It didn't matter to Atlas which side this looming figure was on—although Atlas knew exactly where he stood. And that was exactly the point. *There should* be *no sides.*

Chapter 2

"Breena, where the hell have you been?" Jordan's crystal blue eyes had darkened to hurricane oceans.

"And what happened to your skin?" Lilly wanted to press a finger to it but thought better of it.

Bree trudged through Jordan's front door at 7:30pm into the full-on scorn of her friends. Her head had its own pulse, and she shook away their questions with closed eyes. Seemingly simultaneously, Lilly was at her side offering her water and dinner, cold an hour ago, but supposedly delicious. Breena held her hand up to silence the chatter and pushed her way through to the stairs.

"Aren't you going to give us an explanation, Breena?" Jordan followed her up the steps with room enough only for air between them. "Dammit, Breena, talk to me!"

Breena reached her room without acknowledging Jordan, squeezing her body and bag through the slim opening of the door. Her effort to keep Jordan from following failed as he pushed in behind her, leaving the door cracked. Light from the hallway seeped in, but neither of them flipped the switch inside his father's office. She chucked her backpack to the floor, spinning on her heels. "I didn't invite you in, Jordan."

"I don't care. This is my house, so I can be in here if I want. I also want to know where you were. You were supposed to sit in on the followers' meeting at Christ Church with Lilly. You know, the group you put Linda in charge of before she bolted with your brother?"

"Well, how did the meeting go?"

Jordan threw his hands in the air. "It was just a social gathering. Drinks, chips, testimonials about how Linda saved them from Atlas' misguidance. No clues to where she took off to. But don't pretend to care, Breena. If you were actually interested, you would have gone with Lilly like you were supposed to. So, spill it. What was more important than following up on the first lead we've had on your brother in a month?"

"Nothing! Getting Ari back is still the most important thing to me."

"Bull. If that were true, you wouldn't have bailed on your best friend and left your brother out there a day longer than he has to be. So, what were you doing?"

"I went to the river to canoe with a friend."

"The truth, Bree."

"I swear. Where do you think I got so sunburned?"

Jordan scanned her body, incredulous.

Breena squirmed under his gaze, acutely aware that he was studying her. *My lips are still puffy. He'll know.* Breena put a hand to her mouth and picked at her lip. *Stupid, you're just drawing more attention.* She spun away from Jordan then, unable to tolerate the inspection any longer.

"Tch. You're unbelievable, going out to play when things are so serious right now. You're so selfish."

Back still toward Jordan, Bree squeezed closed her stinging eyes and willed the tears that sprang up to stay put. *Can't I just mourn myself in peace?* Jordan shifted his weight. The floor squeaked. Breena locked her lips, wriggling out of her clothes one limb at a time in an effort not to rub past her radiating skin. Jordan watched with pained adoration as one stretch of flesh after another was revealed to him—flesh that he loved. Breena's heart raced in a combination of thrill and spite.

Her actions mirrored months earlier, when she and Jordan first became a couple, except for the quick reveal and spiteful intentions. *Am I doing this to be cruel or because I want his attention?* The light from the hallway cast a yellow stripe across her back and down to her hip. A cool hand on her arm interrupted the impending downward spiral. She swayed. Jordan reached back with his foot and pushed the door shut. The room receded into a collage of dark figures. He stepped closer and leaned down to Breena's ear. She smelled like trees and grass.

"I don't understand what happened to you."

Bree hugged her arm around her torso to cover his hand. She stared off into the darkness of the room. "Everything has happened to me." *I'm saying goodbye.*

The next morning, Breena held the phone away from her splotchy face and whispered to Lilly, "My mom's still with Grant. Says he doesn't want her back at home alone."

Lilly rolled her eyes. "We have to talk to her about this soon. If she's not going home, just tell her now. Tell her we're leaving to look for Ari, and if she wants to come with us we need to know."

"Mom, Ari's been gone three months. We're going to look for him." Breena squeezed the bridge of her nose. "No. I'm not just going to wait around for the police anymore. I *know* he's with Linda." She put the phone on speaker and set it down on the big oak desk.

The electronic tin of Lexa's voice prattled on. "It's just not safe. I don't like that you're not here with me, but you—"

Breena cut in. "Then come with us, Mom, geez. I can't believe you've waited this long."

"Breena, you know it's just not that simple. The police investigation doesn't need our interference, and it's not practical for me to pick up and go like that."

"You don't like that I'm not there with you when I'm staying just a few miles down the road, but you won't do anything about your son who's God knows where? Stay in Grayling with Grant. Whatever. We're going to bring Ari home." Breena snatched the phone back from the desk and disconnected, lamenting the bygone days of physically slamming a phone into its cradle. Lilly looked at the ground shaking her head.

"What? I'm eighteen, now."

Lilly scowled at Breena anyway.

"Don't give me that face. You know it's what we have to do. Besides, going off to find him will be like a replacement for our canceled beach week."

"I really don't think this is going to be anything like a vacation."

Breena picked at her lip and shrugged.

Lilly pulled her strawberry hair into a ponytail. "And what about Jordan's parents?"

"What about them? They never paid attention to him before. Why would they care where he goes now? As soon as we graduated, their minimal parental instincts went into retirement." A thump issued from the front of the house, and Breena stood up. "Jordan must be home from the grocery store."

The girls padded across the dense green carpet and out of the darkly shelved office.

"You home, Jordan?"

No response.

"Wow, Bree, he's giving you the silent treatment now? Jordan, did you remember my cheese puffs?"

Bree glowered. "Maybe he locked himself out." Breena walked quicker toward the staircase. "I'm sure he got your cheese puffs and conveniently forgot my frozen yogurt. We had another moment last night."

Lilly trailed slowly behind her, always suspicious rather than curious. "I'm not surprised. He was really mad at you. Honestly, so was I, but I know you're under a lot of pressure so—"

Breena bounded down the stairs and peeked in the kitchen. Jordan wasn't in there, so she strode to the front door. Lilly watched her pass the landing from the top step, her toes curled around the highly polished wooden edge. Bree reached for the doorknob and, as she turned it, the door was shoved open from the outside. Two brawny men busted into the foyer, quickly overtaking Breena, who shrieked muffled screams as the taller of the two men pulled a black sack over her head then hoisted her on to her tip toes, his forearms under her armpits.

Lilly, who had come far enough down the steps to see past the wall where the banister ended, sprang into the only action she knew how to take. She texted 911 furiously, giving Jordan's address and describing as much of the men as she could see:

-5'8" and 6'5", over 200 lbs, wearing all black, masks
but no gloves, Caucasian or Mediterranean, can't see
vehicle.-

She stared on with her freckled hands over her mouth as Breena's feet were swept from under her, held by the shorter man, and they shuffled their claim to the door.

Adrenaline kicked in once Breena's mind caught up with what was happening to her. She flushed with a hot, buzzing sensation, remembering one of Lilly's many tips on avoiding a kidnapping, and twisted wildly in their grip. The guys were so huge it didn't seem to make a difference, and Breena was carried into the sticky air outside. Panic rose in her throat. Pleas pressed against the back of her gritted teeth, but Bree choked down the impulse to call for Lilly. *They can't know Lilly's in there.*

Bree's back hit a hard surface, propelling the air out of her lungs. Hands were upon her again, dragging her arms around to the front of her body and down toward her ankles. Cold metal encircled her wrists. The same sensation linked her ankles. With a final, jerking tug, all of her limbs met in the middle and were secured like a pig on a spit. The foreign hands left her and a door slammed. Two more doors thumped afterwards, in quick succession. *I'm in a vehicle.* The engine rumbled to life.

Under her, the vehicle squeaked and popped as it tore out of Jordan's driveway and into the road. She rolled slightly toward the back of what Breena could only imagine was the cargo area of a van. The vehicle veered right at the stop sign at the end of Jordan's street. She was only so familiar with it because she had gotten a ticket for doing the same thing a month after getting her driver's license, and the month after that, too. As they motored away from her safe haven, she breathed a chorus of directions into the hot air of the hood still stuck on her head.

Right, straight forty seconds, stop. Left, straight three hundred seconds, stop. Straight one, two, three, four. . .

Bree came to in a dim room with wood-paneled walls and faux ceiling beams. Her arms ached and, when she moved to stretch them, she found that they were cuffed to the headboard behind her. It didn't look like much, the old 70s furniture, but as she rocked her bodyweight forward and back, hoping to snap the frame, Breena thought of what her mom always said about things not being made like that anymore. *Sturdy.* Bree glared at the three wooden ducks flying over the TV on the wall opposite. The air conditioning unit under the window to her left roared to life, making her jump. The cuffs bit into Breena's wrists again, and she swore.

The heat of anger flooded Breena, then, as if someone poured a bucket of steaming bath water over her head. First her eyes burned, and then the sensation moved downward, her face flaming to life. She couldn't see herself in the TV screen, but she knew she was red. As the rage traveled, the metal cuffs heated.

Right, straight forty seconds, stop. Left, straight three hundred seconds, stop. Straight... Hell! What number did I make it to? We were on that road a long time, but when did I pass out, and how much longer after that did we drive? Just as Bree was about to start in on berating herself again, voices sifted in through the large gap under the door to her right. She froze. *Stay awake so I can put up a fight? Act asleep so they leave me alone?* The key card slipped through the lock. The handle turned. *Fight.*

Two men moseyed into the room, still absorbed in their conversation. Breena instinctively pushed an image through her mind, only to be met by the searing pain of her still-broken connection to the astral plane. Illusions failing, she relied on her fire, hating that she had to wait for one of them to touch her to have an effect. Pulling against the bed again, the wood, which, in her panic she hadn't noticed was smoking underneath her handcuffs, gave.

She leapt off of the bed, hooking the short one around the neck with the chain between her wrists as he lunged forward to tackle her. Yanking him down and forward with both arms, she rammed her knee into his face, crushing his nose and rendering him limp on the floor. An angry line of chain-link-shaped welts tracked the back of his neck tattoo where she burned him.

The big one moved as clumsily as Breena expected given his size, though he was obviously the more intelligent of the two. It was clear in the wide-eyed fury he wore that his brain moved faster than his body could, and by the time his body caught up, she had already snatched up the unconscious one's gun from the waistband of his jeans. She cocked it and aimed at the immense target in front of her.

"What the hell? How did you get off the headboard?" He froze with his hands mid-reach.

The little one roused and looked up. "Shit, Galo, she got my gun!"

"Idiot, don't use my name." The taller, Galo, pulled his gun from his hip in the second Breena glanced down. He unlocked the safety and pointed it at her. "Get on the ground."

She trembled. Her hands had lost feeling between her grip on the gun and the radiating heat pulsing from them. Unable to take her eyes off of the gun trained on her, a new wave of adrenaline pumped through, and the room around her grayed. The searing headache materialized in the form of blue and black floaters in her vision. *Maybe they're like me.* With her last push of energy, Breena sent out a pulse of heat and persuasion toward her kidnappers. *Nothing. I'm too weak, or they're only human.* "Where am I?"

"Get. On. The. Ground. I don't mind shooting you."

"Galo! He said we're supposed to bring her alive."

Galo cut an incendiary look at his inept partner. "Shut up. She doesn't need to know."

Breena swayed. *Atlas did this.*

"Breena, drop it."

Bree shook her head. She knew it came across as the gesture of a disobedient child unwilling to comply rather than confident defiance, but her vision was red, and she lacked the coherence to posture more formidably.

"What do you think will happen to you if I shoot you? Do you think you can survive it? I've heard how tough you are."

No one moved or spoke for a few seconds. The other kidnapper wore a strangled look of satisfaction, like he was having a hard time waiting for the next move.

Galo broke in. "OK, then. Let's find out." He raised the gun again and pulled back the hammer.

In the instant between Galo cocking the gun and firing, a thought inconsistent with the gravity of the situation flitted to Bree's mind. *Where's this guy from? That revolver looks hundreds of years old.*

Galo started to curl his finger around the trigger. Breena inhaled until she couldn't fill her lungs any further, and closed her eyes. *He said he couldn't kill me.*

The shot rang out and she flinched, dropping the gun, but nothing happened to her. When she looked up, she saw Galo on the ground. *Wait, did I shoot* him*? I didn't think I...* The ringing in her ears prevented Bree from hearing what the men were saying, but Galo looked up at the other guy with rage. Sounds returned with a hollow, under water hum, and she caught the end of their argument.

"Don't you ever shove me while I'm holding a gun again, or you're the one that gets the bullet. You're such an imbecile." Galo stood, holstering his gun and turning his attention to Bree. "Well, now that we've been distracted out of our standoff," he glared at his partner again, "let's have a little chat."

****

Jordan walked up his front porch as the police cars filed into his driveway. He glanced behind him, pausing with his hand hovering above the door knob, his arm loaded with plastic grocery bags. An officer stepped out of the first car and approached the porch.

"What's happening, Officer?"

"I'm Officer Lovette. Emergency dispatchers received a 911 text message at this address."

"Breena!" Jordan turned his back on the officer and burst through his front door shouting for his friends.

"Jordan!" Lilly flew down the stairs and into Jordan's chest. "They got Breena. Jordan, what are we going to do? They took her somewhere. I couldn't do anything. I'm supposed to know what to do. I just sat there and watched."

He let the plastic bags slide over his hands and onto the floor. When Jordan was free, he wrapped Lilly up and pulled her close to him. "It's going to be OK. The police are here. You need to go tell them what happened."

"I know, but. . ."

The officers had already filed into the foyer while Jordan and Lilly hugged. He grabbed Lilly's shoulders and looked down into her eyes. "This is how you can help."

Jordan cleared the kitchen table, the least frequently used piece of furniture in the house, and sat down beside Lilly. Officer Lovette stared levelly at them from across the glass. Lilly launched into the events starting at Breena's phone conversation with Lexa, mentioning the thump they'd heard, and then the forced entry and kidnapping. Lilly stared at her hands as she confessed that she hadn't left the steps to see what kind of vehicle they'd driven. Jordan kept a hand on Lilly's knee the whole time while Officer Lovette scribbled notes silently, but it was a white-knuckled grasp more useful for holding himself together than for comforting Lilly.

"And so you didn't get to see their faces at all?"

"No. They were both wearing ski masks."

"No identifying features visible? Tattoos, piercings, scars?"

"Both of them were wearing black cargo pants and black long sleeve shirts. I could really only see their hands. They might have been tan Caucasians, but it's possible they were southern European, too. I remember being surprised they didn't have gloves on."

Officer Lovette held a hand up to stop Lilly and talked into his walkie. "Look for prints around the front door." Returning his attention to Lilly, he motioned for her to continue.

"The tall one had his back to me, so I didn't get a good look, but the short one had small eyes, close-set. Dark. Brown or even black, maybe, and his eyebrows and lashes were just as dark."

"Were they armed?"

"Maybe. If they were, they didn't show their weapons. They shoved into the house so forcefully that Breena was hit by the door. She stumbled back. There was no real way to fight back, so they didn't need a weapon to get her."

"Very good. Thank you."

"Officer, I'm sorry I don't have more information. I feel so bad for hiding, but I knew they'd take me, too, if they saw me."

"You did the right thing."

Tears filled her hazel eyes and she stared up at the ceiling. "It doesn't feel like it."

Officer Lovette stood. "Thank you, Miss Ledford. We'll be in contact."

Lilly and Jordan followed the officer to the door. The others finished searching the outside of the house for signs of tampering then got into their cruisers. Lilly called a thank you after Officer Lovette, and he waved a hand without turning around. After the police were out of the driveway, she looked over at Jordan. He ignored her gaze and went back into the house.

On the couch, Jordan sunk into the deep maroon cushions and put his head in his hands. Lilly stood in the open doorway not knowing what to say. After a minute of still silence, Jordan reached into his pocket and withdrew a folding knife he had taken to carrying during the weeks of rioting. Absently, he flicked it open and closed, blade out, blade in, blade out. He gripped it, then, by the blade, his fingers wrapping around it.

"Jordan, don't—"

"How could you just sit there and watch them take her?"

Lilly recoiled. The flat tone struck more harshly than if he had yelled. She ran up to the bedroom the three had been sharing since graduation.

He curled in on himself more, knees to face, holding the back of his head, knife still in hand. "Why did you say that, Jordan?" Standing suddenly, he buried the blade in the wooden coffee table in front of him.

Upstairs, Lilly sat blindingly close to her computer screen digging away at Ari's old emails to Linda, screen name Dreaming_of_Madrid. "Madrid. Is that where you went, kid? Is Breena there with you?" She scrolled through the attachments in one of the emails, all pictures of Spanish Baroque church spires. Linda wasn't in any of the pictures, so it was hard to tell if the photos were souvenirs or Linda's wishful thinking, a bucket list of sorts. Lilly shifted on the pile of dirty clothes she used as a floor cushion muttering curses about London, where Linda, Tabitha, and Atlas had lived, and all the loonies it had birthed. "Harold Shipman-Doctor Death, Michael Lupo-Wolf Man, Colin Ireland-The Gay Slayer, Thomas Neill Cream-The Lambeth Poisoner, Beverly Allitt-Angel of Death, the illusive Jack the Ripper, Atlas effing Thorley."

An electronic ping beside Lilly snapped her out of her sleuthing. A text message from Jordan scrolled across the screen of her cell phone.

-I'm sorry.-

She scrunched her nose and entered a reply.

-I'm busy. Come upstairs and say it to my face or help me by calling Lexa and telling her what happened.-

****

In the musty hotel room, Galo exhaled cigarette smoke directly into Breena's face. Her eyes watered, and she tried to turn away, but he grabbed her by the chin and held her in place. She closed her eyes, unable to stare confidently into his golden gaze. His appearance was at once human and pleasing, and a little uncanny, unlikely. His hair, eyes, and skin all conveyed tones of honey or amber, like he'd been airbrushed into existence. And it didn't matter that he was seated on the mattress directly across from her, legs crossed like a preschooler, knees pressing against hers. The pose wasn't young or childish on him; he hulked over her.

Breena knew why they took her—she didn't have to ask Galo— but there were still other questions buzzing. *Where am I? Where's Ari? Is he still with Linda? Is Jordan OK? Poor Lilly.* She clamped her mouth shut, a difficult effort amidst the acrid smoke lingering around her. It smelled like swamp, nothing like the cherry cigarillo she had tried in her car after school last year when her emotional withdrawals from the prescriptions and Atlas were at their worst.

"Look at me."

She shook her head.

"Let me see those eyes. What color are they?"

Breena looked up at him trying to channel all of her rage and loathing through her stare. She wanted to burn him with it.

"Oh, ho, ho. Tawny rings of fury. The family eyes. Hey, Mestif, the master was right about this one, wasn't he?"

"Galo, you said we couldn't use our names."

"Well, she already knows mine, thanks to you. Why should I go protecting your identity?"

"Right." Mestif flopped across the end of the mattress on his back, arms stretched over his head. He sniffed an armpit and huffed out a gust of air, crinkling his face. "Oof." He winced again as the movement of his face wrinkled his bashed nose.

Galo rolled his eyes and grinned back at Breena. "He's loyal, but he's no genius. What do you think?"

"I think you're shit."

Mestif cackled and rolled off the bed. "I love this girl."

Galo swung at Mestif and easily closed the distance with his impressive reach. "Breena, you just need to hang tight here until we get the go ahead to take you home."

"He's not going to let me go home. Atlas sent you to take me away from Jordan because I didn't call the guy he wanted me to. He's so petty. Tell me what you did with Jordan."

"We don't have Jordan. He wanted *you.*"

Breena rolled her eyes. She had heard those last words so many times before, or, at least, it felt like it. Every time she got safely out of Atlas' reach, he pulled her back in. She resigned to the voice in the back of her mind; she had asked for this in a way, too. *I wanted to know how to get to Hell. Atlas hasn't heard that Vos already told me. He'll show up soon enough. He never could resist telling me things himself.*

"You know, I'm surprised you ended up with that kid—"

"Atlas is my chosen. Why would that be surprising?" She shook her head. "It doesn't matter. We're not together."

"No, I meant Jordan."

"We aren't together, either."

"Sure you're not. I'm surprised you ended up with that kid because Atlas seemed to know you pretty well. He had you pegged."

"Again, Chosen. But why are you talking about Atlas in the past tense? Didn't he send you to take me?" Her hands started to sweat.

"You know, none of us back home ever liked Jordan, and we would have been happy to take him off your hands, but it's always been about you, Breena. We had no use for Jordan to begin with. He's a waste of a boyfriend. What can he offer you that's better than power?"

It had been months since she last contacted Atlas, but worry crept in anyway. "I said we're not together! Now, tell me who sent you."

Chapter 3

As Breena fought with Galo about the state of her relationship with Jordan, she thought back to the night of their break-up and how Jordan had pulled her down to the pile of blankets and covered her with kisses like he was praying to her skin. She had laid there, silent tears rolling from the corners of her eyes to her pillow, as he whispered empty wishes into her neck and pressed love dressed as distractions through her ribcage and into her heart. After he had gone back to his room for the evening, she stared at the ceiling wondering if she was even real. The detachment crept in and swallowed her as she slugged back some water and another pill.

Galo prattled away in front of her. She focused back in on him. "What I still don't get is how you managed to stay off the radar so long after taking out Tabitha and then all of a sudden you just popped back up, like you wanted to be found. What made you change your mind?"

"I don't know what you mean. Change my mind about what?"

"You met Atlas the other night. Drew a lot of attention, actually."

"No I didn't."

"Yes. You did. That's how we knew you were back."

"Back? I never left. I was just hiding under an illusion screen."

"We were ordered to go get you after you showed up on his astral plane."

Breena shook her head, about to dispute Galo's claims again when an image prickled its way into focus. *A memory. A dream? I did meet him. Just not in person.* "I never meant to. I was dreaming. It wasn't real."

"You know that's crap. All of your dreams are real. That's your born gift. All of Tabitha's family has some ability. Dream manipulation is yours. I can't believe they never told you this."

"But I wasn't trying to reach him. And I thought that ability was destroyed. Even if I wasn't broken, I still don't understand how I contacted him. I wasn't trying."

"Is it so hard to imagine? You weren't trying when they first found you years ago, either. You must've had similar conditions."

A hand flew to her mouth, and she spoke into her palm. "Oh my hell, the pills."

"What?"

"Sleeping pills. They must have relaxed my mind and caused me to unintentionally astrally project. And that's how you found me?" Breena doubled over as her stomach sickened. *It's like I sent out a beacon asking to get snatched.*

Galo nodded. A startling snore ripped out of Mestif, who had fallen asleep near Breena's feet. "'Ya know, kid, if it makes you feel any better—"

"It won't."

"If it makes 'ya feel any better, we're only doing this because it's right for the family. We would've gotten you back eventually."

Breena drew her eyebrows close together. "If this is all for the good of the family, then why were you so ready to kill me earlier? You said Atlas wanted me alive."

Shaking his head, "I *wasn't* ready to kill you. But, threatening people with force is the surest way to get them to do what you need them to do for you. I needed you to *think* I would, to comply."

Mestif kicked as if fighting in his dreams, and Breena snorted. "What's with him? He's like a puppy."

"You're not wrong. Mes is. . . well, Mes is a mess. He's the family's sentry, a half-breed born on Earth and given to our service by his family. I know what you're thinking, that he's not smart enough to be our guardian. You're right. He's no genius strategist or nothing. He's an accessory. Our family chose him as a favor to his folks. Family name's 'Sala.'"

Breena startled. *Jet's name. Does that explain the fire when we kissed? Of course it does. Who am I kidding?*

Galo chuckled. "Literally means 'worker in a manner house.' It is his purpose. Now, they owe us. Also, Atlas didn't send us."

Breena blinked a few times. Something tingled at the edge of her recognition, a memory she didn't realize she held from the night she killed Tabitha. "Now's when you tell me who did."

Mestif, whose mouth hung open, choked and sat straight up from his sleep. "Where'd he go?"

"You were dreaming. Be useful and go get us some dinner. And put some ice on that nose. You're ugly enough without the swelling."

"OK, Galo." Mes stood, stretching, joints crackling, and wobbled to the door with his deep-set eyes mostly closed. He shrugged through the door and pulled it behind him.

When the room fell silent again, Galo looked back at Breena. His flaxen eyes shimmered. "Think about it. You know who commands us."

Bree studied her lap, unsure of what else to say. The memory of the moments after Tabitha's murder sharpened and she saw, in the background of the gory scene, the man who had peered through the window. *It could only be one person.*

Galo stared out the window through a small gap in the curtains. In the silence, Bree's hands began to shake. Anxiety crept in, along with a thrashing heartbeat. "Untie me."

"Eh?"

"My hands. Uncuff my hands."

Galo crinkled his forehead.

"Fucking untie me, Galo!" Breena snapped. Before Galo moved from the window, she leapt up and started smashing her restrained hands against the wall. Her breaths came quick and shallow. Galo approached her, hands outstretched to unfasten her restraints. She screamed, seeing tentacles on each of his hands instead of fingers.

He caught her wrists. "I'm unhooking you. Stop screaming."

Breena wailed more.

"Breena, shut up! Hell. You're going to get the cops called on us."

"The gun shots didn't," she sneered.

He jiggled the tiny key into the lock, Breena sniveling on, her horror having dwindled into an injured whimpering. When the cuffs fell free, Bree bolted into the dingy bathroom and slammed the door behind her.

Against the wooden door, she resigned her weight and slid to the floor, hands over face. She couldn't look. Everything in her sight shifted and morphed into vile visions. When her rear hit the tile, the lump in her back pocket caught her attention. *Halcion.* With one hand, Breena lifted off the floor, and with the other, she fished the baggie from her jeans. Opening the bag forced her to open her eyes, and she was thankful the pills looked like pills the whole time she gazed into the pile of redemption. She hadn't taken any in two days, hoping to stretch the purchase as long as she could. In an effort to speed the absorption of the medication and stave off the withdrawals, she crushed one of the pills into the floor, cursing when it only broke into little white shards rather than powder that would dissolve on her tongue. She picked up the pieces and popped them into her mouth.

Breena swallowed at the bits ineffectively. *Up, up.* Gripping at the edge of the sink, she hoisted herself to standing and put her mouth in the faucet stream. The sharp chunks scraped down Bree's throat, and she popped the second pill into her mouth, downing it without effort. The medication didn't kick in immediately, but the cold water sobered her senses. *I'm in great shape.* The noise of the room rushed in after her warped visions receded. There was banging at the door.

"Open up. Breena, come on. Let me in."

"Are you going to let me go home?"

"Yes, I'm taking you to Luce in the morning."

"Who's that?"

"Luce. Lucifer? Oh, you've been calling him Satan, haven't you? FYI, he hates that."

"That's not home."

"Of course it is. I'm taking you to your family. Now let me in so I can make sure you're OK."

Breena braced herself over the sink and watched the water swirling down the drain. *My life.* She thought back to the argument with Jordan. *Why'd I do that?* The hypnotic flow eased her shakes a bit. *To be back in the fray.* She grimaced as the words resurfaced, and then a sense of thrill overcame her. *I got what I wanted.*

"I'm going to kick the door in. Stand back." Outside, Galo readied his stance, but the doorknob turned, Breena quietly stepping out.

"So Gehenna wants me back sooner rather than later."

****

One-hundred miles south, at an abandoned Methodist church, a group of Tabitha's followers, wrangled together by R, gathered around the large cross on the front of the property. Atlas sat in an RV at a house across the street—it wasn't his—a baseball cap pulled low over his eyes. No one was home. He wasn't concerned. The wind whipped through the group, blowing hair into faces and carrying the voice of their leader away. He shouted over the gusts. "Now, take down this cross and show the religious community what it looks like to feel betrayed."

Atlas rolled his eyes at their drama but itched to join in. Two women in jeans and tank tops hefted axes and approached the mammoth wooden cross. A small group of zealots holding ropes backed away from the monument, the cords pulling taught between their hands and the top of the structure. The rest of the group formed a ring around the destroyers. As the women chopped away at the base of the cross and the other group pulled on their lines, the circle of bystanders chanted.

As the crucifix crashed to the ground, the chanters dispersed to a pile of glass bottles lying near the church's entrance. They stuffed dripping cloths into the openings and set them afire. In chaos, the church blazed, each rioter hurling a few Molotov cocktails through windows and into wooden doorways. They reveled in their destruction, dancing and hollering with victorious ire.

****

Lilly paced across the bedroom, mumbling to herself without embarrassment knowing the thunder would cover it. "So, Linda took Ari on a cruise, supposedly, and then returned to London, leaving her and Atlas' hotline callers with no guidance and no reason to do what they'd been instructed. Tabitha or someone under her control got to the followers before Breena took Tabs out. Missing their leader, they took it upon themselves to avenge her, and that's why they riot. The devotees might not be able to help me find Linda and Ari, but I bet they lead to Breena. I'm sure they want her life in repayment for Tabitha's."

One terse knock on the door interrupted her theorizing. Jordan entered, raising his hands by his head, before Lilly responded. "It's my room, too."

"I never said you couldn't come in." She sat back at the computer and pulled up Ari's electronic banking account. She prayed he had used his debit card for something. There were no airline or train ticket purchases, no snacks at gas stations or trinkets at souvenir shops, so, not wanting to defeat hope, they all assumed he had used cash. None of Linda's emails had indicated anything additional, either.

Jordan flopped on the bed and inhaled deeply. "It doesn't smell like Breena anymore."

Lilly checked on him over her shoulder. "I changed the sheets."

He wore a drawn expression as he considered his hands, which he held out in front of his face toward the ceiling. "Lilly, about what I said. I'm sorry."

"It's OK."

"It's not."

"Well, it wasn't nice, but it wasn't wrong, either."

Jordan propped up on his elbows. "They were supposed to take *me*. Atlas always hated me. I figured to get to Breena he'd want me out of the way first. Should've known he'd go straight to the source." His face twisted. "Or not find us at all. My illusions weren't good enough to keep her safe."

Lilly massaged her temples. "I don't know what to tell you."

He shook his head and laid back. "I talked to Lexa."

"And?"

"Angry, but not like I thought she'd be. Think she might have used up all her caring when Breena was in the hospital. Gotta say, I know how she feels." After a few beats of silence, he probed, "Have you seen the news yet?"

"More storms?"

"You could call it that, I guess." He clicked the remote to the small TV in the bedroom and held the volume button until all the bars on the screen were full. The newscast was just loud enough to hear.

"—at the Methodist Church Camp in Vestaburg. As you can see behind me, the buildings are still smoldering, but the fire chief has confirmed that the blaze is under control. First responders will be monitoring the scene until the last of the embers burn out. As for the suspect in this case, the person partially revealed here by security footage has identified himself as 'The Disorder,' which is burned into the grass in front of the church's parking lot."

On the screen played a pixelated loop of security footage on one half of the screen and a still of the man's face, filmed from the side, on the other half. He wore a zip-up sweatshirt, hood up, and masquerade mask over his eyes. The still showed the perfect moment, the only one in the entire video capture, where he looked directly into the camera. The hairs on Lilly's arms stood and her heart skipped a beat.

"This has already been labeled a hate crime and arson. Authorities believe he worked with a group based on the scale of the attack. Unfortunately, until the recording can be enhanced, this is the only face clearly recorded by the security cameras. A search for those responsible is underway."

"That was Atlas."

Jordan gave a solemn nod and turned off the TV. "*That's* the meeting we should have been at."

****

Parked at the back of a truck stop lot off of I-94 East, Atlas watched the same news report from a rusty lawn chair outside of the RV he decided to steal. The analog television hung outside the cabin door by a precariously mounted swinging arm. A smug grin played across his face as the crime scene footage looped behind the reporter's head.

"Hell of a thing to do, 'ya know?" Atlas turned. A ruddy man with no hips moseyed toward the camper holding on to his shapeless jeans. His left arm was darker than his right—a trucker's tan. He nodded at the screen and looked expectantly back at Atlas. "People, I tell 'ya."

Atlas' lips twitched up at the corner, just a flash of a second, in concealed pride. He shifted in his seat, propping his ankle over his right knee. Stretching back with his hands behind his head, he ventured, "Must have taken a lot of planning, something of that scale."

"Name's Roy. Don't see many RVers in the truckers' lots. Usually just fuel up, grab a bite, roll out."

Atlas rolled his eyes. "So what can I do for you?"

"Thought I'd come chat. Where 'ya from?"

"London."

The bean pole's eyes narrowed. "Where's your accent?"

Atlas stood, crossing his arms over his chest. "Assimilated."

"Ah, so you been here a while. Where you headed?"

"I don't know yet."

The trucker rocked back on his heels and laughed. "You're one of them free spirits."

"Hardly." The men stood shoulder to shoulder regarding the news. After a heavy pause, Atlas feigned a glance at his watch. "Well, looks like it's time for me to get back on the road. It was good talking to you, um—" He held his hand out.

"Roy."

"Right. Apologies. Have a nice evening, Roy." Atlas grabbed the remote from his dilapidated chair and folded the creaking metal hinges. He threw it all into the cabin without regard and maneuvered the TV around on its arm and back into place inside the door. Keys already in hand, Atlas hustled around to the driver's side and vaulted into the air-ride seat. He turned the ignition and drove from his parking space not looking back to see if Roy had gone.

"Hey, yeah, it's Roy. Tell the group I found him. No, he didn't recognize me from the hotline group at all. He's headed east on 94 in a tan RV with two gold stripes down the side. Probably a 1970s model by the style of it."

In the windowless room they reserved for their action meetings, Jo scrawled the message as it was relayed to her across a wall-sized white board, and then she hung up the phone. Behind her, the mix of people cheered and shook hands. Leigh hurried to reassemble her gun, which was in pieces on the table for cleaning, and others hovered by the door, car keys already in hand.

From the corner of the room, dark energy loomed, waiting. Determined to see to it that Galo and Mestif brought his granddaughter home without Atlas' interference, Lucifer had decided to go into the human world for the first time in eons. Typically, he sent his daughters or servants to do such messy work as possessions. But, this cause mattered more than stoking the flaming side of the balance between Heaven and Hell, and Tabitha and Atlas had already upset the balance enough. He needed this done cleanly.

When the bustle of excitement settled, Jo put her phone in her back pocket and gave a rundown to the group of vigilantes. "Roy said he'd be easy to find. The RV he's in is old, stands out, and the guy's got an arrogant attitude—over confident in himself and bound to slip up. If we get ahead of him, we can beat him to his destination, give him a little surprise welcome."

"How do you know it's him?" A round man with glasses shifted his weight impatiently.

Ted chimed in. "And how are we supposed to know his destination?"

"You saw the news. The missing spokesman from the hotline fundraiser last year suddenly reappears, takes us all on as recruits in what I can only describe as a cult, and then this guy trashes the church, which is exactly what Reid—"

Leigh interjected, *"Atlas."*

"—*Atlas* wanted us to do. Don't you think they look like the same person? The eyes. . ."

"They resemble. But how do you know he's the cause of all of this?" Ted squirmed under Leigh's typical glare.

Jo chewed on the cap of her red dry-erase marker. She opened her mouth to answer, but Leigh spoke up instead.

"That *is* the man who caused this. He's the one who answered the hotline when I called last year. He's the one I met at that hole-in-the-wall café. He's the one who tried to recruit us into the riots and then passed us off to that woman, Linda," she rolled her eyes, "who told us to do the opposite of anything he said. He's the one in that church-burning video. I know it."

Ted let out a heavy sigh. "I'm all for holding someone accountable for the chaos that's been unleashed, but if we get the wrong people, we'll be no better than they are."

Leigh scanned the room for shocked faces to match her own. There were only tense stares and rigid postures. "Who is this guy?"

"It's me, Ted. Leigh, we've met."

She stuck out her hand for a handshake. "I'm sorry. I didn't catch that. You said your name's Coward?"

"Easy, Leigh." Jo pressed her temples between her palms. "I'm sick of being your referee."

From the corner, Lucifer agreed to himself. *Yes, Leigh, do calm down. This is such tedious business even without your braying.*

Leigh gesticulated with her gun at the woman with the marker. "I'm fine, Jo." Facing Ted again, Leigh went on. "Look, you're new here—"

"I'm not!" Ted wrung his hands and tried not to cry.

"—so I'm going to catch you up to speed. This *is* the right person. I know because he drew me out, tried to brain wash me into thinking I had some kind of power, some royal blood."

What rubbish my daughter created.

"Calls himself Atlas like he's got the world in his hands. He's a manipulative bastard. So your concern, however valiant, is not needed. If you're not into helping us, then leave."

"I know who he is. I was at the meetings, too." Ted mumbled just above a whisper, "I'm invisible."

OK, Leigh. That's quite enough. Lucifer surged. Leigh swayed like someone shoved her in the shoulder as Luce took his target. Her vision blurred momentarily and weight settled in her chest. It was like drowning, and she tried to scream. She could hear herself talking normally instead.

As if listening in on herself from a separate place, Luce made her say, "As for how we know his destination, I've got that covered already."

Jo raised an eyebrow, curious how Leigh had more facts when they hadn't known anything before Roy's call.

Luce dissembled for Leigh. "Something he said to me during a session last year. I've just been holding on to the information until the time was right. Sorry for keeping it from you. You understand."

Chapter 4

Galo guided Breena back to the squeaky bed with a hand on her back. She had the urge to pull away, but no energy to do it. "When do I have to see him?"

"You make it sound like you don't want to see him."

"I don't."

"I don't get you. Everything you did was planned specifically so you could take over, to rule, yet you don't even want to go back home, much less meet your relatives. How did you think you were going to lead without them?"

She rolled her eyes. "I thought I was going to change things. I guess it was stupid to think I could change the world without changing myself, my way of life. Hey, where's Mestif? He never came back."

"Your guess is as good as mine. Don't concern yourself. He gets distracted sometimes." Breena picked at her lip. Galo swept her hand away. "He said you did that." He stood, shrugging on a jacket. "OK. Time to head out."

"Is my brother there where we're headed?"

"No, and he's human, so it's probably for the best."

Breena rose, groaning as the room spun around her. *There's no point in making a break for it. I guess Vos was right. I'm going to die. Thought it would be on my terms, though.*

Before he opened the door, Galo paused and looked back at her. "Do I need to tie you up again?"

She glared at him.

"Then go get in the van." Galo held the door wide for her and followed Breena, hanging a "Do Not Disturb" sign from the doorknob on his way out.

The pair shuffled into the van and drove out of the lot. Breena leaned her head against the warm window. Through the glass, the summer night looked clearer than it felt to stand in the humid air. *I guess I need to get used to the heat.* Every few minutes, a large pothole in the road jolted the van, smacking her head against the window. Breena pulled the sweatshirt from around her waist and stuffed it against the hard surface. "How long is this going to take?"

"Three and a half, four hours."

She couldn't bear to ask what about dying would take so long and didn't venture any questions about what she'd have to go through. It dawned on her that Galo might have meant the drive would take that long, and she prayed it was just a misunderstanding. *But what business do I have praying anymore? I guess Tabitha got her way, in a sense. Hell has no leader, I'm a traitor to my own religion. . . It's exactly the chaos she was after. I wonder what Atlas is doing to find his happiness.*

Breena resigned herself to the capture, gave in fully to her exhaustion, and closed her eyes. "I'm going to sleep." The lingering drugs in her system made it easy. She woke to the harsh overhead lights of a gas station and looked over to Galo as he stepped out of the van.

"Come on. Bathroom break."

"I don't have to go."

"Well, I'm not leaving you here."

They walked across the vast parking lot. Breena thought about one of Lilly's safety lectures from years ago and wondered if the police were already looking for her. Following her friend's advice, Breena tried to find all of the security cameras nestled above the gas pumps, in the ceiling of the overhang, above the convenience store doors. She made an effort to look squarely into the ones she found, wanting each to record her face unobscured.

"You're acting nervous."

"I *am* nervous!"

She hurled herself into the ladies' restroom and stooped over the toilet, expecting to be sick. *I'm going to die. He's going to kill me. I don't get a goodbye with Lilly or Jordan. Lilly's last memory of me will be seeing me hauled off with a sack over my head.* Tears stormed down her face. *Jordan's last memory of me will be—* She heaved, picturing their exchange in Arthur's office. *That's a terrible goodbye.* Regrets piled on, and she sank to the floor under the weight.

A few minutes passed then Galo banged on the door. "Come on, Breena. Don't do this again. We have to go."

She caught her breath and flushed. "Galo, I can't get up."

"What?"

She shouted louder. "Come in here. I can't get up."

He went in cautiously.

The door creaked, and she heard his slow footsteps. "It's fine. No one else is in here. I'm in the last stall."

Galo peered in. "You OK?"

Bree shook her head.

"I know you're scared. I'm sorry. This is the way it has to be. You took too long to come back to us on your own. We need you. We have no queen." He held out his hand to pull her up.

As they crossed the parking lot, they passed a junky RV filling up at the pump. Turning to cross in front of it toward the van, Breena's heart jumped in her chest like it was coming back to life after a long spell of stillness. Atlas stood against the front of the vehicle, a foot propped against it behind him. "Hello, Love."

Breena's cheeks heated at the familiar address. The reaction inspired inward curses. The last thing she wanted was to admit she still responded to the sight of him. She thought back to the day she went out with Jet and how exhilarating it had been to kiss someone different. *But different's not always better.* Breena's hands began to sweat. She worried at the skin around her fingernails.

Atlas looked toward the pair coming at him and shoved off of the bumper of the RV. "There's my girl." Breena flinched at his loud and cheerful greeting, unsure of its true nature. He walked to meet them. Breena stopped and Atlas closed the gap. "We need to talk. Why don't you come with me instead." It wasn't a question.

Galo threw an arm between Bree and Atlas. "No way, man. Luce sent us to bring her home. I'm not leaving without her. You have to come with us, too."

"Thanks for your diligent service, but it's no longer needed."

In a movement quicker than Breena could process in the moment, Atlas reached behind him, swept Breena aside with his other arm, pulled a gun from the waistband of his jeans, and shot Galo, gun directly to his chest. Breena screamed and stumbled back as Galo collapsed. The gaping hole gushed blood into the oily pavement of the gas station lot.

"Come on, Breena. Time to go." Atlas seized Breena's wrist and tugged her in the direction of a black sports car, leaving Galo to bleed out in the security camera blind spot the RV provided.

This isn't happening. He opened the door and covered the top of her head with his hand as she bent to get inside, like she was being arrested. Her heart pounded so hard she could feel it in every finger, in her stomach, behind her eyes. *Why am I grinning? Is this shock?*

Atlas ducked into the car, pulling his door behind him. They drove casually out of the parking lot and waited at a stoplight before merging onto the highway in the same direction Galo had been taking her. At the light, Atlas grabbed Breena's hand and studied her fingers. Then, he held it up in front of her face. "What did I tell you about this?"

Breena stared in stunned silence, a broad smile spreading across her face. *I can't hold it back anymore. What is wrong with me? I don't even want to be near him. No, I'm not smiling at* him; *I'm smiling at the* excitement.

Atlas smirked. His assumptions about Breena had never been wrong. Even though she was trying to set things right, and even though he was trying to forge a happy, peaceful path, there was no escaping their true make-up. *We do belong to Hell, after all.*

Breena shook.

"I'm not here to hurt you, you know."

"I figured if you were, you would have shot me, too. Where's Ari?"

"He's with Linda."

"And where's Linda?"

"How should I know? You're the one who told her to run off with him."

"OK. Why are you here? I thought you were done with this."

"I tried. I'm so tired of chasing you. But, Luce had other plans, which I found out about from you, by the way. Thanks to your little nap-time news bulletin, I was able to save you from those guys."

"Save me? I thought you *wanted* me to ascend."

"I do, but I thought you should know that you don't have to die to do it. You don't have to go back to heal your illusions. They just want you for themselves, forever. In case you forgot, death is permanent."

She blinked at him. "I don't *need* to die, or you don't *want* me to die?"

"Both. Why do you think I told you to call R? He could have set you up with as many people as you needed in order to ascend and rule from here. But no, you had to call your little puppy, Vos."

"You can understand why I didn't want to take your advice, right? I couldn't exactly trust you. Tabitha's influence or not, you've always been manipulative." Breena knew he was likely being manipulative still, but the idea of keeping her life a human life appealed deeply.

"I know. At least humor me for now. You might change your mind." *If she ascends, I'll have to go with her, and there's no way she'd approve of tearing everything down to rebuild for a happier world. She made it quite clear that it didn't matter my intentions, good or evil. Anything that upsets the balance is evil in her eyes. I wish she heard how she sounded. She doesn't realize that the balance itself is off balance. God set these rules and put us here to counter his work in a fair way. But that just means that we're still working for him. He's contracted out his havoc to a third party, meaning he's in charge of both sides. How is that balance? The system has to go, and she can't become queen if there is no need for Hell.*

Breena scooched down in her seat, oddly relaxed in Atlas' presence. In the silence, she fell asleep as the night grew pale and he drove, dawn just beyond the horizon. He glanced at her, noticing the shadows that made her sleep look as troubled as it had always been.

****

Jordan dashed out the front door wearing his best suit. Lilly tottered toward Jordan's Jeep moments after him, dressed up in a navy pencil skirt and blazer, and red pumps.

"Did you remember the recorder, Jordan?"

"Crap. No."

"You have to go get it. If I try to walk over this grass in these shoes again, I won't make it back."

Jordan grunted in irritation and pulled himself out of the car. It was the coolest day they'd had all month, but he acted like the heat made his body too heavy to maneuver. By the time Lilly made it to the car and got in, Jordan had already gone in the house and come back out with the audio recorder.

"OK, now we're ready. Do you know where this place is?"

"Yeah, I talked to a lady named Jo last night. I found her in the comments section on the arson video the news station posted. She gave me the address and said she'd meet us there."

Jordan flicked on the blinker and headed out of the neighborhood. "Was she a member of the church?"

"No, she's part of a group that's been searching for Atlas. Leigh, one of the ladies in the group, met Atlas last year when he tried to recruit her. Jo said Leigh got handed off to Linda before she split, and now that both Atlas and Linda are out of the picture, she's just angry. She's put all her emotions into setting things right rather than going through with her suicide."

"Noble."

"I wouldn't be so fast to say that. They've got intentions as bad as Atlas as far as I'm concerned. You know, a whole Judge Dredd kind of thing going on. They'd rather bring him to their own kind of justice."

At Lilly's comic book reference, Jordan's face scrunched up and Lilly explained, "Judge Dredd's a cop that has the right to judge and sentence on the spot in the field. Atlas deserves it, moral or not."

Jordan nodded. The chunky red-rimmed glasses he wore on contact-free days slid down his nose. He pushed them back with a knuckle. "Maybe so, but regardless of our opinions on how they're doing things, we're not getting involved. Jo wanted to talk to the press about Atlas, and that's what we're going to let her think she's doing. It's safer if she thinks she's giving info to reporters. She won't try to involve us in any of her group's radical efforts."

They sped down the highway to the church they'd seen on the news countless times in the last twenty-four hours. The GPS didn't need to tell them they had arrived. The nostalgic campfire smell hit first, and then the scorched brick, crumbling wooden columns, and broken glass came into view, belying any fond memories triggered by the scent. Most chilling, though, was the charred earth tagging ownership of the destruction and the crudely constructed gallows the culprits erected in place of the ruined cross, which Lilly scowled at with half-admiration, not for its symbolism but for its gall.

"Well, they didn't show that part on the news, did they? Too creepy for prime-time."

"The Disorder, huh?" Ignoring Lilly's morbid fascination, Jordan considered the crispy grass with a mask of blasé interest across his face. Lilly scoffed.

From behind them, a woman interjected. "That's what Atlas is calling his group of followers, now. Pretty apt if you ask me."

Jordan and Lilly turned.

"Hi, I'm Jo. We spoke in the forum."

Lilly stepped forward with a hand extended. "Hi, Jo. Thanks for meeting us. I'm Lilly, this is Jordan."

"Great to meet you. Follow me and I'll show you the church. I assume you have questions for me?"

Jordan leaned back into the car and grabbed the voice recorder then followed Jo and Lilly across the parking lot.

"So you said your group is run by someone named Leigh. How did she know it was Atlas who did this? How can you be sure you're after the right person?"

"Leigh and I run it together. Someone's got to temper her mean streak. She was in a rough place last year. Long story short, she called the suicide hotline looking for advice. Unfortunately, Atlas was the one to take her call. She got brainwashed instead. Well, nearly. After their conversation, he had her meet him across town from the call center. She says he gave her this long spiel about how people like her deserve to get their power back, that the establishment wanted suffering rather than prosperity. His whole objective was to collect people who felt they had no happiness and nothing to lose in order to do his work of taking down the government, the churches, anyone he saw as obstructing the happiness of the general population through their rules and restrictions."

Jordan dawdled behind the two women and scanned the damage as they passed. Lilly's wide eyes and rosy cheeks said "fangirl" rather than "reporter." She was rapt, intensely interested, as always, in the psychology of crime.

Jo continued, stepping over a singed rug in one of the doorways. "Leigh was in such a low place that his tactics worked on her, at least over the phone, so she met with him. What she thought was going to be a private chat over lunch turned out to be a massive recruiting operation. There were many others there, including me, all snatched up from the hotline calls. She stayed to hear him out, but didn't like his radical talk. I had my doubts, too. Leigh said doing terrible things to others was no better than what she and the other folks felt had been done to them in one way or another. You'd think we would have ditched the group at that point, but Atlas brought in some woman named Linda who spent a few meetings after that contradicting everything Atlas had said. Leigh figured Atlas was just some rogue employee of the hotline and stayed on to hear Linda speak, and she convinced me of the same. Then, Linda disappeared."

"So she feels misled and abandoned."

"Exactly. We all do. She kept quiet about her experience, not wanting to reveal how low she'd gotten. But when the riots happened—Linda had promised they wouldn't—Leigh had no faith in her and realized Atlas had been telling the truth about his plans. That's when she did some recruiting of her own. All of us here have been victimized in some way by Atlas, whether directly or as a result of the destruction he caused."

Lilly and Jordan shared a look as the group walked through the blackened halls of the church. Jo clearly didn't know about Tabitha. Jordan paused. "So let me get this straight. Leigh didn't want to join Atlas because she thought his actions would make her no better than the people who had wronged her. Yet, she has formed a group that's out to hunt him down? What's the end-goal if she doesn't want to be like him? What will you do if you find him?"

"Bring him to justice, of course."

"Your own justice or legal action?"

"I'll admit that Leigh is a little gung-ho about that part. She'd rather just take him out than wait for prosecution once the government gets back into running order after all this is over. We've tried to convince her that isn't the way to go about it."

Jordan pointed at Jo. "Leigh's contradicting herself."

"Leigh's *desperate*. There's little rationalizing with her."

"So right now you're all just—"

"We're just trying to find him for now."

Lilly crinkled her nose. "I thought you already knew where he was. You told me you tracked him after this incident occurred." She gestured around them at the ruined building.

"He was seen at a truck stop a few hours from here. He drove east on 94 in an old RV when he left the stop. That's the last we've heard."

"Did he have anyone with him? Any teenagers, in particular."

"Not that I'm aware of, although Roy—he's the one who spoke to Atlas at the truck stop—didn't go in the RV. I guess there could have been others."

"What's your next move, then, if you let him get away at the truck stop?"

"Jordan, let me stop you right there. We did not *let* him get away. We had no intention of capturing him at that time. It was a fact-finding operation. We were simply seeking confirmation that it was him at all. We got our positive ID, and that's all we were looking to find. As for what we plan to do next? Hopefully beat him to his destination."

"How do you know where he's headed?"

"Leigh told us where. To be honest, I'm not sure where she got her information. She started acting differently yesterday. Calmer, more rational, like she knew exactly what she was doing instead of living off the fuel of her anger. Frankly, no one likes to argue against her anyway. She really loves her guns." Jo led Jordan and Lilly into a dark annex at the back of the church. In the far corner, a figure sat in shadow. "But last night, listening paid off. She led us to this guy."

"Who's that?" Lilly raised her camera to snap a picture, but Jo shooed Lilly's hand away.

"No pictures, please. This one's ours. We grabbed him from a burger joint last night. Leigh recognized him from the recruitment meeting." Jo continued with her misinformation, unaware that her hostage was Luce's spy who had been keeping tabs on Atlas' meetings for Luce all year. "This is one of Atlas' little helpers, not a recruit. Meet Mestif."

Through Leigh, Luce had taken his own guy for a hostage knowing he had to give the group something that felt like a win while keeping them from interfering with Atlas. He had placed Mestif on

Atlas' radar a year ago knowing Mestif's inborn nature to serve would make him the perfect right hand for Atlas. Luce monitored both Atlas and Tabitha in this way, deciding to let the drama play out to test how Breena would handle it. In stopping Tabitha, she passed, but she failed to reign in Atlas.

Leading Jo's group to one of his own was a small price to pay for affording Galo an advantage with Bree, leaving Atlas for himself. Atlas ruined that, too, but Lucifer was powerful, not omniscient. On the plus side, Luce could handle Atlas and Bree at once. Breena couldn't be expected to overpower biology and put an end to Atlas herself.

****

Breena looked around her. She recognized the place, although it had been a year since she had been in her London summer flat. *Dreaming.* There were donuts on the kitchen counter packaged neatly in a white box with a sticker on top. Corner Café. She padded down the hall to the spacious bedroom at the end and flopped across the rumpled sheets. The shower in the attached bathroom was on, sending little wisps of steam from the open door and into the much cooler bedroom. She wondered, without alarm, who was in there and rose to check it out.

The glass shower door was thickly fogged. She couldn't see through it. The rhythmic patter of water cascading to the tiled shower floor and down the drain babbled uninterrupted, as if no one was in the shower moving around. Still, she was not startled by the strangeness. Breena reached for the door. She gazed upward as she pulled it open, toward where a back or chest would be, expecting to see someone. At first, the shower appeared empty, but something prickled at her subconscious telling her to look all the way into the stall.

Poking her head into the stream, she looked to the right and screamed, stumbling back and out of the room as she scrambled, dripping, to run away. In the corner of the shower, crumpled on the floor, was Jet, his black hair plastered to his lifeless face, and bright red blood trickling down his neck from a deep slit that ran across it.

As Breena tumbled out of the bathroom, she smacked into a hard chest. *Atlas*.

"You are not for him or his peasant family. You are mine. I am yours. Do you understand?" Atlas enclosed Breena in his arms and pulled her tightly to his chest. She fought against him unsuccessfully, having barely any room to move or wiggle away.

Breena shouted into Atlas' arm. "I hate you!" She bit as hard as she could into his bicep, which was conveniently pressed against her mouth. He shouted, and Breena tasted the penny-like tang of blood. He pulled away and shoved her across the room. As he contacted and then disconnected with her, Breena was thrust out of her nightmare.

Atlas, parked in a narrow space between two tall pick-up trucks, glared down at Breena with barely-contained rage. "I know what you've been doing while I was gone."

Atlas was at Breena's car door in seconds, throwing it open, grabbing her by the arm, and hauling her out of the stolen vehicle. Breena tripped out and tumbled into his chest. She recoiled from the contact, hating how similar to her dream the motion was.

"I meant what I said, Breena. You are not for him."

"Stay out of my dreams, Atlas."

"It's been months since we spoke. How else was I supposed to keep tabs on you?"

"You weren't."

"Breena, you can't act like nothing ever happened. I had to make sure you were OK. I didn't know what you might do."

"The only thing I had planned on doing was staying away from you. And how were you watching my dreams with my link broken?"

"That's what I've been trying to tell you. Your link isn't gone. You don't have to die to get it back. It's all in your head. You were traumatized. I know what it's like to kill someone with your bare hands. It messes with you. Just because I wanted to be rid of this fight doesn't mean I stopped caring. I'm your chosen, and now you're also my queen. It's kind of impossible not to care. Come on. Let's get inside." Atlas took her arm again and led her up the stairs to a second story apartment.

Breena warred with herself. The urge to give into his seemingly protective nature was strong. *It's so much like when we first met. His intensity is scary, but oddly charming. He goes about everything in the wrong way, but it's almost always for me. To find me. To get me. To keep me. No, don't confuse possessiveness with love or protection. There's always an end-goal. He's not bidden to anyone anymore, but that doesn't mean his dreams have changed. His actions are his own, now.*

She plunged past Atlas into the apartment, looking around the corner into the filthy kitchen, storming down the hallway, and peeking her head into each room. Of the three bedrooms, only one had furniture in it, a mattress on the floor and an old box TV also on the floor across the room. "I'm taking the room with the bed." Rolling her eyes, Breena turned on her toes and marched down the hall.

"You always were quick to get into my bed."

"That was before I knew you were just using me to suck up to my mother!" Breena shouted and slammed the door behind her. She plodded to the mattress and crawled to the middle of the king-sized expanse. Bree plopped down and pulled her legs to her chest. *That wasn't fair. He had no choice but to obey her.* Bree shook her head. *Stop making excuses for him.*

There was a knock on the door, and Breena didn't plan on responding, but Atlas came in without waiting for the invitation. He sat on the edge of the mattress, mirroring Galo's form from a day earlier.

Galo was a better kidnapper.

"Let's clear this up early and there will be a lot less fighting later on." He stared at Breena with a legitimate expression of patience, but the look didn't transfer to his methods. Atlas continued. "I understand if you have a hard time putting Jordan out of your mind. You've cared about him your whole life, and it's hard to leave a boyfriend behind—"

"We're not together."

Atlas furrowed his brow, but continued as if unfazed. "— you've proven to me how hard it is to leave behind a significant other. But Jet, you have to forget about him. He doesn't play that role in your life. I need you to stay with me. Marry me. We'll stay here, lead human lives. We'll pick up where we left off before Tabitha, back when we shared the same goal of making a happier world."

Breena slapped her hands down on the mattress in front of her. "Marry you? You don't *love* me!" *Why didn't I say, 'I don't love you'?*

Atlas rubbed at the arch of his foot as he sat in front of Breena. He almost looked coy, but the expression passed. "Yes, marry me. It can be that simple if you let it."

"It's never been that simple. I just didn't know it when we started."

"*We*," Atlas gestured widely between them, "are supposed to be the next generation of royal blood. As queen, you can simply choose not to go back. Stay here, make this place a little more suited to people like us. Some people like to use a little phrase, 'Hell on Earth,' but, that's so passé."

Breena leaned back on her elbows. "You're crazy. I'm not marrying you. And I've already explained that changing the world to fit your little fairy tale will upset the balance just as badly as Tabitha's plan did."

Well it was worth a try to see if she'd agree. It would be so easy if she did. "You will marry me. That's the way it works in royal families. Queen has daughter, queen finds suitable mate for princess, princess marries suitable mate without debate. Didn't you take history class? Clearly not. Matricide isn't part of that narrative, typically, although I agree it had to be done."

"It's absurd that you still want me. You must have a selective memory. I used you as much as you used me. We aren't healthy together. You won't find your happiness with me."

"Royal marriages are just public representations of the strength of the family. We don't have to be in love. That *is* your concern, right?"

Breena choked out a derisive laugh. "I *did* love you once. So, yes. That's the problem. At some point, we both loved each other, and you betrayed me. It doesn't matter that you had no control over your actions. I should have been your sole focus, and your foolish plan to kill off Tabitha led her to make you a hostage. She was perfectly content to let you serve her in normal ways as her assistant, an employee, until you crossed her. Everything went to shit after she caught you. You could have just let her age and die, said, 'Come what may,' and let me ascend years and years in the future—chaos free."

He shook his head. "I'm sorry that's how you feel. You have to realize that there would have been chaos if she had lived a full life, too. You know what she wanted in this world. Even if she hadn't caught me, she would have come to you for help. The end would have been the same. She was losing her sight and didn't feel it coming, but this result was always in our cards. You simply accelerated it."

"Me?" Breena shouted, incensed. "I accelerated it? Again, I point to your foiled assassination plans."

"I did it all so I could have you. I didn't want her to come for you. I didn't want this to turn into such a fiasco."

"This is so much more than a fiasco. It's a damn cluster-fuck. I don't believe you were ever going to tell me I was her daughter. You only did because you had to. Were you just going to explain away my 'family gift' as a fluke? Tell me I'm a natural?" Breena's hands flew around in her own brand of sign language as her volume escalated.

"I thought it best if you were genuinely interested in being by my side, even if you weren't aware that you already had a place by default."

Breena scooted toward the wall and leaned her head back against it. She massaged her temples for a moment, and then looked back at Atlas. Her heart didn't flip. Its beat had receded into a steady indifference toward him. Her mind wandered back to the dream she had in the car and wondered how Jet was doing. *He probably thinks I'm avoiding him.* "Why is Jet such a threat to you? If you and I don't have to be in love, and if you don't want me to go back home in order to ascend, why can't I pursue my interests?"

"You're right, I don't need you to love me anymore, now that you know who you are—"

"You think I know who I am?"

Atlas ignored Breena's interruption of doubt. "—but he's a peasant. His family serves yours."

Breena swallowed. "Wait. His family does what?"

"The Sala family. They're our servants. Not Jet, but his relatives and ancestors."

She put a few fingers to her lips, remembering their fiery kiss as her suspicions grew into facts. *Mestif's last name. Jet's last name. Drug dealer, servant. Is he just fulfilling some subconscious duty to me to provide? No, no, he liked me. It's not like that.* "I will love who I want—"

"Love?"

Love? "—because you're delusional to think otherwise. Count all the things you've done to me while all I was trying to do was get a break from my life." Breena sprang to her knees, smiling wide, and clapped once inches away from Atlas' nose. "Come on, list it with me! Imposed on my dreams, terrified me, stalked me, lured me away, lied about your identity, seduced me, abandoned me, hunted me down, held me hostage, oh, and don't forget all the blackmail!"

"Look, when you say it like that, I know it sounds horrible—"

"Hell yes, it does."

"And you obviously are reluctant to believe me, now."

"Yes. . ."

"But I'm done playing games. Think of all the things I did right, all for you. Tried to get rid of Tabitha before she could mess with your life, lied to her and played along to feed you information, saved you from Galo and anyone else Lucifer sent to bring you home permanently. Plain and simple, I need you to ascend the throne, and I want you to do it here. I've been groomed to help you to that position. And, before you continue your indignant interrogation about that whole concept, let me remind you that you were always looking for another world anyway. Don't let your hatred keep you from your happiness."

"Ugh," Breena threw her head back and stared at the ceiling. "Still with that happiness mantra?"

"It's true, Breena. Tabitha took me from my family so I would experience pain. There's no way I could have waged this war without the harsh upbringing, without seeing the truth about people."

That's the first time he's called it a war.

Atlas' eyes illuminated. The dark expressions he used to wear when he talked about his past never crept over him. "I could have grown up coddled and soft like all the peasant class kids down there who weren't important enough to be considered as a chosen, but I was born with some nobility. If I'd had an easy life, I wouldn't know the unfairness in the world. I wouldn't feel called to fix it. The universe wanted me to be able to lead the people living here to a new reality. Through you."

"I thought you resented her for your hard life."

"I did, but I'm seeing more clearly now that she's gone. Ironic, really."

"Because. . ."

"Because now I have a purpose, one *she* gave me."

Breena wrinkled her nose, shocked to hear him give Tabitha such glowing credit. "I supposedly have a purpose, but I still resent you both."

"She let Luce send you away for the same reasons, you know."

"That doesn't make me feel better."

"Not yet."

****

Mestif squirmed in his bonds. Jo paced a circle around him. Jordan was wringing his hands, but Lilly looked like she was about to pounce the captive. Her pen and pad were ready for clues.

"So, who is he? Why'd Leigh want him?"

"Leigh said he's part of Atlas' team. She recognized him from some of the meetings."

"Now what?" Jordan encouraged.

"Now we wait 'til he gets too hungry to keep his secrets." Jo grinned with pride.

"You're starving him?"

Lilly's eyes widened to saucers. "That could take weeks! I came for answers *today.*"

"No, this one's food-motivated. Remember, we took him from a restaurant in the first place. He was already hungry. Plus, look how he's drooling."

Mestif made eye contact with Lilly. "You got something for me?"

She walked around his left side to avoid his unnerving stare. "I don't know. Do you?" On the back of Mestif's neck, Lilly noticed a tattoo of a skyline marred with healing burns, and her breath caught.

"Lilly, we don't—"

Lilly shushed Jordan with an upheld hand. "I'll give you one bite of the burger in that bag if you tell us what city your tattoo represents."

Mestif squeezed his eyes shut. "OK. But, I want five bites. The food's cold anyway."

"Done. Now, tell us."

"It's Madrid. My family is from there." Mestif chomped his teeth a few times. "Now, food."

"I've seen that skyline in one of the pictures Linda sent to Ari before they left." Lilly partially unwrapped the burger and held it out to him. With the first bite, he reared back, pulling the whole burger out of her hand. The wrapper fell away and he ate, laughing around the food in his stuffed mouth as the toppings fell out of the bun into his lap.

"Mestif, do you know Linda?"

"Do you have more food?"

"You can have the soda. Liquids are more important to staying alive than food."

Jordan gaped at Lilly. *How ruthless. But, I never doubted she knew how to handle this kind of stuff. She watches way too much crime TV.*

"Yeah, I know Linda. She's the pretty lady that Luce had a thing for. We were sad when Breena sent her away. I miss her."

"Where did Linda go? Is Breena with her?"

Mestif shrugged. "I bet Luce knows. He knows everything. Fries?"

Lilly fed him a few. "Who's Luce?"

"Nuh-uh."

"More french fries?"

"Freedom."

Jordan laughed, incredulous. "No one calls them Freedom fries anymore. That was like a two-year thing."

"*My* freedom."

They all looked to Jo for permission.

"No way."

With her thin hair pulled back into a ponytail, Jo looked more severe than usual. They accepted her answer. Lilly handled the setback with expertise. "That's fine. I understand you want to keep your leverage. But what would the town, maybe even the nation, think when I go back to work and report that a bunch of vigilantes are holding hostage people they merely *suppose* were involved in the riots instead of turning them over to the police?"

Jo blanched. "Mestif, how about a milkshake instead?" It was a lame offer compared to freedom, and she knew it.

"No way. That one's melted anyway."

"A fresh milkshake."

"Freedom. I have a job to finish, and Luce is going to be mad if I fail. But he'll be madder at you for keeping me from doing my job. You don't want him mad at you."

In that moment, Leigh walked in through a floor-to-ceiling opening left by a busted out stained glass window. Mestif recoiled, feeling Lucifer's energy within Leigh. "It's fine, guys, you can let him go, but only if you give me a minute to talk to him in private."

While the others stood at the back of the room pacing, Leigh whispered in Mestif's ear, coaching him on how to play the next moments. They all turned to stare when Mestif shouted. Leigh held his shoulder in an odd movement of consolation.

Jordan leaned over to Lilly and whispered. "It's like they know each other well."

"Uh-huh."

Leigh waved them back over. "So this is how it's going to go. He's going to tell you who Luce is, Jo's going to let him go, and the two of you," she pointed at Lilly and Jordan, "are going to wash your hands of this little investigation. I know you're not reporters. I know you're just children."

Lilly straightened. "Podcasts can be legitimate sources of journalism when the reporter takes it seriously. I have plenty of followers."

Leigh didn't acknowledge her. "And I know you'll be safer and happier if you stop looking for your friends. Let us take care of it."

To humor Leigh and get the information from Mestif, Jordan and Lilly nodded, turning off the recorder in a show of compliance.

"Luce is the devil."

"OK, so you hate the woman. But who is she?"

"No, I mean *he* is Lucifer. He has owned my family for a very long time. He is my boss."

"Your boss is Satan." Lilly's hands rested on her hips, her expression deadpan.

Luce cringed and it showed on Leigh's face. He hated it when people called him that. *Humans.* No one caught the expression. They were engrossed in Mestif's confessions.

"Yes. So it's true that you should stay out of it."

Leigh walked behind Mestif to untie him. "You might want to leave before I let him go. You, too, Jo. Wouldn't want a mauling on our hands." She laughed musically. It didn't fit her sour expression. "He's still hungry." There was no way they'd catch the truth in Luce's veiled threat.

When they settled in Jordan's car, he slammed his hands down on the steering wheel, half thrilled, half furious. "What the hell was that?"

"That was a map. We need to go to Madrid."

Chapter 5

"A lot less destruction than I thought there'd be." Linda turned away from the painting she was admiring while she spoke. "The people probably think their god saved it from the looters." Linda chuckled with a bitter scowl on her face. "The opposite of everything they hold dear is keeping their city alive and thriving. Don't you just love the irony, Ari?"

"I love *you*." Ari leaned in for a kiss, but Linda turned to offer him her cheek and then brushed casually past him.

She exited onto the balcony and stared wistfully into the park across the street. *I loved Tabitha so blindly. I shouldn't grieve her. I would have never listened to Breena if I'd known what she was really planning. Tabitha was* mine *to toss to the curb. Breena robbed me of any closure. And Ari. . . that kid is only a band-aid. A band-aid Breena gave to me in advance because she* knew *she was about to rob me by killing Tabitha.*

****

When Jordan and Lilly returned home, Lilly kicked off her heels in the car and raced to the house across the grassy patches in the driveway. She beat Jordan up the steps and had the emails waiting on the computer screen by the time Jordan entered.

"Look at these pictures. They were attached in one of Linda's emails to Ari. At first I didn't give them much credit. Her user name clearly suggests she's a fan of Madrid, but her profile says she's had the account for years—well before Breena sent them away. As much as I wanted to believe they were there, nothing concrete suggested the pictures had any connection to their location. I figured they were just Linda's wishes, not clues. But, this is definitely the same skyline as Mestif's tattoo." Lilly pointed at the third photo down. "See, it's not the actual skyline of the city, but a representation of some of the major landmarks. There's the capitol building, the crystal palace, Atocha Station. . ."

"How do you know so much about Spain?"

Lilly shrugged. "I read. So, I figure this can't be a coincidence. Linda is somehow connected with him or his family. I just don't know if it goes beyond Luce and Mestif, and their little crush on her."

"Or maybe she just happens to be there on vacation because Breena asked her to leave with Ari and she really took the instructions to heart. Be realistic, Lil. Not everything has some sinister, underlying meaning. For all we know, these pictures happen to match the tattoo simply because they are some of the most recognizable landmarks in Madrid. Lots of people have seen them; lots of people love them."

Lilly shrugged. "I know you're right, but you know I can't resist the idea of a grand scheme."

"Right. So are we going to talk at all about this whole Lucifer thing? It's kind of hard to believe. I'm surprised you haven't mentioned it."

"Eh, the shock has already worn off. Breena told me about him months ago. It only makes sense that he's getting involved in this mess. He *is* the grand scheme at play here."

****

Lucifer waited in the burned-out church with Mestif until everyone was gone. "You know who I am, yes?"

Mes sat in a blackened window sill sipping the melted milkshake and nodded.

Luce bothered with Leigh's shirt sleeves. "You're a liability, now, Mestif. You know how I hate loose ends." When Leigh's long sleeves were rolled neatly to both elbows, Lucifer moved her toward Mes. "I'll have to reassign you."

"OK, sure."

Luce closed the distance between them by cupping Mestif's cheek. On contact, Mes crumbled into ash, his form a temporary carbon statue and then a gritty breeze through the shell of the sanctuary. Behind Lucifer's consciousness, Leigh was screaming. Lucifer pinched the bridge of her nose. *Mortals.* After he finished the nasty business with Mestif, he shrugged out of Leigh's body and went to assign the task of bringing Breena home to the next servant in line.

****

"Why do you love it here so much?" Ari stood behind Linda on the terrace and put his arms around her. She pulled out of his grasp and stared at him for a beat.

"Isn't it obvious? Everything's more interesting. That monument over there, for example. Given to Spain by Egypt. The toilets? Square! Pastries? Any time you want them, there's a bakery to sit in for hours. Except during siesta, but that's so charming, too." Linda's flint eyes glittered like a fairy tale cartoon character. She hoped he was too oblivious to notice that it was tears, not excitement that made her eyes glassy and bright.

"Huh." Ari stared at the Templo De Debod across the street, behind it, a valley of businesses and homes.

"And someone very special to me came from here."

Ari scowled at her knowing she wasn't talking about him. "Tabitha? Come on, you've got to forget about her."

"No, not her. You met him once, I think. Mestif?"

"That guy? What a dope. You're into him?"

Linda put her hands on her hips. "Don't be mean. He's a very sensitive guy, and he caters to me so well. I'm not interested, but he always had a fancy for me, I think, while Atlas and I were working at the hotline. I let him help me out with stuff sometimes. He got us this flat."

"So he's your sugar daddy?"

"Oh, that sounds so crass. No, he's got family connections. It was no trouble for him."

"But you're OK with taking extravagant gifts from him?"

"What girl wouldn't?" She twirled away from Ari to continue her gazing.

Ari stalked back inside mumbling. "I should have never come here." For the first time since he left home, he dug his phone out of his pack, plugged it into its charger, and called Breena.

****

Breena's cell phone buzzed across Arthur's desk and onto the floor by her abandoned pillows. Lilly heard the thump from the other room and went to see what the noise was. She had searched the study the night of Breena's kidnapping for anything that might suggest who took her. Jordan attempted to look through Breena's phone that night, too, but the fingerprint lock kept him out. Lilly hadn't been in the room since. The phone continued to ring, and Lilly breathed a sigh of relief that voicemail wasn't picking up. She hurried to grab the thing and answer without looking at the caller ID.

When the call connected, Ari dropped his tense shoulders. "Hello? Breena?"

"Ari! Ari, where are you? We've been so scared you were in trouble. *Are* you in trouble?"

"I'm fine. Annoyed, but fine. Now, give the phone to Breena."

"I can't." A beat. "She's missing."

"What do you mean she's missing? I thought everything was fine now that the riots had stopped." He started to pace, his preppy white tennis shoes squeaking across the marble floor.

Unsure of how much Linda had told Ari, Lilly struggled with how to respond. "There was a break-in. Two men took her."

"Dammit. Linda promised me Breena wasn't in any danger, that we were just extending our vacation until the riots calmed down. She said she talked to her two days ago!"

So he still thinks that his was a real vacation rather than a plan to get him out of town. "Ari, that's a lie. We haven't known where you were since you left. You could've come home weeks ago. Breena hasn't talked to Linda. We've all been looking for you. Linda's hiding something. You should come home. And call your mother!"

"I need to talk to Linda. Gotta go." Ari pulled the phone away from his ear to disconnect.

"No! Wait, tell us where you are." *He hung up.*

Lilly bounded from the study back into their bedroom calling for Jordan, who had vanished into the sizeable home. She pounded down the stairs to the living room and then to the kitchen expecting to find him in the only rooms they really used. From the kitchen, she went into the back yard where Jordan had cobbled a sad-looking darts board with the little energy he could spare from cloaking the house. He threw two more darts, which appeared one after the other in his hand before each toss, before he noticed Lilly approach him. She rounded the corner of the back deck and tried to take noisy steps toward him so he didn't startle mid-throw. "Jordan, finally." He turned when Lilly spoke, not bothering to soften his expression. "You didn't book those tickets to Spain yet, right?"

"No. Why?"

"Guess who I just talked to."

He released one more dart. "Umm. . . Jo?"

"Better. Ari!" Lilly danced around in a small circle, unable to contain her excitement.

Jordan let the images dissolve as he threw his hands, and his handful of darts, into the air. "Alright, yes!" His eyes brightened and he stood a little straighter. "So, where is he?"

Lilly's exuberance fell like a forgotten party balloon. "I didn't get any information."

He stared at her for a beat. "You? Supersleuth McPreparedness got nothing?"

Lilly jabbed Jordan with her elbow. "Come on, cut it out. As if I don't still feel bad about not getting enough info when Breena was taken, you don't have to make me feel like that with this, too. He *hung up* on me. He wasn't in a telling mood."

Jordan scoffed. "Well, at least we know he's alive."

"We also know that Breena isn't with him. He asked to talk to her. And, Linda has been lying to him about having contact with Breena since they've been gone. She's up to something."

"So you told him what happened?" Jordan shivered like he was replaying that day in his mind.

"Only that she was missing and had been taken." Lilly moped back to the deck and sat on the bottom step. Jordan plopped down beside her. The first signs of nighttime twinkled to life—stars, lightning bugs, and the motion-sensing porch light. With the dim yellow glow pooling around their seated forms, long, squiggly figures came to life on the grass, mirroring their motions.

"And you didn't get his number?"

"Nope. He hung up and then Breena's phone locked before I could go back to the call log. Probably a burner phone anyway. His real number still isn't working." A breeze gusted through the back yard and Lilly shivered. Jordan threw his arm around her shoulder, a simple motion made awkward by its users. "But this is a good sign. He's OK, he knows Linda lied, and he sounded determined to get the truth out of her. I think we should stay here in case he comes home soon. He'll want to help with finding Bree."

"What makes you think Linda will let him come home?"

"Just because he's been missing doesn't mean he's her hostage. He was with her willingly, under false pretenses, but still. Now, I'm sure he's less willing. He'll come home."

Jordan hummed in exhausted agreement. At his feet, a soccer ball took shape. Lilly watched as its many lines of black and white solidified. When they did, Jordan kicked it without gumption to the middle of the yard. From there it rolled, unhurried, to the fence.

"What are you thinking?"

On a deep exhale, Jordan voiced a dark thought, the words whooshing out of him like they'd been stuck for a while. "Maybe we should stop looking for her, now. Now that we know Ari's OK."

Lilly froze like the world had stopped, gaping at Jordan's outrageous idea. Her shock turned to disgust and then defeated sadness. She stood with her hands limp at her sides. "How could you say that?"

Jordan put his face down in his hands and tugged at his hair. "She may not have gone voluntarily like Ari did, but she wanted to go."

"But—"

"She told me." Jordan shoved off the step and marched past Lilly. As he passed through the kitchen door, he looked back over his shoulder and told Lilly he wanted his bedroom to himself for the night. "You can stay in the study."

"With all her stuff?" Lilly issued the question into the empty darkness of Jordan's back yard. He had already gone inside. She shivered again. "I'll sleep on the couch."

Lilly retrieved her bed things, dragging a blanket behind her down the stairs, and made a call to the police station on the way. She figured Bree's phone would be most useful in their hands, especially if Ari called again. *I don't know why they didn't collect that for evidence in the first place.*

Jordan slammed his bedroom door so hard the trim popped away from the wall in three places. He stood in the middle of the room just staring at his surroundings for minutes. No longer with a need to search or analyze, he crossed the room and got into his bed, fully clothed. Jordan sank into his pillow heavily, as heavy as his problems felt, and tried to pick something to dwell on, but sleep overtook him. The next morning, he stayed in bed despite the knocking on his door. "Yeah, Lil, I'm gonna need the room for another few days."

"Fine. I'll just meet with Leigh on my own."

Jordan started, half with interest and half with fear, but he fought back the urge to take part. "Be safe," he called through the cluttered room. Lilly clicked her teeth, pausing on the other side of the door, and then padded away. Jordan leaned out of the bed and pulled the curtains over his black-out shades then drug himself back into the bed by the sheets, only to burrow deeper and close his eyes again.

****

Jet paced in his back yard staring at his phone. After days of unanswered texts, his nerves no longer allowed him to sit still. "Well, does she like me or not?" Jet's black lab, Cinder, drooled from around a muddy tennis ball as he looked up at his human. "It was going so well, but now she's not speaking to me. I don't know what I did." Cinder made a soft boof sound from around the ball and dropped it at Jet's feet. Jet picked it up and threw it half-heartedly. Before the dog returned with it, Jet was back in his house, fumbling around for a coffee mug. He hadn't slept much since his meeting with Breena. He was unwilling to call a drug-deal a date, though that's what it ended up feeling like.

Jet stumbled, his mug shattering on the kitchen floor as he fell to his knees. A heavy, invisible force weighed him down. The setting sunlight from the window above the sink dimmed, and when his vision regained focus, he looked into the darkness to find the imprint of feet in the small throw rug before him. The prints shifted, as if someone stood there.

"Woah."

"You're needed, Jet."

He scrambled back into the wall. "What the hell?"

"Indeed."

"Who's there?"

"Don't act like you don't know your family's stories. It's your turn."

Jet blanched, his complexion going from summer to winter. "I don't want to go there."

"You won't be alone. I need you to bring Breena to me."

Jet's jaw dropped. "Why? What did she do to deserve that?"

"Don't tell me you didn't recognize your own queen."

Jet's heart knocked a few agonizing beats. *My queen. . .*

As if waking to a new life, visions of every moment he'd had with Breena bombarded him. There were more than he had realized. It appeared that his whole existence had absently revolved around hers. *Why didn't I notice her sooner?*

"Don't mistake this for something it is not. Though you are currently our best shot—it seems she cares for you for some reason—she is not your chosen. Your family is not entitled to take part in that tradition. You are to bring her to me only. We need her at home."

"You mean deliver her to her death."

"Aren't you already helping with that anyway? Those pills have her half way there."

Jet's heart skipped a beat. He knew from the gossip at school during their senior year that Breena had a problem, and even she admitted it to him in fewer words not a week earlier, but having someone tell him he was the cause made it impossible to rationalize his side-job. *Well, she only bought from me twice. . . Breena's issues began long before she sought me out. That doesn't make me feel better. Enabling is just as bad.* She wasn't the only person he had helped into a dangerous situation for cash.

"Don't just sit there looking like you lost your puppy. You knew you could be called on to assist me."

"Yeah, but I never believed it. Thought my abuelita was just trying to scare me with her stories."

"What a shame. Now go find my granddaughter and that idiotic chosen of hers."

As if his legs were not his own, Jet jolted from the floor and into his room, tugged on clothes and a pair of shiny black combat boots then headed out, phone in hand.

****

Leigh came to in a silvery beam of moonlight beneath the window where Luce had left her body hours earlier. The thick, drowning sensation gone from her chest, her breath swam alone in her lungs, and the fog cleared from her head. No one moved her limbs against her will. No one watched the crumbling sanctuary through her eyes. She took a deep breath expecting to feel relieved, but instead she felt hollow. Too alone. Beside her, a sooty ring was all that was left of Mestif's ashes. Her hands trembled as she looked at her palms, which were clean. She remembered it all and wondered why they weren't black. *No one's going to believe me.* At the thought, the impression of Luce's subconscious entered her own, an echo, but real enough to convince her. *'And that's why you won't tell.'* She agreed. *I don't know what I would say, anyway.*

****

Steam drifted out of the bathroom as Atlas stepped into the barren bedroom. He let the towel fall from his waist.

"Atlas, put some clothes on." Breena stared into the hallway with her hands blocking her peripheral vision.

"Really? Nothing?"

"Nothing."

"You used to—"

"Let me stop 'ya right there."

Atlas expected an angry tirade about how he shouldn't expect anything from her and that she still hadn't forgiven him, but instead she got up and walked out of the room.

In front of the closet, he stared at his only clothes—two pairs of jeans and two shirts, and a few boxers and socks in a pile under them. A month after the riots began in Grayling, Atlas had gone back to London to pack up his apartment. Without Tabitha supporting him with a job and a home, his only options were to move permanently to Grayling where Tabitha's safe-house was long-since paid off, or to go back to the itinerate ways of his childhood. He tried the former, but there were too many ghosts living there. In the week leading up to reacquiring Breena, Atlas arranged to rent the shabby apartment and stocked it with the only items he could still bear to look at. He left everything else he owned in the house where he'd killed his brother.

A sudden wave of fury shot through him and he ripped his jeans from the hanger and stumbled into them on his way down the hall. Breena was staring out the window overlooking the mucky puddle that was supposed to be a duck pond. "Aren't you going to berate me or something? I'm kind of surprised you haven't tried to escape."

She shook her head.

"Why did you come with me?"

Breena choked on a laugh. "You act like you invited me on a ride and I hopped in. You're as out of touch as ever."

"And?"

"And I know what you're doing."

Atlas stalked over to her and clapped his hands down on her shoulders. "Then humor me!"

She shrugged out of his grasp. "I don't have any humor to give. You saw to that. Now. Explain to me why I'm here. You said I don't have to go back with Galo and Mestif, you made sure that I couldn't, and now I'm here. If you know how to fix me, start talking."

"Tsk, tsk. Remember all the trouble caused last time you asked me to 'fix you.'"

"I'm not that person anymore. I fix myself, and I was well on my way, with Vos' advice. I don't need you to do it for me, but since you have information, I might as well take advantage of that. And that is why I haven't left yet."

"Look. I just wanted a peaceful life. I wanted you by my side. I wanted to finally find out if my mom's spirit is at rest and maybe feel like a human for once. I'm so tired of fighting, and I never wanted it to be you I was fighting. But I cannot allow you to go back to your family."

Breena turned to glare at him. "You don't want me to ascend because it will ruin whatever you're scheming next."

"I don't want you to ascend because I don't want you to *die*."

She tangled her fingers. *I don't want to die either.*

****

Tabitha stormed down the gleaming hall of her childhood home. The click of her heels echoed off the metal walls and stone floor. "Daddy!" Her ruby hair rose around her face, waving, as if her hostility gave it life. The servants carting linens, platters of glistening fruits, and boxes of chains and shining blades scattered as she passed. "Daddy!" She shrieked through gritted teeth like a bratty, spoiled teenager.

When she reached the door to his office, she incinerated it with a touch instead of bothering to use the handle. "Daddy, you've got to do something." She looked around. "Daddy?"

A throat cleared behind her and Tabitha turned, expecting to see her greying father. It was his assistant. "I'm sorry, My Queen—"

A glint of fire blazed across her expression at the invalid title.

"Forgive me... Miss?"

This enraged her even more. She snapped at the shaking squire. "Why are you here?"

"To tell you that your father has gone to retrieve Queen Breena."

"Get out."

****

Jet paced through the aisles of the book store, a coffee in one unsteady hand and his phone in the other, praying to get a reply from Breena. The shop was the only place he could think of to linger a while and not draw attention—other than his home, which Luce had compelled him to leave. Every few minutes he'd pick up a book and pretend to read the back, stare at the cover for a bit, and shelve it.

The text message vaguely greeted her, just checking in. He hadn't decided whether he was going to go after her for Luce or not, so he thought it was best not to open with a question about her whereabouts even though he desperately wanted to know, wanted to see her, wanted to find out why she hadn't talked to him since their kiss. If he didn't have that information, Luce couldn't force him to disclose it.

Chapter 6

"Get your hands off my egg rolls."

"You kidnapped me. You owe me dinner."

Atlas rolled his eyes and shoved two egg rolls from his plate onto Breena's. "You never were satisfied with your own food. Do you really think I needed five egg rolls? I know your game."

Breena chewed on her words. It wasn't like she didn't miss moments like this—quiet, average—but it was only because these moments let her be around him guilt-free. No scheming, no killing. *But it's only superficial. There has always been a wrong that leads me to him.* "There's something I've been thinking about since the last time we were together."

Udon hanging out of his mouth, he hummed in question.

"After I cut my way out of that last illusion, I saw you find me. I was having some sort of out-of-body experience between both worlds. Didn't you know I was still alive here?"

Atlas winced away from Breena. "No. I didn't. I don't want to relive that, though."

"What happened afterwards? There's a gap in my memory from the time you found me to the time I woke up in the hospital."

He could almost see Breena's blood covering him, still, from where he had held her astral body, bleeding out in the hotel room. Unable to save her, he had used her remaining energy to attack Tabitha, turning himself in to a monster in the process. It was probably one of the reasons Breena still hadn't recovered from the event. If he had left her with some of her astral energy, the ties to that part of her would remain, at least in part.

He set his heaping plate of noodles and dumplings aside and looked her in the eyes. "After you died there, I was so full of rage. Blinded. I didn't stop to consider that you were alive in your physical body. My first concern was finally ridding myself of Tabitha. I used the rest of your energy to do it."

Breena narrowed her eyes at him.

"You're probably thinking I'm the reason that you can't manipulate your surroundings anymore, and maybe you're right. But

I swear to you that you do not have to die to fix this. All you need to do is stay with me."

Breena bolted to her feet, huffing. "I've heard that before."

"Think back to before Tabitha starting messing with us. We wanted the same things back then. We wanted each other. We wanted to find something better about this life. We wanted to make the world better."

"Nope. I wanted an escape. And now that I'm at a place, mentally, where I'm trying *not* to run from my problems, I have an out that's better than anything you tried to offer me. Illusions? Pft. I'm going to Hell!"

"I don't get you."

"You're never going to get me. Go have your 'peaceful life' alone." She threw air quotes around herself with a glare. *There is no way his plans are peaceful. He just doesn't have it in him.*

"You really want to go, don't you?"

"Yes. No. I don't know. I *want* to make up for what I've done to everyone."

"Except me."

"*Especially* you. My existence necessitated your harsh upbringing. Your upbringing spurred on all the things *you've* done to people. We're a destructive pair, and everyone would have been better off without me. So this time, my going isn't an escape. It's a—"

"Martyrdom. You don't have to martyr yourself for me."

"I'm not a martyr. I'm a queen. And I'm leaving." Breena couldn't draw out her capture any longer, his answers coming too slowly and her doubt surging too strongly. She shoved her feet into Atlas' shoes by the door—she hadn't had any on when Galo and Mestif snatched her—and unbolted the chain and lock. Behind her, a familiar click sounded, and she turned wearing a bemused grin.

Atlas pointed a small gun in Breena's direction. It had been the best deal in the local newspaper's trading post section and an acceptable backup to the one he'd used on Galo and ditched.

"Aww, you bought me a little pink gun." She went to take it from him. "How sweet."

When she reached for it, Atlas lunged past her reach, jabbing the muzzle into her chest. "You're not leaving."

"*You're* not scary." She leaned in to the pressure of the gun and willed the metal to warm just enough to warn him. Unlike her approach to Galo, she, for some strange reason, didn't actually want to injure Atlas, and she worried the ammunition would deploy under too much heat.

Atlas looked down at his hand. "Cute. Is that all you've got left?"

Breena held her tongue.

"Thought so."

"Then shoot me. I thought you wanted me to live, but if you don't, then go ahead and kill me. Express route to my inevitable death." She shrugged out of his grip and stomped back to the door certain there was no way he could take her seriously while she wore his enormous shoes. "Bye, Atlas."

Atlas was frantic at the thought of losing her. Logic fell away and desperation launched him into action. As Breena crossed the threshold into the mildewed stairwell, Atlas fired a shot at Breena, piercing her left shoulder under the clavicle.

A beat passed where Breena stumbled against the railing, blinking. She touched her fingertips to her shoulder and looked down at the blood blooming across her shirt. Then, she started to chuckle. First it was low, and Atlas thought she was beginning to sob, but the laughter rose to a cackle. Breena threw her head back, howling.

"You. You colossal. . . *bitch*!" She slapped a hand over her shoulder like she was pledging her allegiance to the darkness inside her. Through heaving breaths, she continued to laugh, manic in her state of shock.

Atlas had assumed she would drop, maybe roll down a couple of stairs, fall to her knees or cry out for help like in the movies. He had never been truly afraid of her before, only Tabitha. But she was her mother's daughter.

After the shock of injury and the hysterical laughter that came with it wore off, Breena realized her failure to escape had been a win. *I've always had more power over him when he's afraid. He's actually shaking.* She plucked the gun out of his hand, stumbled inside, and shoved it back between the couch cushions. "Moving on from that bit of unpleasantness. . ." Breena picked up Atlas' plate and resumed eating after stuffing his napkin in her shirt. Even though the shock had worn off, through all the prescription drugs, she couldn't feel the wound yet. *Although that will need attention soon.*

"You need to get that cleaned up. Let me see."

"Get your hands off me. I might have thought I needed a savior years ago, and I might have even thought you were it, but I didn't, and you aren't. Go to the store and buy me a sewing kit with *silk* thread, a pair of tweezers, some antiseptic, gauze and medical tape. I'll sew myself up." *Thank you, Lilly.*

"I'm not leaving you here alone."

"You really think I'm going to run out of here like this? Covered in blood and woozy? The last thing I need getting in the way of my death is a cop or a doctor."

"In the way of your death? You're *glad* I. . ." He drug a hand over his mouth and down his chin in distress, then scoffed.

He acts like I'm the one being unreasonable.

"Don't do anything stupid while I'm gone."

"Just go!" She accented the statement with all the heat she had left and it seemed to be enough to compel Atlas to leave.

She had told Atlas the truth. She wasn't leaving—not physically. Breena made use of the alone time by settling into the corner of the couch and attempting for what felt like the millionth time to make some sort of connection to the astral self she left behind months earlier. As she relaxed into the pile of pillows, letting her head fall back and eyes close, the absurdity of the situation set in.

I'm shot. I'm in Atlas' apartment. I guess I got what I wanted. Am I dying yet?

She was unconscious before she could actively attempt to send her spirit outward to contact Vos or anyone else, but Atlas was right. She didn't need to die to get back to that part of herself, and she *wasn't* dying, just slipping into a slack state where her anxieties receded enough to allow her genetically-enabled traits to breathe.

She walked through the back door of Vos' modest home where he was parked in front of the TV with a hawk's concentration. Breena stepped in front of him expecting a surprised and warm welcome, but he looked through her. *Ah, I'm only dreaming. Failed again.* "Vos. Vos, look at me."

He glanced around the room then shook his head.

Bree sat beside him on the couch. "It's OK if you can't hear me. I'm going to talk to you anyway." She studied her hands. "I need you to take care of my friends. You told me you're bound to me, now, right? So that's what I want you to do. Forget about me, and keep them safe."

A key turned in the lock and the door to Atlas' apartment swung open. Atlas dug through his bag of groceries as he made his way inside. "OK, so I got everything you asked for, Bree, and I brought you some tea, too." Atlas looked up. "Breena, I'm back."

It wasn't enough to stir her.

"Bree?" He ran a hand through her hair not wanting to jostle her injury by shaking her shoulder. Atlas hadn't stopped shaking, himself. "Wake up. We've got to clean that wound." *I can't believe I shot her. Stupid! Now I feel like laughing. She won't wake up. I brought her here to keep her from dying, and I killed her.* With a final desperate shout, he called her name and gave her a rough shove hoping the pain would rouse her.

Breena had finally gotten Vos' attention by throwing his glass to the ground when a searing pain shot through her arm and neck. Instantly, she was back in her body and waking up to Atlas' frantic face peering down on her.

"I'm so glad you're alive." His breath whooshed out.

She blinked a few times and brushed away the hair sticking to her sweaty forehead. "Then you shouldn't have shot me. Did you get everything?"

He dropped the bag in her lap.

"Move so I can get up."

"Let me help you to the bathroom."

"Don't." Breena sat up from her pillow cocoon and threw her hands to her sides, mindless of the burning in her shoulder, to steady the spinning room. *I'm starting to think he's right about not having to die. That was more than a dream with Vos. I was there. I probably shouldn't tell Atlas that, yet. Find out what he's planning first. Decide if I want any part of it.* She swung her legs around to the edge of the couch to stand, and the room rose to meet her.

As her knees hit the carpet, Atlas lunged to catch her, clotheslining Breena before she face-planted on the floor. "That's why I wanted to help you up."

She nodded not trusting her words. *It's nice being taken care of sometimes, I guess, but he's the last person I wanted to allow back into that role.*

"Up, up. Can you get to your feet?"

"Of course I can." She pressed her weight into a foot and swayed. "No."

"As I thought." He grabbed her hands and pulled her arms around his neck. "Here. Hold on." With an easy sweep, she was against his chest going down the hall like a bride after the wedding.

This is not a sign.

He set her on the closed toilet. "You still want to do this yourself?"

No. "Yes. Where's the alcohol?"

Atlas held up a finger and left the room.

I'm so cold.

He returned with the bag of first aid, but not before she had gotten lost in a debate over his character. *Has he changed? Of course not. He shot me. I wonder what his life's been like since I . . . since Tabitha. . .* She slumped toward the sink. *Has he been as lonely as me?* Around her, the bathroom shifted, walls warping into a dark tunnel, tub and other furniture curling in and turning to stone.

"Here." Atlas thrust the bag in front of him as he rounded the corner into the bathroom. When he caught sight of Breena sliding into darkness, unconscious and wrapped in the first illusion she had cast in months, he dropped the bag and lunged for her. "Bree!" In that moment of discovery, the fear shooting through his gut only came *after* the bolt of thrill and pride that he had been right about her. *She can still do it. She doesn't have to die. I get to keep her.*

He grabbed her shoulder and pushed her against the damp wall of the bathroom-turned-cave. "Wake up. You need to see this. You did it, Bree. I knew you could." He casually regarded the blood on his fingers. Then, after a second of marveling, it struck him. *She is dying. The blood loss, her proximity to Gehenna. It's unlocking everything she lost.*

An enraged growl tore through his throat, echoing in the rocky cavern. "No! You will not go." He shoved his arms under her neck and knees, hauling her off the stone. Atlas hoped carrying her out of the room would shatter the illusion and break death's grip, but it followed. Into his bedroom, the murky stones transmuted his walls into monoliths. It sounded like an earthquake.

He ran with her into the living room. The cavern grew. Before the kitchen distorted in her descent toward death, he laid her on the counter and turned on the faucet. The cup in his hand couldn't fill fast enough. When it finally had, he poured it over her face.

She revived, sputtering, and the illusions halted. Nothing else transformed, but what had already turned stayed solid. "I can't see."

"You've lost a lot of blood. That's what you get for not letting me help you right away." *Don't lecture her, now.* "We need to close the wound. I'm going to do it for you. Stay there."

Atlas tore open a packet of cauterizing agent. She hadn't asked for it, but he was glad he had bought it. He pulled her shirt carefully from the edges of the bullet hole under her left collar bone. "Breena, this is going to suck. Hold on to me."

She grabbed his hip with no force, tucking her fingers into the top of his waistband.

Atlas' stomach turned. "OK." He poured the powder into her open wound and she screamed, coming fully to and yanking him toward her with a sudden return of strength.

Breena saw white, the color of the hottest flames. As if a tether attached her mind to consciousness, she was dragged out of the blackness, through a blazing world in between, and back into the yellow light of Atlas' grimy kitchen.

Atlas tossed the packet aside and pressed a piece of gauze firmly onto her shoulder. *I hope it's good enough to cauterize the entry wound only. . .*

She writhed under him, and in the background, the cave crumbled, revealing his apartment again. "Are you with me?" She couldn't put together words through the pain, but she could dig her nails into his side. He winced as if his pain was equal to hers. "I need to sew you up."

Breena couldn't imagine being able to feel that over the silver nitrate working inside her, so she nodded.

Atlas popped a needle out of its packaging and threaded it with the only silk thread he'd been able to find—a vibrant rainbow number. As he slipped the needle through her skin the first time, certain that he would be sick, it occurred to him as each pass got easier to stomach that killing someone with bare hands had numbed him considerably. *Is that why I was able to shoot her?* The ease with which he had succumbed to panic and done it sickened him more than the act itself.

"At—"

"Shh. Don't talk. You have a lot of healing to do."

"No. I'm—"

"I mean it, Breena."

After he tied the stitch off, she shoved him away from her as hard as she could. It wasn't much, but it got his attention. "I'm burning," she managed.

He took a real look at her face for the first time since hauling her to the kitchen and saw the new scarlet streaks of hair at her temples. Her eyes appeared as if backlit, radiating with energy despite her pale and sweaty skin. He didn't want to tell her what he saw. Atlas held her hand to pull her to sitting. "It's almost over, but I need to stitch the exit wound, too."

She nodded her feverish head.

When Atlas examined her back, he expected to see the same evidence of a gunshot wound as he had in the front, but there was nothing. Fear spiked through him and he couldn't help but let out a strangled gasp. *The bullet's still in there. Shit, I sewed the bullet in there!*

"Atlas, what's wrong?"

"I . . . your back . . . the bullet didn't come out."

"Yes it did. It's in the stairwell. I felt the blood dripping down my back, too."

"There's no wound back here."

"Look harder."

"I don't think that's something I could miss, Breena." Atlas circled to face her. It was hard to look Bree in the eyes, not because of the huge mistake he had just potentially made, not because he shot her in the first place, but because her eyes were continuing to change and because he knew, with dread, that she had gotten a taste of what her rightful place in Gehenna had to offer—a repaired ability to manipulate reality, accelerated healing, and an escape. *She's never going to stay with me, now.*

"It's OK. It doesn't matter. I'm feeling better somehow."

I bet you are. "Well, I'm glad to hear that. Do you. . . what do you remember?"

"If you're hoping I've forgotten that you shot me, you're a dolt."

"Not that. What do you remember after I returned with the first aid supplies?"

"I lost a lot of blood. I tried to stay awake, but I couldn't. There was a dream. What was it? Something about walking down a tunnel and into a pitch-black room. When the lights came on there was applause. People bowed to me and smiled. Then I woke up. I was wet."

"I threw water on you to wake you." Breena hopped down from the island like nothing had happened to her. "Do you know what was happening here while you were unconscious?"

She shook her head. "How would I?"

"You've done more impressive things than that."

"So what happened?"

"You made an illusion. Practically turned the whole apartment into a cave. Could've been interpreted as a tunnel of sorts, I suppose. Like your dream." *Don't tell her she was dying. She'll leave.* "I told you you didn't need to die. Once your subconscious took over, it came right back. You've been reaching out in your sleep, and now it's more than just astral projections. You're back to your old self."

"And you're excited because you think you've gotten your way."

It hadn't occurred to me that she might want to go even if she had her connection back. "Well. Fine, I guess I can't stop you. Not even a bullet stopped you from—"

"Are we going to talk about that, by the way? You shot me to keep me here." *And I'm still here. Get on with the leaving, Bree.*

Atlas avoided the prompt and went to the door. He opened it for her, gesturing widely, noticing the bullet that was, indeed, lodged in the mossy wooden siding that lined the stairwell. *The wound in her chest is probably already healed by now, too, unless she was only healing like that while she was near death.* "Just go. You don't want me."

Against all reason and expectation, her heart lurched at the statement. She softened. "You're right. But it didn't have to be like this. Not just today, or yesterday, but any of this." She approached him, holding her aching shoulder. "I know you didn't have total control in the things that pushed me away before, but it doesn't change the fact that you are hard to trust. You've got bad people in your life—"

"And you don't? Jet is not the kind of—"

"Let me finish. You've had bad people in your life and. . . and. . . Hurt people *hurt people.*" Bree coughed. "Ugh, I sound like an Oprah special or something." She pinched her nose. "Neither of us have been good to or for each other. It doesn't matter that you're my chosen. It's nature versus nurture. Despite our bloodlines, we're human first, and humanity can do a number on a person. You are misguided, and you do horrible things to me. But for some reason I'm still standing here talking to you. For some reason I'm attempting to *comfort* you."

"Fantastic job, by the way."

"Shut up." She stepped into the hall. "You have two minutes to explain this plan of yours, and then you lose me forever."

Atlas reached for her hand.

She snatched it away. "Just talk."

Chapter 7

With the spoken version of a throat-clear, less like a need to scratch an itch and more like a shy attempt to say excuse me, a blonde woman around Jet's age—nineteen, twenty-two at the most—sat across from him in a plush chair at the back of the book store.

The sound startled him out of his worrying and he looked up, lifting his head from his hands. A beat passed. "Can I help you?"

The exhausted expression on his face confirmed her concerns. "Oh, right. Sorry for staring. I. . . Well, I was over there," she pointed to the aisle of romance novels, "and I noticed you all alone over here. You look upset." She nodded like that answered his question.

"And?"

"Uh, and. . . and I wanted to make sure you were OK."

A smile touched the corner of his mouth. She wore genuine concern on her face. *She's not Breena.* The smile disappeared.

"Oh, damn. I'm doing it again, aren't I?"

"Doing what?"

"Meddling. My therapist says that there's a difference between kindness and nosiness. I guess she's right. She says I need to wait for a cue from others that shows me they're inviting me into conversation. She also says I have to stop trying to fix everybody and fix myself first. Guess that means I'm broken. You look broken, so I thought I could help."

Jet's eyebrows jumped up.

"Yikes. That sounded abrasive. Sorry. You just, you just look like something's wrong with you." She cringed. "That's not much better is it?" Her hands fluttered around her face, scratching and messing with her hair. "Like, you needed help, and you've got that hair, and those arms, and those mean boots, and that head was in those hands. It's like a calling card. 'Hey, Shianne, come here and make me right. I'm so wrong, I'm perfect. I'll destroy your life.'"

Jet took his keys and cellphone from the small table beside his chair and moved to stand.

"I guess you're like the rest, though. Too afraid of a commitment. You're ditching me already. Way to go. Boys one hundred, Shianne zero."

Jet started away from her wondering what he had done to have this nonsense descend on him the same day Lucifer came to recruit him. She bolted out of her seat to pace him, chattering the whole way out of the store.

"This is so sudden. I can't believe you're taking me home with you. We just met. I don't even know your name."

"What? No. Do you ever shut up?" His tolerance for insanity and bullshit snapped. He stopped in the middle of the parking lot and hit her with a stare that likely stopped her heart, her perfect lethal combination of danger and smolder. "Look, woman. I don't know who the hell you are or how this act has ever worked for you in the past. I do not need or want your help, and I am not interested in being your project, or lover, or downfall. Go hunt somewhere else."

She stared back at him with tears welling as he crossed the lot to his car. Fighting the urge to scream and bash some windshields, she tore her phone from its pocket inside her purse and dialed.

"Dr. Bullard? It's Shianne. I did it again."

Linda stepped over Ari's unconscious form and meandered back to the balcony with a phone to her ear. "Tell me what happened."

The voice on the other end of the line recounted the events and Linda rolled her eyes. "What did I tell you last session?" She nodded. "Right. That you're not going to change someone's mind so easily. What does it take to change a person?"

Linda thought about her own answer to that question—love, loss, anger. She had never intended on going down this route, posing as a therapist, doling out bad advice to lunatics too lost in their minds' chaos to take part in the world's chaos when the riots broke out.

These were people she had wanted to help—lost people who took a liking to her during her work for Breena at the hotline. At Breena's instruction, she had picked a cover name, coached them through their confusion as she had to train Atlas' teachings out of them, and make sure they would not involve themselves in Tabitha's destructive plans. Even after she went on the run with Ari, some of them kept contact. After Tabitha's death and her own heartbreak, things got ugly for Linda, and her advice grew just as toxic.

Unable to sort her grief from her rage, and unwilling to make a distinction between Breena's people and Tabitha's, Linda's helpful encouragement had turned into a full-fledged alter ego. She blinked back what might have been guilt if she still considered herself an emotional being; she had moved past the highs and lows of emotion and settled into a blank fury.

"Exactly. So you're going to need to do more than confront strangers with compliments that sound like insults. Who was he this time, anyway?"

"I didn't get a name."

"You can do better. Remind me, again. What's your goal in all of this?"

"To live in a world where people love me. *Only* me. Always."

"And how are you going to get that love, Shianne?"

"By listening to you."

"Try again."

"By fixing broken people."

"Do better!"

"By taking what's mine."

"There she is."

Shianne's stomping fit in the parking lot had settled into pacing between rows of cars as the sun set. A smile flowered on her face and she thanked Dr. Bullard and hung up, renewed.

****

Unwilling to wait for Atlas' explanation any longer, Breena pivoted on her toe and stepped away from the door.

Don't let her go. Tell her. Tell her. "It's 'the new vision.'"

Breena wheeled back around. "Now *you* sound like Oprah."

"You know, like Jack Kerouac and Allen Ginsburg. I told you when we met that there was more to literature than Neruda. They got the concept from Baudelaire. He wanted people to confront social conformity. Seems fitting."

"The goal?"

"Come back in and I'll tell you."

She glared at him.

He didn't test her threat of leaving for good. "Same as always. Free people from their rules and their rulers, but I don't want the chaos. That was Tabitha, not me. You've got to at least believe that."

"I don't *have* to believe anything."

"That's the spirit! 'I don't believe in this society, but I believe in man.' Jack Kerouac wrote that in a letter to Allen Ginsburg in 1949. How much has changed since then, really?"

Breena stared at him.

"Not enough, that's how much. You and I both know what man is capable of, and you've seen their patterns. The only reason humans act the way they do is because of their rules. They ravage and pillage under the guise of good intentions and following instructions, instructions given by leaders who are themselves slaves to the perceived expectations of their station. It's time, and you know it. Help me. You always wanted change, and I think deep down you always wanted to live no matter how self-defeating you got."

Breena stepped back in to Atlas' apartment and shut the door behind them. His eyes lit up like he had won her over. "I knew you'd see it my way."

"Who are The Disorder, Atlas?"

He blanched. "The who?"

"Don't."

"How do you know about that?"

"When I was passed out earlier, I was able to visit Vos. He was watching the news. And you know whose face was in the security footage beside a picture of a charred lawn with that title emblazoned on it?"

Atlas pulled at his hair. "I had nothing to do with that. They organized it. They did it. I only watched. I walked through after to look at the damage. I swear this is not how I want to do it."

"You watched? How is that better? If you don't want it to go on like this, you could have stopped them. You created them, indirectly or not. They would have listened to you."

He shook his head, a grim look of cynicism darkening his exhausted face. "No they wouldn't. I'm no one. I'm Reid Case the hotline worker, the face of calm and contemplation, not drastic action. They wanted to burn something that night. Nothing would have stopped that mob mentality. They are Tabitha's remnants. Maybe not directly. She didn't start that group. But they are what's left of her M.O."

"If you weren't there with them, and you weren't there just to watch, why did you just so happen to be a hundred miles from home at the same church they were?"

To steal an RV. No, she won't buy that. There are RV's closer to home. Meet with a friend. Psh, who do I know in this country that wouldn't seem suspicious to meet in the middle of nowhere. Unable to settle on a suitable lie, he ventured the truth and hoped it would show her that he was changed enough.

"The Disorder formed within a group of my recruits that never got Linda's message. You sent her off with Ari before she could tell them I was just covering myself to look like I was helping Tabitha and to disregard my advice. They needed something to hold on to and, unfortunately, Tabitha was it. I don't really know why I went. Guilt, maybe? And I guess a little bit of nostalgia. Sometimes I still feel like I should be doing her work, not because Tabitha is compelling me to, but because it was a way of life for so long. Like muscle memory. I don't want to change the world *that* way, but the energy of the scene was hard to resist. I still have anger in me. It feeds on things like that. But I swear I did not get involved." *Not to feed chaos, anyway, but to warn off Lucifer. He's as much of the problem of power, and he's not getting Breena.*

"For some reason, I believe you." Breena swept her hair out of her face. "I'm going to bed. I've been through a lot today."

Atlas watched her shuffle out of the living room and down the hall to, he could only assume, his bedroom. *She's staying? She's staying.* He smiled down at the floor, shocked and grateful.

Breena shrugged out of what was left of her shirt and kicked her pants off. In the bathroom, she braved the mirror knowing that she needed to visually assess the damage. She regarded the cherry streaks of hair with wry amusement. It was as much like her mother as she hoped she'd become. *I can't pull off a full head of it.* Over the sink, she peeled the tape and gauze away from her chest with her eyes closed. *If I only look at it in the mirror, maybe it will feel like it happened to someone else.*

At first glance, all she could do was blink a few times to make sure she was awake. In the past, she had slipped effortlessly into many dreams that looked and felt like real life—that was, until something fundamentally off occurred and the recurring terror part of the dream began. But she hadn't had one of those dreams since her astral suicide, and she was nearly certain that this wasn't the same. She gulped a breath and looked down at her chest, ignoring her own plan.

Just as the mirror reflected, there was no wound, no stitches. Breena had uncertain expectations of what she might see there— some bruises and swelling, maybe a smattering of cauterizing powder that hadn't made it into the bullet hole, a hole itself, or rather, a sutured one. None of these were the case. All that remained of her injury was the dried blood. *Even the ridiculous rainbow stitches are gone.* She picked up the gauze pad and, in the center of a blood clot, was the small length of thread. *Atlas was right when he said there was no exit wound. I healed.* And the healing was so complete that it had pushed out everything he used in and on her skin to do the very same thing.

"Well, that's new."

****

Jordan roused around nine that evening. It had been almost three days since Breena was taken and one day since he had angrily suggested to Lilly that they let Bree stay missing. He took to moping and slept whenever his brain finally allowed it.

Lexa arrived to his house earlier that day saying, "You kids need some good old fashioned momming. I'm staying until Ari and Breena are home safe. To heck with Grant." He'd looked incredulous, he was sure, but Lexa interpreted it as a different brand of speechless—thankful. Her presence made it difficult to maintain his opinion that Breena had gotten what she wanted and should be left to it. He would never dare to say something like that to a parent of a missing child.

Sitting at the edge of his bed, he looked across his trashed room. In a normal situation, his own parents would be fussing for him to clean it up, but his life was too upside-down for something so typical. The giant jar of coins Breena had spilled last school year sat in the corner. It was hard to look at, still full of all its money he hadn't gotten to spend on beach week, or an apartment, or any sort of future with her.

Lilly knocked on his door. All he managed was a grunt.

"Lexa wanted to talk to you about the search."

"I can't."

"You can't talk to her?"

"No, I really can't."

Lilly barged in and threw her slipper at Jordan. "Get out here and help us, Jordan. I don't care why you feel like you can't. I'm pretending like you never said what you said the other night. And *you* need to pretend like you care."

She's right.

She swept her arm toward the door like a flight attendant and waited while he pried himself from the mattress. "And at least put on some pants. You're such a slob."

Downstairs, Lexa spread butter on huge slabs of bread and popped them into the oven. She assumed correctly that it was the first meal Lilly and Jordan had eaten together since Breena disappeared and thought it might make Jordan more comfortable with her presence. She had cooked so many dinners for the three of them over the years. Everything about the night was familiar, but nothing was right.

Chapter 8

A week later, the energy in the house was still fragile, Jordan's tension and Lexa's worry clashing with the clear-headed logic of Lilly's persistence.

"So you're saying that The Disorder is involved in the kidnappings?" Lexa paced circles around the coffee table waiting for a satisfying response from the lead investigator. "Ari has been missing four months, and now Breena. Our family is some sort of target. I want to know why." Nothing they said had brought any relief yet.

"We don't have any reason to believe they'd seek out Ari or Breena specifically, or anyone else, for that matter. It's not their style. They want to impact as many people as they can with their actions. Until now, at least, they've hit *places*. However, the group has some connections in common with Breena and Linda. Besides Reid Case—"

Lilly interjected over speakerphone, "You mean, Atlas."

Lexa scowled, still furious and disgusted by him. She had only recently found out about his and Bree's relationship after Ari's disappearance and held on to the feeling to fuel her search.

The investigator cleared his throat. "Besides *Atlas*, some numbers in your daughter's contacts led us to people we had already come in contact with during the riots. It's good you brought us her phone, Lilly."

Lexa threw a hand over her mouth. "You mean she was out there fighting with those. . . those. . . She's one of *them*?"

"I didn't say that, Ms. Scarlet. Phone records show that many of the numbers in her contacts have never actually been called from her end. There's no evidence that they have tried to call her, either. The people she talks to most often are probably in that room with you."

Jordan and Lilly shrugged like they weren't surprised.

"There is one new number that has called repeatedly since we seized the phone."

"Why all of the sudden?"

"There were text messages to and from it in the days leading up to her disappearance as well, but not in this quantity. The only link is that they went to school together. Jet Sala. His name and number aren't saved in the contacts, but his voicemails are of a close nature. Seems to really care about her. Miss her. They were together the day before it happened. Any of you know the story there?"

It had been almost two weeks since Jordan came home to a yard full of police officers and just over a week with Lexa in the house. She insisted on eating together, researching together, and talking to the police together—the latter mostly because she hadn't been there when it happened or when the police report was filed. She was making up for lost time.

Jordan considered his patience a miraculous thing given the proximity, the constant buzzing in his head, and the knot of hunger in his stomach that he just couldn't bring himself to feed. But at the mention of Jet's name and what Jordan *thought* was the insinuation that Jet might have been able to protect her better, Jordan's fist flew through the wall he had been leaning on. He pulled his hand back through the plaster and regarded the abrasions. *People who say outbursts don't help clearly value their walls too much.*

In the background, Lilly and Lexa had settled back into listening to the detective ramble through evidence and suspects. Before they hung up, Lilly jumped in and asked for Jet's phone number.

"It couldn't hurt for me to talk to him. We didn't know there was anything worth noting going on between them."

"I suppose that would be helpful. We haven't been able to get in touch with him. Judging by the voicemails, it was new, their relationship, and Jet isn't sure if there's anything worth noting, either. He doesn't seem to know where she is. Thinks she's avoiding him."

"OK, OK, this isn't gossip time by the lockers. I think we know everything there is to know at the moment. Thank you for calling, Officer Thomson. Lilly will handle this next part and be in touch." Jordan pressed end and rubbed at his bruised knuckles. Lilly stared. "What?" Jordan stalked to the kitchen for some ice.

Lexa finally sat down beside Lilly and looked at her with a strained rigidity. Lilly put a hand on Lexa's knee. "This is progress.

Jet will have a new point of view on this. They hung out the day before she. . . he might have noticed if there were any odd people watching from a distance or if she had been planning something we weren't in on. I'll find out. I'll find your kids."

For an instant, the fog and tension cleared from Lexa's face and she sat up straight. "If Bree's phone had so much info, why didn't they take it as soon as she went missing? You shouldn't have had to offer it to him. I don't think that Detective Thomson is very good at his job."

Lilly grinned, a rueful look. "He's not."

****

Jet had just turned the shower on to warm when the doorbell rang. He pulled his sweaty gym shorts back on and jogged to the front door. Hand already on the knob, he decided to look through the peephole. Only Breena would be worth opening the door for at that moment. Anyone else was a waste of the water he had left running.

At first, he didn't see anyone, but then he heard a sigh and some shuffling against the door. From under the peephole, the top of a head rose into view, revealing the back of a white-blonde head. When she turned, Jet cursed and jumped back from the door whispering to himself. "It's that girl. Why is she here?" *No. No.* 'How *is she here?' is more like it. Crap. I bet she heard me.*

"Jet, honey? I'm sorry to intrude, but we left on such a bad note the other night at the book store. I wanted to make it up to you."

He went back to the peephole to observe the crazy. *How did she get my name?*

"I got your mail from the box. Look, I even brought you a basket of cookies. I made them myself. I hope you're not still sad from the other night, but if you are, they'll help. I promise."

Yeah, they're probably laced with something to make me feel real good.

"Jet. Baby. I know you're home. I saw you pull in. You came from the gym, right? You look so good in that muscle shirt."

He knew he wouldn't answer the door, but for some reason he couldn't pry himself away to either turn off the shower or get in it. Seeing Shianne out there with that big granny basket of baked goods and a genuine smile that gave away none of her lunacy was like a train wreck. He wanted to see how it ended for everyone. *But I suppose that part's up to me. Just go get in the shower.*

He tiptoed back to the bathroom and prayed she had the sense to leave. With Luce's presence a possibility at any moment, at least until he found and returned Breena and Atlas to him, no one was safe at his house—psycho or otherwise.

On Jet's front porch, Shianne swayed side to side with the basket. Any other day, she would have stayed all day if necessary, but she had an appointment with Dr. Bullard in an hour and, even though it was by phone, she wanted to eliminate any possibility of Jet overhearing her session. She reluctantly set the basket atop the welcome mat and left.

Jet took a longer shower than usual in the hopes that Shianne would be gone when he got out, and she was. He checked his phone as he toweled off his hair and listened to the voicemail left by a number not in his contacts. To his pleasure and surprise, it wasn't from Shianne.

"Jet, this is Lilly Ledford, Breena's friend. I really need to talk to you. Please call me as soon as you have time for a long discussion."

I guess I know what this is about. No more pretending not to know that she's missing. He dialed her back immediately and settled in for what he assumed would be a very complicated chat about his lineage and things most people believed were religious doctrine or myth.

After Lilly got through the thorough intrusion into his relationship with Breena, the pair swapped information, including what he expected to be a messy reveal. He was relieved to find out that Lilly already knew about Breena, and she took his role in the situation in stride.

Jet played up to Lilly's lack of confidence in the police investigation knowing that it would help him deliver Breena and Atlas to Lucifer without additional involvement of human law. Luce didn't want police finding her, and he definitely didn't want Atlas tried by human standards. Lucifer wanted his granddaughter home, and he wanted her chosen to give her a family then cross over to eternity in the pit as it had always been done. For all Jet knew, Luce was deliberately influencing the police investigation away from answers so Jet would succeed, although Jet assumed that wasn't the case because allowing him to fail would mean affording Luce the opportunity to punish him instead, and that was what the guy was really all about.

Lilly babbled away about Mestif and his tattoos, and Linda, and how she thought Linda's choice to disregard Breena's instructions and keep Ari hostage might be some sort of retribution for killing Tabitha—it was—and that maybe Linda had sent the two men to take Breena—she hadn't.

Jet nodded along knowing that Breena's kidnappers were dead, otherwise Luce would never have given him the job of retrieving her.

"The police mentioned that Breena had a number for a person named R in her phone but that she had never called it. It's an alias of some guy they'd busted for rioting months ago. He's out already—apparently they had only been able to charge him with protesting without a permit at the time—but they're trying to bust him for his involvement in The Disorder."

"The Disorder?"

"Have you been under a rock?"

He thought about the first few days when Breena wasn't answering calls. He'd felt like crawling under a rock. Then, along with his great purpose in life bestowed upon him, a stalker was also. "No, not under a rock. Just dealing with some personal stuff."

"Fine. They're an organized group of. . . terrorists, I guess you could call them, although they'd probably call themselves revolutionaries or something. Most recently, they destroyed a church and burned their calling card into the lawn. The only face caught in security footage from that night was Atlas'. So, the police figure if Breena has this R guy in her phone, and R is connected to The Disorder, and Atlas was with them that night, R is the next new suspect to check out after Atlas. Even if R isn't linked to Breena's disappearance, they still want him for arson."

"And Atlas?"

"No official news. All I can tell you is that there's this other group looking for him, too. They're basically the opposite of The Disorder in terms of end-goals if not methods. They're vigilante justice types angry at what Atlas set into motion. They're the ones that captured Mestif. Maybe he can give us some more tips. I can get back in touch with Leigh."

"Mestif's dead."

"What?"

"Luce."

"Oh." Lilly held her breath waiting to gauge his upset.

Jet didn't wait for pity or condolences. "Anyway, I think The Disorder is our better bet for finding them. We could use the existing police info on The Disorder to lead us to R, and to Atlas, hopefully beat the police to them."

"I have been unimpressed so far with the investigator working on this case. It just seems like he's really slow to connect the dots, so I think we could make it first. But I do believe in the police as a whole and in criminals going to trial for the things they've done. Why do you want to keep them out of it so badly? Maybe you should join Leigh's group."

"Luce wants to handle it, says these problems are of his domain, not humanity's. And, frankly, I'm scared shitless of what he'll do to me if I don't deliver."

Lilly heard herself agreeing to feed the police and Lexa only bits of the whole picture, comforting herself with the excuse that limiting human intervention would in turn limit human suffering and injury. She knew she wasn't wrong in her conclusion, but it was hard to accept that she was entrusting her best friend to the devil.

****

Breena stared down at the geese milling about the land behind the apartment building. The sun had just peaked over the trees and a cold wind funneled through the open stairwell. It was morning, but she hadn't slept yet.

Why am I still here? I'm healed, he's sleeping. . . I could just go. I could've gone every day for the last week. I could've snuck his phone away and called Lilly to let them know I'm OK. I should have. And Vos. He could come get me. I owe him a wine glass.

The soft footsteps behind her didn't register until a hand settled on her shoulder. "You're out here again."

"Yeah."

"It's freezing."

"Why don't I want to leave, Atlas?"

"I uh. . ."

"I have to go. I should *want* to go."

"Come back inside. I can't feel my toes." He wiggled them through his socks.

Breena tore her eyes away from the geese and squeezed past Atlas. He followed her back into what he had started to think of as *their* apartment—a dangerous thought, he knew. She put a pot of coffee on for Atlas, and it was all so average. *Why is my face smiling?*

She had never wanted anything in her life to be average. After years assaulted by memories of her father's death, the fire, the nightmares, and the weight of her more recent choices, Bree assumed the churning in her gut and tension in her neck were the marks of a challenge overcome, some sort of participation badge or medal. And, even though she knew there was a new storm swirling outside of Atlas' little apartment just waiting to crown her with another achievement, she couldn't deny the rare peace settling over her. That was always the signal to run.

He just wanted a simple life and for me to be a part of it, but this is not real. I hated him. When did it stop? Did it? She searched her feelings. *Nothing. This is not how it would be.* This galvanized her.

In front of her, the coffee dripped onto the hotplate and sizzled into acrid stains, the empty pot still in her hand as she confronted her situation.

As nice as it is for a change, I don't belong here. A simple life to him just means he's not going to kill and terrify to get the kind of change he wants. He's not content to stay in this apartment and let the world live around him, without him. That's not what he meant.

"Breena—"

She frowned.

"Breena! Give me that." He reached to snatch the pot from her, but that was the moment she snapped back to reality, the whole of the situation with Ari, Vos, Tabitha, her friends once again descending on her.

Before he had it in his grasp, she thrust the pot in his direction and let it go. "I'm leaving." She was already out of the cramped galley kitchen when the carafe hit the floor and shattered.

"What the hell, Breena?" He glanced down at the mess, but managed to pry himself away from the urge to immediately clean it up. "You can't leave."

"I am." She grabbed his shoes again and briefly hoped to avoid a repeat of the last time she did this.

"I wouldn't have bothered bringing you here in the first place if your presence was optional."

"I have a responsibility, Atlas. You know what it's like to take a life—"

His heart lurched.

"—and in *my* case, there was a purpose, a purpose I need to fulfill."

"That's not fair. You know I killed Reid for you."

"Don't even try to put his life on me. You couldn't handle yourself around Tabitha, and it got you caught. These were *your* plans that started all of this, and if what you told me at the time was true, Tabitha would have had him killed anyway since siblings are not allowed in Gehenna."

"Tabitha ordered me to kill my brother because I am your chosen. There could be no competition for *you*. I said it before. They would have likely allowed him and me to live normal human lives if neither of us had ended up as your chosen."

"So you should understand even more, then, that I have a role to fill—a role that people are dying for. I cannot shirk my responsibilities and allow those deaths to go in vain." She opened the door. "And shall we add to the list for impact, Atlas? You killed Galo. I don't have a good feeling about whatever happened to his right hand, Mestif, either. Anyone else I should know about? Maybe Mercutio, Tybalt, and Paris?"

"We are not Romeo and Juliet."

Her eyes grew wide. "'Ya think?"

"Our families *want* us together." Atlas clasped his hands in front of himself, illustrating.

She stomped a foot. "Yet you won't allow me to go to them."

"Because we could be happy here, and they could learn to live with it."

"Because you don't want me to drag you down there with me and send you to the pit. Let me save you some time, Atlas. I don't want you here or there. I do not want you anywhere. Not in a box, on a rock wearing socks, dressed like Goldilocks, or in Gehenna where I plan to make changes you would not like or understand."

Breena expected Atlas to grab her by the wrist and haul her inside, maybe shoot at her again, but he didn't. He stood there and let her go. If it was anyone else, she might think she had won, but she knew any acquiescence on his part just meant he was changing tack. *I'll see him again.*

In the parking lot, she stepped into his ridiculous shoes and walked to the apartment complex office. A middle-aged woman sat behind the desk filing her nails with concentration Breena usually reserved for trying to see through walls. Bree cleared her throat. "Hi. I need to call my ride, but I've misplaced my cell. Can I use your phone, please?"

"Sure, honey." She pushed the ancient office phone across the desk with the heel of her hand like using her fingers would undo all the work she just put into her nails.

Breena stood with the phone to her ear for a moment debating who to call. *Jordan's probably worried, but does that erase the fight we had? And calling Lilly means I'm essentially calling Jordan. Mom's with Grant.* She rolled her eyes. *Vos would overreact. I don't need a body guard. Although he's the only one who was going to allow me to die to get back to Gehenna.* Her shoulder, though visibly healed, twinged. *Maybe I do need Vos, but no. There's always Jet...*

Chapter 9

On the other side of Michigan, The Disorder filled a pub with laughter and clinking glasses. To look at the group, clothed in typical department store outfits and sharing pleasant smiles with one another, they were as standard as a group of friends could be. They were anyone and everyone. But, in the corner near the door, one table of rioters sat discussing potential targets over a tray of quesadilla wedges and hot wings.

"I'm tellin' you. That guy is still around. I swear it was him in the security footage from our last hit. All you need to do is tell me to make the call and I'll ask him to help us choose the next place."

"R, I just don't think that's a good idea."

"You're wrong. All of this," a slim woman with bouncy grey curls gestured around the room to the other group members, "was his idea. What we are now is because of him. He remade us. Why wouldn't he want to help remake the world?"

"Jen. Be real. Don't you think he would have done more than just tell other people what to do if he had wanted a direct part in it?"

"I think he was following orders just like we were. It's time to liberate him like he did for us."

"So it's settled then? Our next target is Reid Case?"

Someone approached the table, a stern expression of confidence setting his tan face in stone. "Yeah, and I know where he's staying."

The group turned at the new voice. "Who the hell are you, kid?"

He pulled up an unsteady wooden chair and straddled it backwards at the head of the table. "Jet Sala."

R's eyes lit up. "Any relation to Mestif Sala? Good guy. Met him at a planning meeting Reid held earlier this year."

"You got it. Unfortunately, Mes is. . . Mes," he feigned a catch in his voice, "Mes is gone."

The group gasped and muttered apologies.

Jet looked down at the table. "I hope you weren't too close. I'm sorry for your loss."

"What are you doing consoling us? He was *your* relative, man."

"Thanks. Honestly, I didn't know him well. Distant relative. But he's not actually why I'm here." He turned off the solemn mask and straightened the sad tilt of his head. Jet leaned in to the group. "I've been admiring your work. A friend of a friend said Reid was just a figurehead for The Disorder, that the media coverage is skewing your message by misattributing it to him. That's wrong, and you shouldn't tolerate it. I heard Reid speak once at one of those meetings you mentioned. His whole philosophy is that we rule ourselves, right? So why are you going to let him take all the credit? And why would you want to follow more of his directions?"

Jen pursed her lips. "We hadn't thought about it like that."

"You've got a point. Let me interject just one question first. How did you know about me?"

"Friend of a friend. She met you at a meeting once. You made quite the impression."

Jet wouldn't have a successful pill business if he couldn't lie well. He learned early that as long as he used bits of truth, or reorganized reality, he could pass anything off with conviction. It didn't matter to him that Lilly hadn't met R. Before Jet set out to follow R from the address listed on his police report, Lilly had been able to confirm with Leigh that R was an outspoken attendee at all of Atlas' meetings. Jet wouldn't call Lilly a friend, and she said Leigh wasn't hers, but it was close enough.

"And how did you find us *here?*"

Jet made no attempt to conceal his next lie. "I come here all the time." It came out sounding like he wasn't convinced, either. He hoped the example of a poorly-executed deceit would engender confidence in the rest of his word, including the skillfully crafted con he was setting up.

"You followed me."

"'Ya got me. You should be flattered."

R furrowed his brows. "So you want to tell us where Reid's been lately?"

"Yes, I do."

Outside the pub, Shianne paced in the parking lot waiting for Jet for the second time. *It doesn't make sense. Dr. Bullard would normally be furious I was following someone, and now she wants more information on him? Usually a name's enough, too much once she knows how I got it. Maybe she wants to make sure he's worth the trouble. Maybe she thinks he could be* the one.

A giggle bubbled up and out of Shianne. *The one.* She slung her purse over her shoulder and steeled her nerves to go inside. The idea that Dr. Bullard might be trying to play matchmaker lent gravity to her pursuit that hadn't been there before. Her past obsessions seemed silly.

"Mr. Sala, here comes your bride." Shianne stepped into the restaurant and noticed Jet right away. He was in the middle of something, part of a group of heads and shoulders crowded close together. *I shouldn't interrupt.* Shianne sat at the bar and watched Jet's back tense and relax as he talked with his hands.

Jet gave The Disorder their game-plan: go home, pack whatever they usually packed for a riot, and meet in the Grayling Save-A-Lot parking lot at 8:00am the next morning. They dispersed to their cars, but Jet stayed at the table a moment more, pulling out his phone.

He dialed the office number Breena used two hours earlier hoping she was still there. He had told her to hang around unless Atlas wandered in.

When the phone rang, Breena answered it from her seat across from Betsy, the nail-file lady.

"Bree? Good, you're still there. No Atlas?"

"Surprisingly, no. *Suspiciously*, no."

"I got the group on board, but we're not coming until tomorrow. They think they're going to confront Atlas about staying out of their affairs. No more showing up on their scene to steal the spotlight. You, unfortunately, need to go back to Atlas' apartment, pretend to make up, do whatever you need to show him you've changed your mind. Keep him from leaving."

She rolled her eyes. "How did I know?"

"Well, that's all you get to know. I'm sorry to keep you in the dark, but it's safer. The important thing is that with *you* there, he'll stay put. Luce wants you home in a *good* way, but Atlas. . . Luce wants him even more, I think."

They hung up, and Jet shoved out of his chair. With a knowing scowl, he turned around to address the weight of feeling watched. He gave her a simmering glare. "Why are you here?"

Chills rolled up her arms. "Because you're here."

"You shouldn't be." Shianne hopped from her bar stool, but Jet held up a finger. "Stay there."

"I told my therapist about you." Her approach was tentative, coy. She had never been coy about anything. "She wanted me to get to know you better."

"Stalking me is not the way to do it."

"This was the last time I follow you somewhere. I swear. Let me do this the right way."

"Why should I? You're crazy."

Her hopeful expression fell and her eyes darkened. "I am *not* crazy. No one calls me crazy!" In an instant she was across the room, swinging wildly at Jet. "You were supposed to be the one. You're supposed to get to know me." A bartender jumped the counter and grabbed her under the armpits, hauling her away from Jet as she raved.

"Get off of me. Nut." Jet smoothed his black button-down with a loathing touch, like she had left some sort of residue on him.

Shianne's mascara ran in watery black rivulets as she thrashed in the bartender's grasp. "And *you* get off of me. Cretin."

The bartender held the door open and nudged Shianne towards it. "You both need to leave."

"Not until she's gone. I don't want her following me anywhere else." He pegged her with a stare. "I *will* call the cops and file for a restraining order."

"Just try." She stomped out of the restaurant to her car. Jet watched in the doorway. He could hear her singing, 'I love you, a bushel and a peck, a bushel and a peck, and two hands around your neck. Two hands around your neck, and I'll make your life a wreck. I'll make your life a wreck, and I'll watch you while you sleep like I do.' Shianne left, and Jet made sure to drive in the opposite direction she had.

****

Ari sat on the edge of the tub with his head in his hands. Linda had drugged him with something a week earlier, and he had come to in the middle of that night in the only room in the apartment that had no windows. After he had talked to Lilly, he and Linda fought. Linda couldn't—wouldn't—give him any leeway with leaving the apartment or communicating with others now that he knew she wasn't interested in him, that they weren't on a vacation, that he was considered missing and in danger.

Before starting in again at knocking on the walls and door, he ran through the events of the summer. When he and Linda first embarked on their trip, there was a friendly ease between them. Linda seemed determined to show him a good time, planning outings and getting involved in events in the places they visited. The cruise went smoothly, and after they toured Italy, they decided together to visit Spain. It was natural. Linda hadn't started out so angry, and he wondered if at some point she actually cared about him. Slight age difference aside, they shared common interests—soccer, music, travel. He believed she had cared.

Then one day she turned. Linda received a phone call from someone irate at the other end of the line. She sobbed for a long time, but as the long discussion wore one, the tears stopped and she grew louder, angrier, pacing until she went silent. When the call ended, she went straight to bed and slept for two days. Ari didn't know what snapped, only that it did. Since then, she kept her distance and was careful not to make eye contact for too long.

After finding out from Lilly that they could have returned home a while ago, he confronted Linda about leaving. Even though he was angry at her deception, Ari tried to present it as an opportunity rather than a finale. She reacted poorly. He looked around the bathroom. "Really poorly."

On the other side of the apartment, Linda hung upside down off the edge of her bed, phone to her ear. Shianne fumed without stopping for a breath, and it was all Linda could do to keep her fake persona intact. She wanted to rant, too, about how Breena was ruining everything, how the Sala men seemed to be on a record heart-breaking streak, how a threat to Ari's life and wellbeing wasn't enough to pay Breena back for the events of the summer. She needed the whole family in the same location. Breena had to go, but not before watching her friends and family suffer.

When Shianne finally stopped rambling about getting publicly snubbed by Jet, Linda had made up her mind that Ari had been at least partially right. It *was* time to take him back home. She made the call to Breena's cell and left a message. She *wanted* her to know she was coming for her, to expect pain. It was only fair.

****

As soon as Breena left, Atlas had pulled out his ratty duffle bag and stuffed it with the few things he had brought to the apartment. Changing tactics would require changing location, especially if Breena planned to drag him to Gehenna with her. If she came for him, Atlas would fight back with nostalgia, a sweet spot in their history to convince her to join him or at least leave him be.

As Atlas made arrangements to catch a flight to London, Breena plodded back to his apartment rehearsing what she would say when he answered the door. *Regardless of my greeting, he'll probably smirk and say 'I told you so.' I guess it doesn't matter how I put it as long as it sounds real.* She knocked on the door assuming he'd be right there waiting for her to prove him right, but it took a few minutes of knocking to draw him out.

He answered without checking the peep hole and wore an expression of genuine surprise. If their past was an easy one, Breena wouldn't have doubted his shock, but she was suspicious that he'd been counting on this all along. Regardless, she started in on her campaign of apologies.

"I can't believe I brought up Reid. That was harsh. I had to come back to apologize."

"That's the only reason you came back?"

"No. It's these damn shoes of yours. I couldn't get far. Every other step I left one behind me."

Atlas forced a skeptical chuckle at her attempt at humor. "The real reason?"

She chewed at her lip then groaned. "Are you really going to make me say it?" His expression was even. "Of course you are."

"And?"

"You're not entirely wrong about society, your plan might work, and even though I don't want a part in it, it does sound better than dying at the moment. I want to make things right, but that's a little extreme, even for me. You'll have to do, for now."

"I figured. Unfortunately, I'm planned to go back to London. You'll have to take a bigger leap than just coming back to my apartment. Come back with me to the place where all of this started."

"You're leaving now?"

"In the morning."

"No, you can't." *Smooth.* "I just mean, how can you afford that? Last minute flights are—"

"I still have one of Tabitha's credit cards. The bill is set up with auto-pay from her bank account, so until her account runs dry, I'm going to let them think she's still alive."

Breena narrowed her eyes at him.

"A perk of being someone's assistant is having access to everything."

"Fine."

"So you'll come with me?"

"No. I meant, 'Fine, that explains how you're paying for it.' But why are you going back?"

"Is there any reason for me to stay?"

Only the angry mob coming for you. "Atlas, I live *here.* I can't leave Jordan and Lilly, or my mom. We still haven't found Ari."

"Convenient how you leave out Jet."

"OK, yes. I'll miss him."

"You've been away from home for two weeks. Have you missed him yet? You seemed to enjoy playing house again. And let's not forget that the last time we were involved in something like this, you lost track of time and reality completely. You were with Jordan, then, and you didn't miss him, either."

"None of that was real."

"Real enough. It cost you your psychic link to your soul, which is why you're really here. It's the Breena effect, if you will."

Breena gave him a questioning stare.

"Like the butterfly effect, but with more whining."

Jet could have planned this any other way.

"Are there any other reasons I should stay?" He rubbed at the back of his hair.

"I thought I would be enough."

"Why should it matter? You said you didn't want me."

She stared at her once-again bare feet, the shoes dangling from her fingers. "Because usually you do and feel what you want regardless of what I think about it. Thought you'd keep on wanting me even if I didn't want you."

"Ouch."

Bree squeezed her eyes shut for a second. "I know." She picked at her fingernail. "I'll leave. I shouldn't have come back." She looked down at Atlas' huge shoes with exaggerated loathing. *They really aren't that bad.* "Do you have *anything* else?"

Atlas brushed her cheek. She was warmer than usual and, despite her advanced healing, he worried about infection. "Just stay. I'll drop you somewhere with a payphone tomorrow on my way to the airport."

She nodded, praying Jet's group came early in the morning.

Chapter 10

Officer Thomson called Jordan before the sun had finished rising the next morning. Jordan blinked away the crust in his eyes but was still too asleep to make sense of the number on his phone. He answered with a groggy hello.

"Jordan, sorry to call so early. I couldn't get in touch with Lexa, and Lilly must already be out snooping around our suspects as usual."

"You're probably right."

Since making contact with Jet, Lilly had redoubled her efforts to become a part of Leigh's vigilante group. She believed that The Disorder was the more dangerous group but respected Jet's wishes to keep Jo, Leigh, and company out of his hair and away from the police. It was worth the extra investigation, anyway. Some members of both groups had overlapped at one time or another, meaning they were all castoffs from Atlas' shipwreck of a plan. And, at least since Atlas' face became news story number one, their differing plans shared common goals—getting Atlas.

"So why are you calling, Officer?"

"I wanted to apprise you of a new development. Breena's cell phone received a phone call and voice mail from Linda late last night."

Jordan sat up and threw his covers off. "That's amazing!"

"Yes and no. While we do, of course, want her to bring Ari home, we still cannot charge her with anything related to their travels, as Ari left as a consenting adult. If something about their situation changed while they were gone, he can press charges then. As it stands, their little escapade was just that. We can only say that it was rude of them not to check in and to allow you all to worry."

"Right. Breena's not going to like that. Any news on her?"

"Unfortunately not. But there's more not to like. Although Linda does appear innocent in Ari's case right now, she made a threat on Breena's life, which is a chargeable offense. If you hold on one second, I'll play the recording for you.

'Breena, it's your *friend*, Linda.' She sneered the words and Jordan imagined the pulled expression on her face. 'Did you have time to miss me, or were you too busy stealing the love of my life?'

Officer Lovette talked over the rest of the message, saying Linda must have wanted Atlas for herself. Jordan ignored this error in assuming Linda loved Atlas instead of Tabitha. It was better the cops didn't know about Tabitha or how she died, and Jordan wanted to hear the rest of the message.

'I wanted to tell you that we're coming home and to thank you for teaching me a valuable lesson about relationships. Our relationship is one of those rare, lifelong connections—your life, in particular—which is drawing to a close. Hope to see you soon. Ari sends his love. Kisses.'

Jordan cursed to himself and waited for the officer to circle back around to the issue.

"We're optimistic that we can intercept Linda and Ari before they get anywhere near Breena. It sounds like she doesn't know Breena is missing. That could work to our advantage. However, in the event Breena turns up before Linda, we've got to get her into protective custody, so please keep us updated and we'll do the same for you."

"Absolutely. Thank you."

"Of course. Go back to sleep, kid."

Jordan tried. He really did. The longer he lay in bed staring at the ceiling, the lighter and more excited he felt. With Linda entering the scenario, he felt less guilty about suggesting they give up on finding Breena. There was no way the two guys that snatched her still had her. All past patterns pointed to Atlas being responsible again, and she could handle herself with him. It didn't matter that her methods usually hurt everyone else. Jordan was done counting on her not to drag him through the dirt. He always felt like dirt. Linda, however, had turned into an unpredictable threat, and Jordan was thankful Breena wasn't around.

Lilly bolted into Jordan's room talking on fast-forward. "Guess what Leigh told me."

"Um—"

"No, that takes too long. Leigh told me the group found Atlas' new apartment. It took all of their efforts, but they were able to track

Atlas' route with traffic cameras and CCTV feeds. At the end of his drive, he passes a camera and then never reappears on the ones nearby that could have signaled him continuing on that road. There's only one residential area after that camera and before all the others, so they're about ninety-five percent sure he's staying in that apartsment complex."

"*Aparts*ment?" He smiled.

"Shush. I'm just excited."

When the group's hunt started, Leigh was certain of Atlas' location thanks to Luce's residence in her head, but everything she knew because of him during that period had gone with him. The cameras were their only proof.

"That's great. It shouldn't be too hard to spot that crappy camper you told me about in an apartment complex. Not a lot of space for stuff like that."

"Oh. No, he's not driving that anymore. He abandoned it at a gas station and left with Breena in a sports car. They used the stolen car report to figure out which vehicle to follow with the traffic cams."

"And there's no way they're wrong?"

"Not this time. After I spoke to Leigh, I got a call from Jet. Breena contacted him yesterday afternoon and—"

The excitement drained from Jordan in a second, pushed out by rage. "And so why didn't he call us *then*? No. Why didn't *she* call us?"

"He was meeting with The Disorder. He had a cover to maintain."

Jordan rolled his eyes, mostly at himself, hating that Jet had a valid reason. "And what's her excuse?"

Lilly shook her head, refusing to speak for Bree's reasoning. "As I was saying. Leigh has the right address because it matches the one Breena gave directly to Jet."

Jordan stared at his feet.

"Jordan. Do you hear me? It means she's OK."

He couldn't make sense of the situation or why he had wanted to give up on her. Suddenly, relief replaced all of the anger he had held in. He could only nod his head.

"I don't know the whole plan, but Jet and The Disorder are going there in a couple hours to get her back."

"He's working with those people?"

Lilly shrugged. "Luce put him up to it or something like that. They're supposed to distract Atlas so Jet can get to Breena, pull her away from the chaos to deal with Luce in peace."

"Why the hell should *he* get to save her?" Jealousy flared in front of his eyes. "I think I might actually be seeing red." He cracked his knuckles. "No. *We* are her friends. *We* have been in this together since she came back from London. *We* get to save her."

"While I would like to agree with you, especially since I'm the one who hid and watched her get hauled out of this house, we don't have the luxury of debating this. You can't just walk up to Atlas in his home and ask for her back. Jet is required to get her or it's *his* life that's in danger. And I promise, you don't want to get in the way of Luce or whatever Jet convinced The Disorder to do for him. Just let the bad guys be bad guys for a little longer. At least it's currently to our advantage."

After a moment of biting his tongue, he settled on his bed. "So when do we go?"

"As soon as you're ready."

****

The sun made it impossible to stay asleep any longer. Breena rolled off of Atlas' mattress and onto the floor. Beside her were the same clothes she had worn, washed, and worn again over and over since her kidnapping, with exception to the ruined and bloody shirt. After her wound healed, she commandeered one of Atlas' two tees. Bree pulled it over her head and went to see if Atlas was still asleep on the couch.

The flight was at 11:00am, and Breena was fairly certain that Jet wouldn't make her wait any longer than he had to, but she still worried how she would keep Atlas from leaving too early. For the moment, his sleeping would do.

****

Jordan drove like he had never been in a car before. His decision-making was last-minute and full of doubt, his movements erratic. Lilly gripped her seatbelt with one hand and the door panel with the other. She knew he was angry and afraid and tried to say nothing. If she was a dramatic person, she would have thrown herself to the pavement upon arrival to kiss the land and thank God she was alive. Instead, she leaned against the hood and stared up at the apartment building.

"Why are you just sitting there? We're here. We beat Jet. Let's go get her."

Lilly lost her patience as quietly as she could. "Shut up about Jet. Would you prefer to be the hero and answer directly to Luce, or do you want to let Jet do his duty? His family has served Breena's for eternity. Sorry to shatter your male ego, but you can't compete with that. Besides. she doesn't need saving. Jet's not coming for that and neither did we. He's merely her ride home. She could have left on her own, but chose to stay in order to help Jet avoid Lucifer's wrath."

"Fine, you stay here to greet the mob of criminals. What apartment is he in?"

"I'm not telling you. We're waiting."

"Maybe *you* are." Jordan stalked down the ground-floor breezeway for any signs of Atlas or Breena that would prevent him from having to knock on every door. *That kind of commotion early on a Saturday morning would ruin my element of surprise.* He rounded the staircase at the end of the hall and went to the next floor. There were no doormats or wreaths that could indicate which places *weren't* his, and there were no name plates either. As Jordan neared the next flight of stairs, something caught his eye—a neat hole in the wooden siding and a light smattering of red. His heart sank, and he thought he might vomit.

Before allowing himself to panic, he got out his phone and turned on the flashlight setting to try and get a look into the hole. In the back of the small tunnel, something metallic glinted.

Jordan's stomach flipped. *Don't jump to conclusions.* He stood by the hole and angled his body in the direction the hole was made. Jordan was looking just to the right of an apartment door that he both hoped was and was not Atlas'. *Breathe. Knock. Maybe it's not his place. Maybe it's from a past tenant. Maybe Bree shot* him. *Lilly would have told me if Jet mentioned Breena being injured.*

Breena cursed under her breath when the knock vibrated their door. Atlas didn't stir. *Please be Jet, please be Jet.* She tiptoed over. *But who else would it be? Atlas doesn't have any friends here.* She threw the door open and flashbacks of her trip to London assaulted her. Just as he had shown up on her step the first time, there Jordan stood, looking half ill, half excited. This time, at least, Jordan didn't pop out of a giant box. This time, she hoped, he wouldn't try to convince her to be with him.

Before she could squeak out a greeting, Jordan tackled her into a hug. "You're OK."

She nodded her head against his shoulder.

"I saw the bullet hole."

"I'm fine." She pulled away from Jordan and tugged down the collar of her shirt to reveal the healed skin. "He got me here. And it healed almost immediately. So, that's my new party trick."

Jordan blinked at her.

"We can talk about it more later. I don't want to wake him." Breena grabbed Jordan by the wrist and led him down the hall to the bedroom. She nudged the door shut behind them. "How did you find me?" The quiet room swallowed her whispering voice.

"Lilly worked her magic as always." A wave of guilt washed through him. He swayed. "I didn't. . . I didn't do any of it."

"And the plan is?"

Jordan rolled his eyes. "My plan or hers?"

"The one that's least rash."

"Lilly wants to wait until Jet gets here."

"But you're still mad at me for hanging out with him before I got snatched."

"That's not what matters right now."

"So that's a yes."

"*So*, I wanted to rush you home, but Lilly insists that getting involved will make Lucifer target us."

"So Galo wasn't lying." She picked at her lip. "Lilly's right, in that case. While I'd love to go home right now, we're already targets. If Luce wasn't after me, this wouldn't have happened in the first place. Why make things worse?"

A thump vibrated the floor and Breena shoved Jordan into the bathroom. "Shh."

Atlas opened the bedroom door and glanced around rubbing at his eyes. "My alarm didn't go off."

I know.

"I'm going to miss my flight. Have you made your choice? If you're coming, we need to go."

Breena paused for what felt like forever to Jordan, his ear pressed against the bathroom door. *She wouldn't actually say yes...*

"You know I can't go with you."

"Still choosing death over a life with me. I feel so good about myself."

Breena wanted to tell him that it didn't have to do with him, that he shouldn't take it personally, that it wasn't like that, but it kind of was. She could only come up with one lame reassurance. "At least I'm not making you come to Gehenna with me."

At that, Jordan burst out of the bathroom, propelled by pure shock and adrenaline. "You're going *where*?"

Atlas let out an exasperated sigh and cast an annoyed glare in Jordan's direction. "You again." Atlas strode over to him, face cold and expressionless. "Like a puppy."

Jordan crossed his arms. His heart was, of course, safely inside his chest, but the gesture made him more confident that Atlas couldn't see or hear it racing. "I'm taking Breena home."

Breena scoffed, and both men turned toward her. "I never realized how alike you are." Jordan gaped and Atlas' rage rose in his eyes.

"I'm going to need you to explain that one, Bree." Atlas nodded in grudging agreement with Jordan.

"What gave you the idea that I wanted or needed either of you in order to get back home?"

"Because you were *taken* from your home, against your will, in the first place. By him!" Jordan thrust a finger into Atlas' chest.

"It wasn't him, Jordan. It was Luce's guys."

"I saved her." Atlas grinned at Jordan, smug.

"Not that I needed you to, but back to my point. I don't *need* either of you to get back home because my home is in Gehenna. All I need to do is die." She chuckled darkly in her head. *I'm a ray of sunshine.*

Jordan blanched. "What?"

"Lucifer had Galo and Mestif take me from the house because he was tired of waiting on me to make up my mind about coming home. It's something I would have come to on my own, in time, but Luce has no more time. I mean, as an entity, he has eternity, but *Gehenna* has no more time to be without a queen. Nothing either of you do is going to make me go with you."

"Dammit! That's why Lilly wanted to wait for Jet, isn't it?"

"Are you mad that I called him first? I didn't feel like I could call you after that fight we had."

"That fight is irrelevant at this point. Lilly said Jet has been serving your family since the beginning of time and that Luce put him on the mission of finding you. He's supposed to take you home. Did I get that right?"

As if on cue, the door to the apartment slammed open, and Jet stormed in shouting names and curses.

Outside, Lilly approached a member of The Disorder and asked him what the group planned to do as he pulled a can of lighter fluid and a duffle bag out of his trunk. She had an idea, but she needed more than her assumptions.

In less than pleasant wording, he informed her that the group was there to spread their message in a place where Atlas couldn't take credit, by any means necessary. "I mean, who would torch his own place?"

Lilly forced a nervous giggle and agreed. She didn't know Jet well, but in their small interactions with one another during school, she always assumed he was a good guy, drug sales aside. Luce had to be Jet's only motivation to lead The Disorder on a crusade. He wasn't a violent person. *He doesn't think he can take Atlas alone.* She smacked her forehead and ran in after him.

****

Ari stared at the clouds under the plane. He and Linda had been so many places since May that the trip felt like all the rest. He knew he was going home, but the idea didn't stick. Its abstraction prevented any excitement. It didn't matter, in the moment, that Linda likely had a terrible thought driving her sudden change of heart. In the moment, nothing mattered. He was adrift and had been all summer.

Linda, however, was manic with vengeful giddiness. In the lavatory, she read through her list of losses, all the things she blamed Breena for ruining or stealing. It was like a morbid pep rally in her mind, every grievance cheering her toward her revenge. She thought briefly of Shianne, the slightest twinge of guilt constricting her chest. Shianne hadn't done anything but fall for the same lies and tricks she had, and now she was feeding the poor girl lies and bad advice just to soothe herself. Linda wasn't so far gone as to lose touch with the facts of her behavior. She was only far gone enough not to care.

****

Shianne lurked at the entrance to the apartment complex parking lot. She sat in the bed of her truck and watched The Disorder organize. *Dr. Bullard wouldn't want me to be a part of this.* She dangled her legs over the tailgate for a moment then hopped down. *But I want to be where* he *is. And she wants me to take what's mine.* Shianne started across the parking lot toward R. "It's fine. This is fine." She tapped the scrawny guy's shoulder. "I want to help."

"Who are you? Do you even know what we're doing?"

"I know what *I'm* doing." She snatched the lighter out of his hands, grabbed a waiting Molotov cocktail from the ground, lit it, and threw it in the direction of Atlas' apartment. A bush caught fire. "Making an impression."

"Fine." He nudged the hand holding the lighter. "Keep that, I guess." R climbed on top of the car they were beside and a hush fell over the crowd. "It's time."

That's all it took for chaos to erupt in the parking lot. Average-looking people turned into snarling animals wielding torches, hammers, and lengths of chain. Car alarms shrieked as some of The Disorder smashed windshields and slit tires. Smoke had already started to dull the air.

She looked around her for Jet in the sea of madness. *Why isn't he out here with us?* The lighter in her hand felt like a stone. *But I should be able to commit to him even while he's not looking. What would it say if I only did things he liked because he was watching me? How many 'I love yous' is a burning building worth?*

"Stop! All of you, just stop yelling!" Breena shoved Atlas, palms to chest, away from Jet, who Atlas seemed to like even less than he liked Jordan.

"I will not stop. He is not your chosen. He doesn't get to waltz into my house claiming you like his prize. I don't care that Lucifer sent him."

"What, so you *do* get to claim me because I'm your chosen?"

"Exactly."

"Let me tell you this," she whirled, pointing at each of the men, "None of you get to *claim* me. If I have to go back with Luce by. My. Self. I will." Jordan opened his mouth to argue, but Bree shoved a hand in his face, snapping her fingers closed like she was operating the mouth of a sock puppet. "Bzzt. No talking."

Lilly jabbed Jordan in the ribs with her elbow.

Still in front of Jordan, Breena looked back over her shoulder. "Jet, I appreciate that you came, and I realize you are not trying to claim me. You're just doing your duty, exactly like I'm trying to do."

Jordan looked sick.

"Atlas, you're welcome to come back with me and fulfil your duty as well, but I know how you feel about that and, to be honest, I couldn't care less about that particular tradition or the expectation that we create an heir."

Jordan couldn't bite his tongue any longer. "I don't understand why you called him first. You didn't know about his obligation to you until I got here and told you."

Breena rolled her eyes. "If you could hear yourself, you'd understand. And I was already piecing this together without you."

"Why don't you ever let your friends help you? We are your friends! Let us take you home."

Lilly snorted. "Please. You didn't even want to continue the search for Breena before I got that call from Jet."

Jordan's heart stopped, and Lilly clapped a hand over her mouth.

"Gee, thanks, Jordan. Good to know you didn't actually want to help me, you just don't want *anyone else* to help me—"

"That's not it!"

"—and that pretty much settles it. So, Jet, if you'd go ahead and get me out of here, I'd love that."

Jet nodded and grabbed her hand. Despite the mayhem he knew was blooming outside, and the territorial drama unfolding before him, his heart slowed. Everything slowed at the touch. His vision seemed to sharpen and his hearing as well. It was different than when they had kissed after the boat ride. Knowing his family history was true changed the nature of their connection. It wasn't simple attraction anymore. This was some ancient, animal thing. Three words entered his mind, repeating as if they had always been there. *Serve. Guard. Sacrifice.* The argument went on around him as he tuned in to his new instincts.

"Jordan, I know it's hard to grasp the possibility that anywhere but my house or your house could be home, but that's the reality we're in right now. You know exactly where I'm going."

At the entrance of a new voice, Jet snapped out of his introspection—it was hardly the time for it, anyway.

"Let the boy come with us. All queens need a jester." The room fell into hushed surprise as Luce strolled in wearing some unfortunate's body, and went right to Breena. "It's a pleasure to finally meet you. I've been watching so long I thought it might feel strange introducing myself. *I* already know *you*. I'm Lucifer, your grandfather."

He held out his hand, and she struggled to pull hers from Jet's. He looked helplessly up at Luce, embarrassed in his lack of control, which he knew Lucifer would see for exactly what it was even if the others didn't.

"Stand down, Sala. You're supposed to ask me who I'm wearing." Luce struck a suave pose like he was on the red carpet. Lilly cringed.

Jet watched his hand unclasp from Breena's through no decision of his own and knew the rest of his life would follow that pattern now that whatever it was had turned on in his brain. *Or DNA?*

Atlas had reclined against the wall and was watching the spectacle unfold with sad amusement when the first whiff of smoke hit him and he stiffened.

In the same moment, Breena shook Lucifer's hand and the room was thrown sidelong into another plane. It was Lucifer's doing, but Breena and Atlas were the only ones who immediately recognized the shift.

Breena screamed at the sudden pull on her injured psyche. She hadn't been in this parallel environment since the unfortunate, time-stuck Myrtle Beach illusion, where she had been forced to cut herself out of it to survive Atlas and Tabitha.

The night she connected with Atlas in her sleep had been a drug-induced fluke and, in this instance, she was painfully sober. The few pills in her pocket at the time of the kidnapping had been used within thirty-six hours. It was the only reason she was thankful for her new powers of healing, although she didn't know if those were permanent or only induced when near death.

As the shock to her system calmed, Breena noticed her friends around her, each of them trying to shoulder their ways closer, to put a hand on her, to see what was wrong. *I hate seeing those expressions. Fear. Pity.* She let the pull flow through her, relaxing into the discomfort, mellowed, and stood up. "Luce, why'd you bring us here? I assume you know I have no purposeful connection of my own to this place anymore. Your lovely daughter saw to that. I'm broken. You can't sustain me here forever."

"You are not broken, but I can and will keep you here for as long as it takes."

"As long as what takes?"

"For you to convince that one to come back with you and give you an heir." Luce pointed at Atlas, who was already shaking his head.

"She doesn't want me."

"Nonsense. Have you seen how she's looking at you?"

"Yeah, like she wants to kill me."

"In Gehenna, that's a high compliment, to be sacrificed by the queen."

"Then *you* die for her."

Luce chuckled. "If it was possible, I might consider it."

Jordan stepped between Atlas and Luce, throwing his arms out beside him. "Uh, anyone want to explain to us common folk what the hell is going on?"

Atlas ridiculed, pleased, "Jordan, you still don't feel it? I guess practicing with Breena was useless. Got a little too hot for teacher? How distracting."

"Shut up, Atlas. He's made good progress." Breena reached for Jordan's arm to reassure him, but he shrugged out of her grasp and went to stand in the doorway.

"So for those of us who aren't accustomed to leaving our bodies, what happens now?" Luce casually looped an arm around Lilly's shoulder like they were old friends. She grimaced and pulled free to glare at him. "I don't need comforting. Just answer my question. Clearly, you did this."

Atlas couldn't believe she was talking to Lucifer that way, and he began to see why she and Breena were friends. His past interactions with Lilly had been fleeting, but her pragmatism in the situation spoke volumes about her. *At least Jordan's the only limp noodle in Breena's life.*

"What happens now is I bring my granddaughter back to her real family. Say your goodbyes." Lucifer cut his eyes toward the window, but he wasn't taking in the scenery. He looked beyond their plane to the physical world, the template from which their current reality was cut, as smoke clouded the air outside the apartment building and alarms rang out.

Outside, The Disorder chanted for Reid to show his face. They snarled into the flames and cheered as the siding warped and melted off the building in slack sheets. Shianne had lost herself in the craze.

Initially, she had stuck to smashing car windows and lighting the seats on fire. She wanted Jet to see her contributions when he got out of the building. But The Disorder hadn't waited for Jet, and the building was engulfed. She tugged on R's arm, pleading for him to listen to her, to just wait, to go in and get Jet.

R rolled his eyes. "Look. He's not one of us. He was a means to an end, and I suspect he felt the same way about us. This was a mutually beneficial thing, meeting him in that bar, but now that we're all here, we don't need him."

"He'll die in there!"

124

"He knew what we'd do, and it was his idea. No one made him volunteer Reid's address to us. He went in anyway."

Shianne lost it. She screamed and swung at R and screamed some more. Over the din of fire trucks, fanatics, and crackling flames, it didn't make much impact, and R easily forced her out of the way.

****

Linda shuffled through customs, Ari at her side, looking as if a bus had hit her. She clearly had not slept during the red-eye flight, although her mussed, straw-like hair said "bed head." The man at the desk flipped through their passports, looking between them to confirm their photos, then stamped and waved them through. Ari thought Linda's appearance might raise some flags, maybe warrant a search or alert the authorities—*our faces are bound to be everywhere if they've filed police reports*—but as they passed under the "Welcome to the United States of America" sign, he figured security saw plenty of exhausted people in need of a shower and a hair brush.

Her even demeanor startled him more than her flashes of rage. When she was silent like this, there was no definite meaning. Ari had liked that about her—her cool composure. She had seemed to him the quiet observer. There was a rich world of intellect inside her, and it existed precisely because she observed, reserving words for meaningful comments.

As he pulled his luggage off of the belt, Ari knew her current stoicism fueled whatever plan she had in mind for his return. And, perhaps, it contained a bit of mourning as well. Ari wanted to believe that the end of their trip saddened her for the reasons it saddened him. Their time together, uninterrupted time where they bonded and made memories, was over. In the moments where he was able to put his anger at her deceptions aside, he recognized that coming home meant breaking up—if they had ever really been together—and that made him feel a different type of anger entirely.

He palmed the burner phone in his pocket. *Weird that she let me keep it. I should call Breena. Is she still missing? Does Linda know she's missing?*

"Come on, Ari. I got us a cab to your house." She put on a fake smile, and Ari pretended to accept it as genuine. "I can't wait to see your sister. I haven't seen her since she got out of the hospital last winter."

Lies. "It will be nice to sleep in my own bed. I guess seeing Breena won't be so bad either." Ari paused a moment. "'Ya know, I'm surprised Mom was so cool about this whole trip. Even though she was fine letting Bree go to London alone last summer, I wouldn't have guessed she'd be so relaxed about me taking off with a girl. This was impulsive. At least with Breena, her trip was painstakingly planned and had a clear goal." He glanced at Linda. Her façade held. He continued to needle as the taxi carried them away from the terminal curb.

"What was the goal of this trip, anyway? First, I thought it was a good distraction after your break up. Tabitha treated you like dirt. You're better off without her."

Linda winced almost imperceptibly. She hadn't told Ari that Tabitha was dead. The lie Linda used on herself was that publicizing that information would show weakness. She didn't want him to know that she'd been keeping tabs on her ex.

He went on. "Seemed like you were into me, too. Then, I thought our vacationing had turned into more of a marriage-less honeymoon. I admit I was really into it. But, people don't drug their spouse, or whatever, and lock them in a bathroom. People don't take their spouse on a vacation then decide to keep them as a hostage."

Linda's eye was twitching.

"All the while, letting that spouse, or whatever I actually was to you, think they're wanted. You're acting just like her." He paused for effect, but didn't get the reaction he wanted. "You're the same as Tabitha."

She turned toward Ari and struck him with such force his neck snapped back and his head bounced off the window. The cabby slammed on his breaks and veered to the side of the road.

"Hey, Lady! Save your domestic 'til after you pay your fare. There's a cleaning fee for blood."

Still eviscerating Ari with her glare, Linda spat back at the driver through tight lips, "Then drive *faster.*"

Chapter 11

Inside the burning building, everyone's bodies lay limp in the engulfed room, their psyches still detached and fighting it out on Luce's alternate plane. All but Luce remained unaware of the danger encroaching on their physical forms.

"As I've stated. Breena belongs with her real family and has a duty to fulfill. What kind of friends are you to be so selfish as to keep her for yourselves? She has an entire world to influence. You are just five people. Atlas and Jet will come with us. That should make the goodbyes a little easier."

"I am *not* going with you. She doesn't want me, and I have no desire to be bred and discarded like a dog." Atlas moved behind Jordan and shoved him back into the center of the group. "Take him. He follows her around and begs for her love anyway. He'll make the perfect royal pet."

Jet shook his head. "He's not even part of this world. Shit, until a week ago, I wasn't either. But even I have a better shot at getting her than he does."

Luce and Atlas raised their voices, speaking over one another. "You absolutely do not! Remember what we discussed, Jet."

"She is not for you, drudge."

Breena clapped in Atlas' face. "Atlas, quit it. Luce, I am going whether they come or not, so let's just go."

"They come."

"I have a plane to catch. Luce, let me go back to my body, and I'll be out of your hair forever. Bring Jordan for Breena. He can have my place."

"It doesn't work like that, but you will all soon find that it doesn't matter. At this moment, your bodies are dying."

The blood drained from Lilly's always-rosy cheeks. "What did you do to us?"

"I didn't do anything. Jet thought it would be smart to bring The Disorder with him to help do his dirty work of delivering Breena and Atlas to me."

Jet looked at his feet, unable to withstand the daggers from the group.

"Too bad they saw through his show of support and just used him to get here. They have their own score to settle with Atlas. Or do you prefer to go by Reid, as they call you?" Luce nodded toward the parking lot, which only he could see. "Regardless, your being here with me leaves your bodies vulnerable. Unfortunately, your indecision and resistance will result in all of you coming with me. You'll die in the fire."

"Wait." Breena stomped her foot. "No. Just because they die does not mean they go to Hell with us, Luce."

"Breena, you wound me. Will you not acknowledge me as your grandfather?"

"Not if you hurt them. Lilly and Jordan have nothing to do with this. I've been pushing them away for months for exactly this reason. And they're good people. Under normal circumstances, they'd never wind up down there with you."

Jordan paced across the room pulling at his hair and covering his mouth and squeezing his head between his hands. He didn't wear panic well. It bubbled out in thin shouts in Luce's direction. "You're the devil! You're powerful. You're demanding. Prideful. It's what got you into your eternal predicament, right? If you need Atlas and Jet to come with you, why don't you just make them and let us go!" He had grabbed onto Lilly's arm, and her skin whitened under his grip. She shrugged out of his grasp and rubbed the area.

Luce grinned and, for the first time, looked as sinister as one might think the human form of the devil would look. "Where's the fun in that? You know who I am. Does that sound like something I would do?"

Jordan had the impulse to say, "Yes, it *does* sound like something you would do," but then he remembered a conversation with Breena after learning about her lineage. She had said the role of Gehenna in the world was not to directly start or carry out chaos. The purpose was not to do evil to humans. Rather, the role involved planting seeds, enabling humans to make their own evil. It had something to do with the balance of Heaven and Hell, peace and chaos. God's given free will to choose applied to both sides of the balance. "So you won't force anybody, but you'll stand by and let it happen nonetheless."

"Precisely."

Jordan wanted to strangle Jet. He knew the line of cause and effect that got them all to this point was long, but it was so easy to cut it down to the most recent events presently threatening their lives. Jet brought The Disorder. The Disorder brought the fire. *Even Atlas is less guilty of threatening our lives right this second. Should have stayed away and let him skip town.*

The fire had spread to every unit in the building. High-powered hoses doused the flames enough to allow firefighters to go in to put out hot spots. In the alternate plane, Jordan and Lilly wavered. Their bodies were dying and their links between the two locations weakening. Breena expected to be in the same condition since her connection had been forced by Luce, but as the fire undoubtedly neared her body, she felt as if her insides were knitting back together. She heard Tabitha's voice, something she had choked out before her death.

Burn? You're going to burn it? Me, the queen of Hell? You do know there's fire there, right? We're not susceptible to fire, daughter.

Luce interrupted her thoughts with something about doing her duty as queen, and she snapped back to reality as he finished with "—I won't force them, but you can."

Breena stared at Atlas and Jet. Jordan and Lilly stood behind them against the wall, wincing as their bodies died. *How do I doom two people I love to save two more?*

"Quickly, now, Granddaughter."

I owe Jordan so much.

"Breena!"

"I can't. Luce, I can't do it." Her knees buckled. "I don't want to be like this. I don't want to be *this*." Her hands glowed a soft, luminous yellow like she had put her hand on top of a flashlight.

"You already are."

The fire outside and the proximity to Luce supercharged her. *I wonder if I can break this plane and get us all out. Am I stronger than Lucifer?* The energy under her skin roiled, an aurora in her palms. *Try.*

She shook off her denial, stood up, and went to Jordan and Lilly. Breena put her hands on their shoulders. Looking over her shoulder at Luce, she grinned. "Then you'll be proud." With all of her pent-up energy, she shot a surge through Jordan and Lilly, hurling them back to their bodies abruptly enough to revive them.

A gap in the parallel world remained, large enough to see through to the firefighters who carried Jordan and Lilly in their arms. Another rescuer checked for Atlas' and Jet's pulses then shook his head.

No. No, no, no. I was going to force them out next! She gripped a hand over her mouth not sure whether she was going to scream or vomit. At the sight of Atlas' dead body, the first thought that hit her was not that his death was her fault, not that she would miss him, and not even that she might still have some twisted feelings for him. Instead, her mind jumped immediately to the fact that he wouldn't get a funeral, that no one would claim him from the morgue, that he was alone in the world and had only been trying to remedy that and the life of sorrows that had come with it.

Breena's fiery glow intensified and radiated from her hands and into her arms, neck, and face. Instead of the tears she assumed would flow, the heavy press of fury like fists pounding to get out of her chest overcame Breena. She whirled on Luce, fire lighting her eyes. He stared down at her with smug pride.

"You. You did this to them. Your pathetic attachment to your traditions killed them." Her volume rose as she tore into him. "I told you they didn't need to come with me. I told you to let them go." And then she was flat-out screaming. "I'm the *queen*! *I* get to choose how I rule. *I* get to choose who rules with me. *I. Rule. You!*"

Jet and Atlas watched from across the room, their consciousness and astral forms preserved in Lucifer's parallel plane. Jet, grinning and awed, nudged a miserable Atlas in the ribs. "That's our girl. Feisty."

Atlas was livid, but powerless. "She is our queen. Show some respect."

Jet pressed. "You get what you want, now, right? Lighten up."

I should have caught an earlier flight. Atlas loved her, but he never *truly* wanted to go back to Gehenna with her—not even while Tabitha had him under her thumb. Atlas wanted her to live a normal, human life with him. The thought of getting dragged down with Jet, and the fact that Jet seemed more than happy to sacrifice his life to get closer to her, made him want to bash his teeth in. He didn't even know if he could do that anymore, disembodied as he was.

Breena fought on. "You heard me, Grandfather." She spat the name at him. "I. Rule. You. Things are going to change, and I am going to change them. If you don't like it, I don't want to hear it. I *would* tell you to go back home to Heaven where you came from, but, oops. You screwed that up *eons* ago." The pressure from the last year finally boiled over. "And if you hadn't, I wouldn't be here, glowing like fricken' rave kandi under a black light, trying to overhaul the rules of a place created *specifically* to eff with the rules. You should be more receptive to some change, old man. I've lied, I've murdered, I'm Hell's perfect little role model. But Gehenna is not my home, and since I'm going there willingly, and since *I'm the queen*, we're going to do things my way." Fire flared from her fingertips in a concentrated stream like the steam releasing from a pressure cooker or the jet thrusters of a space shuttle. Her hair reddened in fresh stripes—she didn't need a mirror to know. Her scalp tingled, and she could see the new tresses out of the corner of her eye.

She looked at Atlas and Jet. Her feelings about their presence were muddied. Then, she peered out of the cracked illusion and into the charred remains of Atlas' bedroom. It was empty save for two white sheets over her chosen and her servant. As the fire from her fingers stopped, something clicked into place that she had been too angry to notice sooner. "And dammit, Luce, where is my body?"

Luce regarded his borrowed body's nails, bored. "You're in it."

She looked down at herself, suddenly unable to rage anymore. *My whole body goes between planes? My whole body goes between planes. When I first got to London, I woke up muddy from a dream. My whole body went. But then I was in a hospital bed for months later on while I was in these planes.* "So my body stays behind unless—"

"Unless you don't want it to. You'll learn to control it."

"And I wanted it to come with me this time? The fire hadn't even stared yet when we—"

"Guess you want to be queen more than you thought." Luce snapped his fingers and the matching apartment bedrooms fell away.

****

"This is DJ Mix with your evening traffic report. Roads leading out of Livona, Michigan, including all major highway exchanges, have been closed until further notice. Roads into the area remain open. This morning, The Disorder laid waste to an apartment complex in the Livona suburbs, setting fire to one of the apartment buildings and trashing vehicles. There have been two casualties and dozens of injuries as a result of the fire. One of the victims' names has not yet been released, but we are told that twenty-one-year-old Reid Case was found dead at the scene." At the news, Linda darted to the shoulder of I-75 North and slammed on breaks, her heart stopping as suddenly.

"What the hell, Linda? A little warning?" Ari scooted back in his seat.

Linda shushed Ari as the report continued.

"You may remember the name from the missing person investigation that arose after Case, a suicide hotline worker, disappeared for months, leading many to think he had taken his own life. Others in the apartment unit where the bodies were located were found injured, but alive, and have been transported to a local hospital. Fortunately, residents from the other units in the building escaped unharmed."

Linda mumbled profanities through grit teeth. "Atlas can't be dead! I had plans for him." She slammed the steering wheel with both hands.

"Although firefighters have gotten the blaze under control, and rescue crews have transported the injured, police are still working to apprehend many of the suspects. Blocking the roads out of the area will aid in the process, and the Wayne County Police Department asks for and appreciates your patience and cooperation. As far as specifics go, we now know that hundreds of rioters contributed to this massive case of arson and murder, although it is uncertain whether all suspects are members of the hate group. We will return to alert you when roads out have reopened."

After the report ended, the music station's obnoxious sign-off song blared through the speakers, complete with fart noises. Ari shook his head. It seemed vulgar to air something like that after such serious news. He looked over at Linda and, even though he hadn't forgiven her in the slightest, he put a hand on her thigh. "I know you were close."

She shoved his hand from her leg. "Close? No. I never came close to him. Not in Tabitha's eyes. Not in Breena's eyes. My job was to undo all the damage he caused those poor people, to tell them *not* to do the very things that just got him killed. I was the work horse and he was the decoy, yet his work and her work always mattered to Tabitha more. Then your sister had to kill her. I hated Tabs, but I never wanted her dead..."

Ari shrank back.

"Oh, didn't know that? Didn't know your special snowflake of a sister was a murderer? She's the one who sent us on that trip, you know. Told me to get you out of town, keep you safe. Little did I know it was so she could have some space to kill the love of my life. She knew. And she knew the town would fall apart that night. How sweet for a sister to protect a brother that way."

"Linda, I don't think you're right about this."

"I'll prove it." As quickly as she had pulled over, she threw the car into gear and tore back onto the highway, taking the nearest exit to loop around in the direction of Atlas' apartment. "I bet she's there."

When they arrived, the parking lot was roped off with police tape. Linda drove just past the lot entrance and pulled off the road, parking in the emergency lane behind a K-9 unit SUV.

"Linda, I don't think you can park here. You'll block the emergency vehicles."

"No one will notice another car in this chaos. Now, get out."

The pair marched onto the crime scene like they belonged there, or at least Linda did. Ari cast worried glances around him the whole time. His expression didn't arouse any suspicion, though. Everyone looked that way—people who lost their homes, people who witnessed the act, people in handcuffs.

Linda might have even gotten as far as she thought she would if she hadn't obliviously walked right past Shianne, who was sitting on the sidewalk in cuffs with ten other people.

"Dr. Bullard? Oh my gosh, Dr. Bullard! It's me, Shianne. Wow, I'm so glad you're here. I didn't think you'd come. It's been a while, not since Atlas' last meeting before the riots. I'm glad to see you."

Ari stared at Linda staring at Shianne in disbelief. Linda's face had taken on a sickly color, and her expression resembled his when he tried to calculate a tip in his head. He nudged Linda and whispered at a volume meant to be heard, "Who's Dr. Bullard? Why does she think you're a doctor?"

Shianne, scrambling to her feet, still hadn't shut up. "—and I kept telling them you'd be here. I said, 'Let me call my therapist. She'll tell you I'm a good person and I'm trying to get my life right.' And the cop said, 'You just put a bat through that guy's windshield. I don't care who your therapist is. Get 'em to testify in your trial.' But here you are!"

Linda imagined that getting ejected into space without a suit felt a lot like this moment—chest tight, lungs useless, body freezing over, stiffening and inert. *This isn't . . . she is not . . .* "It wasn't supposed to be like this!" Her body unlocked and Linda unleashed a wicked slap across Shianne's cheek. Shianne squealed, but couldn't do anything to fight back except step away from Linda and yell at her.

The outburst drew the attention of a few nearby officers who jogged over, one shoving Shianne back down to her seat on the sidewalk and another two grilling Linda for her presence and behavior.

Instead of answering their questions, she demanded to see the bodies, which came off as more of a red flag than her willingness to wander into a crime scene or assault a suspect. The officers may have understood if she presented herself as a grieving relative or frantic parent wanting to make sure her child wasn't the one whose name hadn't been released. But Linda went full-Shianne.

"It's not supposed to be like this. All my plans are falling apart. I have something to prove to him," she pointed at Ari, "and you're going to let me to do it. Now show me the bodies so he can see his bitch sister dead in a bag beside the one containing her ridiculous 'chosen.' They ruined my life and I want to laugh at their corpses."

Her volume and frantic gesturing escalated until one of the officers grabbed Ari by the sleeve, hauled him away from her proximity, and tased her. After the ugly business of convulsions, cuffing, and removing the probes, the officers shoved Linda in the back of a patrol car. In front, the policeman pulled up her record using the ID removed during her cuff-and-pat-down. Getting anywhere with the case had been hard for Lexa and Breena since Ari was an adult and had gone with her willingly. Records indicated Linda as a person of interest, but were updated with the recent addition of the threat on Breena's life.

Ari knew he should ask questions, but all he could do was stand behind Shianne where the officer had put him and watch Linda scream mutely behind the window and throw herself against the bullet-proof glass. Checking to see if anyone was watching him, he stooped down behind Shianne and whispered low in her ear, "You are going to tell me how you know Linda and why you think she's your doctor, and then you're going to tell me where my sister is." He didn't believe Linda's ranting. Breena wasn't dead.

Before Shianne could finish skootching around to face Ari, two policemen approached, one giving Shianne a "stay put" look and the other guiding Ari away by the elbow. He wanted to take Ari's statement and get in touch with his family.

Ari couldn't offer anything helpful to the officers. He had the same questions they did: Who was Shianne and why did she think Linda was her therapist? Why did Linda want to see the bodies? Did she have anything to do with The Disorder? Why had she returned with him now after all this time, and to the feet of the police at that?

He shrugged. "They're all crazy."

Chapter 12

Jet, Atlas, and Breena followed Luce, who was back in his Gehennan body, at a distance. He stood at least seven feet tall and bore remnants of the same bright hair as Tabitha and Breena's new streaks. What wasn't greying still flowed like magma. Like many others Breena had seen since arriving, his skin was olive-toned and smooth and suggested nothing of his true age. She wondered why she didn't resemble her ancestors more.

As they continued, Bree resisted the compulsion to think additionally on his looks, too weirded out by the realization that he was handsome, and also her ancient grandfather. They hung back as he led. It didn't feel safe to get too close, proven by the fact that he had just spirited them to a citadel at the center of Gehenna. The black marble hallway glittered around them, somehow bright though there were no lights or windows.

Jet and Atlas paced her on either side, competing to be the one to protect her. She ignored them, thinking no one would try to harm her in her own home.

It's a strange sensation. Déjà vu doesn't really cover it. I don't feel like I've been here before, but I'm comfortable. I think I still doubted any of this was true until now. There's nothing going on inside me. No restlessness or pain or. . . She sucked in a breath. *This is what peace is.*

Breena halted mid-step, throwing her arms out to stop Atlas and Jet. As their footsteps fell away from Luce, he paused and looked back.

Still holding Atlas and Jet at bay, she called after Lucifer, "We'll catch up. Give us a minute."

"You don't know where I'm taking you. Come."

"I *said* a minute."

Luce ground his teeth, his lips pulling back into a snarl. Breena figured he was already starting to regret his decision to bring her there. *Maybe he's comparing me to my mother. That can't be good.*

Lucifer rolled his eyes and stalked away. She turned to look at them, expecting some sort of protest or blame. They were dead because of her. Instead, they waited for her to speak.

"I don't know what my grandfather has planned, so I will give you a heads up. If we are headed into a room full of people waiting for me to ascend, or get married, or some other hasty nonsense, there will be a fight. Don't make it worse by fighting over me. I will not be choosing either of you. Understand?" She turned toward Atlas. "You have put me through so much. I don't want you that way anymore." He took a breath and she could feel the agitated energy rolling off of him. Bree put a finger to his lips and turned to Jet. "You, I like. Very much." She blushed. *Get yourself together.* "But I'm going to run this show myself, so please don't expect a relationship just because I've rejected him."

Jet finally got mad. "You can't be serious. Do you know what I did to get to you? I led The Disorder here so they could get rid of Atlas! So that I could save you. *Just* you. I was supposed to do it on my own, deliver both of you to Luce, but I knew why he wanted both of you. Chosen." He spat the word in Atlas' face. "I thought any punishment was worth getting to you and getting him out of the way. I figured if we ended up here together, we'd *be* together. But now we're here. All of us." He jabbed a finger in Atlas' chest. "You should have died with your mother." Atlas recoiled. No one had brought up his mother in a long time, and he wondered how Jet knew about his human mom's sad fate. "How stupid was I to think—"

"That's enough, Jet." Breena spun on her heels holding back tears that surprised her. She had always been empathetic, but in this new place, she found she could feel Atlas' pain as her own. *An enhanced connection. Is this supposed to make me want him more? Ensure we follow through with tradition? Ridiculous.* "Let's go. I'm sure there are people waiting for me."

The sense of ease Breena arrived with was gone. Her bare feet were ice as she padded down the shimmering hallways to the room where Luce waited. *I thought it would be hotter here.*

They entered a dark chamber and were told to kneel by a disembodied voice from the far end of the room. In a row, Breena at the center, they went to their knees. The lights rose and, as she suspected, the room was packed with people and, beside a throne she could only guess was hers, kneeled her mother. Breena swayed and grabbed Atlas' arm. Atlas grinned smugly despite himself. He didn't want to be there, but if it was the only environment in which he truly had a shot at Breena, he would accept it. He would accept *her*.

Lucifer spoke up from behind Breena. "Before you is your mother, whose place you are about to take."

Tabitha smirked at Breena, relishing the shock that she was still alive. Bree couldn't take her eyes off of the puckering, scaly flesh of healing burns in the shape of Breena's hands around Tabitha's neck. *So I really did burn her. But there were no marks on her physical body. Why is she alive? This must be her spirit. Like Jet and Atlas. How am I the only one whose physical body can come here?*

"She who intends to rule will rise to stand before the former queen." Luce put his hands on Breena's shoulders.

Bree leaned to the side to look up at him. "I will not."

The crowd of gentry gasped.

She noticed she was still holding Atlas' arm and let go. "We will change how things are done, starting with this." The sense of belonging crept back. "The former queen will go back to the pit where I sent her. The chosen will go to a cell until I can determine a suitable punishment for his crimes against me, which include attempted murder—" The crowd gasped again and murmurs ran through the group in waves. "—and the servant will escort me to my room." She stood and turned to Lucifer. "Finally, the king will acknowledge publicly that he is just a figurehead and will stay out. Of. My. Way." *If he wanted me here so badly, if they need a queen so much, they won't do anything to me that would change my mind about tradition.*

Atlas' panic rose in Breena's throat as two guards dragged him into the hall and out of sight. *Don't let it get to you. This is the right thing to do.* The crowd gaped at Breena as she walked toward the door. "Why are you all still here?"

Luce, blood red and wide-eyed, seethed. "They're waiting for you to dismiss them."

"Oh. Go home everybody."

One member of the gentry was emboldened by outrage. "You haven't ascended. You cannot make these choices about the fate of our people, your chosen. . ."

"Really? Seems like I did."

****

Jordan sat up in his hospital bed and pressed the call button for the ninth time. When the nurse answered through the little speaker on the remote, Jordan was confident he had finally worn down her patience. She sounded like she might literally bite her tongue. *Perfect.* He jumped into the same speech he had been giving since they checked him in from triage. "I'm ready to go home, now. I'm fine, and I'm pretty sure you can't keep me against my will. Now, if you'll just bring me my clothes, I'll get out of your hair."

The nurse leaned across the work station and handed the receiver to a co-worker. "You deal with him. I'm taking my break."

"Sir. The call button is for emergencies. You—"

"The whole hospital is for emergencies, and I am not one of them. Now bring me my things so I can leave."

"Sir, we can't just—"

"I'm taking up valuable space."

The nurse looked back at her friend's empty station and rolled her eyes. "Suit yourself." She got up and walked to Jordan's room with a clipboard and forms. "You'll have to sign this waiver acknowledging that you realize and assume responsibility for the medical risks associated with DAMA."

"With what?"

"Discharge Against Medical Advice."

"Great. So while I'm doing this, you'll go and find the bag the paramedics shoved my clothes and phone and wallet in?"

She nodded.

"Thanks."

Lilly came out of the procedure well. The emergency doctors who received her from the ambulance elected to intubate the unconscious Lilly before further edema set in. Her smoke inhalation injuries were serious, and they were going to keep her for observation for at least four days.

In the morgue, Atlas' body had been tagged Reid Case—no one knew any better—and slid into a cold chamber. In the adjacent refrigerator, Jet's body lay in wait for a positive identification by his parents.

****

Linda and Shianne sat in side-by-side cells at the Wayne County Jail arguing through the bars about who was more at fault for the way their lives were turning out. Linda earned charges for disturbing the peace, interfering with a police investigation, and simple assault on a law enforcement officer to top off the threat she made on Breena's life. After she had calmed down in the back of the patrol car, an officer went to question her again, letting her out, which was his mistake. She stomped his foot and shrieked at him again to let her see the bodies or else she was going to make some more. Shianne watched in awe of Linda's freak-out wondering how a woman like that ever became a therapist. She still hadn't put together that it was a lie built on the back of those Atlas had told.

In the jail, Linda spent the afternoon explaining her deception to Shianne in that context, trying to shrug out of the responsibility and breed another Atlas-hater, but Shianne didn't want to hear reason—no one's version of it. She yelled over Linda the entire time, cussing her for deceiving her, blaming her for her arrest, making sure she knew that if she hadn't pretended to be a shrink, and she hadn't sent her on a mission after Jet, she never would have been there when The Disorder caused the disaster.

****

Ari sat alone at the kitchen table in his house, an empty house, trying to wrap his mind around everything he had missed. There were newspaper clippings, scribbled notes, and candy wrappers scattered before him. Lexa left the house and her search for him behind when she went to live with Grant. He wanted to feel betrayed, but he couldn't help reminding himself that he had gone willingly and had wanted to stay with Linda. He was a missing person to his mother, but he had never felt lost. Not until arriving at the apartment fire with Linda. *That was the end.*

Ari absently folded a nearby candy wrapper into tiny sections and then smoothed it back out. He repeated the meditative motions, the only thought in his mind that he should have more thoughts in his head—thoughts about Linda, Breena, Atlas, but they just weren't there.

****

Jo rallied the group again, holding up a nearly empty beer bottle for what had to be her twentieth toast. During a planning session for their next attempt at capturing Atlas, they heard the news of his death on a break-in news report. A celebration was cobbled together with the random assortment of drinks and food in Jo's kitchen, which they laid out on the table after sweeping maps and schedules to the floor.

The group watched Leigh with cautious glances. Some wondered whether they should celebrate in front of her at all. It was Leigh's dream and Leigh's planning that had led them so close to finding Atlas and, if not for The Disorder, they would have been the ones to enact justice on him. Jo knew Leigh was peeved that his death hadn't been by her own hand, but Jo's assumptions weren't of much use.

Leigh had all but shut down since her experience with Mestif and Luce. Of course, most people didn't believe that the devil possessed her. She had tried to tell them, despite Luce's lingering compulsion not to, but they took her meaning as a figurative thing, as if a wild streak of mischief had overcome her and led to an impulsive lapse in reason. Since then, her depression and withdrawn ways resurfaced. She didn't take joy in the things she used to, and even though those things included hunting people down and exacting vengeance that she liked to call justice, the change still concerned the group.

Leigh wished she could still call the hotline, but she had lost all faith in the institution. Plus, if her friends didn't believe she had been possessed, why would a stranger at the end of a phone line? She wasn't ready to hear their reassurance or encouragement. Logic told her the hotline was valid and useful, but she wasn't ready for logic, either.

****

In her quarters, Breena paced in front of Jet saying nothing to ease his anxious questioning. She had her own.

Did I really just imprison Atlas? Is it too extreme? He was actually going to leave me this time. Lucifer prevented that. It wasn't Atlas' choice. Do I punish him for being brought here? Yes, *Bree*, yes. *Of course he deserves punishment.*

"Bree, please, just sit down. It's not like you sentenced him."

That got her attention and she looked at him with surprise.

"I know that's what you're thinking about. You love him."

"No?" She shrunk into herself as she heard the response come out as a question. "No. That's not why it's upsetting."

"Stop kidding yourself. Look, you don't need to protect my pride like you did with Jordan." She made a face. "Oh, don't be so surprised."

"You're being harsh."

"It wasn't that hard to figure out. The way Atlas looks at you. . ."

"He's just. . . earnest."

"Anyway, you don't need to protect my feelings. I know I'm not here as your boyfriend, and certainly not your potential husband. If anyone will get that honor, it will be Atlas. It's just the way things are. And that *is* precisely why it is upsetting. You might not have intended to play into his vision of a normal life, but despite your restless nature, some of it seemed nice to you. And now that you're here, you're no doubt feeling a stronger draw to him than usual. It's biology. Even so, I don't think your choice was cruel. He shot you, and that's just the most recent of the terrible things he's put you through."

Breena nodded. "He's the field."

"What?"

"I'm the fire, and he's just the burning field."

"Lucky man."

Breena didn't care whether Jet meant it sarcastically or literally. Neither option gave her any consolation. "Jet, I'm sorry you're. . . I'm sorry you had to. . ." she shook her head like it would help shake the right words from her mouth. There was no good way to say it. "I'm sorry your body died. I feel responsible."

"You don't have to apologize." *Serve. Guard. Sacrifice.*

"Yes, I *really* do. Everything I've done for the last, I don't know, almost two years now, has been to undo the mess caused by my selfish escapism, to prevent harm from coming to my friends and family. Now here we are."

"I understand, although I can't agree. My family is a part of this because of lineage, just like you are. That's nothing you had control over."

She sighed and gestured for Jet to sit beside her at the end of the bed, which was more than waist-high and outfitted in plush purple sheets and blankets, purple so dark it was easily mistaken for black out of direct light. "But if I wasn't queen—"

"Then I would have been summoned by Lucifer to find and protect and serve whoever *was*. My place is by the queen's side. I'm just happy it's you."

Or is that *biology, too? Are our choices our own? Have we ever chosen anything at all?* Despite struggling to decipher which parts of life were conscious decisions and which were biological compulsions set to lead her home, she couldn't keep from grinning. They hadn't had a private face-to-face conversation since their boat ride, and in both instances, the heavy subject-matter didn't clutter the easy exchange between them. "I missed this. You."

Jet had the urge to put his hand over hers. He settled for allowing his thigh to rest against her knee. "I thought you were mad that I kissed you at the boat landing. I called so many times, and you never answered. It's not like I was happy to learn that you'd been taken, and I definitely was less than thrilled to find out all of my family's stories about this place were real, but I'm glad you weren't just avoiding me. This," he gestured nonchalantly around himself, "for some reason, seems small peas in comparison to worrying where you were."

"Are you sure that's how you feel about it? You were so mad before."

"The way I acted earlier was inexcusable. I apologize. My anger was not at you. You are fully capable of choosing what's best for you, even when that means rejecting me."

Bree wanted badly to believe in her choices, in an inner will not tainted by biology. Galvanized by reasoning that biology would never want her to go against Lucifer, deny her chosen, and upend the customs of her home, her confidence swelled. *Atlas might not be a choice, but Jet is.* "You're right. I am." *I am.*

He chuckled. "You've changed."

"I'm sober."

"How long?"

"I don't know. I ran out of your pills not long after Luce's first set of guys took me. Once Atlas saved me from them," she paused on an inhale, screwing up her face, "seems wrong to say he saved me, but I guess in that one instance, he did."

"I hate that guy."

"Right. Anyway, once I was with Atlas, my body stopped needing them. He shot me and the experience of drifting so close to death. . ."

Jet stared at her with a glazed-over distance in his eyes.

"Sorry. I'm boring you." Breena stood and crossed the constellation floor, the white flecks in the dark marble flickering in that rare way a sky does far from the city. "You may go now."

"Wait, no. I wasn't bored. I heard voices in my head. Lots of them talking all at once."

"What were they saying?"

"No idea. All of my instincts are on edge. They're awake here. It's overwhelming." He stood and gave Bree an apologetic grin. "I need to take a walk."

Tabitha threw a pewter goblet across Luce's anteroom and shrieked. "Did you see how she acted in there? Are you going to let her disrespect our tradition like that?"

"She is the queen. She chooses how traditions are fulfilled."

"She is *not* the queen. She refused to stand before me."

"Oh, who are you kidding, Tabitha? Her very capability to resist my orders proves she is."

"And you're OK with this?"

"Of course not, but it is the card we received."

Tabitha growled again and stomped a foot before whirling on her toes and storming out of Luce's chamber, grumbling under her breath. "I am still the queen, and I'm going to make sure she and everyone else knows it."

Atlas slammed himself against the iron bars again, even though he knew it fit the definition of insanity. There was no new result. It was blindingly bright where they held him—the opposite of everything he expected to see in Hell. Human pop-culture painted this picture of darkness, of nothingness. He always imagined a prison in Hell would be no different than the pit itself—sooty blackness, excruciating heat, no space to move around. This hallway was mostly unused. A few other prisoners occupied the cells he had passed on the way to his own. In all of them, the prisoners cowered in a far corner with their heads in their hands or buried between their chest and knees to block the light.

Atlas had yet to resort to the same. He was too interested in his surroundings to give in to the sensory overload created by the size, silence, and glare. The seriousness had yet to hit him, either. He figured Breena was being her stubborn self and that she wouldn't be able to resist their amplified connection for long. The only thing that really concerned him was that she was alone with Jet.

By the time Atlas grew tired, not from the oppression of his surroundings, but just at the mercy of his biological clock—which he was surprised he still had, given he was permanently disembodied—he chose a wall to recline against and tried to sleep.

****

The cold air seeped through the draughty window in the top of Atlas' forest cottage. Breena surveyed the space. *At least I can keep* some *things from changing.* The little hatch in the floor looked down over the same dusty desk and built-in bookshelves on the ground floor, the eaves of the uninsulated roof still housed cobwebs and the occasional moth.

Why did I come back here? Of all places to visit in my first illusion since... She couldn't finish the thought. *But, well, at least I'm back to normal.*

She sat against the wall and replayed the first time Atlas had taken her there. He had hoisted her up and through the hatch with ease, sat her down, and taught her what she could do. The stark comparison to the last time he had taken her there, against her will, captive, and with Tabitha's help, tasted bitter. Bitter and permanent. Until arriving in Gehenna, she couldn't revisit if she wanted to. Going with Luce to Gehenna had simultaneously robbed her and repaired her. *What now?*

Bree tired of the shabby cottage and its memories and shattered the illusion in favor of the vacation she was supposed to have taken with Jordan after graduation. She sat on a concrete barstool submerged in the bluest of swimming pools. The bartender handed her an oversized smoothie in a cheesy plastic souvenir cup in the shape of a pineapple. Jordan treaded water beside her.

"How can you drink another one of those?"

"They're delicious."

"They're fifteen dollars a pop and taste like overripe salad bar fruit."

She stuck her tongue out at him. "After the first one, your mouth gets so cold you can't really taste that anymore."

"Well, you'd know."

Bree jumped off the stool splashing Jordan in the process. He turned and kicked away. Before she could swim after him, the illusion began to flicker. She snapped out of her indulgent daydream noticing her cheeks were wet. The rest of the background images fell away and she berated herself for wishing she was back home with him.

First, you wish away your normal life and chase the fray. Then, you push away your normal friends and snuggle up with the worst people possible. You finally get the drastic change you were after, and not twenty-four hours into it, you long to go back. What is wrong with you?

Falling back on her mountain of pillows, Bree stared up at the ceiling noticing its intricacy for the first time. Unlike the illusory castle Atlas had gifted her on one of their last nights together, this palace in Gehenna—and she could only assume it was a palace—had dynamic ceilings that appeared the inverse of a landscape topography map. *Am I underground? I thought the whole 'Hell is down and Heaven is up' thing was just a human way of grasping the abstract.* Shadows danced across the peaks and valleys.

Where is the light source? Breena craned her neck to look at the head of the bed. There were no lamps, recessed lighting, nothing. The room emitted its own light somehow, and the soft glow enhanced the subtle etchings that covered the hills on the ceiling. She squinted. *They're. . . names?* Breena didn't recognize any of them, but still, the sense that they were queens' names was strong. *Where's mine?*

Glancing at her wrist, she rolled her eyes. *Why would I expect my watch to do anything here?* Knowing only that if she was in Grayling, it would be late, she considered sleep, but the jitters under her skin ensured *that* activity wasn't on the list for the night— or day. *Whatever.*

Rather than trying to force some slumber, she climbed out of bed and pulled the heavy chair from under the vanity at the other side of the room. Bree stepped up on the tufted cushion, bare feet gripping the plum, velvet upholstery, and reached toward one of the low points on the ceiling. As her fingertips skimmed the names of her ancestors, a buzzing sensation ignited under her skin. *Nerves? Excitement?*

She traced a name—Astaroth. Beside it, Sekhmet. *These are old. Are these in chronological order? My name's probably not here. I haven't done anything yet.*

A knock interrupted her marveling. She shouted that the door was open and to come in figuring, as queen, she didn't need to open the door for people anymore. *I've got people for that.* A nervous little boy stepped just inside the threshold and bowed. Jet stood behind him.

"Your. . ." he paused and looked up at Jet, who whispered in his ear. "Your Majesty?" He looked back at Jet again and hissed out, "But she's not even queen yet."

Jet nudged him.

"Your Majesty, you're needed by His Highness."

"It's late. Tell him I'll come by tomorrow."

The child blanched, and Jet stepped around him. "Bree, you can't expect this boy to go back to Luce and tell him that he failed to bring you to him."

She softened. "Guess you're right. What does he want? I'll either go ahead now, or pop my head in just to tell him he can wait."

"I wouldn't push it on this. Just come."

"Fine, fine." She jumped off the chair. Jet flinched, the chair scooting a bit under her feet and his instinct to protect her flaring.

"Get some shoes. Look in the armoire over there. What were you doing on that chair?"

"Reading the names in the ceiling. I couldn't find mine." Inside the massive wardrobe, the floor was lined with two rows of shoes she could never imagine herself wearing and which, at the moment, would look tragically mismatched with her torn and sooty outfit from Atlas. *Why hadn't it occurred to me to look for fresh clothes in here?*

"I know that look. My sister gets it, too. Just pick something and come on."

Breena grabbed the least dressy pair available and shoved her feet down into the showy boots. If not for their black, faceted studs, they might pass as motorcycle boots. An image of a big guy with a long beard and a ponytail popped into mind, all the way down to the glammed-up boots. *Not as bad as I expected.* She threw a plain jacket over Atlas' pitiful shirt, dodged the mirror, and went to Jet. Bree absently slipped her hand into his and gave him a peck on the cheek. "OK, lead away."

As soon as she did it, her brain exploded. *What the heck was that? Why did I do that? I wasn't even thinking. Who accidentally does that? You're still holding his hand!* She snatched her hand out of his and forced a chuckle. It sounded more like someone had kicked her in the chest, all the air whooshing out in one gust. *He's staring. Can't blame his stare on the shoes. Say something. Him, you. . . anyone.*

Jet wasn't about to protest, although her sharp turn in behavior concerned him. The head servant, Itzal, who had given him a room down the hall from Breena's, was a kind guy—if kind could be a thing in Hell. Jet figured he could pick his brain about whether Breena's attraction to him was amplified like it was with Atlas. He assumed it wasn't and that Breena had a lapse in judgement or just needed some contact. *It has to be lonely, the position she's in.*

The little boy poked his head back into the room. "Are you two coming? Lucifer will yell at *me* for making him wait, even though it's *your* fault."

Breena and Jet made awkward eye contact before walking out of the room, close, but without holding hands. "Let's go. For real this time."

"Do you know what this is about?"

Jet shrugged. "I have a suspicion. The servants talk."

Bree groaned. "I can only imagine what they're already saying about me. They don't know me at all. All they know is I showed up, snubbed them, and went to my room. Great first impression."

"You're their queen whether they were impressed or not and, frankly, we have to serve you whether we like you or not, so I wouldn't worry about it."

"Jet, that didn't help at all."

"I tried."

The little boy stopped short in front of them, spinning on his heel and holding a hand up in their face like a crossing guard. "We're here."

Jet and Breena moved for the ornate stone door in front of them, and the boy scurried around to block Jet. "Not you."

Bree gave Jet a pleading look. She did not want to go in there alone. Jet mouthed, "Sorry," as he was led by the wrist to a bench across the expansive hall.

She took a deep breath then leaned into the door with her shoulder, expecting it to be heavy. With unreal lightness, it swung inward and she fell through the opening into Luce's anteroom. When the stumbling stopped, Lucifer shook his head as if her embarrassing moment had been more embarrassing for him. "Sit down before you fall again, Breena."

"I'd rather know why I'm here first. You know, so I can leave if I'm not interested."

"Breena, for once in your life will you stop resisting those around you and just do what you're told?"

She rolled her eyes and sat. *I'm the queen. Why would I start following orders? He shouldn't be ordering me in the first place.*

"Good. Now, we've got a few important matters to discuss. First, your rejection of the ascension ceremony. While I'm happy to play into your hands to help you send the message to your people that things will be changing, you cannot completely skip out on the very thing that gives you the right to make those changes. There will be a ceremony, and that is that."

"But I wanted to—"

"Let me finish." He sat in the chair beside her rather than across from her, behind his sprawling desk. Luce hoped it came off as a gesture of good will. "You don't have to do any convincing. We will do it your way." She opened her mouth again. "Ah, ah. I realize your way includes not having a ceremony at all, and that is the one thing where I must put my foot down. However, you will have whatever kind of ceremony you'd like. You may plan it. My last requirement is that it takes place within the next two weeks. I simply cannot leave our people without a leader any longer."

"Part of me feels like I should say thank you for giving me options, and the other part of me feels like I'm entitled to those options and shouldn't play into your 'good guy' persona. You are *not* a good guy. I have not moved past what you did to my friends." He shifted in his seat. "No. Don't get up. We're discussing this."

"I did what was necessary to get you here." He clasped his hands.

"I was willing to come! We could have just gone."

"Breena, we've had this argument already. Just because you don't want that boy doesn't mean I could just leave him out there in the world, out there to his own devices. You've experienced firsthand the harm he's done. He upset the balance just as much as Tabitha did. Blame it all on her lost sight and persuasion if you'd like, but he's been planning something all his own. I think you know I'm right."

She nodded.

"Actually, I'm rather in agreement with your choice to jail him. It was surprising—no queen has ever had to jail her chosen before—but, you're like no queen ever, and he's not a typical chosen, either. More headstrong."

"What's going to happen to him in there?" Her heart started to ache. "It was kind of impulsive of me."

"Well, that's another thing I wanted to speak to you about."

"Right. He's had no real charges brought upon him, at least not in a human sense. I'm not sure what the rules here are, but where I'm from, I'm used to someone being jailed only when they're caught in the act, formally charged with something based on evidence, or they turn themselves in. Is it like that here? Do you have classes I can take? Queen 101?" She half-giggled, knowing it wasn't an appropriate time to joke. Bree couldn't help it. Gehenna amplified her nerves along with everything else. "What about his trial? Do you use a jury? How do we choose who—"

"Breena, you're babbling."

She fell silent and took a deep breath. "Usually that only happens in my head where no one else can hear it. Sorry."

"Why does the idea of his imprisonment make you so nervous? *You* sent him there."

"I could never stop him back home." Breena noticed the way Luce shrank in the most miniscule way at hearing her refer to Michigan as home, effectively rejecting her place in Gehenna. "Sorry. It's a big adjustment."

Luce waved at the comment. "About Atlas. . ."

"Right. Well. . ." *Huh. What comes after that word?* She tried again. "Well, I'm not doubting my choice. He does deserve to be punished, and it helps to know you agree even if you disagree with my not marrying him. And why *do* you want me to marry him with all that he's done? Don't say 'tradition.'"

"His connection to you, being near you, is the only time he's ever in control. 'In control' is a lot different than 'under control'. You don't have to use your position against him."

"For the most part."

"Yes, recent events excused."

"I see what you're getting at. You want me to marry him to keep him in control. Mellow him. Because he's a liability."

"And because you have a deep bond, whether you want to acknowledge it or not."

Being in Gehenna made it impossible to ignore. "So, what are you getting at? You want me to sentence him or marry him?"

"Would you marry him if that's how I answered?"

"No."

"Then sentence him." Luce cracked his fingers and looked back at Breena expecting her to change her mind. He thought it impossible that, when faced with the reality of Atlas' situation, she would allow him to stay imprisoned. She was an emotional and sentimental being.

"How? What's the process?"

In the hall, Jet had grown restless wondering when they were going to invite him into the meeting. The boy had included him on his errand of fetching Breena because Luce also wanted to speak to him. Jet hadn't realized he'd be left to pace the hall for three hours. He wished he could say that he was exhausted and that he'd just meet with them in the morning. *But apparently, death is called eternal rest so my* body *can sleep, while my* spirit *remains* wide awake *for the rest of time.* "OK, kid. I'm sick of waiting. I'm going in there."

"No!" The boy grabbed Jet's wrist and tugged with his full body weight.

"Watch me." Jet pulled out of his grasp and opened the door without knocking. "Cut to the part that involves me."

Luce would have doubled in size and yelled at Jet until he was pulp on the floor, pulverized by the sheer decibel of his rage, but he couldn't mistake the relief and happiness that passed over Breena's face when Jet entered. Her protests against marrying anyone aside, he knew Jet was part of the reason she would rather sentence Atlas than wed him. Luce moved to usher Jet further into the room. "Jet Sala, you will be present at the ascension ceremony."

Jet shot Breena a confused glance.

"I'm organizing a new ceremony. Apparently my people can't do without their little party."

"Listen to you embracing the changes."

"Only to the extent I'm being forced to." She nodded her head in Luce's direction.

Jet, his brazenness augmented by Gehenna's biological pull, crossed the room and came to rest in Lucifer's massive desk chair. He reclined a bit and put his feet up on the desk. Luce bristled. "So why do I go to the ceremony? I didn't think servants attended."

"You are to be her courtier, responsible for her social, mental, and physical well-being. You will complete any task she asks of you, and you will accompany her to formal functions."

"Like a rent-a-husband."

"I'm not familiar with that concept. You will be presented to the gallery and dedicated to her service after she has performed the rite of ascension. You will serve as her counsel during Atlas' trial. You will carry out his punishment. You will *not* become involved with your queen outside of the duties bestowed on you."

Jet was thrilled to get an official place at Breena's side, but the direct order to stay uninvolved, which he knew was code for "Don't date your queen," only made him want to more. He decided his stubbornness and hers were a lot alike and that it must be their genetic nature. *That's another thing I need to ask Itzal—are we human or something else?*

"Well?"

Jet realized they'd continued to talk to him as he mulled over Lucifer's requirements. He didn't know what he was answering, but he agreed with sincerity.

"Then that settles it." Breena beamed, excited. "You will begin the ceremony in the nude, and then publicly dress in the clothes of your station after you take the oath."

Jet's eyes bulged and Breena doubled over laughing.

"I knew you weren't listening. We simply settled on a date. September first."

Chapter 13

Jordan stepped with care out of the taxi he hired to take him home from the hospital. The plastic ID band around his wrist pulled at his hairs as he shoved a hand in his pocket to fish out some cash for the driver. His thoughts flashed back to the night he and Breena had gone clubbing in London. He could still see the look of disgust on her face after he yelled at her and stormed away. It was difficult not to attach her disgust to the memory of kissing her before the yelling had begun. Although she had been angry at the kiss, it was his overprotective instinct, his gall, to tell her who she could or could not date, that had disgusted her.

Climbing out of a cab without her this time around has to be karma. But haven't I paid enough? The waiting, the worrying about if she would ever wake up again, the constant rejections and mind changes. . . that had to be payback, too.

His phone buzzed in his pocket. It was a text from Lilly's mother updating him on her condition. She would be fine, but the happy news didn't shine like it should have. It still seemed like everything around him was grey and covered in soot, dulled. Before Breena's disappearance, Jordan always considered himself an optimist. When Lilly teased him about his sunny outlook, which she insisted wasn't good spirit but naïveté, he countered with the notion that his relentless pursuit of Breena was proof of his resilience, not obliviousness or unfounded hope. Despite all of the conflict and rejection, he had never been truly depressed. Scared, many times, but not depressed. Nothing could destroy the image he had in mind of a future with Breena. He insisted that one day he would get her.

That's what I used to think.

Since the kidnapping, the rosy picture in his head had started to weather as if years of the blasting sun of his optimism had faded the crisp scene into a vague yellow. *Giving up on the search was my first mistake. It's my fault how things between her, Atlas, and Luce turned out yesterday. If I hadn't suggested we let her go, if I had taken the search into my own hands and gotten to her before Atlas, she wouldn't be. . . wouldn't be. . .* He couldn't bring himself to think the words, although the weight of the idea was no different than the phrase. *I wouldn't have had to lose her all over again. I'm so sick of being powerless.*

He shuffled through the unkempt yard and into the empty house. The impulse to listen for Breena padding around upstairs had fallen away, but the foreign silence of a house without Lilly or Lexa, who he'd just gotten used to having there, was too much. *Bree always saw me as powerless.* He tried to throw a new scene into the room to block out the emptiness of the space, but the illusion flickered and failed when Jordan kicked his shoes off into it as he walked. *I never compared to him.*

Jordan trudged up the stairs, pulling his t-shirt over his head as he went. His pants hit the floor as he reached his room, which also looked a grey-scale replica of the real thing. *I can't stay in this place.* The smoky clothes were replaced by gym clothes and running shoes.

Jordan's feet beat an irregular rhythm into the treadmill, but he pushed through the weakness in his muscles for as long as he could. It was a slow pace limited by his body not his mind. About half of a mile into the slow jog, his lungs began to spasm, and he jumped his feet to the sideboards as a coughing fit set in. Thoughts about what the doctor would have advised had he not discharged himself, including, he was certain, that Jordan shouldn't exert himself at all for a while, made him want to run even harder. But he couldn't.

His coughing fit must have looked and sounded as bad as it felt because one of the gym staff came to check on him, urging him to turn off his machine. Jordan pulled the emergency stop key because he couldn't see the pause button on the dash through his watering eyes. After the coughing fit passed, he wiped his cheeks and blinked a few times hoping that the tears had cleared any remaining fogginess from his vision. They didn't, and he knew it wasn't his eyes making everything look dull. *Pathetic. Can't even fool myself.*

The first thing he did when returning home was put on a CD and blast it through the home stereo system. It was a farce that only partly made each room sound less vacant. In the shower, he attempted to set new goals to find Breena and get her back. By the time the water ran cold and his fingers wrinkled, Jordan had only come up with one step: *find someone to train me to be better than Atlas.*

****

Two weeks after Leigh and the rest of the vigilante group learned of Atlas' death, they disbanded, and The Disorder hadn't made any large statements, either, after losing so many members to prison. For both factions, certain people still held to their groups' respective ideals on the premise that just because the top target was gone didn't mean there was nothing left to fight for.

Leigh wasn't one of those people, though. Her experience hosting Lucifer, which she still didn't fully understand as such, had made her timid. The gun-happy, vengeance-fueled Leigh had been scared into inaction. She realized that her new demeanor was a reversion to the way she was before speaking with Atlas. Leigh didn't see her stint as bringer-of-justice as a sensible choice anymore. She saw it as a slip into greater madness. It was the only explanation for the acts she committed, and suspecting she had been possessed didn't ease her conscience. She figured she was better off, miserable as she was, before Atlas and considered herself lucky to feel now how she had then. She hadn't traded up like it first appeared. *Hindsight is so clear. I'm lucky to get a do-over. Going to do this right. Do right by me.*

With nothing left to lose, she set out to find a reputable group therapy session to join. She reminded herself in moments of panic that Atlas was gone and that his advice, and her resulting actions, was not the norm. She promised herself no repeats.

****

The day of Breena's ascension ceremony arrived in a blur. She hadn't slept. No one had. Much to her consternation, it wasn't something the body needed in Gehenna, and she found it ironic that the only way for a chosen to connect to a future queen was through dreaming during their earthly lives. *I guess it's more fool-proof, though. Face-to-face meetings and physical attractions could result in multiple pairings. In dreams, we have to reside on the same wavelength, the same planes. Anyone outside of my reach—anyone who can't access, recognize, or understand me in my most vulnerable state—would make a poor match once awake.* She chuckled darkly to herself and rolled her eyes. *So how did Atlas get through?*

Breena waited in the dim dressing room for another half hour. Itzal had sequestered her there, saying, "At sun-up—"

Bree scrunched her face. It was an odd phrase to hear in a place with no sleeping and no sun or moon. *Must be something brought back by those who grew up like me, or he's just trying to make me feel at home.*

He continued, "—you became more than just the dishonorable queen's frustrating daughter. You are heiress apparent. *The* heiress. We waited a long time for you to arrive, but tradition says we must wait a while longer to see you on your coronation day."

Tradition. She huffed, bored and mentally exhausted. *Beginning to hate that word.*

"Don't think of it as an inconvenience or a dismissal of your wishes. This is *your* ceremony, and *you* planned it. That's never happened before. We recognize your difference. But, even though you're to be queen, and we will act to honor you, this tradition honors *us.* You honor us by being our leader, but your leadership is largely a one-way street. This is one of the ways you show us you recognize and value our fealty."

Breena flushed, embarrassed at how little she knew about her new home. "You guys really need a cram school for incoming royalty."

"Cram school? I don't—"

"Never mind. I understand what you're saying. Thank you, Itzal, for your fealty."

He beamed like he'd never been complimented before—and knowing her mother, he probably hadn't—then shuffled out of the room never turning his back to her.

For a while, her flickering reflection in the long, antique mirror held her interest. The gown she had commissioned swallowed her frame in layers of black fabrics, some rich and matte in texture, others glossy and bright with their slick sheen. Fine tulle peeked out from underneath the angled layers that cascaded down from the strapless length. Where the mermaid-cut dress fanned out at the floor, hundreds of tiny black sequins glimmered in the candlelight. She gave up on keeping her gown free from wrinkles and sat down in the stiff arm chair, black chiffon, silk, and crinoline bustling up to her chest and over the arms of the chair from under her.

A rattle outside the door startled Breena from her seat. She compulsively smoothed her dress as Tabitha walked in, smug in her finery, followed by the impatient little page boy from Bree's first night in Gehenna.

Tabitha clicked her tongue at Breena. "You know, you always were a sloppy-looking girl. Look at those creases." She approached Breena with a hand outstretched.

Breena pulled away. "Don't touch me. You've done quite enough."

"So bitter. You're where you belong. What's to worry about, now?"

"I don't want you here," Breena growled.

"Now, now. Starting today, you're family."

Bree shook her head in disbelief of what she was hearing. "You're my mother. . ."

"So now you're ready to accept me?"

"Don't read into it."

Tabitha circled Bree, the wind from her ridiculous dress— clearly meant to upstage Breena's—putting out the candles in the room. Darkness enclosed them. "Today, you permanently exit the light of humanity and enter eternal night as a queen."

A burst of laughter bubbled up, and Breena slapped a hand over her mouth. Her mother might as well have shot lasers from her eyes in response. The look was just as caustic, visible in the blackness. Tabitha waited for an explanation to Breena's outburst. Breena ventured a response, the nature of others' expectations dawning.

"You thought this was permanent for me. . ." Breena gathered her skirts and moved closer to Tabitha. "It's not, of course." *I should have seen this coming.* "You know, just because Jet and Atlas are here permanently doesn't mean I have to stay, too. We arrived at the same time, but their circumstances are different. My body didn't die." She waved her arms for effect. "This is me. *All* of me, not just my spirit. Itzal's been teaching me a little about how things work around here. I know that gentry class and royals can leave Gehenna any time they want and that the only way they can return is when that body dies. I know that I'm the only one capable of returning with a living body. It makes sense the more I think about what Atlas used to tell me about how we were born here and sent to grow up among humans, to learn about them, blend in with them, *mate* with them." Tabitha was glaring, but Breena pressed on. "So if you think this ceremony, or you, or a *man* will keep me some place I don't want to be, well. . . I wouldn't have been able to trap you in a cage like an animal and kill you if you were smarter."

Bree turned to the page, who was cowering in the dark doorway. "I'm sorry we scared you. Take her somewhere. We're done."

The page opened the door and the light from the hallway streamed in, lifting Breena's dressing room from obscurity. Her mother's pinched features surprised her, only because it meant the woman was holding her tongue. *Kind of her to recognize that I don't want to hear it. There might be some hope for our relationship after all.* She shook her head. *I'm so funny.*

When the room was empty again, Breena sat on the tufted bench just inside the door. *That was a surprisingly useful conversation. Now that I know for sure it is possible for me to live in both worlds, I can plan my future better. I only needed to come back here to restore myself, get my illusions working again. Vos was wrong. He didn't know I could live and bring my body with me because I'm the only one.* She skirted her next thought for a few seconds, hating to admit it. *Atlas was right. Is it possible that he really was looking out for me instead of planning something else? No. No, don't get sucked into that idea. And how did he know? Maybe Tabitha contacted him somehow after I thought she was dead. She didn't want me to come here after what I did to her, so she told him to convince me to stay on Earth. Or he made it up and fed me more lies to get what he wanted, and it turned out to be true. Dumb luck. It's hard when you expect the worst in everyone to know whether the simplest explanation is the answer or whether something is part of a scheme.*

Breena decided on the spot that her leadership would include a part-time arrangement. Gehenna would always be there, but her life in Grayling, the people she loved, wouldn't. *Especially if they think I'm dead, dead. I hope Jordan and Lilly are OK. Is it bad it took me this long to think of them? Maybe I'm losing my connection with that life, now. It would make sense. Whichever world I'm not a physical part of gets hazy, like it's just an idea. I really do need to get back.*

She hadn't bothered mentioning her desire to go back home to Luce. She knew he wouldn't take it well, and Bree didn't want him to think she was giving him a say. During their last conversation, after completing plans for the ceremony, Luce told her that sentencing Atlas would be her first royal act and that it would take place immediately after the ceremony. *I only have to stick around until that's done.* A pang went through her. Jet couldn't return like she could. *Am I really going to leave him here?*

Bree's certainty about her plans to leave fluctuated, and she settled on a compromise with herself. She would stay. If there was a way to restore Jet's life, then they would both go back. She could return to Gehenna periodically, without Jet, because, after everything Itzal said about honor, she wouldn't leave them hanging. But, Jet didn't need to be a part of that world if there was a way out, and she knew the only reason he was pulled into it was because Luce's first few guys had failed. *He shouldn't have had to give up his life for their mistakes.*

As if her thoughts had summoned him, Jet strode into the room wearing what could only be described as full livery. It was strange and amusing and, she admitted, a little attractive to see him dressed so formally in a tuxedo with tails, a vest and cummerbund, and the white gloves. . . She couldn't get over the white gloves. His inkwell hair was slicked back, revealing the freshly trimmed undercut on the sides. It was a far cry from the floppy mess he usually wore. Despite how handsome he looked, it felt fake. It *was* fake—as fake as she was in her fluffy dress that, though she designed it, was something she never would have chosen for herself. *I wouldn't have chosen any of this for myself. If I'd known my dreams were leading me here, I would have never gone to sleep. Some escape.*

"How long you going to keep staring? We've got to get to the hall."

She shook her head to snap out of her regrets and linked her arm with his. Her heart thumped a heavier beat then resumed, and Jet's vision sharpened, the dim hallway coming into perfect focus as his innate link to her pulsed stronger. In those moments while they touched, the voices of the pit quieted from his head. Despite having been in Gehenna for almost three weeks, it was the first time they'd touched since the night they arrived. Breena's spare time was consumed with planning a ceremony she didn't want. She missed him.

With unwelcome clarity, a new voice rang in her head, pointing out her still-mixed-up heart. *Which him?* Bree picked at the skin around her nails as Jet escorted her to a room full of strangers who, for no other reason than their assumptions, loved her. *Just like high school. Guess I didn't run far enough.* She thought of what Jordan must be going through. She ached to do it all over.

Chapter 14

While planning the ceremony, she had explained to Luce for the hundredth time that she was not going to marry anyone. He suggested that, instead, she symbolically marry everyone in Gehenna.

"You want me to what?"

"Not literally, and not in the romantic sense that you understand it. But consider it. A coronation is the symbolic way of marrying yourself to your people, dedicating your position of power to them, for them. It's not so different. As queen, you have to marry *someone*. If you refuse tradition, this is the only way I see to prevent a riot or, at the least, their poor opinions of you. Give them a chance to see you and know you before you start making them loathe you."

"Gee, thanks. I appreciate your confidence. How do you know they won't like the changes?"

"I *don't* know. I simply suspect."

Figuring it wise to give him a small win, Breena organized her ascension ceremony much like she imagined organizing a wedding—the big dress she wouldn't normally wear, the rows of people invited to watch, the man in a tux.

Now, Breena stood at the end of the aisle, looking down it to the grand chair in front, trying to avoid eye contact with her people. She thought back to all the times her dreams and illusions had shown variations of this scenario, usually with Atlas, and usually with her walking the wrong way down the aisle toward him.

Jet squeezed her hand then stepped back. Luce would present him to her after her oath. The nerves set in, and she began to doubt all of her choices. *Maybe those visions weren't warnings about Atlas. Maybe they were about Jet.* She imagined herself getting too worked up during the ceremony and running out before he could be presented to her, which she realized would only make the visions true as she walked the opposite way down the aisle, toward Jet, and out of the hall. *Or the scenes were trying to tell me to go against the grain, like I'm doing now by refusing to marry.* This thought calmed her a bit, but something still ate at her. *Atlas isn't here.*

Breena didn't want to admit that it bothered her, but in every variation of the scenario, he had been there. *It's fine. I'm breaking the cycle. With Jet.* Try as she might to shake it off, she couldn't deny that she was excited by the thought that Jet would be, for lack of better designation, hers. There was an easy chemistry between them. No tension. Not like with Atlas. Not even like her relationship with Jordan.

She turned to look behind her and Lucifer stood with Jet like a brick wall. Even as the primary authority in Gehenna, Breena couldn't see getting out of the ceremony no matter what she proposed to Luce instead, but she desperately wanted to run away from the spectacle before her, clear her head. She wanted to know how her friends were back home.

****

Lilly came to in a bright, beeping room. She didn't know how she got there or why there were so many tubes and wires taped to her. The bedside machines next to her squawked until a nurse popped his head around the door frame, chirped, "Hey, Sleepy," and turned it off.

Lilly tried to ask the nurse what had happened, but her throat rasped and her lungs burned when she tried to speak. The nurse put a finger to his chapped lips.

"Don't force your voice. It will come back in a few days. You had some thermal damage to the lining of your airways, but everything is healing up nicely."

Lilly looked around the room. There were balloons and flowers, but that wasn't what she hoped to find. The nurse noticed the hurt expression.

"Your mom went to work, and your dad's in the cafeteria having some breakfast. I'll send the doctor in next time I see him so you can get the full details. Hopefully your dad will be back up by then."

Lilly nodded, her eyes watering. She knew the nurse was just saying what he thought Lilly wanted to hear, and his assumptions weren't unreasonable; it *would* be nice to see her parents. Lilly didn't want to make him feel bad by getting upset, but it wasn't her parents she had been hoping to see. To her still-awakening mind, cloudy from anesthesia, pain killers, and weeks asleep, Breena's absence meant nothing other than Breena's death. There was no alternative train of thought, no other reason Bree wasn't waiting in Lilly's hospital room, asleep with her mouth hanging open, on the cushioned bench built into the window.

****

Jordan sat at his computer, still wet from his shower, researching meditation, astral projection, and any other metaphysical practices the search bar suggested as he typed. His drive to find a teacher overpowered the drive to dry off, and he shivered as he scrolled a metaphysics forum for someone knowledgeable. For the most part, the people in the forum seemed to be just as curious and in the dark as he. Those who offered thorough answers appeared to like the way their voices sounded in text. It was a lot of one-upmanship and horn-tooting.

Frustrated, he jumped to the last page of the forum. The discussion threads were years old, mostly abandoned by their authors and readers. At the top of the page, though, was an intriguing subject line: "Learning Through Near-Death Experiences." *If Breena believed she had to die to restore herself, and if she had to go into those comas to find what she was looking for, there might be something to this. Maybe she did* have *to go.* The bile and anger settled a bit.

Jordan clicked the thread and, although there wasn't a lot of activity in the discussion, the original poster had included an email address encouraging readers to connect with him directly to learn more about the practice. A wave of queasiness rolled over him, but he tried to ignore it, reasoning that he didn't know exactly what the author meant by "Learn How." *I shouldn't judge it yet.* Underneath the reason, some hope that the author of the article would know how to get Breena back tried to climb past his denial. *Getting her back would be better than finding a new teacher.* He scribbled down the email address for later and put some pajamas on.

Her body wasn't there when we came out of the other dimension. He stared into the ceiling light, unblinking. *She must have made it to Gehenna.* His eyes watered. *Can she get back from there? Who am I kidding? She wouldn't come back if she could. Not even if this guy can help. Bree wanted this. Do I?* The more he questioned, the less certain his goal seemed. The only certainty looping through his thoughts was that picking up where he left off in his meditation and illusion skills would be easier with someone else, someone with no shared history, someone he didn't love.

When he woke up the next morning, none too pleased with his neighbors' insistence on using the leaf blower almost daily, Jordan decided he might as well visit Lilly. While at the hospital the day of the incident, staff wouldn't allow him to see her. Since then, his excuse had been that he couldn't handle it. *Lame.*

Since graduation, Lilly had been his go-to. Breena was distant, angry, uninterested. Jordan and Lilly connected on a different level—a non-romantic one, which was the reason for its success. They were partners. Their strengths complimented one another, and they did excellent work together trying to find Ari. Jordan shoved a leg into his pants with anger. His train of thought always led to the same place—resentment.

While Breena squandered her time with her useless attempts at repairing her connections, he and Lilly did most of the work. While Breena struggled away, he supported her attempts, cheered her on, begged her to rest. He hated that he had grown to resent Breena. *But there's a difference between perseverance and foolishness. Irresponsibility.* Lilly always had her head on straight. Instead of pessimism, she offered realism. Instead of denial disguised as determination, she offered temperance. She offered results.

He didn't want to be like Lilly in that moment. He wanted to be like Breena, to deny the gravity of the situation and push forward. Lilly never allowed that, though, and in her condition, she drove her point home. Things were, and had always been, serious. There was no escaping that she had almost died, no way around her recovery, and no way to push forward in the same ways they used to.

"If Lilly were here now," he thought aloud, "she'd tell me we need a new approach." Glancing at his desk, he saw the sticky note with the email address from the night before. He folded the glue strip back on itself then pushed the paper in his pocket. On the off chance she was conscious, he wanted to discuss his plan. He wanted her to lecture him about how incomplete and reckless it was. Jordan walked through his empty house. Without it full of people, it sounded as hollow as he felt. He missed Lilly's lectures and, though reluctant to admit it, he missed Breena, too.

****

The string quartet started to play. The crowd stood, looking back at her. For an instant, she didn't register that they wanted to see *her*, so Breena shifted to look behind, thinking something else was going on back there, that she was blocking their view. Looking back, Bree caught Luce's eye. He raised his eyebrows and shooed her forward with his hands.

Right. It's me.

The music filled the hall with a round, gentle harmony. A pang pulled from deep behind her nervous energy. She didn't know the song, and didn't care. It was the first time she had missed playing the cello since waking up in St. Bartholomew's Hospital from what those doctors had called an overdose and later doctors named Sleeping Beauty Syndrome—the days her choice to skip out on the London symphony program fell hardest on her. It made her want to go home.

Two thirds of the way down the aisle, she stumbled, flushing a deep red. *God, get me out of here.* It wasn't a swear, but a genuine prayer that proved two things—she could say "God"—*not a vampire; check*—and her role in Gehenna didn't override her beliefs—*still a Christian; check.* The oddity of her situation amused her long enough to carry her without additional incident to the extravagant chair at the front of the room. She refused to call it a throne out of sheer stubbornness to change the way the role of the queen was perceived, even to herself.

She ascended the two steps to the chair, turned as gracefully as she could while wearing a dress that didn't allow her legs to separate more than a few inches, cursed her choice in attire, and then sat down, layers and crinolines again piling up around her. *How dignified.*

Luce sauntered toward her with an air of annoyance.

I must look worse than I thought. Her assumptions were incorrect.

When Lucifer reached the dais, she got a glimpse around him to the back of the hall where, waiting with a pissed off Jet, stood Atlas in the grips of two unsightly guards.

The guards' eyes rested so low on their faces that there shouldn't have been room for noses. Yet, they had noses, too—flat in profile so that she wondered how they breathed and with three ridges across the bridge. Their lips were pale and blended in to their general skin tones. Breena gave herself some credit. Her revulsion toward them was not cosmetic in a shallow, superficial sense, odd as they were. The distaste came at the sense that their looks, the beings as a whole, had been crafted and altered, not born.

Until then, she hadn't seen anyone that couldn't pass as human. She figured all the pop culture about hell-beasts, monsters, and creatures were fiction. It reminded her once again how much she still needed to learn about the place soon to be under her rule.

Atlas didn't struggle in the men's grasps. They each gripped an elbow and a bicep until their knuckles, and Atlas' skin under them, had lost all color. He didn't appear to notice. His burning focus was on Breena.

Jet willed his mouth to stay shut. Atlas' intensity radiated through the room, and even though Breena bore the brunt of it, he knew, it battered Jet. Intuiting Atlas' intentions and Breena's emotions was exhausting, and Jet didn't understand why he had to have such a connection if he was incapable of doing anything about it. Despite his duty to protect Breena, he couldn't guard her from inner forces.

Lucifer bowed in front of Breena and started orating. Breena's plans to soak in the moment melted away. All she could do was run question after question about Atlas' presence.

Why is he here? Are they going to try to force me to marry him? Is it just a formality because he's my chosen? Are they going to make me sentence him in front of everyone? Does he really need to be present to be sentenced? Did he ask to come? Her mind bounced back to the ceremony.

"...and the queen is presented to her court. Before you is your heir apparent, Breena; the only child of Tabitha, the last of my daughters; the first granddaughter of Gehenna."

He turned back to Breena. "Please bow your head." She didn't want to break eye contact with Atlas, but she obeyed. "From this moment, your court will call you Queen Ashna, a name meaning 'change' for an heir who has so much in store for us."

At the mention of changing her name, the first time she had heard of the matter, she snapped her head back up and shot to her feet. "I am not changing my name." In the back of the room, Atlas couldn't help but grin. Jet wanted to as well, but seeing the endeared look on Atlas' face turned his admiration of Breena's will into a scowl. Jet wished he could punch the grin right off Atlas' face.

Luce chuckled at Breena's defiance. "The queen whose name is change does not want to change her name." He shook his head and the crowd looked on, tense. "Perhaps we should have named you something that means 'stubborn.'" Luce looked into the room and laughed. Court relaxed, a collective, sighing laughter breaking out.

Breena was incensed. "I'm happy you're amused rather than angry, but I have to point out that I have changed an awful lot for all of you already. I changed my whole life, maybe irrevocably, just to be here and to set the balance right. I changed this ceremony. I changed who I am to marry—it's no one, in case you hadn't heard." A few of the ladies of the court exchanged appalled glances. "And I changed my mind about staying permanently." They were all gasping and trading outraged looks. "Sorry to drop the bomb on you like that. Hadn't planned to do it here." Lucifer put a hand at the small of her back and began to push at her, clearly trying to get her off the platform. She pressed on. "So you can understand if I do not want to change my name."

If it hadn't been for the impractical shoes she pulled from her armoire, the only ones tall enough to lift the last layer of her gown from the floor, she might have held her position. Luce's shoving was insistent. As she shuffled out of court with Lucifer, Jet, and Atlas plus guards close behind her, she tacked on, "I'd think you'd be happy there's something I *won't* be changing." The doors to the hall slammed behind them.

"Breena, what were you thinking?"

"What were *you* thinking? You said I could plan the ceremony. It was going fine." Atlas caught her eye and she held the look longer than she should have. Her stomach flipped even though she knew the look he was giving her meant, "Told you so."

"What about me?" Jet immediately regretted his choice of words. It sounded like a sulky child and, even though he was feeling neglected and jealous, he hadn't wanted to come across that way. "I just mean, am I her courtier now, or does the ceremony have to happen?"

Lucifer waved a hand in front of Jet's face like he was a gnat. "That's not what's important right now. Breena, we have our differences, and I can accept your new ways of ruling in time, but you mentioned some troubling things in there. The ceremony will happen today, so we are going to march ourselves back to position and finish what we started. Then, you and I are going to have a serious discussion about your future plans. It seems as if you were withholding before."

Of course I was.

Luce clapped a hand on Breena's shoulder, spun her to face the door, and gave her a nudge. "Now get in there and act happy about it." He guided her forward with an arm around her waist like she might dart if unhandled. She snuck a look over her left shoulder at Atlas and mouthed, "What are you doing here?"

The doors to court opened onto chaos and arguing and Atlas winked at her. She turned to face her mess. The crowd didn't notice her return at first. Bree had to push through groups in heated debates, and as she passed, she caught snippets of conversations: "She's the queen. She can do whatever she wants," was met with, "She's disrespectful and unprepared."

Like a bird that flew into a window, she was dazed at the turn of events. *Everything would have gone according to plan if Luce hadn't kept the name change a secret. How do things keep falling apart? I'm trying to fix things and people keep screwing it up!* Her anger mounted as she climbed the two steps back to her place of power. The members of court weren't yelling anymore, but they hadn't settled, either. Breena stomped on the platform with her massively-heeled shoe. "*Enough!*" Heads turned in her direction. "I believe we have an ascension ceremony to finish."

They stared as if they hadn't expected her to come back, as if they hadn't expected Lucifer to *allow* her to come back. Clothing rustled and chairs squeaked as rows of extravagantly clad nobles resumed their seats and stared on, aghast but curious. Tabitha took it all in with a giddy glow on her face. She fed on the havoc.

If I want to maintain the power in this situation, I have to appease them for now. "Thank you. I apologize to each of you for rocking the boat. Although everything I said was true, I had not planned to reveal that much today. I realize there is a time and a place for each type of discussion, and this ceremony was neither. Please know that I take this as seriously as you do and, even though my methods differ from your expectations, I fully intend on seizing the opportunities for repairing the balance between Heaven and Gehenna that this role provides. Balance is what you all want, right?"

She scanned the room, trying to make eye contact with some of the strangers before her. Hesitancy poorly masked, if they were trying to mask it at all, a few of the ladies and men of court started to nod. Breena didn't expect everyone to show support. *This isn't some 'Oh Captain, my Captain,' moment.* The affirmations spread across the room, those still too angry to hear her out remaining a stolid minority.

"Thank you. Now, let me finish what I started." She turned around and sat down in the chair. Mind more open to cooperation, seeing that being likeable and giving in on certain things was an advantageous way to sandwich unpleasant change with things her people could get behind, was a new concept. *But I'm still not marrying anybody. For now.* Jet caught that thought and straightened.

Luce and the others resumed their positions as well, picking up on the part about changing Bree's name to Ashna. She rolled her eyes, but complied, adding—out of turn—that they would only call her that during official business. "I will not answer to that name in a social situation. End of discussion."

Taking her cue, Lucifer dropped the issue and moved on, grateful that she would take the name in any circumstance. "Before your court, you will stand as Queen Ashna, born Breena Daughter of Tabitha, First Granddaughter of Gehenna, Betrothed to—" the crowd tensed and Lucifer cleared his throat, "Betrothed to None but her People, the Queen of Change." He held his hand out for her to take.

Breena stood, tottered again down the two steps to the aisle, led by Luce, and curtseyed in a quick jerky motion. It wasn't part of the ritual, and even if it had been, she did it with less grace than a potato, but she couldn't stand still there, all eyes on her. *What a spaz.*

Lucifer gave her a quizzical look, as confused by her action as she was. "Breena, do you accept this name given by your people?"

Not wanting it to feel more like a wedding, she responded with "Yes," instead of, "I do."

"Do you accept responsibility for the souls seated before you and all others in this realm?"

"Yes."

"Will you use your place in this society to better it, acting for the largest benefit, regardless of personal gains or losses?"

Until the last clause, Breena was prepared to say yes, but the part about personal gains and losses gave her pause. *If I agree to this, that effectively disallows me from returning to my regular life. Am I admitting that leaving is not in their best interest? But how do I know that yet? I don't know anything about them. Tabitha ruled from Earth. . . but look how that went.*

Her dive into What-If Lake was interrupted by a man of court. He shot from his chair, shouting, "She hesitates to put us first! She'll be just like her mother. Do not allow this, Lucifer."

"Quiet. Does it not speak to her wisdom that she is carefully considering the promise before she makes it?"

This seemed to calm the man and, for once, Breena was thankful for Luce's interference. She clamped down on her spiraling anxieties and prepared to answer in the affirmative again, telling herself that her choice to leave may seem harmful in their eyes because they are not used to it. *That doesn't mean it actually is harmful. I will set them up to thrive. Everything will be OK.* She hated that this last sentiment formed in the tone of a question rather than certainty, but she ran with it. *I can worry after I'm officially queen. That's what leaders do, right? Worry over their people.*

Atlas looked on from his place in the back of the hall. Bree wondered what he was thinking. The ceremony, her leadership—she was certain all of it went against his idea of the right kind of society, whether in Gehenna, Heaven, or on Earth. He had always wanted an acephalous culture where everyone led only themselves. It was no wonder why he didn't want to come back with her, why, even if it meant losing her, he was prepared to get on a plane and seek out his happiness before Lucifer showed up to claim them. *Is that why he came to the ceremony? To remind me of his disapproval? To make me rethink this? Did he really think I would give his opinion of me so much power?*

She flashed back to London, shortly after they had first met in the grocery store, when he had slipped a note into her hand at a club then disappeared into the crowd. As she read it, her brain screamed "Stalker Alert!" but she was flattered by the compliments he had written in the note and by his efforts to connect with her. She couldn't help it. From that moment on, their paths were inextricable. Major life decisions shifted course because of his influence. *Of course he thinks so highly of himself. I conditioned him to think what he says and does matters to me. I taught him how to treat me by allowing it.* She mentally rolled her eyes at herself. *You were so naïve.*

Lucifer cleared his throat. "Shall I repeat the appeal?"

"No. I've made my choice. I will put their needs first, even if it results in personal losses. In some ways that matter a great deal to me, it already has. My presence should be proof enough of my dedication. I lost a lot to get here."

Out of the corner of her eye, she saw Atlas shaking his head. He nudged at one of the guards and whispered something. They turned and left the room, confirming Breena's assumptions.

"With this affirmation I am proud to crown you, in front of your family and your court, Queen." He conjured a white crown with gold flecks onto Breena's head. It was the only part of her ascension outfit she hadn't been able to design or see ahead of time. As it sat on her head, she wished for a mirror.

While Breena marveled at the unfamiliar weight of it atop her, Luce embarked on a long speech about duties and honor, something else he hadn't mentioned being a part of the ceremony. It eventually led to his presentation of Jet to Breena. With an expression of relief on his face, Jet rushed to the front of the hall with no regard for the slow, dignified pace Itzal and Luce had implored him to use.

Just before sending Jet to retrieve Breena for the ceremony, they had pulled him aside to explain.

"Though in service to her, no courtier scuttles around or hurries to his queen's every beck and call. That is for the lowly who bare the label of servant and nothing more. You have risen beyond the class of your ancestors. You are her right hand, her public escort, and her private confidant."

Luce chimed in. "Hurrying makes you appear fearful of your queen, as if you rush to complete your tasks for fear of reprimand. You must maintain as strong and confident an appearance as she. Others in court will try to hold your ear, asking for favors or to pass on propositions for the queen. Some may even try to bribe you for her favor. How would it reflect on her if her right hand was a busy-body like a worker bee or a sneaky rat that darts around behind the scenes?"

Jet scratched the back of his neck. "Bad. It would look bad."

"In response to those simple words, a simple reply: Yes."

In the great hall, Jet approached Breena before the throne, mind blanking at the proper procedure. Jet bowed low, just guessing, and met her eyes upon rising. Lucifer, allowing his exasperation at their ignorance to show for a split second, pinched the bridge of his nose and closed his eyes. When he opened them, Jet was on one knee with his hands behind his back.

Breena stared, a little breathless. *So much like a proposal. I don't know what I'm feeling.*

Luce looked down on Jet and nodded. *So he has remembered something.* His face settled into a neutral mask, but Breena thought she saw the traces of a grin in her grandfather's eyes.

At the end of the ceremony, Jet escorted Breena out of the hall. The court clapped sedately at the completion of the ritual. As similar as it all was to a wedding, she figured there would be cheering, photos, a grand send-off. The crowd looked more like that of a golf tournament. And there was nowhere to be sent off to—

Breena had free reign within the realm of Gehenna, and although there were many parts she hadn't yet visited, there was no honeymoon for becoming a queen.

She grabbed Jet's hand. "Come on. I've got to get out of these shoes." Breena leaned on Jet and hobbled back to her room. After she got the strappy torture chambers off, she dangled them in front of him. "Get rid of these."

Jet rubbed his palms together. "My first official task is to get rid of your uncomfortable shoes?" *Itzal told me not to scurry around.* "I can always do that later if there's something more important, something more symbolic you want me to do first."

"You're really into this."

He shrugged, his resistance playful. He was happy to do that or anything else for her, happy that he was there with her while Atlas was locked away. "I mean, it's not how I imagined my life, but it's history, right? You're a special queen, and I'm the one that gets to help you make things right."

"Fine, fine. What should I have you do?"

"I can't tell you how to order me around."

"You can if I tell you to." She winked. "Queen logic."

He sat down on the bench beside her. "When do you have to sentence Atlas?"

"Lucifer said immediately, but clearly he didn't mean it in a literal sense. Time is weird here. I guess when you live eons, doing something even years later seems pretty prompt." She shrugged. "I don't know. He skirted the date every time I mentioned it. I think he's hoping I'll change my mind and marry him." Breena noticed Jet's knuckles whiten.

"So about that first official order. . ."

"Jet, I don't know. I got nothing going on." She stared up at the ceiling and all of its names. "But, I still haven't found my name up there. If it wasn't there then, maybe it is now that everything's official."

That doesn't sound important, either. He grabbed a chair and climbed atop it. "Maybe the names don't go up there until a queen dies. Or whatever is equivalent to death here."

"The pit."

"Yeah, that."

They started at opposite corners, reading through each name that curled across the ceiling. When they met in the middle, their eyes were so strained and necks so cricked that they decided to abandon the search and leave the remaining two corners for another night.

I have forever to find it. Breena fell back on her bed, bitter. "I was thinking, maybe I'll go back to my normal life before Atlas' trial."

Jet fell across the end of the bed, resting his head across Bree's shins. "You'll have to set a date first. No need to wait out Luce, now."

"I think I'd rather wait."

"What? You mean you're going to let him stay down there indefinitely?"

That's exactly what she had meant, but hearing it aloud made her cringe. "Well, maybe not forever. It can be part of his sentence. I don't know if that's how they do things here, but it's not an uncommon thing back home to imprison people."

"True, but it is something else to imprison people for long periods with no trial in sight. Does he deserve that? So much of what he did was a result of Tabitha's compulsion."

"How do you know about that?"

"Luce filled me in."

Bree swiped a hand in front of her, clearing away the previous statement. "What happened before you came along is a different story. I'm trying not to hold that against him. Most of it, anyway. This is for shooting me."

"I get it."

"Do you? You sound mighty jealous. Want me to hurry up and get rid of him so you can swoop in?"

He rolled to face her and propped himself on his elbow. "Swoop in? You're kidding. I'm in this because of *you*. *You* are the swooper."

"No I'm—"

"Who's the one who did the approaching when things got bad with Jordan? Who's the one who got the other a death-sentence? You started this. And I'm willing to bet that in some way, maybe an unintentional way, you started things with Atlas, too. Finish what you start, for once." The ease between them drained out of the room and left them annoyed and too close. Jet got off the bed wanting to take a walk, but he couldn't leave unless she offered him an exit.

Breena stared at Jet's feet as he paced. It was a rhythmic action that would have put her to sleep in normal circumstances, but she couldn't escape that way anymore. She couldn't escape at all. The click of his feet began to grate on her nerves. "Stand still, Jet! You're driving me crazy."

"I need you to tell me what's going on with you. Sometimes I think you're content to be alone. Other times I get the same signals off of you that I got on the canoe ride. Right now, I think you're reluctant to sentence Atlas not because you'd like to punish him more by drawing it out, but because you don't want to punish him at all."

"Yeah, well sometimes I get the sense you're happy to be at my side even if you can't have me. Other times you act like you might try and break some rules. I kind of like it, but that's not the point. But mostly, you resent me."

"Don't tell me how I feel."

"Ditto!"

The wicked glare he gave her stopped her short. On one hand, she thought he might continue yelling or storm out. On the other, she half-expected him to close the distance between them and grab her saying, "Just shut up and kiss me," like so many predictable rom-coms. *Do I want him to? Sometimes it's hard to tell the difference between premonition and hope.*

As if her thoughts had been broadcasted, a pang of longing for Atlas lanced through her. The echo of that pang shot through Jet, sending him a step back. *This place really wants me to go to Atlas.* An old biology lecture from high school came, unbidden, to the front of her mind. *Like white blood cells fighting an infection. Or was it some other kind of cell? White. Almost certain. Every time Jet gets close, my body screams 'Invasion!' and tries to direct me towards Atlas.* She mulled this over for a few more seconds. *Focus.*

"Jet, we can't be like we were."

"And what were we?"

She frowned.

"It's OK. Just say it."

"We were friends." It didn't sound like a statement of confidence. She knew what he was getting at, what he wanted her to say. She couldn't do it.

"Breena!" When met with an obstinate refusal to make eye contact, he voiced what she would not. "We were dealer and customer. We were retailer and consumer. You might as well have gone into the grocery store and kissed the customer service clerk."

Bree chewed at her lip.

"I realize we didn't have time between that day and your kidnapping or now to get closer, and because of that it might seem crazy to you that I would have developed any feelings—" Bree nodded along. "—and maybe that's why you seem so ambivalent about me."

True.

"I'm trying not to take it personally, especially with this whole 'My biology wants me to want him' thing you've got going with Atlas. Of your two choices, he's the. . ." Jet paced, considering, like he was trying to catch the thought that trailed off. "Well. I will do what my role requires of me, but you have to know that I don't think I can wait out this Atlas thing if you're really going to put off his trial. Now that I'm officially. . . yours," he ventured, "for lack of better terms, it's like I'm linked in to your wavelength and his as a result. I don't want to feel what he's thinking about you. Or you him."

Yes, that would be unpleasant. "Am I worth waiting for?"

"Yes."

"Then you will wait with the understanding that I make no promises. The 'I can't wait, I need you, I have to have you,' isn't healthy—I know—and it doesn't work, not in the long run."

"So you're still going to prolong this?"

"Maybe. If I don't, it won't just be to spare you. For once, I'm trying to put other people first and fix what I've broken. Unfortunately for you, you don't count as 'other people'. Your role here makes you an extension of me. You have to sacrifice as much as I do for these people in order to help me carry out my changes."

Jet sat back down by Breena. These were all things he knew, but it helped to get it out in the open. She knew where he stood, and maybe someday it would make a difference. For the time being, he couldn't help but look forward to meting out whatever punishment was decided for Atlas, even if he had to wait.

Atlas stood with his back toward Tabitha, who was enervating him with the tapping of her toe. *She hasn't changed at all.*

"I asked you a question."

He wheeled on her. "And I said you can't compel me to do anything for you anymore." The words relieved some of the pressure that had settled on his chest. *Guess this is closure.*

"I told you to stop her. You didn't do anything in there. She wasn't supposed to ascend. The throne is *mine.*"

Atlas shook his head, and he wished this kind of clarity had been possible for him from the start. *So much would be different.* "You're the one who wanted her to 'come back home, be with family, fulfill duty.' Why work so hard to prevent it, now?"

"That. Was. Before." Tabitha angled her chin upward, showing the ruined skin around her neck in the shape of two handprints.

Atlas grinned, and Tabitha went berserk. Earlier in the week, Tabitha willed two guards to release Atlas and take him to the ceremony in hopes of changing Breena's mind. When the day came, the guards complied, but Atlas' presence did nothing. When Breena officially became queen, all of Tabitha's remaining powers of coercion disappeared. She wasn't coping well. At her tantrum, the same guards came running from the end of the hall, seizing her like any criminal and hauling her away.

Atlas played at concern, hiding a grin under his hand. *I think I could stay here forever if I saw that every day.* When she was gone, he patted the pristine white wall as if it was an old friend.

Breena sat up from her sleepless rest, gasping. Jet roused beside her. Visions of one of her old illusions, *their* old illusions— Atlas' and hers—strobed through her room in fragmented pieces. It was the white room, full of butterflies and decorated only with a grand bed. Atlas had gifted her the extravagant illusion, which extended outward with a castle, statue garden, and forest, shortly before their time in London ended. *Why now?*

Chapter 15

Shuffling across the gravel in her driveway, Lilly returned to her childhood home to stay for the first time since graduation. She hadn't officially moved out, not in the way that most eighteen-year-olds do the summer before starting college. Her transition to Jordan's house was a trickle. Every few weeks, more of her stuff appeared in their shared room, brought over after visits she only made to satisfy her parents, who believed leaving town and changing their ways of life told The Disorder they had won.

She missed Jordan and Breena and the routine they had fallen into, but, she supposed, it was a routine built on chaos and necessity. Lilly didn't know if their living arrangements would have turned out that way if Ari hadn't gone missing. Being home gave her a hollow sensation. It marked an unspoken finality to the remainder of their routine. Since Breena's disappearance, it crumbled more by the day, especially after Jordan's heartless statement about giving up on her.

Lilly's dad hurried her to her bedroom, insisting that she stay in bed. Lilly didn't resist. She fell into the orange and yellow pillows propped in the corner and fished her phone out of her pocket.

She rasped in a whisper to herself, "I don't know a lot about this world you're part of, Breena, but I think I know enough to be certain you're gone." She gripped the phone and felt guilty that she couldn't cry. "It's real, but it's not."

Beside her on the nightstand sat a mess of sticky notes and paper scraps with scribbled leads. Lilly did a lot of research to set up Ari and Linda's escape during the time before Breena's final confrontation with Tabitha, but Linda didn't stay the course for long, and Lilly's initial findings hadn't furthered the search for Ari, so the notes didn't make it to Jordan's house—unlike three quarters of her wardrobe, half her books, and a binder full of research on crime and punishment.

It enraged her. She swung her leg across the bed, kicking it all to the floor. *I'm the careful one with all the answers and none of it saved her. Why couldn't she be the careful one? Why couldn't she be happy with the life she had? She had to seek out danger to feel alive and it killed her, and I did* nothing.

Lilly's dad knocked on the door. "Is everything OK? Did you fall?"

"It's fine. I knocked over some books."

As much as she resented Breena's pill habit and would never condone it or adopt one of her own, she kind of understood the motivation behind it. *I just want to sleep forever and get away from this feeling.* She shook her head. *No. Don't be like that. Take a nap, wake up, find a new path.*

****

"This is going to cost me a fortune." Linda slid into the back of a cab outside of the prison and buckled her seatbelt. Leaving prison took forever; between the lengthy paperwork, getting her belongings back, and waiting for final approval, the meter ran for over two hours before she came out.

The judge set her bail for $75,000, which she paid off with the remaining money in the account she shared with Tabitha. Her parting gift encircled her leg, a tracking anklet to make sure she didn't try to go back to London, Madrid, or anywhere else. When she arrived to her group home, to which the anklet insured she arrived even though they allowed her to travel there on her own, she would be limited to a five mile radius, and that put her nowhere near Breena or Bree's friends and family.

Since Breena's body wasn't among those found in the fire, and no law enforcement officer knew to or would ever consider the option that she had dematerialized to another realm, they continued to search for her. Linda didn't know what to think. She worried about concluding her manhunt. *If Breena was dead or otherwise removed from the situation, fine, but assuming so is dangerous. What if she shows up somewhere? I can't sit around and do nothing about my anger. Someone needs to pay for Breena's betrayal. Anyone will do.*

****

Leigh sat on her porch step with her chin propped on her knee. She tried all morning to motivate herself to go to work, but it never happened. Instead, she waited for Shianne to arrive with her support dog.

Shianne had been released from prison shortly after the incident, getting off with time served, a fine, and an order to pay for repairs to the cars she had smashed. On her way out of the precinct, she and Leigh crossed paths—Leigh on her way to have lunch with one of her friends on the force. The two recognized one another from their run-ins at Atlas' recruitment meetings. While Shianne had benefitted from Linda's deprogramming—at least it seemed like a benefit before Linda posed as a therapist—Leigh had left worse off than she began.

She said as much when Shianne asked how she had been doing. Shianne was quick to put a stop to the belief that she had gotten off easy, going into detail about Linda's betrayal. Leigh hadn't intended to have a real conversation when she spotted her—she was in no mood—but commiserating was nice for a change. By the end of their chat, Shianne had invited herself over to share her support dog, Bubby.

Shianne pulled up and Leigh stood to greet her. In the back of Shianne's car, Leigh could see the outline of a sedate black lab licking at the window. As Shianne opened the door for him, Leigh hadn't decided if she would talk about her experience with Luce. *Even if I wanted to, how would I explain it? I don't even know what happened to me. What* I *think happened. . . that kind of thing isn't possible. She wouldn't believe it.*

"Go see Leigh, Bubby."

The dog trotted over to Leigh where she stood barefoot on the sidewalk. He sat and gazed up at her with big, brown, understanding eyes. Leigh smiled. After a few unblinking seconds of attention from the dog, she broke eye contact and greeted Shianne. "Hey, Shy. What's with him?"

"He's waiting for a command."

"Oh. What do I ask him to do?"

"Anything, pretty much. You wanna go inside? I'll have him go potty now if you do."

Leigh nodded. "Come on in when you're done." She pushed through the screen door and went to the kitchen. The house was open to the approaching fall weather and Leigh called out to Shianne, "Hey, you want a beer or something?"

She came into the house, Bubby at her side. "Yes, but I can't. Gotta drive. But don't let me stop you. I'll just take a water."

Leigh fixed the drinks and motioned in a wide arc, raising her eyebrows.

"Oh, wherever. Living room?"

"'Kay."

They sat on the couch and Bubby followed after Leigh patted the space beside her. "Maybe I should get a pet. Not a support animal, necessarily. That can be expensive. Just another living being to look after, talk to."

"It makes a huge difference. What would you say?"

"To a pet?" The question caught Leigh off guard. It sounded so rehearsed, so trained, like a therapist. Regardless of Linda's fake credentials, Shianne had learned some strategies or, at least, learned how to mimic a shrink mimicking a shrink. Leigh laughed. "You want the real answer?"

"Mhm."

"I'd tell him about how I think I was possessed."

Shianne choked on her water but tried to hide it as a legitimate swallowing malfunction.

Leigh looked away. "And that's why I'd tell a pet before a person, normally."

"Well don't get a cat. They'll give you more unimpressed and judgmental looks than any person."

"What about a guinea pig?"

"Are you trying to change the subject? You realize you can't bring up something like that and not finish the story."

Two hours later, she had finished the story, and Shianne paced from the door to the kitchen, from the door to the kitchen. "So what are you going to do?"

"What can I do? It was out of my control while it was happening. What effect can I have now? It's over."

Shianne shook her head, thinking. "What if. . ." Bubby and Leigh stared at her with the same probing look, one waiting for a task and the other waiting for a plan. "What if we get someone to ward the house? Smudge it with sage or whatever those hippy dips do."

"Before all of this I would've laughed and told you that stuff ain't real, but it couldn't hurt to try it. Where do I find an expert on that kind of thing?"

****

A lean man with teal hair rounded the corner nearest his house when his phone vibrated. Grey jogged into the grass that ran along the road home and pulled his cell out of his arm band.

As he put the phone to his ear, answering and then swallowing a few deep breaths, he shoved the ocean-hued strands out of his face. On the other end, a nervous introduction preluded a request he wasn't used to getting.

"I'd like you to teach me." Jordan paced his bedroom in his underwear, his nerves making him sweat too much to put anything on upon waking.

"You're not calling about a reading?"

"No, I'm calling about an article you wrote—how near-death experiences affect the astral body. Your contact info was at the end of it."

"Oh, right, right." Grey gulped another breath, the talking wreaking havoc on the breathing rhythm he tried to maintain during a run. Stopping without a cool-down always made him lightheaded. "Huh. No one's ever contacted me about that article. Usually they all just want a tarot reading or cleansing."

"Oh, well, I'm not interested in that, and to be clear, that's not what I'm asking you to teach me." Jordan had no idea how to put his request into brief-chat form. "It's such a long story, so if we could meet up and discuss it. . ."

"Sure, in public."

"Of course, of course."

"I'm not at home right now, so I'll give you a call back after I've had a chance to check my calendar." Grey kicked his feet toward his rear, feeling his hamstrings seize. "Yeah, you're welcome. Talk soon." Grey tried to shove the phone back into its plastic sleeve strapped to his arm. The screen was sweaty from his ear, making it difficult to slide back into place. "Oh screw it." He jogged the last third of a mile home with the phone in his hand, chanting, "Don't drop it, don't drop it," in time with his gait.

****

"Luce, there has to be something you can do. I've *got* to sleep. I'm going crazy here." Breena had stormed out of her room when the flashbacks ended, leaving Jet to stumble after her looking for an explanation.

"You're going to have to get used to the extra time on your hands."

She shook her head, wishing she could be blissfully in denial. The ornate stone and metal walls around her prevented any lasting escape from reality, though. There was no way to ignore the changes that had occurred, and that was precisely why she wanted to go to sleep. Without the option to use her typical means of escape, she was on overload. *It's too much.* "Aren't you powerful? I'm the queen, but you're the one people fear because you have the power to make them regret *not* fearing you. If you're capable of that, surely you're capable of knocking me out for a few hours."

"I'm not. Not here. I cannot create what isn't a part of the world already."

"OK, then where are all the girls my age? I need someone to talk to."

Lucifer straightened. A severe intensity crossed his eyes. "Is Jet not fulfilling his duty to you? He should be listening."

"No, it's not that. Jet's great. I love him—"

Luce raised an eyebrow.

Breena's hands fluttered around. "—But Lilly is my best. . ." she hugged her arms around herself. "Was. So where can I make some female friends?"

"There aren't many females your age in your station."

"I haven't seen *any* girls my age, not just in the upper class, which I don't care about, by the way. Why? Where are they?"

"Female children were discouraged after your birth to ensure more males would go into the world as a potential chosen."

"You restricted families to one child *and* you disallowed female offspring? Disgusting."

"Your mother did it all for you."

She slammed a fist on Lucifer's immense desk. "I don't want that 'honor.' I want a friend."

He pursed his lips. "I don't know what to tell you. It can be lonely to be a royal, not that I care to identify with such a human emotion, but I've been on Earth enough to understand it. It's another state you'll have to learn to be comfortable in. After you've been here long enough, you won't feel anything anymore."

"That sounds miserable." Breena puffed and stalked out of his chambers. Jet was waiting in the hall for her. Before he had a chance to say anything, she held her hand up. "I have to find someone to talk to."

Bree wandered down a spiral staircase to the left of Luce's rooms. *Don't associate with the help, don't make friends with the commoners, don't mind your loneliness, don't, don't, don't. Psh.*

When she stepped into the corridor of the servant level, all their scurrying ceased. A split second of stillness released into a rolling wave of workers dropping to kneel in front of their queen. It bewildered Breena, and she stumbled through a clumsy acknowledgement of their loyalty.

"Yes. Yes. Hi. I'm Bree. Hi. Thanks. That's so. . . wow. OK, OK, please get up. No need to stop for me."

They rose, but remained fixated.

"I really mean it. Feel free to get back to what you were doing. I'm just passing through."

The crowd, who were, to her disappointment, mostly male, scattered. The only females she saw at first were elderly, born before her mother came to rule and dwindle their numbers. Breena moseyed down the hall watching the workers folding linens, washing fruit, repairing broken furniture in their designated stalls lining the corridor. *I don't know what I expected to see, but this almost feels homey. Like a market. Or a renaissance festival.*

One of the rare, young girls approached her then. "Your Majesty? Can I help you find something?"

Bree shook her head. "How old are you?"

"Twelve, My Queen."

"What are your thoughts on friendship?"

"No time for that human tradition."

Breena's hopeful expression fell. "Does everyone feel that way?"

The servant girl beamed, proud of her upbringing. "Of course. We don't share that weakness with humans." She noticed Bree cringe. "I beg your forgiveness. I wasn't thinking. You grew up with. . . them."

"I'll let you get back to work." Breena turned to finish her stroll, abandoning the hunt for a friend that would understand her. In that moment of general longing, her DNA pulled for Atlas. *I have to see him. He's known me longer than anyone else here. He doesn't share these people's views on relationships.*

In the blinding white halls of the prison, every guard she passed kneeled at her presence. She waved away their habitual gestures of fealty, every few seconds having to tell them, "Thank you, but please get up." By the time she reached Atlas' cell, which was down an extensive corridor of mostly-empty ones, she was already tired of talking. *He's rotten, but that's overkill having so many guards for one man.*

As if the pull to go to him wasn't strong enough just being in Gehenna together, the force between their close proximity was almost painful. Her ribcage ached as if it was breaking. Her heart raced. Her feet were almost impossible to control. They didn't want her to stand still looking at him; they wanted her to move closer. *This isn't love. This is biology.*

Despite the discomfort, she took another moment to stare at his recumbent form. He hadn't changed. The same dark hair fell over his closed eyes. The same slow rhythm of his breathing belied his inner turmoil. She found she could separate her current admiration and desire from what she felt when they first met. The origins of attraction differed.

"I know you're not sleeping."

He didn't acknowledge her presence, so she took the time to gather her thoughts, already relieved that the visit proved her feelings toward him were hard-wired, not genuine care.

"I know *you're* not sleeping because *I'm* not sleeping, although I would be if it was possible."

He stirred. "I didn't think you'd come."

"Hadn't planned on it."

"But?"

"There's no 'but.'"

He got up from the floor and strode to the bars that separated them. The expression on his face said, "I don't need to tell you that you're wrong."

"Don't give me that. You always give me that."

"It's not my fault, you know."

She blinked a few times, unsurprised at his stance, but still reluctant to believe what she just heard. "Which thing? A lot of it is."

"The reason you're here talking to me right now. The flashbacks, the aches and pains."

"Oh." Bree glanced at her feet, noticing they were cold. *And barefoot.* She reddened. *Not very queenly of me. Atlas probably thinks I'm ridiculous.* "I didn't realize you were having those, too." *I don't care what he thinks. I don't.*

"Yeah. The last one sent me to my knees just as the guard passed. Managed to get an explanation out of him after he checked me over and said I was fine. Told him I didn't feel fine. Like getting pulled apart. Every time is worse."

"Huh."

"What? It's not like that for you?"

"No, it is. Why is it getting worse?"

"The guard said our bodies are fighting what it assumes is risk of extinction. It's instinct. Apparently, by this point, most people in our position have already. . . well, we were already supposed to have. . ." he shoved a hand through his hair. "People aren't usually able to resist this long, which is why it's getting worse, because our bodies are doing all they can to pull us together and force us to secure the future of our race, including forcing us to relive our time together. Fighting stubbornness with nostalgia."

Breena threw her hands up and turned away from the cell. *It's only going to escalate until we do something about it.* "Can it kill us, whatever is going on with our insides?"

"Doubt it. It wants us to live and to make life."

"Right. But, if no one makes it this long without giving in, and if we continue to resist, no one really knows what harm it can do to the body at advanced stages."

"I guess you're not wrong."

"I have to go. I was going to go back home after the ascension anyway, but I was worried it wouldn't be in the peoples' best interests. Something happening to me because of the unknown power of this thing going on between us would be worse."

"Take me with you. Once we're back home, we won't feel this, but if you leave me, it's going to overwhelm us every time you return."

"Atlas, your body died. Even if you didn't have crimes to serve for, I couldn't take you."

He staggered back a couple of steps. At first, she thought it was a reaction to what she had said. *Surely, he knows about his body. How else would he be here?* Then, it hit her as well—the lancing pain and the disorientation—and she dropped to the floor. At the same time, the guards down the hall were repelled backward. They heard Breena collapse, but were unable to enter the corridor. Something forced them out.

The pulse that emitted from Breena had not only sealed Breena and Atlas in an impenetrable sphere of energy that roiled with flame around the perimeter, but it had blown out the bars on Atlas' cell.

Chapter 16

Atlas and Breena were subjected to a stream of shared memories rolling through their sight like the tape on a film reel. With a dizzying shift, their joint memories diverged, and the reel showed Breena Atlas' memories of her, beginning before they even met.

Breena looked on as a young Atlas sat on his bedroom floor, eyes closed, face serene and with a hint of wonder playing around his mouth and eyes. The view shifted, letting Breena see what Atlas was looking at. It was her. She picked carefully through the leaves and vines until she reached a clearing. *I know this clearing. It's the one from all of my old dreams—the ones that shifted into nightmares the older I got.* She tensed, worried that she was about to witness herself running from the hungry, furious version of Atlas who had haunted her sleep for so many years.

Instead, she watched herself step into the edge of the swaying grass a child, maybe twelve years old. The trees opened up and the sunlight poured down, and across from her, in the distance, was a gentle figure. *I remember this, too. They always played out like this when I was a kid. They were calm dreams. I used to think it was God at the other side of the clearing.*

After meeting Atlas, Bree knew that he was the evil of her nightmares. Until this replay, she had never decided whether the soft version of that dream had also been him watching, pre-Tabitha, pre-corruption, or if her childhood assumptions were correct. *Now, I know. Atlas told the truth when he said he'd been waiting for me a long time.* The figure of Atlas waved at young Breena then stalked back into the trees.

The view reversed back to Atlas' physical presence in his room. He opened his eyes and sighed, standing and approaching a desk. From the drawer, he removed a small calendar and put an 'x' on the date. Atlas thumbed through the pages before it, and almost all had an 'x' written in the corner. *He kept track of every time he saw me? Like it was the best part of his day. . . He* did *have a rough life.*

The memory reel zipped forward in time. She watched Atlas, a little older, cross her path in Michigan years before they met. A flash of a more recent conversation with Atlas interrupted, as if only there to remind her that she had once asked him if it was possible that they were ever in the same place at the same time, and if they were, did he recognize her? They sat in his forest hunting cabin, and he acknowledged that it was possible, but he was unsure if he had. He explained that children didn't stand out in daily life because their souls were too quickly changing.

His memory of Michigan, her proof, resumed. A teenaged Atlas and a young-teen Breena shared a crosswalk, passing one another before diverging into wildly different life paths until meeting again years later. She chose to believe that even though Atlas did look back at her after they passed, his statement about not knowing it was her was true. *At that age, he could have felt a tug of connection and not yet understood it for what it was. He probably passed it off as mild attraction.*

Jumping again to a future date, Breena watched as Atlas tuned in to one of her cello practices. He sat atop his bed, transfixed and with tears rolling down his face, as he looked beyond his bedroom into another plane, a plane Breena had unknowingly tapped into as her music and emotions manipulated the waves of the room around her.

She always visualized her music and used it as a way to travel beyond her body, but until the moment in her London flat from which she awoke muddy after one of her music-induced illusions, she hadn't known the scenes were physical manifestations. As she was starting to see, Atlas had known long before she did what she could do. *He always believed in me.*

She wanted to approach Atlas, ask him why he was crying, but before she could manage a way toward him, the scene was replaced by a replay of herself hurrying down a dark street in the middle of the night. She tripped on a manhole cover. *This is the night I went to the café in London because I hadn't grocery shopped yet. That's the night I thought I saw someone outside the window.* The scene played on, Breena catching her footing and then stopping for another moment to look around over her shoulder. *I stopped because I heard something.* The view panned to show Atlas, not even a full twenty-four hours before meeting for the first time in the grocery store—which he swore was pure chance, and she believed—standing beside the café trying to stifle a laugh. *He was laughing at me?* That's *the noise I heard on after I tripped on my walk home? And he had the gall to say he wasn't stalking me.* She played at outrage not wanting to romanticize his creepy behavior, but a warm fondness swirled its way further into her chest, a chemical caring.

Atlas stared, rapt, at the first memory in which Breena was able to put a definite face and name to his presence. She turned, startled, with a box of detergent in her hands. In the original moment, he had been too wrapped up in his own visceral reaction to her to notice the impact he had had on her, even before their powerful first touch. She swayed, her eyes searching his. They were hard to read, but the slight forward tilt to her posture indicated she wanted to get closer. He introduced himself, and her expression blanked—almost as if disappointed, like she had expected to remember meeting him somewhere once presented with a name and was saddened to realize she didn't know him. Her proximity suggested she wanted to know.

He watched her pupils dilate as he extended his hand and introduced himself. When they grasped hands, they had both been plunged into a fiery vision that was likely the reason she had pursued knowing him despite her fears and doubts and his awful behavior. It was a terrifying sight, but it compelled them both.

In this memory review, instead of reliving the vision he had when he grasped her hand, he got to watch from outside of them both. While their psyches traveled in a vision of their future, Atlas watched their physical bodies shimmer, not in a glittery way, but as if they were partially phasing out of reality and into another plane. Their expressions were blissful, their grasp tight. They faded in and out of translucence in slow waves. The light radiating from the scene intensified, no doubt in conjunction with the intensity of their shared premonition. When they broke apart, Atlas noticed Breena's hand shaking. She smiled anyway.

Atlas always worried that his love was purely instinctual, like an animal in heat desperate to find a mate before dying off. It didn't stop his attraction or pursuit, but it had been a latent concern in the back of his mind that while Tabitha had been in control of his mind and actions, his heart was ruled by his genes. Now, watching her again, he knew that while genetics did play a part, there had been no reason to fret—at least not over this particular issue.

Atlas' next vision stopped on a moment he remembered with a grin. Breena hadn't been in town long at that point, and Tabitha hadn't given approval for him to meet Breena. The pull was too strong, though, and he went to her apartment to introduce himself. When he arrived, concerns about Tabitha's reaction when she found out—and she always found out—started to worry him, and he decided against knocking on her door. The draw to know her pushed him into the grassy patch in front of the window instead of back to the sidewalk. His theory was to look like he belonged in the yard to avoid suspicions from the neighbors.

Before he could watch the events play out exactly as he remembered, the vision propelled him inside. Breena wore a startled expression and cast her suspicions in the direction of the window. She cursed under her breath and ran to the kitchen where she removed a large chef's knife from a drawer by the sink. The grin he typically wore when reliving this moment of risky excitement faded.

He heard her mumbling about knife laws in London, and she picked up her phone. This was a view of that night he hadn't gotten from the outside. A twinge of guilt squeezed at his gut.

She paced the room a while before settling in for what he thought was the night. Outside, the Atlas who had denied stalking Breena backed away from the window and went home. Inside, Breena's reality of nerves played on.

Breena wrapped an arm around her waist. Her stomach growled. She checked all the windows and doors for movement and shadows then decided she had to get food. Leaving the knife on the island, Bree prepared to go out.

He didn't need to see the rest of this scene. Atlas got the point. Her mistrust of him started early, before she even realized it, and had done little to improve her view of him.

As if the force guiding these memory tours knew he had gotten out of it the intended message, the scene zipped forward to the first day Atlas took Breena to the cottage in the woods. He watched through her eyes the cab ride, the walk through the field, and his recount of his past. He saw, as he told it, what she had seen.

His face was stone—it didn't show the pain he felt when reliving those moments with his father or replaying the events of his first murder. He watched through her eyes as she picked at her fingers and worried at the skin on her lips, trying to reconcile her fear with her desire to comfort him. It was obvious that even from the beginning, she feared him. To an extent, he always knew this, but the shame that washed over him at the realization surprised him. All he wanted back then was to trap her, to have her, and if fear and pity worked, so be it. But her hot and cold reactions to him after London were in response to his own. *Why didn't I see that before?* It hadn't been possible for him to love her *and* hate himself, so what he tried to give her was corrupted, even before Tabitha had reprogrammed him into her service.

Again, a change in scenery confirmed he had learned the desired lesson. Breena sat on her front porch in Michigan still wearing the hospital bracelet from St. Barts. Atlas looked down at it from her eyes. On it, in large letters, was, "Suicide Risk." She picked at it and mumbled, "It isn't like that."

Atlas had only heard bits and pieces of Bree's ordeal from Tabitha. Breena only mentioned it in passing, usually while yelling at him about disappearing on her, leaving her alone to search through their dreams and illusions for him. He put it together—what doctors had called a suicide attempt or accidental overdose, and what other doctors later diagnosed as Sleeping Beauty Syndrome had been her withdrawal from reality. *Not an attempt at death, but at a new life elsewhere.* He believed what he had heard, and he was certain she was looking for him during that time, but as his vision panned to look at Breena during a time when no one had been watching in the original moment, he saw it all for what it was—her desperate attempt at escape from a world that had let her down, and he was a huge part of it. Their relationship was proof she had gotten over her fears of him, and just as her trust was fully given, he broke it. *Of course she hates me. I never tried to make this right.*

The view switched a final time, scrolling quickly through snapshots of each frantic and stupid measure Breena had taken between London and Gehenna, direct results of his poor handling of her heart. Before he came to, he swore he heard a voice telling him to make it work. *You* want *to make it work.*

Bree and Atlas thrust back into consciousness at the same time, completely unaware of the other's visions. Instead, they were aware of the undeniable urge to get closer. With the bars between them little more than dust on the floor, destroyed from the pulse of energy, they ran into each other's arms, the biology at work finally in tandem with their emotions. The new perspectives overpowered Breena's previous protest and Atlas' apathy. They didn't talk about what they saw and, through locked lips, they couldn't have if they wanted to.

Jet paced in Breena's quarters. She had been gone for almost four hours. A page for prison security informed him that something had happened preventing anyone from accessing Atlas' cell block. The page wrote it off saying, "It's only queen stuff, sir," as if it was a standard occurrence, but Jet could feel what was going on down there, not with telepathy—and he was thankful for that—but with enough empathy from his bound service to Breena to make him want to vomit. He understood why Breena wanted to sleep—anything to prevent *this,* which was inevitable according to Itzal—and he wished *he* could at least sleep through it if it was bound to happen anyway.

Just as Jet was about to run down there himself to see if his link to Bree would be of any use in separating them, Breena came through her door, disheveled and refusing to look Jet in the eye.

"What did you *do?*"

She put her palms to her temples, shaking her head, and went to her wardrobe. From it, she pulled a fluffy robe that looked like it was made from the fabric of stuffed animals. Bree swung it over her shoulders, shielding herself from Jet, and undressed from underneath the cover. Then, she tied it closed around herself, turned, and met Jet's glare. "If you already know, don't make me say it."

"I don't understand. You're so against him. You wanted to let him rot down there."

"Yeah."

He threw his hands up, incredulous. She couldn't meet his penetrating stare.

"It's always been like this with him." She looked at her hands, which were vibrating and glowing softly with leftover power from the surge.

"That's a separate issue. You don't just sleep with people because you always have. You don't *love* him!"

"Part of me does still, I guess. And I had no choice. This place. . ."

Jet grit his teeth. He wanted to yell, 'There's always a choice!' but he had felt what she felt and knew of all the purposeful choices she'd made in Gehenna, this wasn't one of them. He tried to move past it. "And what does this mean for your plans to marry?"

"Nothing."

"But if you love him. . ."

"*Nothing.*"

"And your plans to go back to Grayling?"

"I'm still going. In fact, I think it's an even better idea, now. I can't stick to my word if I'm constantly distracted by him. He will always be here, and I will always want him in one way or another."

"Where do we stand?"

"Unchanged."

He laughed, but he wasn't amused. "Maybe *you're* unchanged, but I'm not. I need to get out of this place." Jet shoved his sleeves up to his elbows even though his nerves were making him shiver.

"You know it's not possible."

"Make. It. Happen, or, I swear, I'll kill him."

Breena let the thought hang in the air for a moment. She understood Jet, his anger, his jealousy, but she couldn't do anything about it, and Jet's threat was essentially empty—Atlas was already dead, and so was he. "Go spend some free time. I need to be alone for a while, and I don't have anything to ask of you."

"Better not."

"What was that?"

"I said you'd *better* not ask anything of me right now."

"Go, Jet." *I hate this. I don't know him well enough to handle this the right way. I don't know what he needs from me.* She scrubbed at her face, exhausted. *Why don't you just ask him what he needs?*

Chapter 17

Grey walked through the beaded curtain of the hookah shop and sat at the bar. Jordan was already there, but he felt so awkward and out of place that he took a few moments before surfacing from the clearance section at the back of the store to approach the ocean-haired man he'd contacted earlier in the week. After he finally worked up the nerve to sit down and introduce himself, Jordan jumped right in to his request. "I'd like you to, first, believe what I'm about to say and, second, help me with it."

"I'm an open-minded guy. No worries."

"My girlfriend," the phrase made him stumble and correct, "My *ex*-girlfriend—"

"Ah, say no more."

"Oh, there's more."

Grey nodded, easy and laid back.

The guy was so cool Jordan had already started to hate him a little bit. *This is the kind of guy even attractive guys lose girlfriends and boyfriends to.* He tried to reign it in. "My ex, Breena, is, she has. . . a special heritage. She went back to be with her family, and this guy there, who she used to date—rough relationship, by the way—is destined to marry her. Destined according to their family and social beliefs, anyway. I'm not convinced her future is so set in stone. But, I'm nothing like them. I have no natural talent for the things their family can do, yet she tried to teach me. She saw something in me, or at least I always hoped it was that and not her attempt at making me a better replacement for him. I need to learn more, show this guy up. I don't know if it will win her back, and I'm not even sure that's what I want. All I know is he's a nasty guy and deserves to be humiliated by someone who's less than nothing in his eyes."

"Good deal, man. I get it. I need more history about these people and their abilities. Clearly, he's not, like, a soccer star or a genius or else you wouldn't have asked *me* to be your teacher. So what gives?"

"She's. . . she, uh, she's the queen of Hell?"

"You sure? You don't sound sure."

"She's the queen of Hell." Jordan had never revealed it to anyone, hadn't even let it pass his lips. It sounded preposterous, even after all the evidence he had witnessed in proof of the concept, and he expected more a reaction from Grey.

"And you want to learn. . . ?"

"She and her awful ex can both manipulate reality. They can influence dreams, create illusions, and jump astral planes at will. There's more, I'm sure, but that's what my research has allowed me to name. Naming makes it feel less insane. If other people out there know these things, it must be real in some respects. I'm not crazy. See?" Jordan sparked a small fire in the hookah, which sent green-grey smoke tendrils whisping into the air. He put a finger in the glowing embers and emerged unharmed. "Not real. An illusion."

"You wouldn't be able to do that if you were *nothing* like them."

Jordan wanted to feel heartened at that. He didn't. "But this isn't good enough. Their illusions actually *can* impact the world around it. Theirs would have burned me. She *has* burned me." It hit him with as much clarity as he had ever felt about loving her. "You know, I think I just decided. I *don't* want her back." The announcement sat heavy in his gut. "But, I still need to show him where I stand. Atlas and I have an unfinished argument from a year ago." Grey paled. "I may not ever get to marry her, but neither will he." Jordan noticed the look on Grey's face. "What's wrong?"

"Had a run-in with him when I was a teenager. Strong gift. Sick head."

"So you know why you need to help."

Grey groaned. "Yeah."

"Mind telling me what he did to you?"

"What he did to me? Nah. You mean what I did to him."

****

Tabitha stared into the pit from her bedroom window. Below her, there were no distinct figures, no souls who stood out. It was a fiery crater packed to the brim with generations of used-up chosen and queens dethroned. She grumbled. "You'd think they'd treat us better after what we do for our people." Tabitha did not want to end up down there. Technically, she should have already taken a place in the milling masses. The only reason she hadn't was because Breena had been too preoccupied to notice she hadn't complied with tradition. "Although," she thought aloud, "Breena isn't one for tradition, so maybe I'll benefit from her upheaval of our values."

The possibility that Bree's unconventional methods might be to Tabitha's advantage made her rethink her efforts to dethrone her daughter. "If I have no choice but to accept her as queen, I might as well get something from it. It *would* be easier than revenge." The souls in the pit flared up at the word and she grinned. "But where's the fun in that?"

Atlas paced in his blown-out cell. He could have easily walked out of the prison, but there was no place for him, and he was about as far away from Breena as possible without leaving the royal compound. Distance equaled progress. Although the bone-breaking pains and visions had subsided, relieved by Bree's contact, he assumed they would return shortly.

He sat back against the wall and marveled. *I owe her so much. Apologies aren't good enough. I tried that in the past, before I grasped how she viewed me. No wonder they didn't work. I'm floored by how much I miss her. It's probably just the hormones talking, but is that such a bad thing?*

Atlas started to come around to the idea that giving in to their predestined purposes might be enjoyable. He had wanted it before—even if not for the right reasons. Now, all he wanted was to treat her like the queen she was. He wanted to do things her way, be whatever she happened to need. *Maybe she'll marry me after all.*

****

"No, you don't want to hear about that." Grey swept his long hair into a ponytail.

"I really, really do. You don't know how much trouble this guy has caused me. You say you did something to him? I want to hear every detail." Jordan's eyes sparkled.

"Jordan, man, you need to be careful. He's no one to mess with, and you look like you're having too much fun with this. Trust me, I might have won the last round, but—and no offense here—but it's like you said. You are no match for him. I'll teach you everything I can, but keep in mind that *I* was barely a match for him."

"Sure. You're right." Jordan's calm, sensible response masked the almost rabid desire for retribution building inside. "So? What happened?"

Grey rolled his eyes. "We met at my high school. He was trying to enroll himself—I don't know where his parents were—and the front office lady was giving him a hard time."

Jordan had a hard time envisioning Atlas at a school, especially on his own when presented with the option *not* to attend.

"Atlas was getting real worked up with her, which I could understand to a point. It must be hard trying to advocate for yourself when you're basically living like an orphan. So I went up beside him and tried to tell him to calm down. The receptionist was a sweet, middle-aged woman, no husband, no children. I think she loved her work because she got to be a part of the types of lives she didn't have for herself. Family and that sort of thing."

Jordan nodded. It was all he could do not to break in with a, "Get on with it."

"Atlas starts yelling at the lady, right? And she's so calm about it that it makes him madder. He's going on and on about trying to do the right thing, trying to be responsible even though he's on his own, and that she's preventing him from having a fair shot at a future. Noble-sounding stuff unless you heard how he was saying it and the other choice words he threw around."

"Fair enough."

"Yeah, I can't say I really blame him for being upset, but—and I don't know how he handles things now—back then, he didn't have a grip on his abilities. When his temper flared, so did the illusions. Yeah, you see where I'm going with this. As he's chewing out Ms. Bennett, the room starts to waver. The copy machine behind her bursts into flames, and poor Ms. Bennett passes out. It was probably better off for her, though. As she hits the floor, Atlas unleashes this raging wind. Papers were flying everywhere, Ms. Bennett's skirt flew up around her waist—as if her morning wasn't bad enough—and the doors were pinned shut. Luckily, the three of us were the only ones in there for the whole ordeal. It would have been complicated for anyone else to see, and as much as I hate the guy, he was better off *not* getting arrested. Can't imagine what he would have done to the cops or the jail cell."

"So you stopped him, I'm guessing?"

"Had to. Now, my spiritual connections don't manifest like his. I couldn't counter his illusions with my own calming ones or anything like that. I grabbed him, one hand around his neck, one hand on his shoulder, and shoved him into the wall beside Ms. Bennett's desk. It distracted him enough to cause the chaos to stutter, but then the anger turned on me. I pinned him against the wall and forced my chi into his mind. That's my manifestation, by the way. I can get inside people's minds."

"Which is why people go to you for readings. Good scheme."

"It's no scheme. I'm not just guessing at what's in their thoughts. I can access and visualize them. And that's what I did with Atlas. Boy, is he messed up in there. All I saw was blackness. Every turn I took, trying to find something positive to pull to the surface, to neutralize his anger, there was just more rage. I took a turn down one path and the words "just like my father" scrolled through on repeat. Another turn led me to "killer," and "demon." A quarter of his mind was fixated on not being able to stop his mother's death. That one I felt bad about. It clearly wasn't his fault and yet he blamed himself. In the back of his mind, and I mean the very back, a small light glowed around a name—" Grey paused, knowing Jordan wouldn't want to hear it. "It was the only happiness in there. By this point, the room was a disaster, I was bleeding from some flying thing striking my face, and he was drawing on my energy to make things worse. As much as I wanted to continue exploring his head—I was a little out of control in ways, too, at that age. I had a hard time knowing when to stop digging and manipulating—I had to shut it down before I didn't have the strength remaining. So, I strung a web of my own energy around the parts of his brain that were contributing to his rage, essentially strangling it."

"It must not have worked because grown-up Atlas is just as angry."

"It wasn't permanent. It lasted long enough to stop the destruction, tell him to leave, and get him out of the door. Whether it wore off five minutes later or five days later, he never came back, but

I'm sure he has a hard time ignoring the little message I left behind, even now."

"What message?"

"Just a little calling card, if you will. Every time his rage reaches a certain point, it triggers a memory I implanted. It's fake, and I'm sure he knows it, but he remembers *himself* killing his mother."

"Ouch. Preying on his biggest regret. . ."

"Yeah. It was the only thing I could think of at the time. I figured if he connected that level of anger as the cause of her death, it would deter him from acting like that anymore. I don't know if it worked, but I'm sure he was not happy about the intrusion. I didn't make any effort to hide that I had been in there."

"And what happened to Ms. Bennett?"

"Oh, she was fine. After Atlas left, I went into her mind, too, and erased her memories of the whole thing. If he had come back, I guess I would have let her keep the memories the second time around so that she'd call the cops, but he never did. I was thankful this was before the time of security cameras in the school. No footage to worry about reconciling."

Jordan nodded. "Gotta be honest. This is a lot to take in and, I know you did it for the right reasons, but honestly, you sound as cruel as he does in some ways. Messing with peoples' heads is dangerous. Is that what you would teach me to do since I can't beat him with illusion?"

"I can try. I have no idea whether you'll take to it. Some people go their entire lives never connecting with the side of themselves that allows manifestations of their psyche. I think you're farther ahead than that, but I make no promises. As for being cruel to him, isn't that what you wanted?"

Jordan shifted on his stool, suddenly uncomfortable with his approach to the Atlas issue. *This isn't me. But I can't be a push-over forever.* "Don't let me back out before I've tried it."

"Deal." Grey stood from the bar and stretched. "Alright, well, you text me when you're ready to set a date to start. I've got another client to meet, so I'll be heading out."

"Right. Sorry to keep you so long. I'll talk to you later."

They shook hands and sauntered into the parking lot. Grey got on a bike propped against the front of the building and pedaled off. Jordan watched from his car then drove away. His thoughts bounced around between hesitancy and determination. He had originally intended on going straight home, but he was too restless. He found himself heading down the back roads that took him to his and Breena's park, the one they used to wander after school, where they ate greasy fast food after hours, the one where Breena showed him an illusion for the first time. He hadn't been in so long. It was wrong to go without her, like a big middle finger to their relationship, to the trust she had in him, to his promises made to her. He was OK with that.

Chapter 18

Lilly rose from her nap stiff and sad. She needed to talk to someone, but no one was left. Jordan had gotten so wrapped up in his training with Grey that he rarely called to check in. It didn't help that Breena was firmly in his past. He was functioning off of malice alone. She tried to point this out to him. She even compared him to Atlas, saying that his search for happiness had really been a search for revenge, and that Jordan was doing the same. She thought the comparison would startle him into normalcy, but it didn't. Having a friend liken him to someone he hated so much infuriated him further. They hadn't talked since.

After finishing her cereal, Lilly scrolled through her contacts looking for someone to call. Outside of Breena and Jordan, the numbers on her list might as well have been marked off limits. They were the people who she talked to so infrequently that it would be odd to call them up now just to chat. She tried convincing herself that that's how friendships were started—one person talking, at random, to another. She shook her head. *That's dumb.*

****

Across town, Linda crouched in coveralls at the end of her driveway pulling weeds. The chores at the group home rotated weekly. The menial tasks freed her mind to focus on her "Breena Problem," as she had taken to calling it. Even so, she still hadn't come up with a viable plan to release the building pressure of her bloodlust. Breena's disappearance infuriated her, not only because it prevented direct revenge, but because it seemed to have nothing to do with the riot that broke out at Atlas' apartment. *It would have been so easy if it had. . . .*

Despite the front desk attendant confirming that Breena had used the office phone before going back to Atlas' apartment, the trail was cold. Knowing Tabitha's original plans for Breena, Linda forced herself to accept that Breena must have gone to Gehenna. There was no way to get to her. Linda hated settling. She chucked the lump of weeds and tangled roots she held to the ground. *It has to be the friends, then.*

****

A soft knock echoed through Breena's cavernous chambers. Tabitha came in without an invitation. Breena sat up, throwing the plush covers aside. "Why do I even have a bed if I can't sleep?"

"Sorry to disturb you."

"No you're not."

"You're right, I'm not. I'm here to present a proposition."

Bree moved toward Tabitha with an arm out, guiding her back to the door.

"And, judging by your condition, it would be wise to hear me out."

"What condition?"

"The precarious state you're finding yourself in due to Atlas' presence."

"What could you possibly have to offer me that would help with *that*?" After a day, the pains and flashbacks had returned. A week later and it was grating on Breena nearly to the point of madness. Her mother's hinting piqued Bree's interest, and she was almost uncomfortable enough to admit it.

"I know you don't want to be here. I know Atlas doesn't want to be here. I know Jet doesn't want to be here." Her lips curled into a smug expression that was supposed to be a grin. Instead, it was more of a snicker, menacing as always. "As you know, you can go back easily since your body is alive. Your boys, well, for them it's not so easy, but there is a way. Have you figured out how to do it, yet?"

"No. And you want something from me in exchange for learning how to send them back."

Tabitha shrugged. "A body is a hot commodity around here. You're the only soul who has one."

The fact startled Breena. She knew her gift was unique, but hearing it mentioned like a collector's item made her squirm. *No one's going to come after it, right? No, it's not something people can swap out and put on. It's a body, not a sweater.*

"I can see it in your eyes that you're interested. Plus, I know you better than you give me credit for. You're a sweet girl. Don't know how my own daughter could end up that way, but you are. And sweet girls don't let their boyfriend die. Or, in your case, stay dead."

Facing her guilt, Breena admitted defeat. "So what do I do, and what do you want for it?"

"It's really very simple. You've got to send Lucifer to the pit." Breena's eyes bulged and, seeing her expression, Tabitha clarified. "Well, it's simple in that it's one step. The step itself, not so simple."

"And what will sending him to the pit do?"

"It puts you in his place. Every queen is the successor while she is in power. No queen ever gets to take his place because he's a stubborn old man who won't move on."

"So you understand how I felt when I forced you out."

Tabitha scowled, still not over it. "So forcing him out will allow you to take his place and, with it, comes his powers."

"He has the power to send them back to the living?"

"No, but you will."

"Why? He said he couldn't create what didn't naturally exist here. He can't make a body. Why would I be any different?"

"Because you *have* a body."

"Having a body doesn't tell me how to make a body." She held a hand in front of her, pausing their line of discussion. "I feel like this is going in circles. New question. What good does any of this do for you? I know it's not because you only want me happy."

"If you move up to his position, I get my old throne back."

"How do you figure that?"

"Because you have no heirs of your own."

A lump formed in Breena's throat. *I know where this is going. She's telling me that my options are to either marry and create an heir or have her on the throne again. If I don't overtake Luce, we're stuck here, miserable, trying to resist one another. If I do overtake Luce, resisting Atlas means she is queen again. If I marry Atlas and have a child, I don't have to worry about her, but I've compromised all my plans. She thinks I'd rather go back on my word than have her as queen, and she's counting on this awful biology to drive us out of Gehenna so she can get her throne back.*

"Oh, and did I mention you could only do it once?"

"Do what once?"

"Make a body. You'll have to choose who gets to live again."

"That's ridiculous. Why wouldn't I be able to do it for both of them?" Breena held the door open, willing the conversation to draw to an end.

"You only have one body to draw from. I must have forgotten to tell you that you'll be draining your power by half when you make a body from your own. If you make a body for both of them, *your body will die.*"

Bree squeezed her head between her hands. "I need you to go now."

Tabitha leaned forward like she wanted a hug, but Breena couldn't accept any motherly kindness from her. Bree ushered her into the hall then went back into her room and put her feet into a pair of slippers. *How would she even know that if no one else has ever had a physical body here? She just wants me to agree to her plan and let her back in. Then, when I find out it's not possible, she'll refuse to leave the throne and, because I don't have an heir, I'll have no way to force her out. I'll have to wait 'til she dies. No, she's already dead. Until she goes to the pit, at least, or fades out of existence. Judging by Luce, that might be a long, long time.*

Drawn back into her robe, she padded down the long corridor away from her room. She ended up in a large, domed space that reminded her of a planetarium. *She's going through a lot of trouble to force me into deciding that marrying Atlas and having an heir is the best path. She can't be doing it just for tradition's sake, and marrying him doesn't get her throne back. There has to be some other pay-off for her in my choosing that option. Or she wants to see my plans fail that badly.* When the massive stone door slid closed behind her, the dimly glowing room plunged into darkness and the lights of thousands of stars illuminated.

Why would there be a planetarium in Hell? The stone, half-sphere ceiling was pocked with little holes letting the light through, from the highest point of its arch to the straighter edges that met the floor. She put a finger tentatively into one of the holes to try and feel the light-source at the other side. Her finger didn't reach. *Nothing here has lightbulbs.* She marveled.

The room was so still and quiet it almost made her anxious. Other than sight, she was in near-total sensory deprivation. *People pay money for these kinds of experiences back home.* The thought came in Lilly's voice. Since the ceremony had passed and freed up some room for thought, Lil crossed her mind a few times a day, Bree hearing her familiar words of caution and encouragement as if she was in the room. She remembered Lilly telling her about an at-home sensory deprivation tank that some people used to soothe anxiety. She had suggested it to Breena after she got sober saying that if a doctor prescribed it as a way to prevent relapse, insurance might pay for it.

She stared at the stars above her. *I should pretend Tabitha never came to see me and just go back home for a visit.* The idea settled over Breena, and her spirits started to lift. Then, another thought interrupted, crushing the small relief under more guilt. *Visiting might be more harmful to my friends than my death was. If they think I'm gone, and they've done their mourning, how traumatic would it be if I showed up at their doors?*

Her oath as queen, to put her people first even at her own expense, didn't apply to her friends and family from her former life, but the responsibility of ruling had renewed her sense of duty to finally start doing right by others. Her friends were her family, more so than the countless strangers she governed in Gehenna ever could be, and she thought it only right to continue punishing herself rather than risking what might feel like punishment for them. *I need someone to talk to. I have no idea if I'm making the right choices.*

Her next thought she knew was foolish, but she went with it. Replacing parts of the sky view around her with the clearing from her and Atlas' pasts, she relaxed against the same tree he had always lounged on. Breena's nerves weren't on edge here like they used to be. She figured it was because there were no more mysteries to the place. Atlas wasn't a nameless figure in the background, nor was he a furious menace. Her anxieties didn't manifest into any other ugliness now that she had control over her gifts. Tabitha wasn't lurking in dove form, listening in on her confessions or praying on her naïveté.

The stars of the physical room peeked through the illusion-engineered clouds and tree canopy above. The air turned cold and crisp. Breena exhaled, watching the steam of her breath swirl then dissipate. She talked through her problems out loud as she had done so many times before.

After about fifteen minutes, she started to shiver. Bree added a campfire to the center of the clearing and scooted closer, forming a checkered blanket under her. Mesmerized by the popping fire, her thoughts slowed. All but one fell away. *I'm lonely.*

The illusion wavered as the light in the room around it shifted. Breena turned toward the door to see what had caused the disruption. She expected to see nothing, thinking that her skills were still weak from going unused for so long. Jet was leaning against the wall by the door taking in the surroundings.

They hadn't spoken in a week, not since the day Breena and Atlas had experienced their *Allurement.* Itzal told Jet not to use the term in mixed company, that it was a euphemism that many thought cheapened the special experience only a chosen and a queen got to have. The common people dreamed of having that kind of encounter, he said, and most of them revered it as a ceremonial moment. In most instances, Jet learned, it *was* a ceremonial moment that occurred officially and directly after a wedding. It wasn't supposed to be some haphazard, dangerous, inelegant romp on a prison floor. Word had gotten around as soon as the prison guards changed shifts that night, and there were hundreds of scandalized Gehennans. Jet had made sure to apprise her of the fact before resuming his silent treatment.

Is he going to say anything? Do I say something? He's the one who stormed out on me. He has to break the ice. But I'm the one who did the hurting, so maybe I need to apologize first.

She waffled on the decision too long, and Jet spoke while craning his neck to regard the evergreens looming above them. "So this is the place you met him? Hate to say it, but it's pretty. Were you hoping he'd show up?"

She shook her head.

"Then why relive it?"

"Just lonely."

"I have something to say to you, and I need you to listen because I care about you, and I want to help you."

Bree nodded.

"Just because you don't need saving doesn't mean you have to be alone. You can let people love you. You can love them. It's not a weakness."

"No. I was weak before, letting feelings get in the way of good decision-making, relying on pills and sleep to fix the way I felt. I have to do this myself."

"I'm not telling you not to take responsibility. I'm telling you that refusing all support is also a weakness. There's a balance, and you have to find it. You're a queen now, a leader. You have an entire race to support. Doing that alone, letting them lean on only you, might look impressive at first, while it's working, but when you break, they will fall on top of you, crush you. You'll look foolish, or worse, you'll look like you thought so much of yourself that you were flawless on your own. It takes a team to make something difficult appear effortless. Your team gets to see you when you're at your worst, when it's not effortless, when you're a mess and falling apart. I am your team and, if it's necessary, Atlas is your team. I'll deal with it. I'm supposed to make you your best. If he's part of that, I'm still in."

"I don't know what to say."

He waved her words away.

"There's something you need to know." She patted the space beside her and he pushed off the wall to sit next to her. Breena filled Jet in on the discussion with Tabitha. As soon as she finished explaining, he jumped in.

"Leave me here."

"I don't... what?"

"If you're going to go through with tossing Luce, which is another issue and game plan all together, leave me here. Give Atlas the body."

Breena couldn't believe what she was hearing.

"We're supposed to do what's best for the most people, right? Well, leaving him here is not the best for the most people. You come first, and you don't want to marry him or have his kids. If you don't do that, and if he remains here, you're going to continue to feel this compulsion to make it happen. I can see and feel what it's doing to you, and it's only been a couple weeks."

"Did you realize it's been a month?"

Jet blinked a few times then hummed. "A month, huh? Well, imagine feeling like this forever. I know you're strong, but can you do it?"

"No."

"So you have to send him back. My presence here doesn't affect you, and I'd have to come back here with you every time even if I had a body. It doesn't matter what I want anymore. This is where I have to be."

She put her head on his shoulder and continued staring into the fire. "I know that's supposed to sound sweet and noble, and it does, but it makes me feel like a sack of crap."

He covered her hand and placed it on the knee his chin wasn't resting on. "Don't. This is what I can do to help you. I'm your team, remember? You don't have to make a plan that helps everybody. You said it yourself. I'm not part of everybody, now."

"You are to me. I'm responsible for you and—"

"*I'm* responsible for me."

"Yes, but I'm responsible for your life. Tabitha said, 'sweet girls don't let their boyfriends die,' or something like that and she was right!"

Jet pulled away from Breena so he could look her in the face. "Sweet girls don't let who die?"

"Boyfriends."

"I'm your boyfriend?"

"I'm a sweet girl?"

"I said, 'I'm your boyfriend?'"

"Uh, well, I mean. . ." she flushed, but she couldn't blame it on the fire. "I thought about it. Before I got taken, I thought about it. The canoe ride was fun. The kiss was. . . fun. And when I got away from Atlas, I called you, not my other friends."

He smirked, proud.

"Don't let it go to your head. I'm sure Tabitha meant Atlas."

"Why'd you have to ruin the moment mentioning him?"

"Just being honest. And you should know that despite the things that have happened with him since we got here, my thoughts about you haven't changed. I know I was adamant that I wouldn't be with either of you, and I meant it when I said it. I didn't stick with it, but I felt powerless to stay away from him. But, what you told me earlier did get through. I don't have to be alone to prove I'm not using anyone to save me. If you can deal with him being a potential part of my life, maybe we can work on this."

Jet couldn't help but cringe. It was not his idea of an ideal relationship. "I'll do my best. No promises."

"I agree. No promises that nothing else will happen with him. But, if it doesn't?"

"I don't want to be your second choice. Isn't that what you did to Jordan?"

Breena's eyebrows shot up. "How did you know that?"

"We went to a fairly small school, Bree. Things got around. I want to be your first choice. Only choice, really, but if he's going to be around, he's got to be second."

"OK."

"OK? You're agreeing just like that?"

"Jet, I didn't come here to be with him. I didn't have any intention on ever being with him again after London. And here, it was largely out of my control. I plan to fight as hard as I can."

"What about all that love and attachment you felt the other night?"

She put her hands on her hot cheeks.

"Yes, I felt all of it."

"Sorry it had an impact on you. I won't lie and say it wasn't real."

"Don't worry about it. We'll work it out."

Chapter 19

Tabitha left Atlas' cell satisfied with the seeds of conflict she had sewn with Breena and her chosen. Although she no longer had any sway over Atlas, she successfully reasoned with him, convincing him that the moment he and Breena had shared a week earlier was just the start of a slippery slope. He was having withdrawal-like symptoms, so it wasn't a hard case to make. She assured him that Breena was working toward getting him back to the living world, and that all Breena needed from him was his love. Since experiencing Breena's past, his determination to repair their relationship overflowed, and he subscribed to Tabitha's plan without hesitation.

Three levels higher and at the other end of the royal compound, Jet and Breena had turned their encounter in the star-filled room into a date. Breena dissolved the grassy dell and replaced it with a frozen pond. She materialized ice skates on both of their feet and pulled a reluctant Jet into the center of the ring.

"I worried that I'd moved on you too fast after the canoe ride."

"Sorry I didn't call. I was a little tied up."

"That's not funny."

"Then why're you smiling."

"It's only funny because you're OK, now."

"I wanted to call. I wanted to call as soon as I got back that night. Jordan was hounding me about where I had been; he shoved his way into my room and demanded answers. I was fuzzy from the pills—I took some in the car then fell asleep before going home—and he was standing close to me. Everything hurt. I was tired of fighting him, tired of missing him. You don't need to hear all of this. Sorry. All I was getting at is that I wanted to call you, but I couldn't handle my emotions. I was worried by how I felt about you because I had done the too much too soon thing before."

Jet struggled to a stop, tottered around to face her, and cupped her cheek. "You don't have to explain. I wasn't trying to make you feel bad for not calling. I'm glad to know you wanted to, but I wasn't expecting a call so soon, and you couldn't help what happened in the days after."

She exhaled, the fun kind of nerves and butterflies filling her up. It was a welcome sensation, a diversion from the stabs of longing shooting through her chest. Her genes screamed for Atlas, but Jet held her focus, his dark eyes glinting under the twinkling stars. "Thank you for forgiving me. I know I'm not easy to handle. I understand why you reacted the way you did."

He pulled her close by the waist, both of them gliding in their skates to meet in the middle, and he kissed her once on the forehead and then once on the lips. Jet pulled away to look at her, but she followed his retreat, kissing him again, this time with clear purpose. Their mouths didn't need words for the conversation they were having.

Atlas writhed on the floor of his cell. His body revolted at the perceived assault. It didn't matter to his instincts that Jet and Breena were trying to build a relationship. It didn't matter to his demanding genes that Breena sought Jet out. His body only knew that someone stood in the way of his bloodline's survival. He would have charged out of the still-defunct cell and found them if he could move from the floor, but his vision was red and he couldn't take in a full breath. It was so much more debilitating than rage. It was the physical manifestation of heartbreak.

A guard peered around the edge of his cell, curious about the swishing noises he heard. He saw Atlas attempting to crawl toward the hallway and failing. It was a pathetic sight, something no Gehennan should have to see their queen's chosen do. The guard took pity on Atlas, empathizing with the man because he had recently been dumped.

The guard hoisted Atlas over his shoulder and made for the exit of the prison sector of the compound. They got in a glass elevator. Atlas' upside down view of the pit shrank as they rose. When they reached the top level of the compound, Atlas' pain started to ease. He was closer to her, and his body knew it.

"Can you walk?"

Atlas nodded and the guard put him down.

"Want me to help you find her?"

"I'll know the way. Why did you help me?"

"I'm a traditional guy. Short of rejecting her rule, this is the only way I can protest her new ways. My boss isn't so fond of her yet, either, so he won't punish me."

"Breena might."

"If she wants to, so be it. I won't be the man who stood around and watched this happen to you without making an attempt at setting things right. She's going to break our society if this keeps up."

Atlas was thankful for the guard's actions and admired his enthusiasm, but he just wanted the man to stop talking so he could follow the pull in his chest toward Breena's location. When the guard stepped back into the elevator, Atlas began his stumbling search down the corridor to the observatory.

The closer he got, the more his individual emotions surfaced. In the absence of blinding discomfort, he noticed the jealousy, desire, and urgency propelling him.

Breena stopped short in front of Jet, sending him to the ice.

"Oh come on! I was finally skating."

She stood frozen in place, startled at the sudden absence of aches. "Jet. Jet, get up, quick."

Just then, Atlas burst into the room, face alight with triumph. There was a sinister glint underneath. Jet put his hands out in front of him, an instinctual attempt at subduing Atlas.

As Atlas went through the door, Jet inched his clumsy way in front of Breena. It was all Atlas could do not to snarl at him, the vicious urge to claim and protect her at its peak. He kept his mouth shut, grin tight, strained, and approached the pair as calmly as he could.

"Breena, I need to talk to you."

"How'd you get here?"

"A guard helped me. I think he thought I was dying—the distance, it was too much."

Bree stepped out from behind Jet's rigid figure. "OK, let's talk." She gestured toward the bench by the door and skated over. Atlas sat next to her and opened his mouth, but she interrupted. "Oh, do you want skates?"

Jet put a hand over his face. "Ugh. You're kidding."

Breena shot a look at Jet. "Remember what you told me earlier."

He rolled his eyes, more at himself than at her. "I know. I'm trying."

She turned back to Atlas. "So? Want to skate with us?"

Atlas was looking at her with a glazed-over, disbelieving expression. His mouth hung slightly open. "For once, I think I echo his thoughts." He nodded toward Jet with his chin. "I came to talk to *you*." After a moment with no response of concession from Breena, he added, "About us."

"Yes, but Jet is my council. Anything you want to suggest or arrange between us will get run past him before I decide." *That will help me know it's a choice and not a reaction.* "It's easier if we all," she glanced back at Jet, "suck it up and work together on this."

Atlas smirked. "Like a threesome?"

Breena drew back from him, appalled. "That is not what I meant, and you know it. And, if this conversation wasn't so necessary, I'd be sending you straight back down to your cell, painful or not."

Jet skated over and sat on the other side of Breena. She was getting used to being in the middle, but used to something and OK with something were different states. "I don't want to be the reason you two tolerate each other. I think it would be a lot easier if you both found something mutually beneficial to bond over."

Atlas scoffed. "Bond? With the help?"

She elbowed him in the side. "He's not the help, and, also, who cares if he was? I'm not running this place like the medieval times. More like the dinner-and-a-show Medieval Times. Ranks are for job purposes only, not for defining someone's worth or humanity."

"I think we spent too long with humanity," Atlas challenged. "You have to look at this as a different world. We *aren't* fully human, and you can't treat this like we are. There are different needs here, and your rejection of tradition gets in the way of fulfilling those needs. So tell me what you're going to do about our predicament. Or, should I say *your* predicament, because honestly, I've changed my mind about us. I want to be with you, and you're the only one getting in the way of a solution."

Jet couldn't believe what he was hearing. "What, so I finally get an in with her and you decide you want her back? It doesn't work like that."

They had started to lean across Breena to get in each other's faces, and she put an arm across both their chests to hold them back. "Guys, I'll decide how this works. And Atlas," she turned to look at him, "you need to know, I've chosen to see where things go with Jet."

Atlas balled his fists. "What about. . ." He looked over at Jet for a flash and could tell he already knew. "I don't want it to be over."

Breena looked him in the eyes, unblinking. "Exactly. *You* don't want it to be over." She paused to let it click. "It needs to be. For way too long I've based all of my decisions around you in some way. For once, I want to date someone because I really want to get to know them, not just because I'm trying to fix what you broke," he shrank back at the words, "or what *I* broke trying to get over you."

Atlas crossed his arms over his chest, blocking out her message. "It's never going to work."

"Thanks for the support, man." Jet shook his head.

"Jet, I may not like you, but I want her to be happy. I didn't mean your relationship isn't going to work, although I honestly hope it doesn't. I meant that it won't work for me and Bree to try to stay away from each other. I don't think it's actually killing us, but it feels like it's killing us."

"She hasn't mentioned it feeling—" Jet stopped short when he noticed Breena nodding along, agreeing with Atlas.

"And that's why I have to leave."

Atlas put a hand on her knee. Jet visibly flared. Atlas removed it. "Please reconsider."

Breena begged Jet with her eyes to back her up. He knew about Tabitha's manipulations, but he couldn't step in for Bree. Despite her desires, he doubted that leaving, that ousting Lucifer and the other things that would have to happen before she could get out, would change anything. He worried that by the time she'd accomplished those prerequisites, she and Atlas would already have given in. *I barely have her and I already feel like I'm going to lose her.* He gave her a sad smile.

Neither Atlas nor Breena wanted to mention to one another that Tabitha had approached them, Bree not wanting to get Atlas' hopes up about returning to his life, and Atlas fully aware that any mention of her mother's influence would send Breena running from his suggestions. Neither knew how to proceed without letting on, and the room fell into a heavy silence.

Finally, Jet stood, wrapping a hand gently around the back of Breena's neck and locking gazes with her. "I'm comfortable with where we stand, and I want you to make your choices because they fit your goals. You guys need to talk alone. Don't worry about me as you decide how to go forward. I'll be in your quarters when you're done, Bree."

The trust meant everything to her, but she still worried any choices made without him wouldn't be real choices, but predestined inevitabilities. She stood and gave him a sweet kiss on the lips, both to let Jet know she appreciated the space and to make a statement to Atlas.

When they were alone, Atlas reached a hand through the illusion of ice and broke it down. "It's freezing in here." Breena was miffed at his presumptuousness, but waited to see what he was going to do next. In its place, Atlas erected the chapel he had built for Breena in the clearing.

As soon as it formed around them, she swiped her hand across the door like she was erasing a white board, clearing the scene. "No. We can't go back there."

He nodded, hurt, but understanding. "Need to make new memories."

"Right." Breena, first at a loss at what to replace the chapel with, pointed to the far side of the room. A wall with a window popped up. From it, an adjoining wall to the left formed, with a closet door, a dresser, and then another closed door. Behind them, two other walls rose, and she populated the interior of the room with the contents of her bedroom in Grayling.

"I'm surprised you'd have me here. If things go poorly, it will ruin your own home for you."

She laughed. "Hate to break it to you, but that kind of already happened. Had a lot of desperate moments in this room, but, I'm homesick, and you've never actually been in my room, so. . ."

"I'm actually a little nervous."

"Because you're in my room?"

"Mhm."

"Huh. Well, sit. We have to talk, anyway."

Atlas looked around himself not wanting to assume she meant for him to sit on the bed. He pulled the desk chair into the middle of the room and faced her. "Breena, I think we should get married."

"Jumping right in. OK."

"OK?"

"No! Not, 'OK, I'll marry you.' OK, we're jumping right in."

"So you won't, then."

"You're getting ahead of yourself, as usual. At least make your case for getting married. Other than our little relapse the other day, nothing has changed."

"Did you see stuff while you were passed out?"

She nodded.

"That's what changed. It changed *me*."

I've heard that before. . . "What did you see?"

"All the shitty things I did to you. How much you needed me to be honest and present. I can't make up for what I did after Tabitha got to me, but I can make up for scaring you and deceiving you and enabling you to run from your life." *But only if you tell her about Tabitha.* "And it starts right now. I need to tell you that Tabitha came to me earlier." He expected a severe reaction from Breena, but she waited for him to continue without expression. "She wanted me to try to get back together with you. I guess it's the only part of her former plan that's still possible, having her daughter home and with her chosen, but believe me, she's not the reason I decided to speak to you. I've wanted to since the visions. I'd like to think her motivations were as simple as that, but she's definitely up to something."

Breena waited to make sure he was done before taking a deep breath and admitting that Tabitha had visited her as well. "I know exactly what she's up to."

They spent the next hour discussing what Tabitha had proposed—that she either got rid of Luce, took his place and his power, and went home with Atlas in tow leaving her to rule, or Bree got together with Atlas and had an heir. "She thinks I'd rather go back on my word and my plans to keep her off the throne than to allow her to rule again."

"And?"

"And she's right." Atlas' face lit up.

"I wonder why *she* doesn't try to overthrow Luce and get her body back."

"Oh, I actually have *that* answer. I'm the only one who can do it because I'm the only one here with an actual, biological body that was born here and returned without having died on Earth first. She's damaged. Her biological body was killed and she lacks Luce's power to possess. She lost her shot."

"So being queen again is the most she can do for herself in terms of power."

"Exactly."

"We can't let her back on the throne. Are you prepared to stay here to prevent it?"

Breena smoothed the wrinkles in the illusory comforter around her. *Doing what's best for everyone before myself.*

"You know she'll make a move for it if you go back home for a visit."

"Atlas, I miss my friends. I. . ." She wanted to say that she needed to see them, tell them she was OK, that they could stop searching for her. She wanted to tell him she needed to visit her mom, sleep in her own bed, sleep at all. But she didn't want to cry. "My options suck. No offense."

Chapter 20

Rays of sunlight through Leigh's kitchen window illuminated the haze of smoke spilling from the bundle of sage in Grey's hand. He waved the smoldering herbs with methodical purpose around the doorways to her laundry room, back porch, and all of the windows. Backtracking into the kitchen again, Leigh wiped at her eyes.

"Powerful experience, isn't it?"

"Huh?" Leigh stopped following him as he went into the small living room. "Oh, no I'm not crying. It's the smoke. Allergies."

"Oh, sorry. I thought you knew how this was done."

"It's nothing. Continue."

"I'm done with the cleansing, but I'll need to ward the house, too. A pure environment is no use if it doesn't stay that way."

"Of course." Leigh stepped back to let Grey continue with whatever it was he had started doing with his hands. There were moments such as this one where the whole of her experiences seemed so ridiculous that she almost didn't believe herself. *Maybe I should just go back into therapy.* She thought of Shianne. *Poor kid.*

Grey wandered down the hall to Leigh's bedroom mumbling something about needing to protect her sanctum. She rolled her eyes. *Can't believe I'm paying this guy.*

"So tell me, Leigh. How do you think this evil got to you? Most people who call me are having hauntings or nightmares, not possessions."

"I can't be certain. . ." Leigh's reticence to share her run-ins with Atlas and The Disorder came not out of embarrassment about getting suckered into following him for a bit, but that she had had to call the suicide hotline in the first place. Her family still didn't know about the state she was in at that time. To them, mental illness was unacceptable, an excuse. Remembering something Shianne said— that acting out of shame empowers the people who do the shaming—Leigh took a deep breath and admitted to her situation and the events that led up to Lucifer's intrusion.

Though Leigh didn't know it was Luce, per se, or that Atlas had a direct line to Hell, she had been able to feel the immense power of the being who consumed her. "I can only assume that this guy at the hotline, Atlas," Grey groaned, but Leigh kept talking, "who was also going by the name Reid Case—was worse than I thought, and that he had some enemies—entities—out there who wanted revenge on him worse than I did. I made the perfect target."

Grey nodded his slow, thoughtful nod and looked around Leigh's room. His ears rang, the silence mixing in with the shouting of his conscience arguing with itself: "Run," "Fight," "Run," "Fight." She crossed her arms over her chest covering the exposure that came from having a man in her personal space. No one had ever been in her room. Grey tapped his chin then startled the silence. "'Ya know, I can make your protections much stronger if I can imbue them with specific tasks and purpose. Instead of making a blanket ward that keeps out all entities—the disadvantage of that being some entities are harmless, even benevolent—I can program it to keep out all with mal-intent, *especially* those who have harmed you already. You're sure it wasn't Atlas possessing you?"

"Oh yeah. He was rotten, but nowhere near as powerful. And, like I said, this thing wanted me to catch Atlas as badly as I did. It couldn't have been Atlas going after himself."

"Right, right."

"Besides, you don't need to worry about warding off Atlas. He's dead."

Grey's cool demeanor melted off at the heat of his outraged explosion. "What?"

"They found his body in that burnt-out apartment from The Disorder riots a month ago. It was all over the news."

"That kid didn't tell me he was *dead.* How am I supposed to work with that?"

"Excuse me, what? What kid?"

"Another client wants me to teach him a way to show Atlas up. He failed to mention he was dead."

"Maybe he didn't know."

"Maybe he wanted to show him up on *Atlas' turf.*" Grey swung a dreadlock out of his face. "His anger has made him reckless. Sounds like that's what happened to you, too."

"You're probably right. Thanks for your time."

Leigh paid Grey, locked the door behind him, and stood in her living room, considering. She looked around her home trying to see if anything was different. She worried if Grey had done anything at all, or if she had just paid a stranger to fill her house with acrid smoke, lay hands on some of the walls with his eyes closed, and leave. She looked at her aloe plant, which she talked to as if it was a pet. "And if it never happens again, I still won't know if it's because that guy knows what he's doing or because it was never going to happen again anyway."

****

Across town, Jordan sat with Lilly in a diner. Lilly couldn't tolerate the silence of her room, or any room without Jordan and Breena, and had given him a call. His guilt got the best of him and he agreed to meet her.

"Can I practice on you?" Jordan dodged Lilly's questions about Breena—if he had heard from her, and how he was holding up—with his own. Grey started Jordan off with two simple lessons: visualizing the mind and influencing its thoughts. He hadn't promised Jordan would be capable of getting much farther, but he swore anyone could learn persuasion. Jordan waited for an answer from Lilly, whose straight-set mouth and narrowed eyes already answered him.

"Jordan, Atlas is dead. We lost this one."

The comment flew straight over his head, which he was shaking vigorously.

"He *is.*"

"I know that, but don't you think he'll come back?"

"How would he do that? You're just hoping he will because you know if you acknowledge that *he* can't come back, neither can Breena."

Jordan scrubbed his face. Lilly was right, but he couldn't bring himself to tell her that. "There was no body, Lilly. Breena's body wasn't there! Don't know where she went, but she's not dead."

Lilly reached for his shaking hands. "That might be true. She's got a collection of near-death experiences under her belt. But, Jordan, there *was* a body for Atlas, and I just don't see how any amount of training will help you get back at him. He's dead and very likely in Hell. Isn't that punishment enough?"

"They're not like us. Maybe death isn't permanent for them. Maybe Hell isn't *punishment* for them. It's home."

A sad grin spread across her face, but it didn't reach her eyes, which were full of pity. "Jordan."

This is why I didn't want to see you. I need my denial just a little while longer. He wouldn't look up at her.

"I never told you this," she stared out the window wondering if it was the right tactic, not for cheering him up, but for commiserating. "I was in love with her, too."

This got his attention, and his head snapped back up. It was Lilly's turn to avoid a hard gaze.

"Then how the hell are you taking this so well?"

"She was never mine. Makes it a little easier to accept. Can't lose what you didn't have to begin with. But, don't mistake this for handling anything well. She was still my best friend, and I can mourn the loss of that. I'm miserable."

"I don't think I really ever had her, either. Should just get on with life."

"Don't say that. I think you saved her life—starting when you said 'hi' in kindergarten and again when she woke up from her overdose."

"If I'd gone looking for her right away I could have saved her again."

"Don't do that to yourself. You know she had a bigger purpose. I'm starting to think this would have happened at some point no matter what we did."

"That does not help."

"I'm trying."

By the time Jordan got back home, he had four voice mails from Grey. They ranged from easy prodding about Atlas' death to annoyance that he would leave out that fact, to outright anger because he thought Jordan wanted to take drastic action to go directly to Atlas with his new skills.

Jordan couldn't muster the energy to call him back; instead, he lay atop his sheets and unfolded clothes to stare at the ceiling.

Jordan imagined it cracked and splintering away to reveal the sky outside. In his daydream, the earth would spin itself around so he could face the sun, and he would simply dissolve, immediately and painlessly, under its heat. *She was so good at what she did. I actually believed she was real.*

****

After their discussion, Breena sent Atlas to a room down the hall from hers. He was confined to quarters until his hearing, which she still hadn't decided to carry out. Between the physical relief their proximity brought and the fact that the prison guards didn't respect her choice to punish her chosen, it made more sense to keep him where she could watch him.

Atlas milled around the perimeter of his room. He was grateful to be closer to Breena, and the set up was more comfortable—a sofa, bed, lights that turned *off* rather than the constant blinding brightness of the prison, and a wardrobe full of clean clothes. Despite his improved situation, Atlas lamented to himself. *Even though the shattering sensation in my bones is gone, it's almost more difficult to be so close. In the cell, I could shut out the world and handle the pain with meditation. Here, three rooms away from her, I feel more restricted than before. She should have just put me in her room if she really wanted to punish me. That close with no contact? It would be worse than this.*

He sat on the plush leather couch, but it didn't last long. *I wonder if I can still project here.* He hadn't tried since dying, the burning drive of his body too high-strung to get anything else accomplished. Atlas got to the floor and folded his legs. With eyes closed, he tried to push his spirit outward to look in on what Breena was doing. Two things dawned on him: he couldn't project out of body because he no longer had one—instead, his entire constitution, the physical manifestation of his soul started to shift planes—and, he should ask to join Breena rather than looking in on her. It was one of the many options he had for improving her opinion of him. As hard as he denied it when they met, he *had* stalked her, and it couldn't continue.

He went to his door and peeked out thinking there would be a guard. Seeing no one, Atlas ventured a foot into the hallway. *I guess she expected me to stay confined to quarters on my own honor. She's testing me.*

Not wanting to blow his first test, he went back to his door and shouted down the hall. "Hey, Breena! You around?" He waited for a reply or footsteps but heard none. "Bree? Or a guard?" *Now what?*

"So what did you decide?" Jet was playing solitaire on the floor of Breena's room. It was the only thing he could think to do without sleep and without his queen. Gehenna didn't offer the variety of recreation his human life had. He even missed his job at the canoe-rental booth. *A little.*

"You know what I noticed here? Not only does my body not need to rest, but it doesn't need pills. I haven't felt any withdrawal symptoms, not even the desire to take something in the first place."

"That's great, but you're avoiding."

"Because I don't have an answer. We really didn't decide anything. My relationship with him is as in the air as ours." Jet scrunched his face. "I know it's not ideal."

"Peachy."

She sat beside him. He warmed. "Deal me in?"

"To solitaire?"

Breena gave him a blank look, mildly offended that he didn't want to play with her.

"It's a one-person game, babe."

She flushed, first at the nickname and then at her ignorance.

"You've really never played?"

"Until the last year, all of my free time was spent practicing the cello. It wasn't 'til I went away last summer that I let go of that dream. Since then, there's been a lot of drama." She gestured around herself. "Obviously. I never really learned how to fill my spare time."

Bree could hear Atlas calling from down the hall. "Why doesn't he just come knock on the door?"

Jet stretched and moved up to the bed. "He's trying to impress you."

Breena followed. "I *guess* it's working. . . he's not one to acknowledge rules."

"Aren't you glad he is? You don't look impressed."

"To be honest, I was hoping he'd give me a reason to throw him back in the prison. If he continues to prove he's changed, it's going to make our decisions so much harder."

Everything in Breena wanted to prove her doubters wrong— prove she didn't need, and more so, didn't *want* a husband; prove having a chosen didn't mean she had to choose him; prove she wasn't too good for a servant-class man and that he wasn't too lowly for her. She put a hand on Jet's knee. "I *want you.* I don't want the memories I have. I don't want to want him *despite* those memories and what he's done."

"But?"

"But, maybe the whole chosen thing is 'the way things are' for a reason."

While Jet had waited for Breena to finish up with Atlas, he made up his mind to ignore all of his feelings and hopes regarding Breena. His heart couldn't take any more of the hot and cold, the with-him-not-with-him. The emotions that managed to bubble through were popped on sight.

He looked down at Breena's hand on his knee. They sat shoulder to shoulder against the side of her bed. The urge to take her hand was strong, but he resisted, insisting to himself that only after she had a plan she could stick to would he act on his desires. He inched away from her body, the broken contact easing the ache in his chest.

She noticed and pulled away another inch in the opposite direction. "I know this is hard on you. Don't think your patience and understanding has gone unnoticed. I appreciate you."

He flushed, hoping she couldn't see it.

"If I got rid of him right now, for good, what would you do?"

Jet chuckled and stretched his legs out in front of him, leaning back on his forearms.

"You don't want to tell me? It's your chance to convince me you're the answer." She knew she shouldn't bait him, prodding at the little restraint he had. *But I'm so sick of restraint. Everything we've said and done since coming here has been restrained, measured, calculated.* "And if I chose him?"

"Nothing would change from how it is right now."

"And I can't choose both?"

"You know you can't." He pushed the strands of crimson hair at her temple behind her ear. "I mean, you're the queen, you can do anything you want. But you shouldn't. You can't keep us both on a tether, constantly doubting your intentions and commitment."

"I know." She took a deep breath. "I know." Just as Breena stood up, a spell of dizziness washed over her and she fell back against the edge of the bed. She pressed her hands to her eyes and blinked as she pulled them away. It didn't help much, and she eased herself onto her back.

"You OK?"

"Just stood up too quick. It'll pass."

He eyed her, skeptical. "You look pale."

"You've met me before, right? I'm always pale next to you."

"Sorry. Pale was the wrong word. You look like toothpaste—you know, white and slightly shiny." He felt her forehead then pulled his hand away with a grimace. "You're sweaty."

"Oh, you're making it into a big deal. I'm find."

"Find?"

"*Fine.*" Bree hung her legs over the edge of the bed, sitting up with her eyes closed to prevent another spell. Once on her feet, she tested her balance by looking around the room, leaning to the left and then the right, and turning back to face Jet. "See? Fine-*nn.*"

"Where are you going?"

"To get something to eat."

"Breena, what are you talking about? There's no food here, and your body doesn't need it anyway."

"It really is hell, isn't it?" Bree gave him a wry smile. "I miss snacking. There's nothing to do! What do people do if they don't eat or sleep?"

"Well, I don't know about what queens spend time on, but probably making decrees and sending people to the guillotine."

"Ha. Ha. I mean it, though. What do I do now?"

"You could make a messy example out of the guard who let Atlas out. . ."

"I'm not Erzsébet Báthory." She surveyed the room as if something new and interesting to do would pop up. When it didn't, she strode into the hall calling behind her, "I'm going to look around."

During the month in Gehenna, Breena had found the servant levels, the overlook at the pit, the observatory—its stars and light-source still mysteries—and a treasure trove of books and scrolls in Luce's giant library. Bree hadn't felt much like reading, and more than half of what he owned was written in ancient glyphs and languages anyway.

As she passed Atlas' room, she ignored the urge to invite him along. Veering right where the hall diverged beside an intimidating and grotesque sculpture, the black mica walls warped her reflection into a fractured dance. There were no doors in the hallway, leading Breena to believe there must be something large at the end. *Something entertaining, I hope.*

The walk to the end took twenty minutes, or what felt to her like twenty minutes in the strange vacuum of time surrounding Gehenna. When she rounded the last curved section of hallway and the end of the corridor came into view, Breena didn't know what to make of the sight through the glass doors before her. It was a full-scale replica of the castle Atlas had shown her, the same one she envisioned countless times in the days before giving in to Atlas and their *Allurement.*

Why is this here? Is Atlas trying to bribe me with memories? Denying her curiosity to explore its familiar and lovely halls, she took off down the path back to her room, letting her annoyance carry her full-speed. The trip didn't take long, but the odd lighting and repeated shimmer of her reflection in the walls made it appear she wasn't going anywhere. It wasn't until Breena almost careened into the statue that marked her left turn that she noticed she was back in familiar territory.

She pounded on the mammoth stone slab that made up Atlas' door. "Atlas! Atlas, let me in."

Chapter 21

Atlas opened the door with a frantic, wide-eyed expression. "What? What, what, what?"

"Why is that castle here? Are you trying to manipulate me with gifts and, and," she shoved past him into the room, "and the single best memory I have of you, of us?"

Atlas noticed her hands shaking at her sides. He recognized the look in her eyes, too. It was the one that meant, "I'm about to bolt. Forever." He put his hands up, knowing he needed to settle her fast. "What castle?"

"At the end of the hall, right path. Did you put it there to mess with me?" Her volume increased. "Atlas, I swear, I can't handle those memories right now. Not when you're. . ." She swayed. "Not when you're right here and you feel, *I* feel. . ." She shook her errant thoughts and the filmy waves of heat in her vision away. "Just *no*!"

"I don't know what you're on about. I want you to see how I've changed. I'm not doing anything to manipulate you or spy on you."

"Then what is it doing here?"

He shrugged. "I want to see it."

The pair made the long walk, Atlas too tense to take a full breath and Breena visibly livid. Atlas could hear Breena's teeth grinding together between staccato footfalls. When they reached the end of the corridor, this time, Breena pushed through the glass into another section of Gehenna. She took in a small gasp at the sight, her heart skipping a beat. *This is* my *world.* Around the castle were tall evergreen trees swaying in a cool breeze. The night sky, though starless, glowed over the landscape, casting sharp shadows on the angular architecture.

"Should we go in?"

Breena couldn't make up her mind, and she swayed side to side, putting her weight on one foot that wanted to go running into her favorite place and then on the other foot that wanted to run from whatever the appearance of the fortress meant.

Atlas touched her elbow. "I didn't do this. But I think we both recently spoke to the person who did."

Breena warmed until her anger rose to a steady burn beneath her skin. "You might want to let go of my arm, now. I don't want to burn you. Want to save that for my mother." She growled out the last word.

"You don't want to see inside first?"

"Not trying to convince me, you say?"

"Just checking. *I* want to see inside."

"Yeah. We had a good time here." Her eyes held questions. *Did you really love me, then? Do you now?*

Atlas nodded and turned for the door. "Let's go talk to mother dear."

Tabitha answered her door dressed for a soiree, her ankle-length black dress tinkling as she moved. It was covered in glass-beaded fringe, like a 1920s flapper. She held a masquerade mask by her side.

"Going to a party?" Atlas stood with his hand on the frame of the door, Bree beside him in the opening, blocking Tabitha.

"Some of the ladies of court are having a small gathering."

"We need to talk first."

She pushed her lips into a pout. "But I'll be late."

Breena shrugged. "You lived on Earth long enough to use the 'fashionably late' excuse."

Tabitha wrinkled her nose.

"Pass it off as just another annoying human habit, then." Bree gestured past her mother. "Can we come in?"

Atlas whispered to her, "You're the queen. You don't have to ask."

"Right. We're coming in to talk. Sit." Breena perched on the edge of one of Tabitha's frivolous gilt chaises. Jet pressed at Tabitha's back to do the same.

"Well, Breena, I guess a mother cannot complain when she receives a visit from her daughter."

"Oh, can it. You're so fake. We came for an explanation about the castle at the opposite end of the compound."

"That old thing? I'm surprised you're just now finding it. You were supposed to move into it sooner, but you've drawn out many things."

Atlas stood behind the small couch. "It's not an illusion?"

"No, it's as much a part of Gehenna as the pit or the rest of the royal compound. No one created it in illusion and no one built it to manipulate Breena."

Atlas leaned over Bree's shoulder to get a look at her face. He needed to see that she heard Tabitha clear his name.

Bree put a hand up to block his face inches from hers. "If no one put it here to impact me, why did Atlas show it to me a year ago?"

Tabitha grinned, fairly certain of the answer. "Ask him."

It didn't register at first what Tabitha wanted him to tell her. He thought back to that night and the reasons he gave Breena for showing her that particular illusion. Why, out of the endless combinations of images and scenery he could have drawn up, the castle came first. The realization was like a smack. "She's right." He circled to stand in front of Breena and face her. "Do you remember what I told you afterwards? When you asked me what I showed you?"

Her eyes brightened, but she didn't want to say it.

"I said, 'In a perfect world, you could have this every day.'"

Breena pressed into the cushion trying to back away from him. "You two—you've had this set up since then. What to show me, how to build my trust, what to say after you broke that trust. . ." She burned Tabitha with a searing glare. "*You* didn't get what you wanted when I was alive, so you're trying to get it now." She stood. "I know you just want the throne for yourself. You're a bitter woman with no decency. No wonder your own father wouldn't stand behind your decisions." She turned to rail at Atlas. "And *you* haven't changed at all."

Breena gestured wild circles and jabbed her finger in their directions as she laid into them. Realizing he could lose her from this misunderstanding, he grabbed her wrists, careless of the burns to his hands, and pushed her arms down by her sides, holding them there and speaking in soothing tones.

"That is *not* how you calm me."

He let go. "All of that is true of the past, but I swear on. . . well, I'm dead, but I swear on my life that that night and this one have *nothing* to do with her. The reason I showed you that castle last year is because you wanted an escape. You wanted to be a part of another world. I used what I read of your emotions and dreams. Even *I* didn't know it was a real place."

She turned away from him, staring vacantly across the room, tuning him out.

"Dammit, Breena, listen. It was a premonition. The place you wanted most was the place you were actually meant to be."

Tabitha butted in, ignoring Atlas, who shook his head—he did not want her involved. "He's right. Your home was calling. You should be ecstatic. Your dream came true!"

"My dream? How does any of this look like a dream come true to you?"

"The natural order is functioning properly; you saw this place in your future whether you interpreted it that way or not. You clearly inherited some of my sighting gift. Now, you're here. Stop resisting."

The words struck her. *I do* want to stop fighting. But this can't be the way to happiness. Atlas went to the doorway.

"There's something else you should know," Tabitha added. "So that I can't be accused of withholding the truth or manipulating you while you don't have all the facts, and also because, perhaps, knowing will change your mind. That castle is yours. As I mentioned, it is where all queens live with their chosen until an heir is born." Tabitha went to the door and gestured for them to leave. "We would have set you two up there from the start, but, well, you know."

Atlas stood in the hall waiting for Breena to quit the staring match she started with Tabitha, but he realized Breena would never cave and never turn her back to Tabitha before both of them were clear she had won. He grabbed her belt loop and tugged her toward the door. Tabitha followed them out, locking up behind herself.

"Well, children, the party waits." Tabitha relieved herself of their presence traveling the opposite direction she needed to go so she didn't have to walk with them. At the end of the hall, she looked back. "Oh, and if you decide you'd like to move in, what with the baby on the way, get Jet and Itzal to set up the logistics."

Breena stared, dumbfounded and numb, in the hallway. Her stomach quivered, a ball of nerves sick from the rapid cycling between betrayal, fury, and reluctant understanding. *What did she say?*

When Breena came to, Atlas was looking down on her in a room with a grey ceiling she didn't recognize. Unlike her own, it was smooth and bare. He smiled.

"Is this your room?"

He nodded.

"Did I pass out?"

"From shock, I guess. Leave it to you to pass out in a place with no sleep. Must be that body you brought with you."

"Had a dream while I was out."

"Oh?"

"I was still in high school. All the boys kept arguing in the halls. It made me anxious. When I got home, my mom—my Earth mom—sat me down at the kitchen table and said, 'You can't keep letting this happen. Every time you do, it just sets the rest of them up to expect they're next.' I kept asking her, 'Allow what to happen? Next to do what?' But she wouldn't answer. Then I woke up."

"Sounds like Lexa wants you to stop playing with guys' hearts and settle down, already."

"That *would* be your interpretation."

"We need to talk about what Tabitha said."

"What part?"

"Are you in denial or do you really not remember?"

"Both, maybe."

"Breena, are you pregnant?"

Her vision swam, his question confirming Tabitha said what Bree thought she had. "I, uh, I," she held her temples, "I don't know. Am I?"

"How would I know?"

She threw up her hands. "Instinct? I don't know."

"It's true my instinct to be with you, you know, *with* you, has subsided. I thought it was because we were staying near each other. Maybe it's because you're not sending out anymore signals?"

"*Me* sending out signals? What about you, with your, your. . ." She looked him up and down pointing in a wave that included his whole body. "I did not come on to you."

"Fine, then. We'll blame pheromones. Whatever the case, I'm not getting that vibe from you anymore, and I'm guessing it has eased for you, too. I'd bet money it's because the job is done."

"Oh, stop being so romantic or I might come onto you again." She rolled her eyes.

"But we're on the same page, right? It could be true."

Breena put a hand on her stomach. "It's like it's me, but it isn't me, this life I'm living."

"Same page?"

"Yes. Same page."

The pair went back to Bree's room as soon as she could stand without stumbling. Jet was playing solitaire again, their conversation about things to do in Gehenna having gone nowhere. He left his handful of cards on the floor to greet them. Breena's demeanor set him on edge right away. He looked between them. "What is it?"

There was no good way to present the idea to Jet, so she let it tumble from her lips in a whoosh. "Imightbepregnant."

She expected cursing or a shout, or any outward reaction at all, but Jet sat on the nearest chair in silence. After a few terrifying minutes of icy tension that could have shattered into a fight at the sound of a sniffle, he gasped. "You *are*. That dizzy spell earlier, you totally *are*."

"Huh." It's all she could manage.

"This makes our choice easy, then." Atlas drew Breena to the bed and urged her to lie down.

She complied, but asked, "It does?"

"We'll stay here in Gehenna. There's no need to continue avoiding doing again what we already did. That means you don't have to go back home to avoid me, you don't have to play into Tabitha's wish for you to overthrow Luce so that you can send me back. We'll have our heir. She can't do anything to us."

"Atlas, that doesn't make it easier. This changes everything! I was finally getting used to—"

Jet stepped between them and pointed a finger at Bree. "Stop there. Don't act like you were well-adjusted. This changes things, but we're no worse off."

Atlas rubbed his hands together and scowled. "Jet, you don't have to be so nice."

Jet spun on Atlas. "No, and I don't want to, but that can wait."

Bree, overwhelmed to the point of shutting down, imagined herself floating on her back in a pool, the water just covering her ears. As Breena dazed off, Atlas and Jet discussed which of them got to continue pursuing her. Jet's temper intensified as condescending drivel poured out of Atlas' elated mouth. All the unpleasantness muffled into peaceful background noise. Through it, broke the sound of her own crying. Bree came part way back to the present and interrupted. "This wasn't supposed to happen."

Jet's temper couldn't handle anymore, and he snapped at her. "Yeah, well that's the risk you took when you let your body call the shots. You *never* consider how your impulses will harm you. It was the same with the drugs. I never should have enabled you."

She blinked, surprised at his volume. "I didn't think—"

"No, you didn't, did you?"

"Hey! You do not talk to her like that. I am as much to blame as she is and you know she didn't choose to do it."

"Oh, so you forced her? I'll kill you!" Jet shoved Atlas a few feet back from the bed.

"No, and I didn't choose, either. This place, it's Hell, the place people go when their choices weren't good enough in life. We lost our chance to choose."

Breena gasped, affronted. "I'm not here because I was a bad person."

Jet lunged for Atlas, swinging. "Well none of us were great, now were we?"

"Both of you, shut up!" Bree got to her feet. "Our circumstances are different from the souls in the pit, and our lives before now are not up for debate."

"You should sit." Atlas reached for her.

Bree pulled away. "I'm not an invalid. We don't even know if it's true. Tabitha's probably messing with me."

"That does sound like her," Jet nodded.

Atlas calmed. "I feel like I should have known."

She groaned and let herself fall back to the bed. "Why would you have? You don't have a physical body. I honestly don't know how anything here is possible. It's insane that we even, well," she waved as if clearing away the train of thought she started, then continued, "We can't apply our human experiences—"

"—or science, apparently—"

"—to the way of things here."

Chapter 22

Jordan wallowed in his back yard, finally out of bed, but still feeling sorry for himself. Lilly had cajoled him into firing Grey, convincing Jordan that he was not only too distraught to make good choices with his money, but that he was powerless in the face of death—no matter what he thought Grey might know about near-death experiences, crossing planes, or manipulating others.

It wasn't typically Lilly's style to be so defeatist, but she wholly believed that of life's many challenges, death was not one of them, and it was to be accepted. None of her research, none of her preparedness or cautious nature could predict, stop, or reverse it. Jordan needed that dose of reality.

Jordan sat under the tree he and Bree had climbed so many times as children. It was the tree he'd thought of when they read *The Giving Tree*, which always made him sad. Now, the tree seemed to hang even heavier with its memories, drooping under the weight of sunsets and a girl with wind-blown hair he'd never see again.

It didn't matter to him that he didn't want her back. *I don't have to want her back to miss what I had. I'm allowed this.* It was of little consolation, the platitudes and fake proverbs he tried to live by in these tough days. *The grieving process is a bitch.*

Around the back of the tree, their initials filled the space of an open heart carved when they were seven. He couldn't bring himself to go look at it; even knowing it was there prodded at him like he had reclined on a thorn; he checked behind himself to see if he had. *Nope.*

Jordan stood up knowing he needed to do something, be around someone. He thought about Ari. A few nights earlier, Jordan talked to him, and he had mentioned Linda's arraignment was coming up. He was now living with and Lexa and Grant just outside of Grayling, happy to have their support in acclimating to a stationary post-riot life without Linda and, worse, without Breena. *I should call them, give them my condolences.* He walked a loop of the back yard trying to outrun the guilt of skipping Bree's vigil. Lilly had still been in the hospital and he reasoned that he couldn't do it without her. It may have been true, but it also stemmed from his deep denial that Breena was dead at all. That and selfishness. *How could I help them mourn her when I couldn't help myself?* By the time he reached the deck and went inside, the bottoms of his bare feet felt as raw as his insides. He inspected a prick from a burr in his heel. *I deserve it. And I deserve to move on.*

****

Lilly hung up the phone and put on her shoes. She was on her way out of the house to make the two and a half hour drive to Oakland University. Their freshman orientation for the fall semester came and went among the chaos of her summer, but she planned to start prioritizing her future now that Ari was home and the search for Breena had come to an end. The police department declared the disappearance a cold case, their main suspects dead.

She slung a sagging messenger bag over her shoulder and locked the door behind her. Even though she and Breena hadn't planned on attending the same college, it still sat wrong with her that Breena wasn't coming with her. As a child, Lilly had always imagined rooming together, eating cookies in the middle of the night, making pots and pots of coffee during exam season, sharing the typical college experiences.

The highway unfolded before her, and she drove past the exit Atlas had used to make his RV getaway. Lilly lamented, considering that if she had done more acting and less researching, if she had pursued Atlas' location that night, he would have led her straight to Breena. Lilly floored the gas. *After graduation, I don't think I'll ever go back to Grayling.*

****

Leigh struggled to the front of the store with a large box containing a cage, a shrink-wrapped mini-bale of straw and alfalfa, and a stack of small bowls and bottles. At the register, a clerk waited with a small cardboard carrier ventilated with rows of holes at the top. Leigh unloaded her arms onto the conveyor belt then peeked through one of the holes at her new pet guinea pig. He sniffed around the edges of the box. She smiled.

****

In the fall breeze, which smelled of dried leaves and dirt, Lexa looked over the edge of the balcony onto the rolling slopes of the ski resort. It was an odd mix, the trees still partially clothed in leaves and the hills deep with manufactured snow. Grant approached Lexa and wrapped her in a hug from behind. She tensed.

"This is wrong."

"Are we going to discuss this again?"

"I always judged those moms on TV who cried in a news report one minute because her child was missing or dead and the next minute a talk show sends them on a dream vacation to unwind. I thought, 'How could any parent take a vacation during a time like that? Why aren't they at home, working, searching, grieving?' Now, I'm that mom. I can hardly stand myself."

"We will always be waiting, looking. You still have to take care of yourself, though. Allow yourself this. It's just a weekend."

Lexa rolled her eyes and pulled out of his embrace to go inside.

****

"Luce, I need to talk to you." Breena peered into his office from around the door frame. He waved her in. She entered in a huff. "Tabitha told me I'm pregnant. She's lying, right?"

Luce stood from behind his desk. Breena couldn't tell if the heat on his cheeks was anger or embarrassment. *She* felt both.

"She may have lost her sight, but she is never wrong about these things." Lucifer rounded the desk and put his hands on Breena's shoulders. The quick glimmer of approval vanished. "It wasn't Jet that you . . . right?"

Breena shook her head, mortified to share any details about how it happened.

Luce wore a triumphant grin, his full lips turning up to reveal unrealistically white teeth he never smiled enough to reveal. The light came back to his face. "This is what we've been hoping for!" He squeezed her then pulled her into a tight embrace. Breena's arms were pinned to her sides within his, her cheek smooshed against his wide chest. "What made you change your mind?"

She tried to shake her head, not wanting to discuss the nature of the events that led her to this moment.

"We must move you into the queen's palace at once. You will need to choose a guard. Jet is a fine courtier, and he will continue to serve at your side, but you must appoint a head of security if you are to live outside the compound. Now that you're carrying the heir, your safety is doubly at risk."

Bree wiggled out of his ecstatic grip. "Slow down. Are you saying there's no test I can take? We're just going to take Tabitha's word on this."

"Can you not tell?"

She laughed, confounded. "I didn't realize I was supposed to be able to tell. Why does everyone keep asking me that?"

"It must be your physical body. This isn't how it usually goes around here. No matter. I'll send a seer to your room later to confirm. For the time being, let's proceed as if it's true. We have a lot to do." Lucifer, carried out by his excitement and sense of urgency, left to start arranging the details.

She looked around herself and shrugged. "Sure, I'll see myself back to my room." In the corridor, Breena ran her hand across the wall as she walked. The smooth stone with its natural curves and ridges reminded her of the riverbed rocks she and Jordan used to attempt to skip as children. Another memory of him popped up, of their second grade teacher fussing as the class walked single file from the library back to their classroom. Lilly stood in front of them, her pile of books clutched to her chest, hands to herself. Jordan walked behind Bree, his hands on her shoulders like a conga line. She trailed the slick grooves between thickly painted cinderblocks with a finger as the class made its way back to their room. The teachers always hated that.

No use thinking about any of that. She put a hand on her stomach. *I don't see how I can go back, now.*

Jet greeted her at her door. "Well?"

"Luce said Tabitha has a knack for these things and that she's most likely right. He wants all of us to move to the palace."

"Wow. Palace. That sounds so regal."

"And 'Queen' doesn't?" She nudged him in the side. "I need a head of security." At the sight of Jet's almost black eyes lightening to a cheery shade of umber, she interjected, "Not you." He deflated a bit. "Know anyone from the lower levels that could use a promotion?"

"Itzal's the only one down there that deserves it, but if he was in charge of your safety, you'd die. He's too old and frail to fight off the moths in his closet."

She wrinkled her nose and hoped there weren't really moths in Gehenna. "I don't know who I'm going to pick. I don't know anyone here, I think a lot of the older people would *love* to see me harmed, and it doesn't help that tradition says I get Tabitha's team—like an *inheritance.*" Bree refused. "I don't want *anyone* she had."

As soon as the words left her mouth, she was struck with a lightning bolt idea. "Vos!"

"Who?"

"Vos!"

Jet made a rolling motion with his hands. "Need more than that, Bree."

"Vos was Tabitha's lug when all this started, but he was the one who helped me kill her. Everything I needed to learn about getting back here, I learned from him. He did a lot to keep me safe." She noticed Jet frown at that. "I don't blame him for getting kidnapped. There was no way he could have seen it coming." She still didn't know Luce had personally removed Vos from her service.

Jet wore a perma-scowl, unwilling to accept that he would have to relinquish control of her safety to someone he didn't know and who had a failing track-record.

"Even if you don't approve right now, I think you'll like him. He's easy going—"

"Too easy going. So easy going he wasn't watching you."

"He's easy going and careful, loyal—he hated Tabitha but didn't betray her until I used my power to manipulate him."

"So he's easily influenced. Great."

Breena ignored Jet's skepticism. She knew how her statement sounded, but she was confident Vos would stand by her. "I just need to figure out how to get him here."

A flurry of servants hustled about the palace turning it from the sparsely furnished shell Breena loved into a home more suitable for a family. Luce was pointing and shouting in every direction, and the servants scuttled to satisfy him, but really, his orders were counterproductive to their goals, his focus too much on looks rather than function. The ornate chandelier Lucifer had them hoist into the eaves of the foyer clinked as they secured it.

A red-cheeked woman with a bouffant of curls atop her head spoke from behind Luce. "Shall I go to her now? If I see a child, she'll be able to move in right away. They're putting the finishing touches on the suite."

"And the nursery?"

"She and her chosen should decorate it."

Lucifer wrinkled his nose but nodded. "You're right. Yes, go to her now."

The seer curtseyed and left for Breena's chambers in the main compound.

Breena opened her door at the timid knock to find a small round woman with curls that filled the doorway.

"I'm Aisling, one of the seers, Your Highness. His Majesty Lucifer sent me to verify your health."

"Come in, come in."

"Yes, My Queen."

"Please, Aisling, call me Breena."

"Oh, I don't think it would do to be so familiar."

"You're about to be very familiar with me unless I'm mistaken about how this works, so it's fine. Really."

Jet squirmed and wondered if he should go into the hall for a bit.

"You're unfamiliar with our ways." She wore an easy smile. It wasn't her goal to embarrass Breena for her ignorance, and even less her goal to appear as criticizing the queen. Aisling was loyal to Luce's lineage no matter how much things changed from ruler to ruler. "All I need to do is have a quiet moment to hold your hands."

"Oh, well that's not so bad. Would you like to sit?" Breena gestured toward the couch to the right of the armoire.

Aisling nodded and flitted over to the chair. For a woman who Bree guessed was centuries old, and who had the form and skin of a grandmotherly figure, she moved lightly, excitedly. Breena let a small giggle slip out as she mused at the seer. Aisling looked over her shoulder and blushed. "I apologize for my. . ." she suggested her body and demeanor with a small, wiggling shimmy and a smile. Her excitement was alive inside of her. "It's just been so long since there was a child." Sensing Bree's openness to informality, she allowed herself to continue. "Let them say what they will, but I'm so excited to see how you improve this place."

Breena put a hand to her chest. It was the warmest welcome she had gotten.

"Well, actually I *have* seen it, but it's always better in person. First-hand experience versus a movie—you understand."

"I appreciate the support."

Jet raised his eyebrows at Bree from across the room. She knew him well enough to get his meaning. He was getting impatient. Breena cleared her throat. "Ms. Aisling, since all of this was unexpected, well, for me, maybe not for you," she gave Aisling a questioning glance, "can we proceed with the. . . What is this called?"

"Yes, yes, of course. The *Confirmation.*" The seer took Breena's suddenly clammy hands into hers, which were smooth with age and a life that hadn't required their use. Distracted by excitement, Aisling interjected one last observation before she closed her eyes. "You know, your mother trained with me for many years. It's a shame what happened with her sight." Within seconds, they were both breathing the same deep, focusing rhythm, eyes closed. When the seer's breathing hitched, Bree's eyes flew open. Aisling smiled. "Fortunately, you and this little bundle here are going to right the wrongs Tabitha's hubris and defects brought."

On the edge of Breena's bed, Jet flopped back into the pillows with his hands over his eyes. His heart tried to work its way from his stomach back into his chest. Recognizing his selfishness, he struggled against the happiness—a child meant Bree would stay in Gehenna, stay where he could be near her. The anger? It was more like jealousy toward Atlas. "Freaking genetics."

"What did you say, Jet?"

He hadn't noticed he'd been mumbling and blinked a few times.

"Congratulations, Queen."

Breena couldn't feel her face. "Why did her sight have to work on *this*? Why couldn't my mother have been right about, ugh, anything else?"

The seer stood. "You're not happy."

Ashamed, Bree shook her head. Jet sat up and watched. He was grateful Atlas wasn't there. He itched to put his hands around Atlas' throat. But, even Jet's annoyance didn't overshadow the sense that Atlas should have been there. Breena needed someone, and Jet knew he wasn't it in that moment—although he hoped it was *only* in that moment.

Inside Breena's head, the words "no future" ran on repeat behind the ringing of her ears. *My plans never accounted for this. I'll never go back home. I'll never get to apologize to my friends. I'm stuck. Here for eternity, but without a future.*

Aisling put her hands on her hips and cut through Breena's freak-out with a sharp, "Excuse me!" Breena returned. "Forgive me for the harsh tone, Your Highness, but I have to put a stop to this spiral you're indulging in. I have seen your future and hers," she pointed to Bree's stomach, "so you cannot convince yourself there isn't one to live. Everything will work out more closely to your original plans than you can know. You have to live your life to find out." She put a hand on Bree's cold arm and gave it a light squeeze. "So suck it up and get on with living it."

Chapter 23

Atlas had gotten roped into decorating with Luce during the seer's visit. Lucifer explained that the chosen never took part in the queen's confirmations because it wasn't his place as a person who would transition out of the queen's life once the child was born. All Atlas had the power to do was nod and pretend he understood and agreed. Inside, he was almost certain that Breena's distaste for tradition would also apply to his requirement to go to the pit after the birth, therefore welcoming his presence during the seer's visit.

Nonetheless, he was stuck listening to Lucifer gush over the shade of eggplant he chose for the master suite.

"It's, of course, the color of royalty, so there was no other choice in my mind."

"Let me stop you for a second. I have a serious question."

Lucifer closed his mouth around the next thing he was going to say and raised his eyebrow.

"I'll preface this by saying that I'm fine with the way it's turning out for me, but what happened to my sentence? I'm supposed to be in jail. Breena let me off easy moving me into her corridor, but I didn't think that was permanent. Now that she's probably pregnant—"

"Oh, she's definitely pregnant. Tabitha's never been wrong. Sending Aisling was to ease Breena's mind, not because I thought my daughter was incorrect."

"OK, now that we're having a baby, do you plan on proceeding with a trial?"

"I never wanted to punish you in the first place, Atlas. I may disagree with your methods, but I recognize that my daughter influenced you negatively in many of those instances. It was Breena who told me she would not marry. Her options were tradition or jail. You know which one she picked."

"Do you think this will change things?"

"You know her better than I do."

Atlas rubbed at his neck. *She's going to resist all of this for as long as she can. I won't win.*

Breena straightened in Aisling's grip. "Hers? *Her* future? It's a girl." She noticed a tentative grin forming. Bree didn't want to see positivity in any of this. She wasn't finished wallowing in her anger and dismay. She didn't want the excitement that crept in.

"Of course it's a girl. They're always girls. How do you think we maintain our lineage of queens? Only the lower classes bear all genders, and that's limited as a whole."

"Huh. Makes sense," Jet mumbled from behind Breena. Unaware of his approach, Bree jumped.

Aisling grinned at Jet. "How do you feel about this?"

His expression went blank and the seer shifted on her feet. "I'll leave you two to discuss. And don't worry. I won't speak of your relationship."

Breena whipped her head back around to Aisling, expression severe. "Do you see *everything*?"

Aisling smiled wide and left the room, her hands clasped behind her back.

Jet chuckled. "I guess you earn the right to be smug when you know you're never wrong."

Before heading back to the palace, Aisling detoured to visit Tabitha. The seer's loyalty to the throne and her early knowledge that Tabitha's reign would end like it had made her relationship to Tabitha easier. She'd had years to prepare herself for the upheaval. The shame Tabitha brought to Gehenna didn't fall on Aisling as hard as the others. It was one of many expected factors she adjusted to.

Tabitha invited Aisling to sit with her in the small alcove off the left side of her chamber. It hung over a portion of the pit and was pocked with several small windows that let in the eerie orange glow from below.

"I'd appreciate if you leave the predictions to me."

"You don't like that I saw it first."

"I don't like that you use your sight to manipulate. Even worse, you're often wrong. The threats you make are damaging, and they make us all look bad when you can't even carry them out because they were based on false visions."

Tabitha tapped her foot, regretting inviting Aisling in.

"Don't mess with Breena. You got what you originally set out to get last year—she's here, she's giving us an heir, and she's reluctant to take on His Highness to obtain a body for Jet or Atlas, which means she's going to stay. That was a foolish gamble you made, by the way, and an excellent example of what I'm talking about. You just want to get rid of her if she's not going to do things your way."

"That is only a flawed portion of what I wanted," Tabitha spat. "I wanted those things for her *before* she sabotaged my plans and sent me back here. I *wanted* disorder on Earth."

"Well your actions and failing sight brought it here instead."

Tabitha slapped the seer across the face. "Insolence. I am your queen!"

Aisling did not retaliate. She stood up with a pitying smile and a patient tone. "You are not."

"OK, that's the finishing touch." Luce admired his decorating while Atlas rolled his eyes inwardly at the way Lucifer took credit. He'd only given the orders to make the palace look that way. Aisling entered with a nod, confirming the child and her completion of the task. "Well, congratulations, Atlas. If anything is going to save you from your sentencing, this is it. Go see her, but skirt the issue. If she's forgotten about it in the business of these developments, so be it."

"When can we move in? Can I bring her by?"

"Any time."

Atlas took his leave of Luce, Aisling, and the hoard of servants pretending not to listen in. His stomach tumbled at the thought of a having a child. *If someone asks if I'm excited, I don't know what I'll say. Or maybe they won't ask. It's nothing special for a chosen to produce an heir. It's expected.*

The twenty minute walk to Bree's room from the palace gave his thoughts plenty of time to jump around. By the time he was face to face with his queen, Atlas had settled on pride as an appropriate reaction to the news.

Living in Gehenna with Breena and making a family had been the original intention. It was the reason they had connected in dreams, the reason he sought her out upon waking, the reason Tabitha approached him, hired him, housed him. *Maybe I have won.*

"I suppose we should move."

Atlas and Jet read her body language differently, Atlas recognizing the reluctant acquiescence of her cocked hip and the hand that rested upon it, Jet, in his still-new familiarity, seeing enthusiasm that made his chest ache.

Breena called in some servants to gather hers and Jet's things, and she sent Atlas with a group to his room to do the same. None of them had much, just some clothing and comfort items that had been in the rooms when they'd arrived, so the switch took only a couple trips between the compound and the palace.

Sitting in the expansive drawing room of her suite, which the rest of Gehenna clearly expected her to share with Atlas, she wondered why she hadn't seen this portion of the castle during her original shared illusions with Atlas. *It's because that vision was a representation of what I wanted most, and a marriage, a family, wasn't part of it. I wanted the grand room to myself.* If her dreams had always been veiled premonitions, and she planned to begin looking at them in that way regardless, then her course of action was clear.

Atlas entered like he owned the place, leaping to belly-flop on the enormous feathered bed. As his body came to a rest, hair ruffled in the way Breena used to love—the realization that the love she felt was past tense hitting with clarity—she marched into the room. "Out!" Bree threw an arm to the side, pointing to the floor-to-ceiling double doors.

"What?"

"You've fooled yourself if you think this, *she*, changes anything. I moved you into the compound because I thought it would make things easier on both of us, but that wasn't the reason the pain went away. If you stay, you'll try to manipulate me. I will change my plans only as much as she requires."

"You're letting a *fetus* call the shots?"

"I just told you you don't have a say."

"Ouch. You know I meant *your* fetus."

Bree shrugged. "Being with someone I don't love doesn't do her any good." She looked at Jet as he entered the tense silence that followed her declaration. "And if I'm with someone, it's because I want to be, not because I think I need to be."

Jet smiled and pointed to himself, mouthing, "Me?" Bree gave the slightest of nods and turned back to Atlas who was walking on his knees to the edge of the bed.

He stood. "It's bittersweet. You used to need me so much, or at least you thought you did, and I always wanted you to see what you were capable of, but now that you've turned that corner, the part of me that wants to keep you is sad you grew up." He bit his tongue against the questions about his fate. *Another time.*

"But you understand?"

"There were only two possible outcomes once we got here. You'd follow tradition or you'd make a new road." Atlas took her hand. "And I knew better than to think the former. I hoped, but I knew." Jet stepped in toward Breena. Atlas got the message, although it was one Jet didn't need to make a point to send. "I'll move my stuff into one of the other rooms." Atlas dropped her hand and padded into the cold marble hallway.

Jet placed a kiss on her cheek and led her to the bay window. As the largest suite in the palace, its location at the end of the hall allowed a wall-sized view of the statue and topiary garden she and Atlas had danced in. Jet broke through her daydreaming. "We'll have to cover those sharp edges in bubble wrap or something."

Breena gave him a questioning tilt of the head, thinking he was referencing her memories.

"You know, baby-proof it."

"You're embracing this."

He pulled her close and put his forehead to hers. "I'm embracing *you.*"

"Because your duty to me extends to my family?"

"And because I might love you."

Breena pushed back at the guilty thoughts of how she didn't deserve his love after getting him killed and bound into service. She didn't want to think that his affection might be an extension of his duty—a mere exposure effect. Her worry came out anyway. "You don't have to. I'd understand if you were still angry."

"Even when I'm angry," he gestured between them, "this doesn't change."

Breena let out a relieved breath she hadn't realized she held.

"Hey." He pulled back from her a few inches. "What are you going to name her?"

"Too soon. But I do know that I'm definitely staying here. How can I return to my life and friends like this, with a child that for all I know might not even have a physical body given the circumstances. It's just too much. So I need to get on with restoring the balance between Heaven and Hell. It's the whole reason I came. And we need to get Vos down here before I start. Can't imagine people will be too thrilled with me."

****

Vos arrived a week after they all moved into the palace, following Lucifer's orders. Breena didn't want to think about what the orders actually meant for Vos or how he got there. She suspected they meant the same thing as they had for Jet: Serve the queen with your life. She allowed Atlas to stay in the castle, albeit in the wing farthest from her own, along with her courtier and head of security. Breena didn't need anyone as a mate, although she and Jet had pursued their want for a relationship, but she had the maturity to admit she needed as much support with the baby as she could get. The child needed a team. And a father.

Four months later, Atlas, Breena, Jet, and Vos gathered around a low coffee table, cups of what Breena had learned passed for food in Gehenna nestled in their hands. Over their dinner, which they ate out of enjoyment rather than necessity, they discussed names for the baby.

Vos stared with fondness at the squirming baby in his arms. "I know what we could call her."

Chapter 24

On the day of the naming, Lucifer stood on the dais looking down on his elated court, Vos beside him standing just as proud. Luce's voice thundered around in the eaves. "Today is a magnificent day for a party. We're here to honor your queen and her chosen as they prepare to name your princess. The queen has also chosen to honor you with a performance of the cello in closing."

Bree smiled through her nerves and wondered why she had volunteered the idea. It had been so long since she played. Practice had taken a toll on her fingers, and it was just as difficult to put herself back in the vulnerable place of allowing her music to materialize for everyone to see in illusion. *On purpose.*

In the front row, Aisling and Tabitha sat shoulder to shoulder in the closely packed line of chairs. Beside Tabitha, Itzal and a few of the other servants Breena had chosen to serve in her household sat with the honor of being invited to view the ceremony from the family's row. It explained, at least in part, the sour expression on Tabitha's face, her elbow barely grazing Itzal's best suit.

Luce continued. "It's been centuries since we've had a child in the royal house, so in case you've forgotten how this ceremony goes, I'll remind you that Queen Ashna—"

Breena interjected her real name under the obvious cover of a cough.

Luce closed his eyes and inhaled some patience, then revised, "Queen Breena and her chosen, Atlas, will present to Vos and Jet, royal household head of security and Your Majesty's courtier, the child after announcing her name. In receiving the child, they symbolize their oaths to continue serving the queen by serving the princess, an oath that requires no words. Acceptance of the child seals their bond of protection and guidance."

The court nodded and hummed in approval. Lucifer turned to Breena and Atlas. Breena took a deep breath and stepped forward. Of all the traditions she rejected, this was one she embraced with no changes. She and Atlas practiced for months. Bree wanted to get it right, not to honor the court by following protocol but to give her daughter a fresh beginning unclouded by judgements of Breena that the court may transfer to the child.

Beside Lucifer, she started the incantation. She hadn't known Gehenna had a language of its own before beginning to train for the ceremony. She learned as much as necessary to get through the day, but didn't plan on using it for anything else.

Atlas echoed in French, the incantation always repeated by the chosen in his native language from Earth. "J'honore le tribunal avec ma fille, dont le nom est donné ce jour. J'honore ma fille, qui est donnée aujourd'hui à la Géhenne. Elle vous servira parce que vous la servez. Ma fille est à moi; ma fille est à toi."

Atlas' reservations about using the French of his Earth parents dissolved after he internalized the message: "I honor the court with my daughter, whose name is given this day. I honor my daughter, who is given this day to Gehenna. She will serve you because you serve her. My daughter is mine; my daughter is yours." It wasn't something his father would ever say. Even in his father's language, he could choose not to be like him.

After Atlas had finished his part, Breena handed the girl over to Atlas so she could stand before her. Holding the baby's chubby hands, Breena looked back at Luce for a nod that she was still doing it right. He approved, and Breena continued the ceremony in English, representing her previous life on Earth. "My daughter receives a name that befits her purpose. She is Eos, the dawn, and you will call her by name."

Vos and Jet, who had knelt, eyes cast down, on the lower step of the platform as Breena handed the princess to Atlas, looked up at the baby and extended their arms. Atlas approached them. "Vos, call your princess by name."

"Eos, My Princess."

Atlas released her into Vos' huge, protective hands. Vos held her close to his chest, stood with the girl, and handed her back to Atlas. Atlas nodded in approval—he had never had anything against Vos, their time in Tabitha's forced service giving them a shared history. Vos went to stand again with Lucifer.

Atlas passed Eos to Breena so she could repeat the process with Jet. "Jet, in my service and hers, call your princess by name."

"Eos, My Princess."

As Breena extended her arms to hand her over, Tabitha, who had been seething in the background, lunged for Jet, sending him and Bree's ornate Gehennan-crafted cello, to the floor. He fell to the side and landed, clumsy and confused only for a split second. He swept his feet back underneath him and crouched to dive for Tabitha, who was fiercely trying to pry Eos from Breena's hands. Atlas was already at Tabitha's neck, Vos wedging himself between her and Breena to guard the child from Tabitha's sharp, vengeful hands. Jet launched himself at Tabitha's ankles, hoping to topple her as she had him.

As the outcast queen fell kicking and shrieking insults and threats about Eos, Vos hurried Breena and the baby out of the hall. The dumbstruck crowd of ladies and gentlemen of court stared in inaction.

Luce was at the double doors in a flash, barring them closed so Tabitha couldn't follow Vos and Breena if she tried. With his daughter restrained under the weight of Atlas and Jet, who had disarmed her of a small dagger and pinned her belly-down, arms twisted behind her back, legs pulled back like a hog, Lucifer let loose on Tabitha in a way he never had on any of his daughters in all his eons of existence.

"Enough! You are more of an infant than our dear Eos, and your actions more shameful than many of those in the pit."

"She's no princess. She is not the dawn; she is vile night, the death of our race. She is not the heir because Breena is not the queen. It's my throne!" She jerked under the men to look up at Luce, and Atlas slammed her head into the floor, smashing her cheek into the stone. "She ascended before my transition to the pit. It's not the way we do it. Breena is a shameful daughter. You would let her rule when she killed her own mother."

"Shut up, you disgrace. You think I would let *you* rule after attempting to kill your own granddaughter, our heir?"

"We would be better off! The earth will be better off. Breena will not sow chaos as I did, and she will never teach her daughter our ways."

"I can only be thankful you never taught your daughter your ways."

Another growl welled up inside Tabitha and erupted from somewhere deep. "It is *mine*! My body is dead, but I am still alive here!" She twisted. "Get off me, thugs. I am your queen!" Jet angled his head away from her attempts to kick free of his bear-hug grip. "Get off and *bow to me*!" Her commands trailed off into irate screaming, her eyes blown wide, wild.

With a sigh, not of reluctance but of resignation, Luce squatted beside Tabitha's face where she could see him. He put a hand on her hair like a father. "Perhaps you will find some who still kneel for you in the pit." With that, he snapped his fingers and her ethereal body disappeared from under Jet's and Atlas'.

The men landed on their rears on the stone floor, lolling a bit then righting themselves as the court gasped. Luce stood, cracked his knuckles, glanced around the room of slack-jawed faces, and then exited the hall appearing neither angry nor sad and in no particular hurry. When he was gone, but not out of earshot, the room erupted into fervent murmurs. Atlas and Jet looked at each other. After a freeze-frame moment of shock, they jumped up to hurry after Vos, Breena, and Eos.

They burst through the palace's doors to find Breena cradling Eos, both of their faces serene.

"She's gone." Jet beat Atlas to the announcement with a smug smile. It didn't bother Atlas, though. He was too relieved to be jealous. He doubted he'd ever be jealous again after seeing where jealousy had landed Tabitha. A moment passed without a response from Breena. Vos and the others waited another second, and Jet sat beside her. "I didn't mean 'gone' like she escaped. I mean gone, gone. Dead, or the Gehenna equivalent. To the pit."

Breena smiled up at Jet, Eos' tiny fingers gripping one of Bree's. "I know. I felt her shift." Eos sighed and they all looked down at the baby. "I should put her down for a bit." Bree walked across the marble foyer as evenly as she could, not wanting to jostle Eos. They all marveled after the pair.

"I can't believe she sleeps."

Jet and Vos nodded in envy.

Epilogue

Linda, whose friends used to describe her as plain, a follower, sped away from the curb as soon as the engine turned over and she came up from under the steering wheel. Now, she felt vibrant, exciting, alive. Tabitha's death had shocked her into action and revenge had steeled her nerves. "I'll have to send Kris a thank you card for teaching me to hotwire." Adamant about not drawing attention to her escape, she resisted the urge to really push the car. She did not drift around the highway on-ramp, she did not flip off the driver preventing her from merging right away, and she did not speed—not as much as she wanted to, anyway.

Settling on a comfortable five over the speed limit, she steered herself toward Breena's house. *Even if she's still missing, taking out Ari and the mom will feel nice.* The two hour drive from the group home to Grayling unfolded before her. It didn't take long for highway hypnosis, or revenge hypnosis, to set in.

Linda drifted across the lines of the left lane. A shrill honking startled her back to reality, but she overcorrected. Her car and all of the others on the interstate moved too fast for Linda to catch up to what was happening. Screeches, horns, and the dull, crunching pops of colliding metal cascaded over her. Linda's head struck the window and her hands fell from the wheel. In her last moments of consciousness, she heard the warped blare of a tractor trailer horn growing closer. The impact blackened the rest of her vision.

When Linda came to, she was standing in a small room with a desk. A squat woman sat behind it tapping a pen.

"I asked you spell it."

Linda blinked a few times. "Excuse me? Spell it? What?"

"Spell your middle name. I get these things wrong all the time."

Linda nodded and acted like she understood. "That's R-H-Y-A-N."

The clerk wrote the letters out, mumbling. "Of course it has an 'H'. Obviously." She rolled her eyes.

"Remind me why we're here?"

"Answer's not going to change no matter how many times you ask me that. You sure you don't want to wash the ink off your fingers?" She stood and rounded the desk, reaching for a shiny doorknob on a door Linda hadn't noticed before. Linda looked down at her hands. They weren't covered in fingerprinting ink like expected, but blood. The nameless receptionist opened the door. "After you."

Linda stared into blackness and squinted. "Where am I?"

"That answer isn't going to change, either. Now, on with you."

Taking a step into the void, Linda pivoted before continuing. "This isn't jail," she paused and looked back into the dark. "Or the hospital." Linda took a step back toward the woman. "Is this purgatory?"

A hearty laugh burst out of the woman and it echoed around Linda. "Ah, that never gets old. It's just a hallway. See that glow at the end? Walk that direction. You'll know where you are when you reach it." Before Linda could walk back into the little prep-room, the door slammed. Without the light from the desk lamp, the depthless dark took on a slight glow in one direction. She fumbled toward it as instructed.

When she finally stumbled into the orange environment, Tabitha was there waiting for her. "Reputable source told me you'd be arriving today."

Linda shrieked and tried to run back into the lightless tunnel. *I didn't plan my revenge to die so lamely.* She was seized by a hoard of blackened, sooty hands and dragged into the pit screaming for her loss, for her presence, and for her welcoming party. Tabitha chuckled as she trailed after the mass. "Welcome home, darling."

Lucifer's loud laughter echoed from his balcony as he watched her terror unfold.

Thank you for spending time with my characters! If you enjoyed the book, leave a rating or review on GoodReads, and, if you purchased online, on the retailer website. Thank you!
http://www.goodreads.com/RedInkEnthusiast

About the Author

Amanda Marsico is the tea-sipping, cat-cuddling, chocolate-sneaking author of *Nova June: Inventor* (ages 3-7) and the *Humans In My House* series (ages 8-12); owner of Red Ink Enthusiast, a writing services company; and professor of English and Composition. When she's not swimming in post-it notes, she's crafting, baking, or hiking.

www.redinkenthusiast.com
www.facebook.com/redinkenthusiast
www.instagram.com/redinkenthusiast

Look for book 3, the final installment of the *Acephalous* series, Winter 2019 and find other titles by Amanda Marsico on Amazon.
amazon.com/author/amandamarsico

www.ingramcontent.com/pod-product-compliance
Lightning Source LLC
Chambersburg PA
CBHW020749250626
47155CB00003B/993